DUBIOUS ASSETS

Beauty, brains and a brilliant career—Catriona Stewart has the lot. Yet she is a crofter's daughter at heart and less sophisticated than her glamorous friends, so she's easy prey when millionaire Hamish Melville—on his second marriage—turns on the charm. Catriona isn't cut out to be a mistress, and when she meets dangerously handsome Andro, she hopes he can offer something more meaningful than adultery. But Andro's brother Rob could cast some doubt on that—and Hamish might not easily let her go....

DUBIOUS ASSETS

Dubious Assets

by

Joanna McDonald

Black Satin Romance
Long Preston, North Yorkshire,
England.

British Library Cataloguing in Publication Data.

McDonald, Joanna
   Dubious assets.

   A catalogue record for this book is
   available from the British Library

   ISBN 1-86110-009-4

First published in Great Britain by Headline Book Publishing, 1995

Published in Large Print September, 1996 by arrangement with
Headline Book Publishing and Joanna Hickson.

Black Satin Romance is an imprint of
Library Magna Books Ltd.
Printed and bound in Great Britain by
T.J. Press (Padstow) Ltd., Cornwall, PL28 8RW.

All characters in this publication are fictitious and any resemblance to real persons, living or dead, is purely coincidental.

Dem 1/98

For Sophie and all thirty-something career girls
who sometimes consider their assets dubious.

In writing DUBIOUS ASSETS I had in-calculable help and advice from my bank manager who wishes to remain discreetly anonymous, although anyone less likely to succeed in hiding her light under a bushel I have yet to meet! Profuse thanks are also due to George and Katie Halliday for unstinting hospitality in Skye and intriguing nuggets of information which have unquestionably brightened the narrative, and to the regulars of the Ferry Inn at Uig who put up with my tedious interrogations. I also owe a debt of gratitude to James Hunter and Cailean Maclean for their marvellous book SKYE: THE ISLAND which gave me invaluable background material and refreshed my memory of the beauty of Skye whilst far away in the 'precipitous city'. For information on the film industry I must thank Lee Leckie of the Scottish Film Commission, and for allowing me to refresh my memory of location shooting thanks are due to Paddy Higson and Zenith Films.

One

'This is absolutely ludicrous! I wish to see the manager.'

The angry woman in the smart navy suit drummed her polished nails on the white marble surface before her, chipping the scarlet lacquer. Her voice was sharp and clear-cut, like the diamonds on her fingers.

'Of course, Mrs Moncreiffe,' responded the pleasant blonde behind the marble counter, lifting the telephone handset. 'Which particular manager handles your account?'

An impatient sigh greeted this query. 'I haven't a clue. I never bother with such details. I thought Steuart and Company were supposed to be the acceptable face of banking! Well, this double-signature business is totally *un*-acceptable.' Another flake of red polish skimmed across the Carrara marble, attached to a sizeable half-moon of fingernail. 'Damn!' The digits stopped drumming and the diamonds flashed as their owner examined the damage. 'I won't have any nails left by the time this bloody divorce is through.'

'I'll just see who's available,' murmured the obliging blonde, hastily tapping out a number. On the counter between them lay the cause of the trouble, an open chequebook encased in embossed burgundy leather with the top

13

cheque filled in. 'Oh, hello Catriona. If you're free could you come down to the banking hall please and speak to Mrs...er...' a glance at the names printed below the signature. '...Victoria Moncreiffe? She wants an explanation of the new instruction regarding her joint account.'

'What Mrs Moncreiffe wants is some bloody money!' snapped the nail-breaker, clenching her fingers into a fist to forestall another damaging tattoo.

'One of our managers is on the way down to see you, Mrs Moncreiffe,' said the blonde soothingly reuniting the working parts of the telephone. 'Perhaps you'd like to take a seat.' She gestured towards an elegant period settee which stood beneath a gilded mirror in the public section of the room.

Her own side of the dividing counter was more businesslike, equipped with the necessary aids to bank-telling—computer terminal, cash drawer, small safe, calculator and panic button but, significantly, no security screen. Steuart & Company was the kind of bank which liked its clients to feel comfortable with their money because most of them were loaded with it.

'I hope I won't be kept waiting long enough to sit down,' fretted Victoria Moncreiffe, beginning to pace to and fro on her three-inch heels, setting a-flutter a Hermès scarf casually tied to the strap of her expensive stitched-leather shoulder bag. She looked what she was, a well-to-do lady on a city shopping expedition, dressed by Jaeger and distressed by marital breakdown.

A tall, high-beaked man in baggy tweeds and a frayed Tattershall check shirt strolled in from the street and greeted the blonde cheerfully. 'Morning, Gillian. Dig us out a new chequebook, would you please, m'dear?' He flipped a completed request form over the counter and nodded amiably at the pacing lady. 'G'morning,' he murmured.

Victoria Moncreiffe responded with a grunt and a minimal facial twitch. She was off men, even this inoffensive middle-aged stranger who just happened to have wandered into her orbit. So she should have been relieved when the manager who arrived in answer to her request was a woman—but judging by her startled expression, she wasn't.

Catriona Stewart, Manager of Private Banking, was tall and slim with an intelligent, mobile face, a fine, clear complexion, high cheekbones and large, expressive silver-grey eyes, but her most striking feature was a thick, glossy mane of burning-bright red-gold hair. She wore a tailored, daffodil-yellow jacket over a short, straight black skirt and sheer black stockings on long, shapely legs and she approached the fuming lady with a warm, sympathetic smile and an outstretched, ringless hand.

'Good afternoon, Mrs Moncreiffe. My name is Catriona Stewart. How may I help you?'

The creases in Victoria Moncreiffe's brow deepened. 'Are *you* our bank manager?' she exclaimed, taking the proffered hand limply and barely shaking it. It was clear that this discovery did not exactly thrill.

'I am one of the managers, yes. Actually I haven't been with Steuart's for very long, but I hope I can sort out your problem,' said Catriona carefully, detecting a stress-level at Storm Force. 'Perhaps you'd like to discuss it somewhere more private?'

'What I'd like to do is cash a cheque, but it seems I may no longer do so without my husband's counter-signature.' Victoria Moncreiffe's outraged opinion of this restriction was shrilly apparent. 'As Charlie and I are not speaking that is a little difficult, to say the least.'

'If you come with me, Mrs Moncreiffe, I'll do my best to explain.' Catriona held open the door of the banking hall and cast a meaningful glance at the man in the frayed shirt who was now staring curiously. 'It won't take long. I'm sure we can arrange things to suit you.'

'That would take a miracle!' declared the indignant client, but she stalked from the room nonetheless, with Catriona close behind.

'A little marital difficulty?' enquired he of the Tattershall check, twinkling at the blonde he had called Gillian.

She smiled secretively and shook her head. 'My lips are sealed, Sir William,' she said, though in fact they were temptingly parted over pearly teeth.

'Aha!' cried the Baronet with a braying laugh. 'The celebrated Steuart clam system!'

'"Your money is our business—and no one else's",' chanted Gillian primly. 'It's not the bank's motto, but it ought to be.'

16

Steuart & Company, public limited company and private exclusive bankers, occupied a converted Georgian townhouse in an elegant square at one end of Edinburgh's 'Golden Mile' which, despite the glamorous description, was paved with drab concrete and peopled mostly by men in grey suits; against this background, Catriona Stewart's bright taste in jackets came as a welcome relief to many. In a small conference room behind Steuart's banking hall she saw her fractious client comfortably seated before taking a chair herself.

'I'm so sorry you've had this unpleasant surprise, Mrs Moncreiffe,' she said gravely. 'A letter was sent to you yesterday, but perhaps you missed the post this morning?'

'I've not been staying at my usual address,' snapped Victoria Moncreiffe. 'My mail is being forwarded.'

'That would explain it,' nodded Catriona. 'Your husband wrote to tell us that you have separated and that a divorce is pending, and he asked us to institute the normal procedures. I'm afraid that involves placing some control over both partners' access to shared assets, including the money in your joint account.' She smiled sympathetically. 'It's only a temporary move, until the legal situation has been resolved.'

Mrs Moncreiffe's brow, already strip-furrowed like a medieval field, puckered further. 'But what am I to do for money? Surely Charlie can't cut me off without a penny!'

'No, Mrs Moncreiffe, you mustn't worry about that. We can arrange for you to have a

17

limited amount of cash, enough to tide you over for a week or so, and by then the lawyers should have made interim maintenance arrangements. I'm surprised your own solicitor didn't explain all this to you.' Catriona kept her voice soft and placatory, in an effort to lessen the impact of her words.

However, Victoria Moncreiffe was not to be placated, even by this unexpectedly warm and feminine bank executive. Privacy had opened the valve on her emotional pressure-cooker and her pitch of stridency rose as she came to the boil. 'Solicitors are useless! Mine told me I shouldn't have left the marital home. How could I stay? Do you know what my bastard of a husband is up to? He's having an affair with the girl who does his shooting lunches. Just a little pheasant-plucking, he calls it. And I was the one who hired her! Nothing sloe about *her* gin. I caught them at it after the final drive—bonking away in the back of her Frontera, cosy as a pair of Purdys.' She shook her head as if to rid her mind of the memory. 'Do you shoot, Miss Stewart?'

Catriona confessed that she didn't. She could have added that shooting, like most of the activities of the landed gentry, was a closed book to someone like herself, reared on a Highland croft, where a shotgun was only used against rabbits or crows or even, humorously, to describe the kind of marriage her sister Marie had made—pregnant and unrepentant. She could have explained this, but tactfully she didn't. Rich landowners made up half of

Steuart's account-holders and Catriona was fast learning their ways and trying not to find them strange.

'Neither do I. But I'm beginning to realise my mistake.' Victoria Moncreiffe began tapping out distress signals again on the polished surface of the table. 'Charlie's done the dirty on me and now he's trying to beggar me.' The demise of another nail was imminent.

'Honestly, Mrs Moncreiffe, it isn't as bad as that,' Catriona assured her. 'The lawyers will sort it all out soon, but in the short term just let me know how much cash you'd like to withdraw and I'll clear it for you.'

'I suppose you'll ring him,' muttered the betrayed lady. 'Why should I have to explain every penny to that bastard?'

'Well, it works both ways,' Catriona reminded her. 'He can't take any money out without your consent either. The system is supposed to protect each of you.'

'Huh!' sniffed the provoked wife. 'If I know Charlie he's probably got another account somewhere stashed full of money.'

'I cannot comment on that,' responded Catriona guardedly. She had never met the man, but from the bank records she knew that, in addition to owning land, the Honourable Charles Moncreiffe was a prominent businessman with considerable income and several accounts. 'If you give me your cheque, I'll make the withdrawal arrangements immediately.'

'I still think it's ludicrous,' grumbled Victoria Moncreiffe, tearing out the already completed slip and handing it over. 'But you've been very kind,' she added, favouring Catriona with a wan smile. 'I'm sorry to have caused all this bother.'

'It was unfortunate that you didn't get our letter,' observed Catriona gently, taking the cheque and pushing a notepad and pen across the table. 'Could you write down your present address and telephone number for our records? After all, your husband will want access to the account as well.'

'As long as that grubby little cook doesn't get her hands on it,' exclaimed Mrs Moncreiffe, writing busily. 'I think I should bring my jewellery here for safekeeping, otherwise next week she'll probably be dishing up game pie wearing *my* sapphires.'

Catriona acknowledged the cynicism with a sympathetic shrug. 'Please let us help in any way we can,' she urged, picking up the completed address details and moving towards the door. 'I'll just get your cash. I shouldn't keep you too long.'

'Thanks,' said her client, eyeing her appraisingly. 'Perhaps there's something to be said for a woman bank manager after all. At least I feel you're on my side.'

'I'm glad,' Catriona said, hiding a wry smile as she left the room. The role of Agony Aunt had not been part of the job specification as outlined by the professional head-hunters who had lured her to Steuart's two months before, but she supposed it might be a useful addition to her CV.

One of Steuart & Company's prime functions was to accept large deposits of money from the wealthy and invest it in the enterprising. The attraction for Catriona was that they still did it on a personal basis. In the big clearing bank where she had worked hitherto, the friendly local bank manager had become an extinct animal. Even ambitious high-flyers like herself who reached the dizzy heights of Assistant Branch Manager by the age of thirty, were unable to take decisions on loans without processing them through a rigid electronic procedure. For Catriona, a friendly, outward-going personality who sprang from a gregarious island community, this had proved increasingly frustrating. She wanted to use her own judgment, not accept the ruling of a despotic head-office microchip. Some of her crofting relatives had viewed her switch to the rich financial salons of Steuart & Company as a betrayal of her roots, but when they decried the private bank as being cliquey and elitist, she retorted that at least it was human.

After telephoning the Hon. Charles Moncreiffe however, she reflected that some of its clients were less human than others.

'If Victoria's not there to run the house, why the hell should I pay her anything?' he demanded in high dudgeon. 'She ran away like a snivelling schoolgirl for no good reason, there's no one to walk the wretched dogs and the damned heating oil's run out. It's all bloody inconvenient, actually!'

Eventually the Hon. Charlie grudgingly conceded three hundred pounds cash to his

21

estranged wife, but his self-righteous indignation and total lack of remorse left a bad taste in Catriona's mouth and inspired a rush of compassion for the unfortunate Victoria, whom she ushered solicitously off the premises, uttering words of encouragement tinged with female solidarity.

Returning to the large first-floor office she shared with the other two Steuart middle managers, she stopped at the desk nearest the door. 'Have you a minute, John?' she asked the man sitting behind it.

John Home-Muir was a broad-shouldered, fresh-faced, good-looking individual who obligingly lifted his ingenuous grey-green gaze from the spreadsheet he was studying. 'Something bothering you, Cat?'

'Yes—the Hon. Charles Moncreiffe. You handle his accounts, don't you?'

'Only his forestry investments. If you want to know about his multiplicity of other accounts and his multi-farious offshore deposits, you'll have to ask Donald.'

John's face took on an expression of mild distaste as he said this, which surprised Catriona, for the former Scottish rugby internationalist was the least malicious person of her acquaintance. When she had first met him, she'd wondered how he'd ever survived in the violent rucks so frequent on the rugby pitch until he revealed that he had been a full-back, who had kicked long and hard but had not very often been required to risk ears, nose and eyes in midfield battles for the ball. 'Which accounts for my unimpaired good looks,' he'd explained with a grin.

The third occupant of the open-plan office looked up from his computer screen. Donald Cameron was the oldest of the Steuart middle-management team, a dapper, pinstriped individual with a slightly expanding girth and a more than slightly receding hairline who nevertheless contrived to remain abidingly attractive to the opposite sex.

'Did I hear the dreaded name Moncreiffe?' he enquired. 'Tread carefully down that dark alley, Cat.'

'Why? Is he a rat?'

'Yes, and he leaves a lot of nasty stuff behind him for others to step in,' came the response.

'What's he been up to?'

'Well, you weren't here earlier, but there was a bit of an incident concerning his wife.'

'Ah, the non-breeder,' observed Donald, nodding.

'What do you mean, non-breeder?' Disbelief hovered in Catriona's voice.

'I mean she can't have children and the Hon. Charlie wants shot of her. You know what these minor aristos are like about breeding heirs.' Donald gave a cynical shrug.

'But she told me she found him *in flagrante* with the shooting-lunch lady.'

'So she did—by careful arrangement. Charlie wants a quick divorce and Victoria wasn't co-operating, so he made damn sure she found him inside the outside caterer, as it were.'

'God, that's disgusting.' Catriona was incensed. 'Poor woman.'

'Yes, it's amazing the lengths to which some people will go to give good service.'

Catriona stared a few seconds at Donald's bland expression and then gave an indignant giggle. 'I didn't mean poor *cook*, you idiot. I meant poor Mrs Moncreiffe!'

'Any woman who consorts with the Hon. Charlie deserves our sympathy,' intoned Donald. 'Let it be a lesson to you, young Catriona. Do not marry for money or mess with married men.'

Catriona dimpled. 'Instead I mess with money and am surrounded by married men.'

'Some men are more married than others,' he replied airily. 'John, of course, is a hopeless case but I, on the other hand, have seen the light.'

'Come on, Donald. Your divorce may not be final but a certain banking-hall manager's plans for you most definitely are,' observed Catriona dryly, returning to her desk.

'Appearances are deceptive. My freedom is imminent and Gillian and I are just good friends,' retorted Donald.

'Of course,' nodded Catriona without conviction, logging into her computer terminal. 'However, there's a manic gleam in that lady's eye that just keeps us other girls at bay.'

'Don't be put off, Catriona. I'm Donald, try me!' He flung wide his pin-striped arms.

'So you keep saying, but I value my life too much,' she replied robustly.

'Do you two mind?' grumbled John. 'I'm wrestling with a forestry investment here and I can't see the wood for the trees.'

The others subsided, exchanging contrite glances. Their continuous and innocuous flirtation was a regular joke between them.

'Sorry, chum,' murmured Donald and began tapping on his keyboard. A few seconds later Catriona's message icon flashed and she keyed into it.

'Re. the Hon. Charlie: leave that particular aristo to me, Cat. At least I can beat him at golf!' Donald relayed electronically.

Smiling, Catriona tapped a return message: *'OK, but look after Victoria. Big sister is watching you!'*

'I'm Donald, remember? Kind to all ladies.'

'Yes, Donald. We all know you're a duck. Out.' With her finger Catriona made a slicing signal across her throat and her screen went blank. She had a pile of work to do and little time to do it. Small-screen banter with Donald would have to wait.

She liked her two colleagues, especially the usually amiable John Home-Muir, whose wife Alison had become a particular friend. She was an art valuer who worked for the Scottish branch of Wentworth's, an international firm of auctioneers. Exploiting family ties, John had recently acquired the Wentworth's account for Steuart & Company—a coup which had greatly pleased the bank's Chairman, Lord Nevis, an art collector himself who, in recognition of the new relationship, had decreed that his management team should all attend a Wentworth function early that evening. An engraved invitation card was tucked into Catriona's desk-blotter.

The Directors of Wentworth's invite you to attend a Private View of fine paintings and silver...

Leaving the bank an hour or so later, Catriona blinked as if a sudden flurry of street dust had swirled up into her face. After the interior gloom, the dazzling spring light seemed to vibrate the air like bagpipes, playing eight-somes on her eyeballs. It always took her breath away, the triumphant brilliance of this east-coast light. It shafted across the North Sea straight from the blinding whiteness of the Arctic, so much harsher than the gentle, moisture-laden light of Scotland's west coast, which illuminated the mountain crags and sweeping bays of her childhood home on Skye.

'Steady,' warned Donald, offering a support-ing hand as she teetered, temporarily blinded, at the top of Steuart's entrance steps. 'I know you fancy him but there's no need to throw yourself at Bruce's feet.'

Catriona blinked again. 'Thanks, Donald,' she said, countering his teasing wink with a sideways glance. 'I'll try to resist the temptation.'

Now that her vision had cleared she noted with relief that the man who had preceded her out of the bank was far enough ahead to be out of earshot of Donald's remark. Bruce Finlay was Steuart's Managing Director and Catriona had to admit that she did find his powerful good looks attractive. Although she kept her own attitude strictly professional, she suspected that he didn't actively deter female

26

interest, even though he was married and the father of two teenage children.

'We need your banking flair, Miss Stewart,' Bruce had told her gravely when he appointed her, 'but you will also be good for our image. We're too colourless and masculine. Your style will definitely alter that.'

At the time Catriona hadn't been sure whether to accept the compliment or bristle at the implication that she was being recruited more for her looks than her ability. In the end she had smiled gracefully, and relied on the subsequent two months of hard graft to prove that her financial skills vastly eclipsed her decorative qualities.

Lord Nevis, who had offered a lift in his company car, was gallantly standing back to allow Catriona to embark first. 'Thank you,' she said, nodding at the debonair, grey-haired aristocrat and ducking into the rear of his Mercedes.

Bruce Finlay wedged himself in beside her, glancing appreciatively at the considerable length of sheer black Lycra-covered leg exposed by the tilt of the seat and the relative shortness of her skirt. Catriona was unperturbed. In her eight weeks at Steuart's she had come to accept her male colleagues' undisguised physical admiration because she now knew it to be harmless and unconnected with their view of her professional expertise. She even found it rather reassuring, a boost to her female ego. Donald climbed in beside Bruce. John Home-Muir would follow later, obliged to attend a trustees' meeting which he could not avoid.

'You'll enjoy this, I think, Catriona,' Bruce remarked in his pleasant, Anglo-Scottish voice, honed by six years of English public-school education. 'It's usually quite a social event.'

'I'm looking forward to it,' Catriona fibbed blithely. 'Although I know nothing about art, I'm afraid.'

'Time you learned then,' declared Lord Nevis, settling himself in the front passenger seat. 'A large number of Steuart clients invest in it.'

'Yes, so I've noticed,' Catriona said as the chauffeur accelerated into the rush-hour flow of traffic around the square.

'I'm a Colourist man myself,' put in Bruce, referring to a turn-of-the-century school of Scottish artists for whom clarity of hue and line had been all-important, although the hues and lines they chose sometimes appeared rather outlandish to the conservative eye.

'Really?' Lord Nevis's refined tone was slightly incredulous. 'I can't cope with blue rocks and black bottles myself. I prefer the Impressionists.'

Bruce's discreet cough disguised a cynical smirk. 'Hmm. Yes, George, I agree—but they tend to make a somewhat larger impression on the wallet.'

'Many a mickle maks a Monet,' quipped Donald, blissfully unaware of his Chairman's frown of irritation.

'Thinking of buying her, Bruce?'

28

The question made Bruce Finlay swing round. A well-dressed man of medium height and maximum presence was standing at his shoulder, his arresting blue eyes fixed on the painting which Bruce himself had been studying.

'Oh, hello Melville,' he responded, feigning enthusiasm. 'She's not bad, is she?'

The picture under review was a full-length nude by the Colourist artist J. D. Fergusson, a study of a lounging female staring defiantly out of the frame as if to challenge the observer to find fault with her body. Her limbs and the twin globes of her breasts were heavily outlined in black.

'She looks as if she's got silicone implants,' growled the blue-eyed man distastefully. 'A clinch with her would be like cuddling concrete.'

Hamish Melville was one of Scotland's foremost entrepreneurs, having substantial interests in food-retailing, whisky-distilling and the entertainment industry. To date he was on his tenth takeover and his second marriage, and his reputation as both wheeler-dealer and womaniser was formidable. He was also a keen collector of Scottish art.

Bruce gave a sharp laugh. For his own private reasons, his easy charm became a trifle brittle in the presence of this particular individual, but he was careful to preserve good relations since Hamish Melville banked with Steuart's.

'I was thinking of hanging her rather than laying her,' he said pleasantly, 'but I see what you mean. Seen anything *you* like?'

Hamish shrugged. 'There's a Joan Eardley

29

over there I might bid for. It depends how high it goes.'

Bruce had noticed the painting in question in a far corner of the crowded room, a seascape which he personally thought resembled a plate of leftover spaghetti, but he prudently kept his opinion to himself. Casting round for a change of subject, he caught sight of Catriona peering closely at a landscape in a nearby alcove and gestured in her direction with his wineglass.

'Have you met our new manager, Hamish?— Catriona Stewart?'

Hamish followed the direction of his gaze and his eyes widened momentarily as they came to rest on Catriona's intent figure.

'No, I haven't,' he said ruminatively. 'And at the risk of sounding sexist, she looks far too good to be a bank manager, even at Steuart's.'

As they watched, Catriona straightened and tossed back her russet mane to sip thoughtfully at her drink. Her attitude was fluid, relaxed, chin slightly raised, back straight without being rigid. She had unbuttoned her rather severe yellow jacket to reveal a white silk blouse which softened her image so that she looked less the smart, efficient banker, more the elegant, leisured female. Absorbed in the painting, she was unaware of their eyes upon her, heedless of the ebb and flow of people around her.

'In her case I think you'll find that looks aren't everything,' murmured Bruce, moving in her direction. 'What have you found there, Catriona?' he asked, intrigued by the intensity of her interest in a picture which turned out to be an unpretentious watercolour of a Highland coastal scene.

Cariona jumped, abruptly jerked from her reverie, then smiled as she recognised who it was. 'It's of Uig Bay—in Skye,' she explained. 'My home. Look, this is our family croft.' She pointed to one of five or six small houses strung out along the foreground shore of a wide semicircular bay surrounded by steep hills. 'It's so strange to see it here, completely out of context.' She swallowed hard on the lump which had formed in her throat as she scanned the familiar contours in the landscape. It wouldn't do to let these hard-nosed businessmen see the sudden wave of longing which the little painting had inspired in her. It was several months since she had set foot on Skye and she felt starved of the spiritual transfusion which a visit to the island infallibly gave her.

'Catriona, I'd like you to meet Hamish Melville, one of Steuart's most important clients.' Bruce effected the introduction smoothly. 'Hamish, this is Catriona Stewart.'

'How do you do,' responded Catriona, feeling her hand seized in a firm dry grip while her own eyes were held by a pair of penetrating blue ones which gave the impression of perceiving not only her recent surge of nostalgia but also every other repressed emotion. 'I know *of* you, of course,' she assured him quickly, to deflect this disturbing concentration. 'Your name is legendary in financial circles.'

Hamish's tawny brows rose slightly. 'Legendary, indeed? From *you* I'll take that as a

31

compliment.' There was a slight but un-mistakable stress on the pronoun and a slow smile spread across the entrepreneur's deceptively cherubic face. Catriona didn't yet know it but when it came to legend, Hamish Melville's charm was equally eligible for such classification.

Colour tinged her cheeks. She was used to handling brash businessmen but she found his subtle cordiality rather unsettling. 'I hope you will,' she said, retrieving her hand.

A pinstriped arm jogged Bruce's elbow, spilling his drink. 'Pah! It's becoming a bit of a scrum here now, isn't it?' he observed irritably, shaking wine off his hand. 'You don't need to stay much longer, Catriona, if you've had enough. I think we've done our bit for bank and business.'

Catriona shook her head. 'I'm enjoying it,' she told him. 'More than I expected, to be honest.'

'Is that because you found the painting of your home?' enquired Hamish, turning aside to inspect the watercolour. 'Does the artist do it justice?'

Catriona gave this question some thought. 'I'm not really qualified to say,' she admitted, 'but I like it. It was painted before the ferry terminal was built so the scene is rather different today. Uig is now the main port for South Uist, and the Calmac jetty dominates the bay, jutting right out from here to here.' She indicated the dimensions on the picture with grim deliberation. 'It's either a hideous example of planning blight—or an essential element of transport links with the Outer Hebrides, depending on your point of view.'

Hamish shrugged and smiled. 'I don't know the area so I'm glad I don't have to argue either case,' he said. 'Will you buy the painting?'

Catriona looked startled. 'I never gave it a thought,' she said. 'How much do you think it will fetch?'

'Let's have a look.' Hamish consulted his catalogue, leafing swiftly through the lots. 'Between four and five hundred pounds, according to Alison Home-Muir's estimate. She's usually pretty reliable.'

'Do you know Alison?' asked Catriona in surprise.

'There can be few art collectors in Scotland who do not. Dealing with her is one of the more pleasant aspects of the game, isn't it, Bruce?'

Bruce looked distracted. 'What? Oh yes, quite right. Look, I'd better go and hunt for my wife,' he added. 'In this crowd she could have been here for ages without setting eyes on me. I'll see you tomorrow, Catriona.' He laid a hand on Catriona's arm and squeezed it in farewell. 'Goodbye, Hamish. See you soon, no doubt.'

Hamish acknowledged the other man's departure then turned back to Catriona. 'What we need is another drink,' he declared and instantly acquired the attention of a passing white-aproned waitress. 'Do you like Bollinger?' he asked, as they watched champagne fizz into their glasses. Wentworth's enjoyed a promotional partnership with importers of the high-class French wine.

Catriona gave a small laugh. 'To be honest, I can't tell Bollinger from German Brut,' she confessed. 'Isn't that sinful?'

Hamish smiled and shook his head. 'There was a time when I couldn't tell it from Irn Bru,' he confided. 'Except I probably enjoyed Irn Bru better. Not any more, though. Here's to our very fortunate meeting.' He tilted his brimming glass and sipped appreciatively.

Catriona followed suit more cautiously. As she did so she caught sight of a tall dark-haired girl in an eye-catching red suit, breaking off what looked like an acrimonious conversation with a ruddy-faced man with a built-in sneer. 'Alison,' she called, raising her low voice to help it carry through the chattering throng. 'Over here!'

The dark girl's expression was transformed from irritation to delight and she came hurrying over. 'Catriona! Thank heaven for a friendly face. That man is one of those journalists who give reptiles a bad name. How are you getting on? I thought you'd be yawning by now, art not really being your thing.'

'I'm learning,' laughed Catriona, leaning forward to plant a kiss on the other girl's cheek. 'With a little help from an expert.' She gave a smiling nod in Hamish's direction.

Alison swung round, recognising her friend's companion at once. 'Hello, Hamish,' she said, exchanging more kisses. 'I hope you're feeling in a buying mood. There's a wonderful Eardley over in the other corner.'

'Yes, I've seen it,' he said. 'It's certainly interesting, but I find the company more so on this occasion. Why didn't you tell me about your husband's charming new colleague?' He gave Alison a reproachful look.

The dark girl's eyes danced. 'She's not just John's colleague. Catriona's my friend—we play squash together. Which reminds me, I booked a court for tomorrow evening—six-thirty.' Catriona acknowledged the date and fielded a slight wink. 'And I didn't introduce you before, Hamish,' Alison went on, 'because she's not to be trusted with rich, handsome men.'

'Oh, thanks a lot,' cried Catriona with mock indignation. Her silver eyes widened into an expression of injured innocence, only her curling mouth betraying the fact that she was playing along with a game. 'I was behaving myself for once and now you've ruined it.' Early in their friendship, Alison and Catriona had discovered a mutual mischievous streak and enjoyed exercising it in tandem.

'Hamish would have seen through your angelic disguise in no time,' Alison scoffed. 'This man is a master of boardroom strategy.'

'You did say *boardroom*, didn't you?' came Hamish's swift riposte, amusement softening his bright blue eyes.

'Why? Are you suggesting you're also a skilled operator in some other sort of room?' queried Alison coyly. 'You see, Cat? You can't employ your cunning feline wiles on Hamish Melville with impunity!'

'I'll bear those in mind,' smiled the entrepreneur, relaxing now that he had assessed the score. 'Meanwhile, all cats must eat. Why don't you two have dinner with me after this?' He waved to indicate the crowded room where the decibel level had risen commensurate with the flow of Bollinger.

'And what about Mrs Melville?' enquired Alison archly, her fine dark eyebrows elevated. 'Will she be joining us?'

'Mrs Melville is in Paris,' replied Hamish somewhat grimly. 'Probably being wined and dined by Christian Lacroix or Karl Lagerfeld. It's the least they could do, considering the millions of francs she's squandered in their respective salons.'

'You can't say squandered when she always looks so sensational,' objected Alison. 'You must meet Hamish's wife, Cat. Linda is Edinburgh's best-dressed woman.'

Catriona's veneer of sophistication had all but crumbled at the idea of shopping in the Faubourg St Honoré. 'Does your wife dress at Dior?' she asked incredulously, sounding a little breathless.

Hamish shrugged. 'Well, someone has to,' he murmured disparagingly.

Alison ignored this calumny. 'Since you're a couture widower, Hamish, we'll take pity on you, won't we, Cat? I'm sure John won't mind if you join us for dinner—especially if you're going to bid for the Eardley.'

'What won't John mind?' The husky Borders' burr of John Home-Muir broke into the conversation as he bore down on their small circle, unmistakable with his wide shoulders and bashful smile.

'Oh Johnno, you made it!' exclaimed Alison with delight, reaching up to throw an affectionate arm around her husband's neck and plant a quick, enthusiastic kiss on his lips. 'Brilliant! I thought you'd have to go straight to the restaurant.' Although she appeared the epitome of a sophisticated career-woman, Alison was at heart quite a simple creature. She ran a gloriously muddled Victorian terraced house, adored her somewhat shy and unassuming husband and secretly longed for the baby that would complete their three-year-old bed-of-roses marriage.

John received her hug with a slight blush and said rather guiltily, 'Don't tell Bruce but I left the other trustees to argue a clause on inheritance law. It's not my strong point, as you know.'

'I'm sure Bruce would want you to support your wife's endeavours,' Alison said approvingly. 'Hamish is going to join us for dinner.'

'Good.' It was only a year since John Home-Muir had played in his last rugby international for Scotland and he gave the entrepreneur the full benefit of his full-back grip in greeting. 'I hope you like pasta and plonk. That's about all you can get where we're going.'

Hamish surreptitiously flexed his fist, grateful to discover that it had survived the Home-Muir handshake. 'I like pasta as long as it's cooked by Italians,' he assured the banker. 'Only they know how to treat it.'

'Oh, Giuseppe's Italian all right,' John agreed. '*Very* Italian.'

'Look, now he's here I must take John

37

over to speak to my Chairman,' Alison said apologetically, tucking her arm in her husband's. 'For some reason he thinks the sun shines out of his brow—but then, he's a rugby fan. We'll meet you both in half an hour or so, when the crowd has thinned out.'

Catriona watched her friends disappear into the throng. 'I don't know how Alison can put a value on some of these paintings,' she remarked to Hamish, surveying the nearest alcove where several figurative still-lifes rubbed frames with lush Victorian landscapes and inscrutable contemporary abstracts. 'Some of them look worthless to me and yet the estimate is in thousands. If you pay a lot for a picture, does that make it a better one?'

He laughed, raising his hands as if under fire. 'Now we're getting into deep critical water! In art, one man's Picasso may be another man's poison.'

'Or woman's...?' she prompted with an instinctive spurt of feminism.

He made a gesture of resignation. 'Yes, all right—or woman's. Are you very touchy about such things?'

'Not very, a wee bit, perhaps. I just like to think that one day I, as an independent, self-made woman, might be able to afford a Picasso. Have you got one, by any chance?'

'Yes,' he said with quiet satisfaction. 'As a matter of fact I have.'

'How amazing!' Breathless incredulity fleetingly resurfaced in Catriona's voice, then it steadied back into its natural contralto. 'Did you buy it because it was valuable, or because you liked it?'

Hamish considered this carefully, as carefully as he considered Catriona. God, she was beautiful, this lady bank manager, with her lissome figure, porcelain complexion and tumbling Titian mane!

He crinkled his clever blue eyes to veil the thoughts in his head. 'I can't answer that easily,' he replied at last. 'You'll have to come and see it some time. It hangs in my office.'

Catriona looked intrigued and nodded. 'I'd like to, very much.'

Two

The restaurant was full and noisy. At one end a long table was abuzz with laughter and repartee. A birthday celebration perhaps, or an office outing, thought Catriona on entering. Under bright lights behind a tiled barrier, two sweating chefs juggled with dough and steaming pans of pasta, while a pizza-oven emitted waves of heat through its ever-open door.

The proprietor was a small dynamic Calabrian called Giuseppe, who wore an eye-catching lurex waistcoat and a wide effusive smile in which a gold tooth glinted as he greeted Alison and John, frequent and much-valued customers of Ristorante Il Castello. He led them, chatting enthusiastically all the way, towards a corner table where John introduced him to Hamish Melville, whom he greeted with a polite but perfunctory nod of the head, and to Catriona, whom he acknowledged with exaggerated gallantry, pulling out her chair and shaking out her napkin to place it across her lap. Had he been aware that Hamish could have bought the street in which his restaurant was situated, the nearby fortress after which it was named and half the crown jewels housed in the castle's strongroom, Giuseppe might have adjusted the balance of his attentions but, being a red-blooded Italian male it is equally probable that he might not. It was his habit to court the approval of the men who ate in his restaurant by charming their lady companions.

'If you're happy and you know it clap your hands!' sang the occupants of the long table, suiting their actions to the words of the song and gesturing to the other diners around them to join in, which several goodnaturedly did.

'The place is lively tonight,' Alison said to Hamish a little ruefully, 'but we like it and the pasta is terrific. I take it you've never been here before. Giuseppe would have remembered if you had. He never forgets a face.'

'He's quite a character,' observed Hamish, watching the wiry Italian weave his way skilfully between the tables, directing his team of waiters like an orchestral conductor, waving his expressive hands. 'He obviously runs a very popular restaurant and works very hard to make it so. He deserves to do well.'

Catriona noticed that Hamish's voice held a

deep clarity which rendered it audible through all the hubbub and clatter without any apparent effort on his behalf. Was this the result of commanding a business empire, she wondered, or the reason for his boardroom success? She watched as he automatically rearranged carelessly placed cutlery so that it lay neatly beside the raffia place-mat set before him, displaying hands that were lean and deft, the little finger of the left one adorned with a large gold signet ring. As indicators of character they revealed him to be confident and controlled, with a reservoir of well-harnessed energy.

Catriona studied the menu. 'Have you decided?' she asked Hamish, noticing that he had hardly glanced at the garish list of available dishes.

A puckish smile illuminated his round face. 'I'm considering Spaghetti Puttanesca,' he confided in an undertone, 'but Alison might not approve. I believe it means "lady of the night" and she suspects that I have far too much truck with naughty ladies as it is.' He cast a mock-accusing glance at the other girl. 'Don't you, Alison?'

A saucy grin greeted this sally. 'I'm just waiting for one of them to tie you up in knots, Hamish,' she responded, her sharp ears having picked up every word. 'A plateful of Spaghetti Puttanesca might just do that!'

'A fate to be avoided, even when offered on a plate.' Hamish frowned. 'What do you suggest, Catriona? I'm sure you know your gnocchi from your noce.'

Catriona pleaded ignorance. 'Italian cooking's not really my forte,' she said. 'I'm better at Gaelic than garlic.'

'I wonder what Giuseppe would produce if we ordered Gaelic bread?' cried Alison irrepressibly.

'Yuk!' exclaimed John, shuddering. 'I had something they called Spaghetti *Buchan*ese once in Fraserburgh. Never again. I'm sure the sauce was based on haggis. I think I'll stay faithful to penne—Penne alla Mare.'

'And I'll have Lasagne,' said Hamish equally firmly. 'It's usually a safe bet.'

'I'll have that too,' agreed Catriona, 'and some tomato and mozzarella salad.' She began to unbutton her jacket and shrugged it off her shoulders. 'It's hot in here, isn't it?'

Hamish leaned over to help her. 'For which much thanks,' he said flatteringly, eyeing the soft cling of her white blouse.

'God Hamish, you're such a smoothie,' Alison intervened. 'Don't listen to him, Cat. He's all silk.' She reached out boldly and felt the thick cream cuff extending beyond the sleeve of the entrepreneur's alpaca suit-jacket. 'Just as I thought. Do you always wear silk shirts?'

'Yes, why not?' responded Hamish. 'Silk is more comfortable.'

'Hell to iron though,' remarked Alison. 'But I suppose you wouldn't know.'

'You suppose wrong,' he informed her. 'I have been known to take an iron to mine if I don't like the way they've been laundered.'

'Help—a perfectionist!' exclaimed Alison as the waiter came to take their order.

Catriona listened to this exchange with amusement, thinking that Alison was a little 'hyper'—overexcited by the level of interest expressed in the paintings which she had been responsible for assembling and cataloguing for the auction. Watching the entrepreneur endure her friend's teasing Catriona thought him surprisingly easygoing.

Giuseppe's obliging attempt at Gaelic bread arrived smelling strongly of garlic but also of some other ingredient. 'I think it's whisky,' Catriona ventured, taking a small bite. 'He's sprinkled it with whisky.'

'And oatmeal,' observed John, prodding at a crisp flake on the surface of the buttery dough. 'He could serve this for Burns' Night. "Fair fa' your honest sonsie face, Great chieftain o' the *pizza*-race"!'

'Poor Rabbie,' cried Alison indignantly. 'You'll have him turning in his grave.'

'Actually I think Burns would rather like this place,' remarked Hamish, surveying the lively restaurant with its crammed tables, rushing waiters and steaming pans of pasta. 'I bet it's not unlike the howffs of his day.'

'Only the décor would have been sootier and the songs bawdier,' Catriona laughed.

Behind her the long table was becoming more rowdy. Giuseppe passed by, carrying a heap of dirty plates. 'If you're happy and you know it clap your hands!' sang the girl whose birthday it had proved to be, standing up and clapping pointedly in the direction of the laden restaurateur. She was a pretty girl

43

and Giuseppe had never been known to resist a challenge from such a source. Grinning broadly, he stopped, casting his eyes to the ceiling with a look of exaggerated resignation—and clapped his hands.

Plates crashed to the floor and the whole restaurant fell momentarily silent before exploding into general hilarity. The birthday girl giggled hysterically, hands over mouth in astonished delight. 'I never thought you'd do it,' she cried wildly. 'Giuseppe, you're absolutely mad!'

Later, over the pasta, Hamish took Catriona by surprise. 'What made you leave Skye?' he asked suddenly.

Catriona started, her fork halfway to her mouth. Beside her John was head to head with Alison on the matter of whether to put a conservatory on the back of their house.

'I got promotion,' she said, lowering the fork. 'From Portree to Paisley.'

'Didn't you find it hard to leave?'

She stared at him, surprised at his insight. 'Yes, I did at the time. But you must know what it's like. Didn't you have to leave somewhere to get somewhere?'

'I was brought up in Motherwell,' he revealed. 'In the shadow of the Ravenscraig steelworks. I didn't find it hard to leave.'

'Do you ever go back? To see your family?'

He shook his head. 'There's none to see. My parents are dead, my brothers and sisters scattered. Occasionally one of them surfaces, looking for a hand-out.' His face clouded, anger mingled with regret.

'And do you hand out?' she probed gently.

'Yes, usually.' He did not elaborate. 'Skye is a much more interesting background. Not easily forgotten.'

'No, but then it doesn't forget you,' she frowned. 'It doesn't let you go. Sometimes it might be better if it did.'

'Why? You have a sense of place and worth, surely, when you spring from a crofting community.'

'That's right.' Yet again his insight surprised her. 'But sometimes it can tug a bit too hard.'

'Tell me about your family.' He leaned forward on the table, his meal temporarily forgotten.

She was flattered by his interest, unaware of any possible ulterior motive. 'My father is the Uig harbour master. He used to be a merchant seaman but there was a terrible accident when I was a small child. A hawser snapped and recoiled, catching him on the head. He lost an eye and a chunk of his skull, but he survived. It doesn't ever seem to have made him bitter or resentful. He's amazing.' Her admiration was obvious, love shining in her eyes.

Hamish was impressed by such fierce loyalty. She seemed so genuine, so lacking in guile. 'And your mother?' he prompted.

'Also amazing. She isn't a native of Skye—she comes from the Clyde. My father met her there when his ship docked. She reckons it was love at first sight. We didn't settle in Skye until after his accident. Mum can't have found it easy on the croft at first but now she runs it almost

45

singlehanded—drives the tractor, turns the hay, dips the sheep.'

'So it's equal opportunity down Uig way?' He smiled but his question wasn't entirely in jest.

'Completely.' Her chin was up as she returned his smile.

'So how come you're a banker? It seems an extraordinary leap.'

'From croft to counting house, you mean?' Catriona shrugged. 'A lot of people think that. But when I left school there was an opening in the bank in Portree. I just seemed to drift into it. Then I found that I rather liked it.' She didn't elaborate further, thinking he must be bored, and bent to her plate.

On an impulse Hamish reached out and touched her gleaming hair, smoothing back a loose curl, but as she jerked in surprise, he hurriedly withdrew his hand. 'I'm sorry. I was just wondering where the colour comes from. The Celtic side, I take it?'

She gave a self-deprecatory laugh. 'How d'you know it's not from a bottle? No. My father's family are all redheads. My mother is blonde. I suppose I'm a bit of a mixture.'

'It's a wonderful colour,' he averred. 'Like a summer sunset. I do some sailing on the west coast and the sunset there can be spectacular. But of course, you know that.'

She grinned. 'Yes—but I didn't know I walked around looking like one.'

'Perhaps it's only me who sees it,' he said softly.

'What are you two talking about?' Alison broke in curiously, the matter of the conservatory shelved. 'Are you up to your tricks, Cat? You'll have to watch her, Hamish.'

'With pleasure,' he replied enthusiastically.

Alison shot him a sharp glance and aimed a second at Catriona. Her friend looked markedly less composed than usual, grey eyes wide, cheeks tinged with pink. Warning bells sounded in Alison's head. She had only known Catriona for a few weeks but in that time she had become extremely fond of her. They had discovered much in common—a similar sense of humour, ambitions, interests—but they had not yet had time to fully assess each other's strengths and weaknesses. Nevertheless Alison strongly suspected that however much they joked about Catriona's flirtatious nature, when it came to handling men the island girl was still metaphorically in the first grade of her Skye primary school—easily led, easily deceived and easily hurt. Hamish, on the other hand, had a PhD in charm and seduction, and no visible scars. His emotions, like his businesses, were under tight control and highly profitable.

Alison bit her lip, pondering. She was not sure what she should do about it but Hamish appeared to have made a play and, rather effectively, struck a chord...

It was not an ideal night for sabotage—the moon was too full and the cloud-cover too sparse, leaving the sleeping glen bathed periodically in bright moonlight—but then the intending saboteurs were not experts in their field. Until now, 'Scotland for the Scots'—or SFS as it styled itself—had restricted its activities to the written word. Letters, crudely phrased and invariably anonymous, were sent to people with English names and English accents who'd had the temerity to buy houses or set up in business in Scottish rural communities and bring their bossy imperialistic attitudes to bear on the local population. In the village of Laggan in the hills of South Morar, however, recently transformed from a sleepy hamlet into a luxury timeshare holiday development by an English-based property company, the SFS was about to change from a vituperative group of pen-wielding xenophobes into a more sinister band of activists.

Faces obscured by hand-knitted balaclavas and half a tin of boot-polish, two silent figures in dark clothing glided stealthily from rock to gorsebush to birch grove, wherever the moon cast black shadows, picking an invisible route down the glen towards a cluster of whitewashed houses, standing stark and new at the burn's edge. At a prearranged signal, they paused to wait until the moon plunged behind a cloud before making their final hectic dash over a grass-covered clearing surrounding the paling fence which enclosed the houses.

They crouched with heads together. 'Bliddy moon,' muttered one in a soft Highland voice. 'We shoulda waited till the morra.'

The taller of the two shook his head and spoke in a deeper tone, less markedly accented than the first. 'No, man. I must be away tomorrow. It'll be OK. Come on—just think of it like going after the deer.' He raised his gloved hand, flicked the lighter he held in it and bent to unzip a black nylon holdall at his feet to reveal a square container that looked rather like a six-pack of lager. There was a strong smell of petrol. His teeth gleamed in the flamelight. 'You spray—I'll burn.'

There was an answering grin from the other blackened face. 'Right. You're lucky there's no wind—you shouldna get any blaw-back. Just gie us ten minutes afore ye start.' The speaker vaulted the fence and soon, from beyond it, came an intermittent hiss like the sound of a burning log.

After the specified time, the man with the lighter bent and selected one of the containers from the 'six-pack'. It was a crude Molotov cocktail with a rag wick which he proceeded to light then swiftly toss through the nearest cottage window. The sound of shattering glass and a *whoosh* of flame split the night air as the arsonist cradled his bag and sprinted along the fence to the next building, where he lit another 'cocktail' and hurled it through the window. In this fashion he torched six houses before darting into a plantation of spruce trees which bordered the western edge of the development.

'They don't seem to burn for very long,' he fretted when he met up once more with his companion. 'I expected more of a blaze.' Behind him the flames had died to a flicker inside each of the targeted houses and the glen

49

was quiet again, except for the screech of a disturbed owl.

'No' enough petrol p'raps,' muttered the other darkly. 'And the hooses are empty—so there's no furniture to burn. You lit up my handiwork quite well, though.'

Sprawling black hieroglyphics could now be discerned on the whitewashed exterior walls, disfiguring their pristine neatness. The first house bore the letters ENG, three foot high and crudely drawn but unmistakable. On the next were LISH and on the third OUT, and the message was repeated on the other trio of scorched and vandalised cottages. ENG LISH OUT. ENG LISH OUT. In the light of day the meaning would be plain to see, and in case anyone was in doubt as to the identity of the organisation responsible, on the wooden fence the two men swiftly sprayed their calling-card initials several times—SFS—before pocketing their paint-cans and sprinting off up the glen.

The phone rang on Catriona's desk early next morning.

'Hi Cat, did you get home all right?' It was Alison.

Catriona was in the midst of her early morning routine of checking the money-market deposits and assessing the overnight crop of unauthorised overdrafts. 'Yes, fine. I thought you'd be banging a gavel by now.'

Alison's tone was effervescent. 'I will be, very soon. It should be a good sale. The place is heaving with punters already. I just wanted to

50

check that you're OK. Shameless Hamish can be a bit persistent at times. I thought he might come on to you last night.'

Catriona laughed. 'You're digging for gossip, Ally,' she exclaimed accusingly. 'But you're out of luck. He was impervious to my wiles.'

After dinner she and Hamish had shared a taxi from the restaurant, leaving John and Alison, who lived in the opposite direction, to take another. Before Catriona stepped from the cab outside her home, Hamish had kissed her chastely on the cheek and she had been conscious of a small, guilty stab of disappointment. Guilty because the deep and honourable part of her knew that it was wrong for the wild and frivolous part to find him attractive. Anyway, she told herself, if he *had* come on any stronger she'd have run like a scalded Cat—wouldn't she?

'Good.' Alison's disembodied voice sounded relieved. 'So you're fighting fit and ready to take me on this evening?'

'I'd forgotten we'd booked a squash court. Oh God—another chastening defeat.' Catriona was new to the game and not yet up to Alison's standard.

'The winner buys the drinks! Six-thirty—see you then. Bye.'

'Bye.' Catriona replaced the receiver and jumped as the telephone immediately buzzed again.

It was Gillian from the banking hall, who also handled reception. 'Some flowers have arrived for you,' she said. Catriona could hear the curiosity in her voice. 'A fabulous arrangement.

51

Shall I get Ronnie to bring them up?'

Ronnie was the doorman, a cheery ex-Gordon Highlander who sat in the bank's entrance in his medal-decked commissionaire's uniform and smiled a welcome to all comers except those he didn't know, who were politely intercepted and vetted before he would press the hidden switch that electronically admitted them to the banking hall.

'How lovely!' Under her smart charcoal-grey suit and bright green polo-neck Catriona could feel her heart begin to beat a little faster. 'But don't disturb Ronnie, he's got his finger on the button. I'll get Moira to come down.'

Moira Campbell was Catriona's secretary, a General's daughter, twenty and twinkling, bonny, efficient, eager and mischievous. She returned from her errand partially obscured by her fragrant burden, a glorious riot of hot-house lilies and roses. 'Someone's stripped the Botanic Gardens' she said. 'Shall I open the card?'

There was a small white envelope tucked among the stems.

'No, I'll do it,' said Catriona, suddenly conscious that her hands were trembling.

The card said simply: *Thanks for your company, Hamish.*

'They're from a client,' she told Moira half-truthfully, laying the card face down on her desk, unable to decide whether to smile or frown. A confusion of emotions surfaced in quick succession—delight, unease, joy, guilt. She was grateful that John and Donald were out of the room, aware that they would undoubtedly have teased and goaded her over the identity of the giver.

'I think they should go in the Steuart Room,' she added hastily, seeking to avoid her colleagues' speculation altogether. 'If they come from a client then the clients should have the benefit of them.'

The Steuart Room was the most elegant of the three reception rooms set aside for meetings and interviews. In it coffee or drinks might be served while loans and investments were discussed in privacy and comfort. Like the bank, the room was named after the eighteenth-century Scots economist, Sir James Steuart, whose fiscal theories had first inspired his more famous and analytical successor, Adam Smith. Obligingly Moira departed with the bouquet.

Bruce passed her in the doorway, eyeing the flowers with interest. He approached Catriona's desk. 'From an admirer?' he enquired.

'A client,' she replied succinctly. 'Are you looking for me?'

'Yes.' Bruce placed the letter he was carrying on her desk and sat down in the chair opposite. 'I think these are your sort of people,' he said. 'Would you do the necessary, please?'

She glanced at the letter. 'Carruthers, with a Kent address. They're English.'

Bruce raised an eyebrow and tutted. 'Dinna be sae biased, lassie,' he said, affecting a brogue more pronounced than his usual RP. 'They are English but they've been recommended by one of our established clients and they sound like Steuart material.'

Catriona reddened slightly. 'I didn't mean...' she faltered and then continued more forcefully, 'I'll get in touch—make an appointment.'

'Right. They're not in town long—staying at the Caledonian Hotel.' Bruce glanced at his watch. 'I think I'll pop along to the Wentworth auction, just to see how things are going.'

'Will you bid for the Fergusson?' Catriona asked.

'Why? Don't you think I should?'

'Of course. If you like it.'

With a curious expression Bruce leaned towards her across the desk. 'Why do I get the distinct impression that you don't?'

'I thought she just looked a bit...aggressive, that's all.'

'Yes, you may be right. I'll go along all the same.' Bruce stood up, then added on an afterthought: 'By the way, what did you think of Scotland's answer to Richard Branson?'

At first Catriona couldn't think who he meant. 'Er...oh, Hamish Melville!' She smiled delightedly at the comparison. 'He was interesting,' she said carefully. 'Do you really think he's like Richard Branson?'

'Not entirely,' Bruce conceded. 'He doesn't have quite the same cuddly image—and he'd never call a company Virgin.'

'Good of you to see us so quickly, Miss Stewart.'

The man who shook Catriona's hand in the bank's entrance hall was in early middle age, with brown hair greying at the temples and

54

thinning visibly above his forehead. His face was slightly pudgy and veined, but he had candid hazel eyes set wide on either side of a substantial nose. He wore a blue blazer, old school tie and dark grey trousers. His wife looked about five years younger, with blond hair lifted by highlights, upper body lifted by corsetry, and cheekbones lifted by blusher. She wore a pretty printed-silk dress under a bright blue coat with pearls knotted loosely at the neck. They were both of above average height and above average self-confidence.

Nick and Sue Carruthers were former proprietors of the Talbooth Restaurant in Ashleigh Weald, Kent and intending proprietors of a similar establishment in rural Scotland. In her brief introductory telephone conversation, Catriona had discovered that they were in Edinburgh on their way north, and she had invited them to come and discuss their financial requirements that afternoon. She guided them up the stairs and into the Steuart Room on the first floor, where a tray containing a silver tea pot and gilded porcelain cups and saucers stood waiting on the low table between two sofas.

'What lovely flowers,' said Sue Carruthers appreciatively, gesturing towards Hamish's arrangement which stood on a dresser at one side of the room. 'Don't they smell wonderful?'

Catriona, busy with the tea pot, did not glance up but merely said, 'Yes, lovely. We have a contract with a local flower shop. Milk and sugar?'

The Carruthers expressed their preferences,

accepted a cup each and were soon enthusiastically explaining their intentions of moving their
family and business lock, stock and barrel
to Scotland. 'We're good restaurateurs,' Nick
declared frankly. 'Sue takes charge of the kitchen
and the menus and I control the finances and
the front-of-house. We had a large and faithful
clientèle in Kent and we intend to build up the
same in Scotland.'

'But if you were so successful down there,
why have you decided to move?' Catriona asked
pertinently.

'It's the children,' Sue Carruthers told her
earnestly. 'Our boys are twelve and fourteen.
They go to an independent day school in
Sevenoaks but the influences on them are
frightening. Drugs, joy-riding, drink, girls—even
at their age. In the Highlands they may not
develop into angels but at least they stand a
chance of not becoming Hell's Angels.'

Catriona consulted the slim file which
contained all the information she had been
able to find on the Carruthers. 'I see you're
prepared to deposit a hundred thousand with
us immediately.'

'The profits from the sale of our restaurant.'
Nick Carruthers nodded proudly. 'But a
substantial proportion of that will go straight
out again to pay for this property we've
bought.'

'Oh? Where is it exactly?' enquired Catriona.

'On the road to the isles,' declared Sue
Carruthers triumphantly, as if she had pulled a
rabbit out of a hat. 'Between Fort William and

Mallaig—I think it's pronounced that way, isn't it?' She had carefully stressed the first syllable of the second place-name.

Catriona agreed that it was indeed *Ma*-llaig. 'Actually I know that part of the world quite well,' she added. 'What is the name of the village?'

'Glendoran. It's near somewhere called Glenfinnan. Do you know it?' Nick asked.

'Glendoran,' repeated Catriona thoughtfully. 'Yes, I do. It's Bonnie Prince Charlie country. He raised his standard in Glenfinnan before the Forty-Five.'

'That's one of the reasons for buying it. The local tourist officer has given us the figures for the area. Visitors flock there apparently, even in winter, on the Jacobite trail,' Sue enthused. 'The property we've bought used to be farm buildings. A steading—would that be the right name for it? And there's a shepherd's cottage nearby. It's part of a large estate but it's become run-down and redundant. It's ideal for our purposes though, and only a few yards off the road.'

Nick had been searching in his document case and now drew out several paper-clipped sheets headed with a well-known estate agent's logo. 'We bought it subject to planning being granted for the conversion, but that should be through any day now, I'm told. Here's a copy of the details.'

Catriona leafed through it. 'What kind of sums are we talking here?' she asked.

'Well, our offer of seventy-five thousand was

accepted for the land and the buildings but the conversion is the major financial commitment. The estimate is over a hundred thousand. We should eventually get a grant from Highlands and Islands Enterprise, but that may take some time so we'll need interim funds to furnish and equip the place and we still need money to live on until we open. We're hoping to move up here at Easter and be ready to open by the end of May. Here, I have a breakdown of all that and the estimated yearly income.' Nick produced another sheet of paper. His financial outline was concise and clear and Catriona began to warm to him. He looked the part of the genial host but he seemed also to have a firm grip on the cash flow.

'So, you'll basically be looking for some more working capital, a loan to top you up.'

'Yes, though I can't be specific about the amount at present.'

'We'd need securities, of course. We could do it in the form of a mortgage and then we would hold the deeds of the property.'

Nick looked dubious. 'Is that necessary? We may not need as much as fifty per cent of its value.'

'We never lend more than sixty-five anyway, and that depends on an independent valuation once the work is finished. Of course, we'd have to do our own survey and clear all this through solicitors. I see you've given me the name of your lawyers here.' Catriona made a note on the breakdown sheet and then looked up and smiled. The Carruthers were just the kind of people she liked dealing with—so different from the Charles Moncreiffes of this world. 'It all looks very promising,' she told them. 'Why don't I come up and see the place? Then I'll have more of an idea.'

'If you wish. We're on our way up there now for a few days,' Nick told her. 'Come as soon as you like.'

'Right. I'll ask my secretary to check the diary.' Catriona rose to use the telephone on a side-table. 'Moira, how am I fixed for Friday? Good. Make a note that I'll be away from the office, would you, please.' She glanced up at the Carruthers. 'Friday suit you?'

Nick and Sue exchanged a brief nod of agreement. 'Fine,' they said in unison.

As they left the room their footsteps shook the Georgian dresser and Hamish Melville's flowers shivered on their stems. Catriona caught a whiff of their sweet scent.

'Cheer up, Cat, you'll beat me yet,' Alison remarked in the changing room after their game of squash. She appeared maddeningly cool for someone who had been on the court for the past half-hour.

Catriona, who was not so fit, finished towelling-off from the shower, her face still pink with exertion. 'You run me ragged round the court and then you expect me to sparkle?' she said wryly, stepping on the weighing machine in the corner and glancing at the needle as it hovered around the fifty-two kilo mark. 'Still, I suppose it keeps me fit.' She rummaged in her bag for a pair of white stretch-lace panties and pulled them swiftly up long, smooth legs.

'You're so skinny,' admonished Alison, surveying her friend critically. 'You'll need to put on a bit of muscle if you want to beat me.'

Catriona laughed and shrugged on a silky camisole, flicking her damp hair off her face and neck. 'You're no Amazon, Ally. It isn't muscle you beat me with, it's skill.'

Alison peered down at her own body, sleek but more rounded and with fuller breasts and thighs. 'I'm getting a tummy,' she complained. 'I wouldn't mind if I was pregnant, but I'm not.'

Catriona smiled sympathetically. 'Still no luck?' She knew of her friend's desire for a baby but was unaware of the heart-wrenching misery the other girl experienced each time her period arrived to drown hope once more.

Alison reached for the skirt of her Black Watch tartan suit. They'd both come to the sports club straight from work. 'No,' she said through clenched teeth, fastening the zip. 'Better luck next month.' She shrugged on her jacket and hid her dejection behind a bright smile. 'And still no sign of your prince coming, Cat? It seems neither of us can have everything, can we?

Catriona gave a brief laugh. 'I'll just have to keep kissing frogs,' she said lightly. 'All I've achieved so far are some flowers from Hamish Melville.'

Alison paused before responding. 'Wow, you must have made a hit,' she said without enthusiasm. 'What did you do to deserve that?'

Catriona stared at her in surprise. 'What are you accusing me of?'

'I'm not accusing you of anything, Cat. I'm your friend, I'm allowed to worry about you.'

'Well, I wish there was something to worry about. I could do with a good affair actually, if the truth be known.' Catriona brushed vigorously at her hair and it sprang up in waves around her head like a sun in splendour.

'Yes, but not with Hamish Melville. Why don't you have a fling with Donald Cameron? He always seems ready, willing and able.' Alison applied red lipstick skilfully, flattering the somewhat sallow tones of her face.

Catriona gave her a look of reproach in the mirror. 'Perleese! Donald's flirting is all hot air. Besides, he's thirled to Gillian, as you well know.'

'Yes, but they're not married.'

'Meaning that Hamish is, so hands off?'

'You're just not the sort, Cat. And Hamish is so—*ruthless.*'

Catriona gave some thought to this description and then shook her head. 'No, I don't think he's ruthless. Shrewd, yes. Resourceful, yes. Ruthless, no. Anyway, why are we discussing him? It was only a few flowers he sent and at this moment he's probably watching his wife try on her new Paris gowns and foaming at the wallet!'

Alison laughed at the image she conjured. 'Yes, I suppose you're right.'

61

'Of course I am,' said Catriona blithely, closing her sports bag. 'Come on—let's go and have a drink.'

Leaving the club half an hour later they emerged into darkness, relieved only by one arc lamp attached to the side of the building. Alison's car was parked in its beam and Catriona lingered chatting with her for several minutes before waving her friend off. Her own silver Volkswagen Golf was in shadow, under a row of bare-branched sycamore trees which bordered the car park. As she pressed the battery-powered gadget to operate the locks, the door of the next car, a low black Jaguar, opened suddenly and a figure reared out of the driving seat.

'Hello, Catriona.'

She nearly jumped out of her skin. 'Hamish! God, you scared me. I thought you were a mugger or something.' Breathing fast, she slumped against the Golf, her heart skipping and jumping like a kid on a bouncy castle.

'Since when have muggers gone about in Jaguars?' he scoffed on a laugh and then came closer to put a steadying hand on her arm. 'I'm sorry. I didn't mean to frighten you. I've been waiting to talk to you.'

'Why didn't you come into the club?' She opened the hatch of her car and threw her bag into the back.

'I wanted to talk to you alone. I remembered that you were playing squash with Alison. Did you get my flowers?'

'Yes, I did. Thank you very much. You really

shouldn't have sent them though.'

'Why not?' She could see his teeth gleam in the darkness. 'A beautiful girl like you deserves flowers.'

'Somehow I don't think your wife would agree.'

A disarmingly wicked chuckle accompanied another gleam. 'Probably not—although I've sent them to her often enough. Will you have dinner with me?'

Catriona was taken aback. 'I don't know,' she replied, flustered.

'What do you mean, you don't know?' She could hear the smile still in his voice. 'Aren't you hungry?'

She was ravenous, had been heading for the nearest Chinese takeaway. 'Yes, I am,' she replied honestly.

'Well, then.' He opened the passenger door of his car. A seductive smell of real leather wafted from inside. 'Do you like fish?' he asked.

It was Catriona's turn to laugh. 'If an island girl didn't like fish she'd starve,' she told him almost indignantly.

'Ah, but *I* know where they cook Dover sole that melts in the mouth, and serve it with ice-cold Pouilly Fumé.' He opened the door wider and the interior light flickered and beckoned.

Catriona relented and swung her legs gracefully under the walnut fascia. 'OK, I'm hooked,' she said recklessly. 'But Alison wouldn't approve.'

'We won't tell her,' he winked and closed the door.

Marinette's was a small unobtrusive bistro in an obscure street in Leith, a port which had once been an independent and thriving community on the shores of the Firth of Forth but was now enveloped in Edinburgh's urban sprawl. Nevertheless it managed to maintain a unique identity as a Bohemian enclave filled with restaurants and art galleries and 'interesting' blocks of flats converted from old warehouses. Where Edinburgh sometimes projected an image of bourgeois repression, Leith was a place of much freer spirit.

Hamish and Catriona were shown to a table in a candle-lit corner where pretty, Provençal-patterned curtains covered the lower half of a window overlooking the street. The floor was polished pine, the table and chairs plain and functional. It was a restaurant where the emphasis was clearly on the food. It was full but not crowded.

'I've only been here once before,' Hamish confided. 'It hasn't been open long.'

'I take it you didn't bring your wife,' said Catriona, studying the cutlery.

'Now why should you assume that?' he asked gently, moving the candle so that the flame did not interfere with his view of her face.

'Because I imagine you have your life carefully organised,' she replied, raising her gaze to challenge his. 'One place for the wife, another for the girlfriends.'

'So, you imagine I have several girlfriends?'

'Probably one in every port,' she teased, showing him her even, white teeth. 'But I'm glad I'm the Leith variety. I like Leith.'

'Good. Because it happens to be my favourite,' he declared solemnly. The candle-flame seemed to isolate them in an intimate glow. It danced in their eyes, the blue pair and the grey, as if sealing a pact between them.

Hamish picked up the menu. 'Do you want to see this, or are you having the sole?'

'Oh, the sole—definitely,' she said. 'And the ice-cold whatever-you-called-it, or I shall think you are not a man of your word.'

'I definitely can't allow that. Dover Sole and Pouilly Fumé twice then, as promised.'

The sole came, moist and succulent, sprinkled with parsley and anointed with butter, and accompanied by a basket of hot, crunchy *pommes frites*. They ate with slow enjoyment, easing the flesh off the bones and savouring the crisp, smoky wine alongside.

'You really know how to give a girl a good time,' teased Catriona in mid-sole. 'Fish and chips in a seaside café.'

'It's the secret of my success,' he responded with mock gravity. 'Tell me—what's the secret of yours? A bank manager while still a child.'

She laughed at his flattery. 'Hardly. And being a bank manager, even at Steuart's, is not exactly the big league.'

'Oh?' He raised an eyebrow. 'What is the big league, in your opinion?'

'Running a business, controlling millions, taking huge risks. It must be mind-blowing.'

She leaned towards him intently. 'Isn't it?'

He shrugged. 'As the elf-man told the child in the nursery rhyme—*I'm just as big for me, said he, as you are big for you.*'

'I didn't have you down as a quoter of nursery rhymes,' she said, shaking her head with bewilderment.

'Which just goes to show how wrong you can be,' he admonished. 'But it's nice to know you're not perfect.'

'I don't believe for a moment you thought I was.'

He gave a small secret smile and raised his glass to her. 'Almost perfect,' he declared, his eyes soft as blue velvet, his voice like liquid honey. 'Especially right now, in this place, in this light.'

She was silenced by his look, by his words, by his whole mesmeric presence. A sudden, deep suffusion of warmth spread through her veins as he gazed at her in the light of the candle-flame. No island youth, no eager boyfriend, no suave man-of-the-world escort had ever inspired such a rush of fire through the core of her being. It was unbelievable, unignorable! Her breathing quickened, her pulse raced, she wanted to cry out from the sheer force of it. But she sat, quivering, waiting for it to pass.

She thought he must have felt the volcanic flow of heat which had transfused through her slight frame, but he gave no indication of it. Quietly she brought her knife and fork together and placed them on the plate.

He lowered his glass. 'I thought you were

hungry,' he said, eyeing the substantial remains of her fish.

'I was,' she agreed huskily. 'But I've had enough. It was delicious.'

He picked the cold green bottle out of the ice bucket. 'Well, you can't refuse to help me with the wine,' he told her. 'Not if I'm to drive you home.'

She watched him refill her glass. The fierce inward fire had subsided and she shook herself free of its last embers. 'It's lovely here,' she said, glancing round at the room full of relaxed, murmuring diners. 'Much quieter than Il Castello.'

'Well, I thought it would be nice to talk. Giuseppe is a character, but his restaurant doesn't exactly encourage intimate conversation. Tonight I don't want to share you with a gregarious Italian, however charming he may be.'

'He doesn't have the monopoly in charm,' she murmured, sipping from her frosted glass. In a louder tone she asked, 'Did you go to the auction, by the way?'

A small twitch of his lip revealed that he had not missed the compliment. 'Yes, I did. It was quite a circus. Alison must have been pleased.'

'She seemed to be. Did you buy the Eardley?'

He shook his head. 'Someone wanted it more than me and paid well over the odds for it, in my opinion.'

'Do you often buy at auctions?'

'No. Mostly from dealers. They let me

know when they've got something I might be interested in.'

'Is that how you bought the Picasso?'

'Ah, the Picasso. No.' He looked mysterious in the dancing light of the candle. 'That sort of fell into my lap.'

'A Picasso fell into your lap—just like that?' She was incredulous. 'Like falling off a lorry? It sounds very dodgy.'

He grinned a little sheepishly. 'Not dodgy, a bit fortuitous maybe. It belonged to an American art dealer who wanted something I had. We swapped.'

'What on earth could he have wanted that was worth a Picasso?' she asked.

'My wife,' said Hamish laconically. 'He wanted to marry my first wife. He thought she was worth the Picasso. He didn't know I'd have let him have her for a Punch cartoon.'

'You're joking,' Catriona cried accusingly. 'You are, aren't you?'

Hamish shrugged. 'Not entirely. He did run off with her and it was his way of salving his conscience. Should I have refused?'

'Yes!' she exclaimed stoutly. 'You can't go bartering people's lives like that.'

'Oh.' He looked chagrined, boyishly ashamed. 'Well, I did.'

She stared at him for several seconds.

'It is a very beautiful Picasso,' he said with fervour, as if pleading for understanding.

Catriona was bewildered, not knowing whether to believe him or not and whether to condone his action if she did believe him. She shook her

68

head in confusion. 'I don't know what to make of you,' she sighed.

He gave her a puckish look. 'Don't try to make anything of me,' he said, taking her hand. 'Just come and see it.'

Three

The headquarters of Hamish Melville & Associates was on the top floor of a large purpose-built block in Edinburgh's New Town, one of the few modern buildings to interrupt the graceful progression of Georgian houses which lined the streets and squares of this part of the city. From there Hamish conducted his business empire, buying and selling shareholdings of varying size and importance in a surprisingly eclectic range of companies. He liked to remain a mystery man in financial circles, keeping the investment world guessing as to where his interest would next focus. In industry he was regarded by some as an angel of mercy, stepping in where disaster threatened, and by others as a harbinger of doom, bringing his considerable talent for asset-stripping into play like an evil son of Lucifer. But fans and detractors alike were unanimous in their admiration for his money-making acumen.

The nightwatchman seemed unsurprised by the arrival of the entrepreneur and his companion so late in the evening and admitted them through the main entrance with a polite, 'Good evening, sir—madam.' Behind her back, however, as she accompanied Hamish down the echoing hall towards the lifts, Catriona thought she could sense the man's prurient stare and it made her feel uncomfortable. She wanted to tell him that they were only going to look at the Picasso...

In the dark corridor on the top floor there was emergency lighting but she wondered vaguely why Hamish did not provide any other illumination as they passed down it into a large, spacious room with extensive plate-glass windows framing a cloud-scattered moonlit sky. She guessed that in the daytime the lower half of the view would include a panorama of the Firth of Forth and the hills of Fife beyond, but these were presently only discernible as an anonymous pattern of street-lights, swirling, silvered darkness and distant, shadowy humps, rather like a stage backcloth. Underfoot the carpet was thick and soft.

'Turn around,' Hamish said quietly and pressed a switch by the door.

Obeying, she gasped with surprise and pleasure as a group of spotlights beamed into focus and a painting almost literally sprang into life on the wood-panelled wall, leaving the rest of the room in shadow. It was an early Picasso, painted during the artist's period of fascination with the characters of the Harlequinade, and it depicted a full-length Columbine in a diamond-patterned dress of blue and grey, her white shoulders hunched, her red hair scraped back and her eyes huge and black, expressing powerful sensuality. In it, an art historian might have found indications of the painter's future preoccupation with cubism and abstraction but, despite a certain asymmetry of form, this figure was recognisably female and visibly aroused with a wide, ripe mouth and hands reaching ardently towards the invisible object of her desire.

Having been brought up on Skye and denied any early opportunity to study great art at first-hand, Catriona had never felt the urge to do so since, and she was unprepared for the emotional force provoked by such a masterpiece. She was astonished by her own response to the painting, instantly recognising the sensuous longings of the subject as if Columbine's fervent desires were her own.

'God, it is wonderful!' she breathed unevenly, her voice almost hoarse with awe. 'I never imagined...'

'Never imagined what?' asked Hamish, coming up behind her and placing his hands lightly on her shoulders. 'That mere paint and brush-strokes could evoke such sensuality? That you, too, would feel what thousands experience when they catch a glimpse of genius?'

Enraptured by the painting Catriona hardly noticed his hands at first but, as his grip grew gradually firmer she could feel his fierce pride of ownership, his own release of pent-up emotion, and something else—something more urgent and demanding and intimate which communicated itself with a speed that overwhelmed her. He was driven by an urge to possess beautiful things. The Picasso was one and she was another. He bent his head and pressed his lips to her throat.

Catriona felt her senses, already teetering off-balance in Picasso's thrall, plunge from their secure foundation. It was as it had been in the restaurant, her body suffused with a wildfire heat and her mind consumed in its flames. Her will vaporised. She had never encountered a man like Hamish Melville, who wielded sexual power like a blow-torch. He smelled of lust and money and there was something else, a musky, pungent aroma which she could not resist. It was desire, but it was not only his, it was hers. It engulfed her. As his lips explored the sensitive contours of her throat, denial became impossible. Under the sultry gaze of Picasso's Columbine, she turned recklessly in his arms.

'You are so beautiful,' he murmured, brushing her ear with his mouth and plunging his hands into the fragrant masses of her hair. 'More beautiful than Columbine—more glorious than any painting!'

She was hardly conscious of thought, except to register the powerful, deep pulsing of her blood. His lips found her mouth and their contact seemed to send undulating waves of pleasure through her body. She abandoned herself to her own self-gratification, helping him eagerly with buttons and zips and returning his caresses with equal fervour as their clothes fell to the floor. The carpet was deep and welcoming and as Hamish scattered kisses over her quivering, naked belly he cried out exultantly before burying his face in the bright, fire-glow tendrils that curled at the confluence of her thighs.

She was heedless, climbing rapturously to climax, but at the crucial moment he revealed himself as the experienced seducer. 'Beauty should make no mistakes,' he insisted, swiftly completing protective precautions while she remained scarcely aware of it, then lifting her bodily to cradle her over his thighs. His blue eyes glittered into her flaring silver ones and his sudden, thrusting entry made her gasp anew. 'But I need constantly to see it, especially when it writhes with pleasure!'

The battered Land Rover drew to a halt in the Laggan Glen road and an elderly man climbed slowly out of the passenger door. His tweed cap and baggy windproof jacket were well-worn and ancient, and his old black-thorn stick, which seemed more of an accessory than a prop, was as gnarled as his hands. He wandered between the vandalised holiday homes, stopping briefly to lean on each garden fence, gaze through the scorched windows and study the crude letters scrawled on the pale stucco-clad walls. Apart from these jarring marks of desecration the houses appeared to be in pristine condition, each with its neat paved patio complete with stone-built barbecue and carefully stacked woodpile, low-walled enclosure for dustbins and somewhat suburban-looking circular clothes-line. They were all built to a similar design incorporating three double bedrooms, two bathrooms, an open-plan living area, luxury kitchen and laundry, and had just been waiting for the furnishings that would have made them habitable for the start of the forthcoming tourist season.

'ENG LISH OUT,' intoned the old man to himself, reading the spray-painted message and shaking his head. 'Well, there won't be any English families spendin' their Easter holidays here now,' he mused, staring past the houses to where the glen stretched away behind them, rocks, grass and gorse bordering a rushing burn which tumbled down off a high, craggy ridge. The clouds were low and a fine drizzle misted his glasses. With an irritable click of his tongue he turned, walked back to the vehicle and climbed in.

'SFS,' he said gruffly to the driver who had remained in his seat. 'What does it stand for, that?'

'Scotland for the Scots,' came the reply.

'Scotland for the Stupid, more like!' sniffed the old man, shaking his head. 'I'm all for us standin' on our own feet but this will just make the English worse. These developers will get stubborn and next thing we know we'll have guard dogs and security patrols and the glen will be like an open prison.'

'Well, you should never have let the land go, Gamps,' the young man pointed out.

'Had to pay the death duties, damn it! You know that. How was I to guess, all those years ago, that it would end up as an English holiday camp?'

'Well, maybe it won't. Perhaps none of them

74

will come now and they'll have to sell the houses off cheap to local people who need them.'

'Huh! That's what those SFS types hope, I suppose. But that just shows how stupid they are.' The old man pulled the seat-belt over his torso and clunked it into its fitting. 'What Scotland needs is a few of her bright people to stick around instead of takin' their brains off to London or overseas. Then we wouldn't be left with just the stupid ones. Still, no one listens to me. I'm just an auld buddie! Come on, laddie—let's go home. I've got work to do.'

'Perhaps I shouldn't have done it,' said Catriona without conviction. 'But I can't regret it, Ally. I suppose you think I'm awful.'

'No. I could murder Hamish bloody Melville, that's all,' responded Alison vehemently, stabbing at her salad with a fork. They were in a wine-bar where Catriona, driven by the urge to talk, had begged her friend to meet her for lunch.

'He mustn't know I've told you. Obviously it's got to be a secret.'

'Obviously,' observed Alison dryly.

Catriona turned a reproachful gaze on her friend. 'Try and be pleased for me, Ally. He's such an incredible person, honestly. You just don't know him properly.'

'Yes I do. He's a serpent. So charming and plausible and slithery and slimy—and rich.' Alison's voice went thin and cold.

Catriona giggled a little wildly. 'I like snakes.

I spent ages in the reptile house when I went to Edinburgh Zoo.'

'Really? Ugh!' Alison shivered and shook her head despairingly. 'You are a case, Cat.'

'Am I? I suppose I should feel guilty, but I don't. He didn't seduce me, Ally, as you seem to think. I wanted him as much as he wanted me. I've never really broken out that way before but now that I have—well, I don't want to stop. Is that terrible?' She gulped at her glass of white wine and glared at Alison, challenging her censure.

They were seated at a table in a vaulted alcove which had once been a wine bin in the cellar from which the bar had been converted. It was a low-ceilinged retreat, quiet and private.

'Well, I'm glad we sat here,' Alison remarked, glancing about her, 'since you seem determined to make a full confession. No, Cat, I don't think it's terrible, I just don't think it's you. You're not the type to be jumping in and out of bed with married men without a qualm. You're much too nice for that. Still, if you want to get your fingers burnt, Hamish Melville is certainly a pretty hot flame to burn them on!'

'How will I burn my fingers? I'm not going in with my eyes closed.'

'Maybe not, but you're pretty dazzled,' retorted Alison. 'Admit it. You've never encountered anyone like Hamish before. And if he wasn't as rich as Croesus you wouldn't have let him near you. You're playing with fire and you know it.'

Catriona made a face. 'It's nothing to do with

his money,' she declared indignantly. 'I wasn't seeing pound signs last night, I was seeing stars. Anyway, we have to cool it for a bit because his wife comes back today.'

'God, you're already talking like a mistress. Listen to yourself!' Alison looked troubled. 'I don't like it, Cat, and I wish Hamish Melville would do the decent thing and leave you alone. You're just not the type to be grabbing a quick bonk whenever His Majesty can ditch the wife. You're worth more than that—and the sad thing is that he knows it. He wouldn't be interested in you if you weren't.'

Catriona smiled apologetically. 'I'm sorry you don't approve, but please don't write me off. I need you so much as my friend. But you will keep all this to yourself, won't you?'

Alison's dark brows beetled. 'Why? Because we're on His Majesty's Secret Service?' She caught Catriona's helpless shrug and raised her hands in surrender. 'OK,' she agreed reluctantly, 'but I don't condone it, remember?' Then she sat back and folded her arms as if, as far as she was concerned, the subject was closed. 'Now, I have something to tell you.'

'Oh, what?'

'I've decided to go to the infertility clinic.'

'Really? Are you sure?' It was Catriona's turn to look concerned. 'Do you think it's necessary?'

'John doesn't but I do. We've been trying for eighteen months now and we're neither of us in the first flush. The old biological clock is ticking on and I want to find out what's wrong.'

'You're thirty-three, Ally—hardly in your dotage. Still, I suppose it's sensible. Can you get an appointment quite easily at this clinic?'

'Yes. My doctor said I just have to say the word and she'll book it. I've told her to go ahead.'

'So when are you going?'

'Next week.'

'Good for you.' Catriona reached out and squeezed her friend's arm. 'I'm sure you'll get all the support you need from John but let me know if you need any more.'

'You can do one thing for me,' Alison said seriously.

'Yes?'

'Have your fling with Hamish if you must, but don't you dare go and get pregnant!'

Walking home through the city centre at the end of the working day, Catriona dodged through cohorts of shoppers and crossed at the West End traffic lights to walk down the relatively uncrowded pavement flanking Princes Street Gardens. The drizzle of the afternoon had ceased but a heavy bank of blue-grey cloud still hung low to the east, while a startling sunset was building to the west, behind the stark outline of Edinburgh Castle.

This was a sight she never tired of, the castle a sleeping giant, its perpendicular stone walls appearing to grow naturally out of their stern, volcanic rock foundations, enveloping and uplifting a sprawling mass of buildings with their diverse ranks of chimneys and buttresses and sloping, crow-stepped gables. It was a proud remnant of history standing sentinel high above the busy streets—the stronghold of Malcom Canmore, the fortified fist of David I, the solid fortress of Scottish government—and it looked like a castle should, strong and impregnable, no fussy, turreted Victorian-baronial Balmoral-lookalike. But of course it was all a sham. Edinburgh Castle was a monument to a moribund state. There had been no government there since King James VI had ridden south to London and been gulled by the English establishment into thinking he was uniting the thrones. Scotland had been submerged and nullified until even its parliament had migrated to Westminster. As the evening sun gave its last fiery gasp the castle was silhouetted against a scarlet backdrop, magnificent and proud, like the once-fierce nation it represented. It brought a lump to Catriona's throat.

At the top end of the long spine of rock that sloped east from the castle lay the great Esplanade and against its lower edge, fringed by trees, rose a glorious buff, white and sepia muddle of turrets, gables and leaded windows which reminded Catriona vaguely of a Disney castle. It was, in fact, a series of Victorian tenements and in one of them she had been thrilled to purchase a small third-floor apartment. She revelled in its central location and breath-taking views over street, roof and spire.

As the sunset turned the wet pavement to Crimson Lake, she climbed the hill towards her home. Via a cobbled lane, a stone ogival arch and a circular turret stairway she reached her front door and there, propped against it, was a large, flat package wrapped in brown paper. She used her Yale before stooping curiously to pick up the package and carry it through to the living room. Standing by the window, with the dying sun making a flaming splendour of her hair, she tore it open.

It was the painting she had seen at the Private View. Uig Bay, minus the jetty, a half-moon of blue-grey sea lapping a black-pebbled crescent of shore and the hills climbing steeply to their purple summits. And, nestling among tall, flowering grasses in the foreground, the croft that was her home, rustic and more run-down than it was now but still achingly familiar with its sturdy triangular gables and sloping, slate-covered roof.

Clutching the frame in both hands Catriona sat down suddenly on the padded bench-seat in the window bay. Her legs had gone weak but her mind was racing. Hamish must have bought it at the auction. Why? Just to please her? Surely not! It was too much. It was weird. It was wonderful. She began to smile and then to laugh and soon tears began to slide down her cheeks. They sprang partly from amazement but also from the sudden surge of homesickness which the little picture inspired. He must have noticed her emotional reaction to it when they first met, must have known how the painting affected her and wanted her to have it. How thoughtful and generous—and how wild and extravagant. He was mad and outrageous and brilliant!

There was no note but it had to be from Hamish. The lack of a written message caused a niggle of disappointment, a reminder of the one moment of discord which had occurred between them the previous night.

After making love under the Picasso they had left the office and gone to his flat nearby, the place where he told her he stayed when it was too late to drive back to his country mansion a few miles south of the city, and there they had fallen into bed and composed orchestral variations on the theme they had merely strummed earlier. Catriona blushed at the memory of their mutual passion. Their ardour had been like nothing she had ever shared with a man before. With Hamish's encouragement her hands and mouth had performed actions undreamed of even in her wildest fantasies, and her flesh had shuddered with the impact of orgasm until she felt as if her veins and arteries would burst with the exquisite agony of it.

In the early hours they had drunk champagne, apparently always on ice in his otherwise-empty refrigerator. 'I must go home,' she had said reluctantly, as he poured the second glass, wishing she could curl up against his shoulder and fall into exhausted sleep. 'I don't know how I'll drag myself to work tomorrow as it is.'

His abrupt reply had taken her completely by surprise. 'But you will, won't you, darling? Otherwise people will ask questions.' He put down the bottle and got up suddenly, winding

81

a sheet round his naked body. 'I'll call you a cab.'

Reality impinged like a cold, wet sponge, languor rapidly evaporating. Catriona abandoned her full glass untasted, and began to pull on her clothes, listening to his businesslike tones as he made the call on the bedroom phone, wondering where the sweet nothings had gone. By the time he finished she was dressed.

'Don't worry,' she said, trying to keep her voice steady and scrabbling in her bag for the small hairbrush she always kept there. 'I'm not going to jeopardise my job for a one-night stand with a married man, even if he did buy me fish and chips.'

All at once the charming Hamish was back, as if he had never left. He took the bag from her hands and wrapped his arms around her, kissing the damp, wayward curls on her neck. 'Don't be angry, Catriona,' he crooned gently. 'I know you're a trusty banker with heavy responsibilities. The fact that you are also a super-sexy lady with a sensational body will be our secret and I promise not to tell.'

She relaxed in his embrace but relented only slightly. 'That's just your sneaky way of saying no one must know about us. I'm not fooled, Hamish Melville, even though I may be infatuated.'

He looked offended. 'I think you're incredible, adorable and infinitely beddable but I want to keep all that a secret known only to myself. Is that so dreadful?' His hand moulded her breast through the soft wool of her sweater and he smiled as he felt the nipple harden. 'And I'm glad you may be infatuated because I'm intoxicated.' As he kissed her mouth the doorbell buzzed. 'Just in time,' he said huskily. 'I may be a married man, my silver-eyed darling, but this is *not* a one-night stand.' He stepped back and staggered theatrically, as if his knees were buckling. 'In fact, I may not be able to stand at all if you don't go soon.'

She had left the flat laughing.

The sounds of the city wafted up to her on the still, damp air—traffic and bustle and, periodically, trains rattling in and out of the Waverley Tunnel through the cutting deep under the edge of the Castle rock. Unconsciously fingering the gilded moulding of the picture frame, Catriona laid her flushed cheek against the cool glass of the window, remembering. Overnight she felt as if, sexually, she had grown up, or perhaps 'come out' would have been more accurate, aroused from a rather hesitant diffidence to discover a recklessness she had not been aware of. The memory of it disturbed and excited her. Even hours later she could feel her body tingle.

But should she keep the painting? She had received flowers and chocolates and even small presents from men in the past and thought nothing of accepting them but this was different. Couldn't such a valuable gift be seen as a reward for favours granted, turning her into just the kind of money-grubbing opportunist she abhorred, and Hamish into the kind of sugar daddy she neither wanted nor needed?

What was she to make of Hamish? He was charming and attentive but was he also scheming and ruthless, as Alison maintained? In business, perhaps, but surely not with her? Last night he had been considerate and warm and impulsive. He had been as carried away by the circumstances as she had. She may not have intended to become his lover but now that she had, she could not bring herself to regret it and with this gift surely he only wanted to show her how much it had meant to him?

'Hello, darling. How have you been without me?' In the hall of their elegant home Linda Melville planted a kiss on each of her husband's cheeks, French-style, and one cool, brief kiss on his lips. 'You look tired. Have you been working hard?'

Hamish pulled her towards him and kissed her more thoroughly. He had learned that it was wise never to play extra-marital games to the exclusion of inter-marital relations. 'I have been desolate without you, you wicked witch! Cold and lonely.'

Linda laughed and broke free, tossing her glossy dark bob of hair, her heart-shaped face creasing into a wide, glazed-ginger smile. 'God, I've only been away three days, darling. Don't go all cave man on me.'

Hamish hid his sensation of mild relief at her rejection. He liked to appear the ardent husband but sometimes appearances were enough—especially after last night. 'How was

84

Paris?' he asked, shrugging off his overcoat.

She took it from him, calling from the hall closet as she hung it up, 'The collections were magic. You should see Dior's beaded bodices—you could just eat them!'

'Rather an expensive snack, I imagine,' Hamish drawled. 'How many did you buy?'

'Only two. I can't wait to show you.' Linda re-emerged from the closet. She was wearing a blond cashmere tunic and trousers and looked as if she had just stepped off a catwalk. Even though it was ten years since she had done any professional modelling she still photographed well and her enormous, burnt-caramel eyes often sparkled from the pages of glossy magazines, but these days it was in the social columns rather than the fashion features.

'Are these bodices attached to anything as mundane as a skirt?' Hamish enquired laconically, picking up his briefcase and preparing to head for his study.

Linda paused at the foot of the stairs. When the Melvilles had bought and restored Laverock-bank, their substantial Georgian mansion in its extensive landscaped grounds, the original dark oak staircase had been found to be riddled with woodworm so they had replaced it with one of pale, pinkish ash, a wood not as much used in Scotland but which suited the light airiness of the house with its graceful moulded ceilings and Adam-style fireplaces.

'Oh yes, but very diaphanous and floaty. Quite romantic. You'll love them.' She gestured impatiently towards the briefcase. 'Don't be too long, darling, will you? We're dining with the McEwens tonight.'

'No, I'll only be a moment. Run me a bath, will you?' He was pleased about this social engagement with an influential industrialist and his wife. It was a talent particularly useful to Hamish that Linda, despite a rather drab suburban upbringing, knew instinctively how to cultivate the right people. Since marrying him she had raised networking to an art-form.

In his study he snapped open the locks of his briefcase and extracted a long grey velvet-covered jewel-box and a document. It was an invoice bearing the crested heading of a famous Edinburgh jeweller's and on it, in copper-plate, handwriting, was inscribed *One diamond and platinum snake-link bracelet, £8,500.* He crossed to the television, built into an audio-visual unit which covered most of one wall of the room, and pressed a switch hidden underneath. The television swung out to reveal the door of a small safe let into the plaster of the wall behind.

As she had one of her own concealed in the wall of her upstairs dressing-room, Hamish didn't think Linda knew about this safe but if she did, she certainly didn't know the combination which consisted of his weight in kilos, his collar size and the length of his erect penis in inches—77.15.08. The personal associations of this code pleased him. Hamish was a self-made man and the combination of his safe was equally self-oriented. He punched the numbers into the mechanism and, when the door opened, placed the box and the receipt among a number of other items already inside.

Wardour Street in London's Soho displayed the usual theatrical bustle as self-consciously 'now' people hurried between offices, studios and seedy theatres carrying the props and products of their work in garish carrier bags or fashionable hold-alls—demonstration tapes and videos, photographic portfolios and make-up cases, or the diaphanous scraps of sequinned netting that might cover crucial areas before a stripper went full-frontal. The location was a crossroads for the entertainment business—a place where music met film and money met opportunity, where careers might be launched and fates sealed, where blockbusting movie producers rubbed shoulders with peddlers of video skin-flicks and disc jockeys hobnobbed with recording managers in an atmosphere reeking with cigar smoke, cocaine, stale sweat and sour grapes.

In an office on the first floor of what had once been a thriving strip-club forced out of business by the rise of the video nasty, two people sat on the visiting side of a desk presided over by a good-looking, city-suited man in his mid-thirties with a square, strong-featured face, short, curly, light-brown hair and an air of pleasant implacability. His visitors were a man and a woman, both unconventional-looking in their different ways, the female a thin, earnest-looking brunette with long straight hair falling from a central parting, wearing an austere olive-green Armani trouser suit and John Lennon spectacles, and the male a dramatic figure in a black leather jacket over a loose, collarless unbleached linen shirt and white jeans, with a shock of curly, uncombed brown hair and a seriously handsome face, straight-nosed and fine-lipped.

'But we can't have got it that wrong,' the brunette was protesting, frowning over a spread of papers lying on the desk. 'It was all so carefully costed.'

'The film is a million pounds short, Isabel,' said the man in the city suit, using a tone of voice which suggested that he was sick of repeating himself. 'Your production estimates are skimped and you haven't allowed enough for the actors' salaries. Even if Gil Munro will do it for what *he* calls peanuts, his agent assures me he will still demand at least a million on top of his five per cent of the profits. The smallest of the other parts will command the Equity minimum—that's two hundred pounds a day for at least ten weeks, and you can multiply that by four for the bigger parts. And your leads may be young but star parts command star salaries, whatever the age of the actor. So you're talking another three million, plus three million for the crew. So you're up to seven million before you add your estimates for costumes and accommodation, which are too low anyway, to say nothing of catering and facility fees and your own pre-production costs. I've broken it all down for you, and ten million is just not enough. We can't grant a Completion Bond on the strength of these estimates.'

'But the guys at Minerva were happy with them, Rob,' said the other man, glancing sympathetically at the stony face of the brunette. 'Isabel was in LA a fortnight ago and they gave her the thumbs-up. She's even been confirmed as Line Producer.'

'But Andro, no job can be officially confirmed until the Completion Bond is in place.' Impatience lent Rob's voice a distinct edge. 'Look, I know you and Isabel have been on this project for months, and it must be terribly frustrating to hear what I have to say, but no one else will start work until they know for certain that they'll get paid whether or not the film is completed.'

'But if a mega-production company like Minerva are happy that it's viable,' Isabel persisted indignantly, 'who the hell are you to say they're wrong?'

Rob shrugged and laid his chin on his clasped hands, elbows planted squarely on the desk. 'Come on, Isabel. You know that's my job. Your backers at Minerva may be dollar whizz kids but they know nothing about the pounds and pence of making a movie in Britain. They rely on us for that. Now I don't work for the most reputable Completion Bond company in London without knowing what the hell I'm doing. I can't issue a Bond based on these figures, however much the Hollywood moguls may like them.'

'And without a Bond we can't make the film,'

muttered Isabel, flashing a grim look at Andro. 'So much for favours. Bang go your chances of becoming the new Hugh Grant, darling.'

'I don't owe Andro any favours,' contradicted Rob, 'and I'm no happier about this than you are. You can get another opinion if you like, although I can guarantee it'll come to the same conclusion. But look, it's not hopeless. You only need another million. Surely you can find some philanthropic movie buff with a spare bit of cash? Films are fashionable these days. Don't give up yet.'

Isabel stood up and took off her glasses, closing them up with an angry click. Although she was frowning deeply she was still a striking woman, with a pair of highly intelligent hazel eyes above a fine Grecian nose and full, sensuous lips. Even the dull green of her trouser suit couldn't diminish the forcefulness of her personality. She gathered the papers on the desk into an envelope file and packed it into the black briefcase which had been resting at her feet.

'Come on, Andro, let's go and follow some little leprechaun to the end of the rainbow,' she exclaimed bitterly. 'That's about the only place we're likely to find a million pounds in time to save this project from extinction. And at least there won't be any miserly Completion Bond brokers there!' She shot a withering look at Rob, wrenched open the door of the office and disappeared down the stairs.

Andro rose lazily and jerked his head in her direction. 'Sorry about Isabel, Rob. The film means a hell of a lot to her, as you know.'

Rob shrugged. 'I thought it meant a lot to you, too,' he remarked. 'Make an effort, Andro—find an angel. The film's a good one. Scotland's the "in" location this year and Gil Munro is a box-office buster. It's only a million you need.'

'It's certainly a good site,' remarked Catriona, climbing stiffly out of the driving seat and greeting the two Carruthers. 'Easily seen and reached from the road but not right on it.'

She sniffed appreciatively. It was good to breathe the sharp, tangy Highland air again after the salty bite of Edinburgh's maritime breezes. On a soft, grey spring morning it had been a pleasure motoring over the wide open spaces of Drumochter, along the winding shores of Loch Laggan, through the pine-clad verdure of Glen Spean and past the deep romantic waters of Loch Eil to reach Glendoran.

'And no other hostelries for six miles on either side,' enthused Sue Carruthers, her bleached-blond hair dishevelled by the wind, revealing dark, unforgiving roots. 'Come and see inside.' She urged Catriona forward with a hand on her elbow and an eager smile. 'It's terribly dusty so try not to brush against the walls.'

The steading was a relic of a failed agricultural experiment. Like many landlords of the preceding century, the local laird had been much taken with the idea of clearing his crofters out of the glens and parcelling his land into larger units which might command high rents from ambitious tenant-farmers, some of whom had tried to develop dairy herds. The Glendoran steading had been built to shelter one such but the herd had not thrived in the harsh Highland climate. Eventually sheep had replaced the cows and the steading-buildings were demoted to henhouses and garage space. Now the present laird, a radical and a reformer, had taken the farm back in hand, returned much of the land to crofters and sold off the redundant steading.

In the byre, the hundred-year-old wooden cow-stalls were miraculously still intact and free from woodworm and rot. 'We're going to keep these,' Nick announced with pride, thumping one of the partitions and raising a choking cloud of dust. 'They're genuine antiques. This part of the building will be turned into a family-style café with tables in each of the stalls. Then we'll add a floor above for a more exclusive restaurant and bar with picture windows looking down the loch.'

Catriona nodded. 'It's a good idea. Certainly lots of families come to this area, particularly in the school holidays.'

'So we've been informed by the local tourist office,' Sue concurred. 'We went to Lochaber District Council to get the facts and figures. There are several timeshare schemes and hundreds of furnished holiday homes and B and Bs around. And the Jacobite trail attracts a constant stream of pilgrims from North America, Europe and even Japan.'

'The Highlands are a tourist gold-mine,' Nick said excitedly.

'Oh yes, you'll do fine with the visitors but the locals might be more problematic,' put in Catriona. 'Did you see the reports about an incident not far away at a place called Laggan?'

Sue looked worried. 'No. What happened?'

'Some new timeshare houses were spray-painted and fire-bombed. A group known as SFS claimed responsibility. It was in the Scotsman yesterday but the incident took place three nights ago and there've been others in Galloway and Ayrshire.'

'Firebombed, why?' echoed Sue faintly.

'What are they, these SFS people—apart from mindless vandals?' demanded Nick testily.

'The initials stand for Scotland for the Scots. They're anti-English protesters,' Catriona told him.

'Nutcases, you mean?'

'Well, zealots anyway,' said Catriona uncomfortably, wishing she had let the Carruthers discover the existence of SFS for themselves. As far as the bank's loan was concerned she could protect it with insurance.

'Does this mean the boys will have a hard time at school?' asked Sue with concern. 'They won't be picked on for being English, will they?'

Catriona thought about this. From her own experience at Portree High school she couldn't remember anyone being subjected to bullying or abuse simply because they were English. More recently though, Highlanders had begun to talk about 'cultural imperialism' and 'Anglicisation', long words with political overtones often bandied about in the pubs and bars.

'You might ask the school principal but I'm sure he'll tell you there's no need to worry. We Highlanders have a reputation for being hugely friendly!' She smiled encouragingly. 'Let's have a look at the rest of your new empire. What's most important is that your schemes justify the bank's confidence.'

The Carruthers proudly showed her the shepherd's cottage which they intended to be the family home, the old stone fank or sheep-pen which would be floored and roofed and turned into kitchens and the site for a new, purpose-built toilet block. It was an ambitious scheme and one which, given the Carruthers' obvious commitment and experience, was clearly worth the small risk the bank would run in lending them a proportion of the funds needed. Catriona was almost certain she could recommend the loan.

After they'd completed their internal inspection the three of them stood outside beside the burn which chattered around tumbled boulders, under a road-bridge and into the loch. The brae climbed steeply behind the steading and the stream had gouged a deep fissure in the earth which was lined with slim graceful silver-birches, their purple twigs still winter-bare. In the other direction, looking across the loch, the mountains of Moidart seemed to rear out of the water, rising swiftly over rough, heather-covered foothills into breathtaking rugged peaks.

'This is the view they'll get from the bar and restaurant. Isn't it splendid and beautiful?' breathed Sue Carruthers, lifting her face to the sharp wind that drove them all to dig their hands into the shelter of their coat pockets.

'Makes you feel privileged to be part of it,' agreed her husband. 'I can't wait to get started.'

'When do you hope to move?' asked Catriona.

'As soon as the school term ends,' Nick replied. 'We have to get out of our Kent house then anyway so we'll just have to bivouac in the cottage here until the restaurant's finished. That must have priority because we need to open before June.'

'Oh yes!' exclaimed Catriona. 'The high roads and low roads will all be jammed with cars and caravans by then.'

Bruce Finlay edged his Audi slowly forward, pointing the remote-control device to operate the electronic gates which protected the driveway of his south Edinburgh home. 'Damn!' he muttered, noticing a silvery-grey Volvo estate car parked in front of the garages. It belonged to a golfing friend of his wife's, one whom he found particularly trying on the nerves and demanding on the gin bottle, and he'd been looking forward to a peaceful evening with his feet up in front of the television.

'Is that you, Bruce?' called his wife's voice from the upstairs drawing room. 'Sorry about

Elizabeth's car. Can you put yours away later?' Her cheerful, smiling face appeared over the stripped-pine bannister rail, blue eyes brightened by alcohol. Felicity Finlay was the typical product of a top-class English girls' public school—light-brown hair, fresh complexion, lively and pretty in a bouncy, exuberant way. She was nearing forty, preferred wearing tailored trousers and immaculate sweaters rather than skirts and blouses and dressed them up with gold chains and chunky earrings. 'Come up and have a drink,' she said encouragingly.

Bruce made a face. Felicity knew he didn't seek Elizabeth's company gladly. With ill-grace he plonked his briefcase down in the hall and removed his overcoat, throwing it irritably over a chair. He climbed the stairs slowly and unwillingly, wishing he could disappear into his ground-floor study.

'How long has she been here?' he whispered as his lips brushed one of his wife's cheeks. 'And how long is she staying?' he added as they brushed the other.

'We're trying to plan a charity campaign,' she told him, declining to answer his questions but tucking her arm in his and almost dragging him into the drawing room.

Bruce forced a smile as he came in sight of the unwelcome visitor. 'How good to see you, Elizabeth,' he lied. 'How are you?'

'Never better!' exclaimed the guest, a thin, loud-voiced woman of fifty-plus with short grey hair and a long distinctive nose. Elizabeth

Nicholson, widow of a once-prominent lawyer, lady-captain of Murrayfield Golf Club and gossipmonger *par excellence*. She raised her glass ostentatiously and knocked back the rest of her drink.

'Another?' enquired Bruce laconically, reaching out to take the glass. 'It's gin and tonic, I presume.'

'Of course,' nodded Elizabeth with relish. 'Thanks.'

'Felicity?' Bruce raised an eyebrow at his wife. 'Are you on G and T as well?'

Felicity picked up an empty tumbler and handed it to her husband. 'Yes, thanks.'

'Right,' Bruce said, moving towards the corner cupboard that served as a drinks cabinet. 'What charity are you adopting now?' he asked over his shoulder.

Felicity resumed her seat at one end of a well-stuffed chintz-covered sofa, tucking her legs under her in a characteristic position. The Finlay house, an early Victorian stone-fronted villa in a street of similar though not identical residences set in half-acre gardens, was comfortably furnished with antiques and traditional flower-patterned curtains and upholstery which complemented the delicate plasterwork and fine proportions of the rooms.

'It's the children's hospice appeal. Elizabeth's chairing a new committee which is going to raise money through sporting events and she's asked me to join in.' Felicity grinned at her friend conspiratorially. 'We're to be known as the Jolly Hockey Sticks!'

From the corner there was a fizzing noise as a bottle of tonic was opened but no hint of a laugh. Bruce was having a sense of humour failure. 'I'd have thought if you join another committee, Flick, you'll have no time to actually play any sport yourself.'

Felicity was a keen tennis and badminton player as well as a golfer, and not many days went by that she didn't hit a ball of some kind. When friends expressed admiration for such a high level of activity, she told them that she had to do something to work off the gin and tonic.

Elizabeth cast a look of mild exasperation at Bruce's back. 'It's only for a year, and since we're raising money by sport she'll be able to take part in all the events.'

Bruce turned and carried their drinks to them. 'Forgive me if I appear to be a killjoy, Elizabeth, but Flick is already on a charity ball committee, two school councils and has just become a director of her tennis club. Isn't that enough?'

Elizabeth raised a quizzical eyebrow as her hand went round the glass. 'Do I detect a man who is worried that his shirts won't be ironed and his dinner won't be on the table?'

'Bruce thinks that charity should begin at home,' murmured Felicity equably. 'Of course *his* work on the Sports Council and the Fine Arts Trust doesn't count.'

Bruce grimaced as his first gulp of gin hit the spot. 'I'm thinking more of the children actually,' he said. 'Where are they, by the way?'

'Iona is at hockey training and Gus is at Scouts. They both came in from school, downed a microwave cottage pie and dashed out again.' Felicity made a placatory gesture towards her husband. 'So we can have a lovely Darby and Joan evening, darling.'

Bruce shot a glance at Elizabeth which said eloquently, *If it weren't for her!* and decided to change the subject. 'I nearly bought a new picture for this room the other day, Elizabeth,' he said. 'I wonder what you'd have thought of it?'

'Why, was it a nude or something?' enquired their imperturbable guest.

'Yes, as a matter of fact it was. A J. D. Fergusson. I thought it might look rather interesting over the mantelpiece.' He indicated the spot, where an indifferent landscape presently hung. 'It was in the Wentworth sale, but I didn't bid in the end.'

'Oh, why not?'

Bruce shrugged. 'I just didn't,' he said, shifting uneasily. 'Saving our pennies.'

'Tell Elizabeth the truth, Bruce,' exclaimed his wife merrily. 'You thought that Iona would giggle and Gus and his spotty friends would have erections every time they looked at it. Go on—you did! Be honest.'

Elizabeth's peal of laughter confirmed once more for Bruce the main reason why he didn't like his wife's friend. She was coarse and vulgar, for all she was a respectable widow.

'I merely thought that it was unfair to make them feel uncomfortable in their own home,' he retorted, taking another large gulp of his drink.

'No nude is good nude,' spluttered Elizabeth irrepressibly, catching Felicity's eye and sharing a fresh attack of mirth.

'Perhaps you think I should have hung it and be damned?' enquired Bruce, grimly trying to keep a grip on his temper.

'And then Gus could have charged all his friends fifty pence each for a peep and given the proceeds to our appeal fund,' giggled Felicity, going, in Bruce's opinion, over the top, as she often seemed to do in Elizabeth's company.

'I've got a bit of a headache,' he exclaimed suddenly, putting down his half-full glass. 'I think I'll go and have a bath.' He stood up and smiled bleakly at Elizabeth. 'You will forgive me, won't you, Elizabeth?'

'Oh dear!' cried she, struggling to regain her composure. 'A headache. What a shame. Just when you and Flick were going to have a nice night in.'

Bruce ignored this quip. 'There's more gin in the cellar if you need it,' he said pointedly, moving towards the door. 'You've nearly finished that bottle.'

Linda Melville removed the last of the make-up from her face and peered into the dressing-table mirror, stretching the skin at her temples. Not many more years before you'll need the dreaded face-lift, my girl, she thought glumly. You couldn't let the chin sag too much before you began to tuck, or it didn't work properly. And the eyes! They were always the first to go, so you looked like a Chinese mandarin. That was the trouble with straight, dark hair; it made you look Oriental and you couldn't do justice to Dior gowns if you resembled a refugee from the Cultural Revolution.

It had been an ego trip in the Paris salons. The murmurs of approval when she tried on Karl Lagerfeld's creations had been like a sniff of cocaine. Even the great man himself had twiddled his pony-tail in excitement. It took her back to when she was eighteen and had won a magazine competition to find the model of the year. The prize of a place on the books of a big London modelling agency had whisked her away from the dreary housing estate in Airdrie where her father worked as a plumber, and five years later, at the peak of what had proved to be a flourishing career, she had met Hamish who was busy losing his first wife and gaining a Picasso. Getting him to marry again had not been easy, but Linda considered that she had made him a good wife, providing the son he craved and oiling the social wheels of his business bandwagon. But now she was thirty-six. Thirty-six!

She stood up and ran her hands over the thin silk of her wrap, feeling the flesh beneath. It was still firm, but she knew that the skin was beginning to crepe slightly on her breasts and buttocks. Fortunately Hamish was far too caught up in business to worry about her crinkly bottom. He was usually too distracted to notice very much at all concerning his wife, thank goodness.

'I forget to tell you, I've said yes to *Introductions*,' she called through the door of her dressing-room. Their bedroom suite was arranged around a large white bathroom with an oval spa tub and marble pillars. Three separate doors led from it to a dressing-room for each of them and to the central bedroom with its carved bedstead, quilted covers, French hand-blocked wallpaper and thick cream cable-weave carpet.

Hamish poked his head around her dressing-room door. 'What did you say?' he asked. He wore a red and gold Indian sarong wrapped around his waist and above it there was remarkably little sign of flab, his chest showing hard and white, hairs tidily confined to the space between his nipples. On his head the thick tawny thatch, only faintly streaked with grey, was damp from his ablutions. He looked sleek and well-preserved.

'*Introductions* want to do one of their special features on us. They come to the house and take lots of photographs and then write lovely things about the way we live. It sells millions.' Linda picked up her hairbrush and began to jerk it briskly through her springy bob.

Hamish made a rude noise. 'It's gross invasion of privacy,' he declared angrily, sleekness giving way to ruffle. 'We don't want to get involved in anything like that, for Christ's sake.'

'I thought it would be good for our image. You know, darling—beauty and business in perfect harmony! Don't you want to boast about our wonderful life together?'

'No, I don't. And I certainly don't intend to stand around while some poncy photographer takes endless snaps of us looking like a pair of morons. If you must do it, you're on your own.' Hamish moved back into the bathroom and picked up his toothbrush.

Linda prowled sulkily after him. 'It'll look pretty funny if people have to read about our blissfully happy marriage with one half of it conspicuous by his absence,' she muttered.

'Just tell them no, for God's sake! Surely they can make do with minor royalty and major movie stars?' He began scrubbing his teeth, temporarily inhibiting speech.

'Well, I think it would be fun. I've worked bloody hard to make this house photogenic and it would be nice to have some decent shots of it.'

There was a tense pause while Hamish finished his teeth and Linda leaned sinuously against the door jamb wondering whether to vamp him or nag him into agreement. Then she realised she need do neither. Queenie would persuade him, she thought. The next night they were invited to dinner with Lord and Lady Nevis, and even the aristocratic and sophisticated 'Queenie' Nevis in her grand West End house, surrounded by her glorious collections of antique furniture and porcelain and her husband's comprehensive gallery of nineteenth-century French and Scottish art, had been unable to resist an invitation to appear in *Introductions!*

Four

On Saturday morning Catriona rang Alison in a panic. She had been so caught up in the Carruthers' development plans that only on her return home from Glendoran late the previous evening had she recollected the weekend's crucial social engagement.

'You must help me over what to wear for the Nevis dinner tonight, Ally,' she begged. 'I haven't got anything suitable.'

'Cat, you must have,' Alison scoffed, still chewing her breakfast toast. 'What about that natty little number you wore to Donald's party last month?'

'That was a disco,' wailed Catriona. 'I can't wear a skintight red mini-dress to a dinner party, especially not *this* dinner party. I have to have something stunningly elegant.'

The penny dropped in the Home-Muir kitchen. 'Oh, God...I get it. Hamish and Linda Melville will be there.' Alison's voice turned arctic. 'If you're thinking of trying to compete with Linda, it's either going to have to be a Versace or a sudden virus.'

'Well, I'm certainly not crying off sick,' declared Catriona defiantly. 'Where can I get Versace in Edinburgh?'

'You can't,' said her friend flatly.

'Ally, help me,' pleaded Catriona. 'Don't treat me like an unauthorised overdraft, please!'

Alison relented. 'Oh, all right. But it's against all my principles.'

'I don't want anything from Principles. It's got to be classy!'

'They're *very* classy. I get lots of my working clothes from them,' sniffed Alison.

'Yes I know, but this is different. You're not going to the dinner—haven't you got something I could borrow? You told me you bought some fantastic gear in London last autumn.'

'Well, I suppose I could lend you my Caroline Charles. It's dead classy, but it's short.'

'What's wrong with short? My legs are my strong point. Can I come over and try it?'

'Yes, but it'll probably be too big. Unless adultery has suddenly made you fat and contented.'

'Hardly. By the way, can you be an adulterer if you're not married?'

'I don't know. You'll have to go to adultery education classes and find out.'

'Oh, Ally. Thank goodness you're joking about it. I thought you'd lost your tickle.'

'Just get round here and try on the dress, pronto. My mother-in-law's coming today and I've got housework to do.'

'I'll be right there.'

Twenty people were seated around the most magnificent table Catriona had ever seen. Its delicate moulded gilt ribbon-edging and intricate marquetry were Italianate, reflecting the ornate

Florentine embellishment of the whole palazzo-style Nevis residence. Mellow stone reliefs of urns and laurel wreaths decorated the outside of the house, and gorgeous fabrics the inside—rich gleaming satin stripes of emerald and ruby shot with gold, damasks and velvets figured in glowing hues, draped and swagged and luxuriously braided.

A huge mahogany display cabinet along one wall of the dining room exhibited Lady Nevis's collection of Sèvres porcelain—dishes, vases and plates delicately handpainted with scenes of classical mythology, framed in gilded scrollwork and bordered with the profound pinks, greens and blues exclusive to the famous French ceramics factory.

Three silver candelabra illuminated the glittering array of cutlery and glass laid on the table and instead of a cloth, which would have hidden the glories of its inlaid surface, each setting had an individual silver-filigree and glass mat, another relic of Florentine craftsmanship. There was no central floral decoration, which would also have obscured the table's prized marquetry, but thick ropes of interwoven lilies and ivy were slung between the candelabra with delicate clouds of stephanotis entwining their branches, exuding a sweet, heady fragrance in the warmth of the candles.

Reine, Lady Nevis, or 'Queenie' as her friends called her, with a subtle Anglo-French pun on her name, had spent thirty of her fifty-five years perfecting her technique as a hostess, priding herself on providing elegant and unusual surroundings in which to entertain her frequent guests.

Catriona had arrived feeling a little self-conscious in her borrowed finery. Alison's short, black ribbon-strap shift made of several layers of silk chiffon which fluttered and clung and revealed and concealed all at the same time, displayed her flaming hair, slender figure and long legs to advantage but also contrasted rather daringly with the more sedate gowns of most of the other ladies present, the exception being Linda Melville.

Even though she'd been expecting it, her first shock of the evening had been bumping into Hamish himself, wearing an impeccably cut black silk dinner jacket and tartan trews, his thick hair brushed into strict order, sharp blue eyes constantly on the move. He'd been standing in the doorway of the drawing room talking to Lady Nevis, who introduced him to Catriona as if they had never met.

Seeing Catriona's confusion, Hamish had taken her hand and immediately enlightened his hostess. 'I have to confess, Queenie, that Catriona and I met the other day at Wentworth's Private View, but I don't recollect quite such a stunning outfit on that occasion. We have you to thank for providing her with a suitable time and place to delight us by wearing it.'

Lady Nevis threw back her immaculately coiffured grey head and laughed delightedly. 'I never tire of hearing a well-turned phrase on the lips of a skilled performer,' she said, smiling warmly at Catriona. 'Hamish manages to flatter both of us with one flick of his silken tongue. He is quite incorrigible.'

'Do you think she means encourage-able?' whispered Hamish to Catriona as Lady Nevis moved away to greet another new arrival. He didn't pause for further asides, however, taking her elbow lightly and steering her across the room. 'You must let me introduce you to Linda before someone else does,' he said, providing the next shock.

The lady towards whom he guided her was quite the most glamorous woman in the room, slim, dark and graceful with a pointed chin and a heart-shaped face like a gamine ballet dancer. She was wearing a deceptively simple dress which had a tiny, sleeveless jewel-encrusted taffeta bodice with a plunging neckline and wide white reveres and a long, gossamer black chiffon skirt which made her look as if she floated on and in a dark cloud. The skin of her arms and neck was translucent, like the inside of a cowrie shell and diamonds sparkled at her ears and throat. Linda Melville, thought Catriona grimly, was Audrey Hepburn without the air of vulnerability.

'Linda, I'd like you to meet Catriona Stewart. She is one of our bank managers, only recently appointed. Catriona, my wife, Linda.' Hamish smiled blandly from one to the other as if he had never brought either of them to climax.

Catriona shook Linda's hand in a rather dazed fashion, thinking, 'He has a wife like this and he pursues me?'

Linda looked at Catriona and thought. 'This

must be the one Bruce can't stop talking about.'

Neither noticed the expression of supreme satisfaction which darkened the blue of Hamish's irises as he gazed upon them, without question the two most beautiful women in the room.

From a far corner Bruce Finlay watched the introduction with interest, thinking, 'here are two birds of completely different feather; a hummingbird and a goldcrest, flying in separate spheres, each as conspicuous as the other. Between them even the charismatic Hamish looks almost dull—no, perhaps smug is the right word. Bruce frowned. Why should Hamish be looking smug?'

'I gather you're from Skye,' Linda said to Catriona conversationally. 'You'll know all the reels and country dances, I'm sure. You must come to my charity ball.' It was not clear from her tone whether she was claiming ownership of the ball or the charity.

Catriona wondered who had revealed her background. Surely Hamish wouldn't have discussed his lover with his wife. 'I'm afraid I'm no better at them than anyone else,' she demurred.

'Really? You *must* have been to that annual ball in Portree where they do all those complicated reels with the outlandish names— Speed the Plough and the Reel of the Fifty-First and so on. I thought you country girls learned them almost before you could walk.' Linda looked rather pained at Catriona's defiance of her imagined stereotype. 'I find it's always such

109

a help when a few pretty girls can do them well. It gives other people something to watch when they can't cope themselves.'

'Yes, I suppose it does,' smiled Catriona, adding sweetly, 'but I don't think I'd be much help to you. I've never been to the Skye Gathering, I'm afraid. We just used to bop wildly to disco music at our ceilidhs on the island.'

'How disappointing,' drawled Linda with a shrug. 'I think it's terrible when these country customs die out.'

'Well, fortunately you seem to keep them going admirably in the city,' observed Catriona, turning her head in response to a brisk announcement by the rather twinkling Irish butler that dinner was served, thus failing to register Linda's frown of irritation.

Hamish was seated between Catriona and Lady Nevis, while on Catriona's right was Bruce Finlay and beside him, Linda. At the other end of the table Lord Nevis had Felicity Finlay on his left and on his right a glamorous and witty knitwear designer called Fenella Drummond-Elliott who was there with her new husband Tally McLean, a taller version of Mel Gibson who, Lady Nevis informed Catriona, owned 'one of the most beautiful hotels in Scotland. You should go and stay there, my dear. You'd love it!'

'This is a beautiful house,' Catriona remarked to her hostess across Hamish as the butler poured dry sherry to accompany the consommé. 'And this table is quite extraordinary.'

'Yes, it's a rather special piece, isn't it?' Lady Nevis agreed, gratified by the younger woman's appreciation. 'I bought it in Lucca, if you can believe it, at a house sale I went to during a holiday in Tuscany. It was years ago—in the sixties when such things were going quite cheap over there. I think it cost more to have it shipped back than I paid for it.'

'It seems to be in perfect condition,' remarked Hamish.

'Yes. Better than its owner, even though I've had more beauty treatments!' Lady Nevis laughed and leaned forward to ask him confidentially, 'Can you quite get used to the idea that one of your bank managers thinks like Adam Smith and looks like Claudia Schiffer?'

'I'm trying to come to terms with it,' he responded glibly. 'Sadly, I don't seem to merit her personal attention during banking hours, however.'

'Well, I hope you don't expect to receive it *out* of banking hours, you wicked man,' cried his hostess archly. 'Queenie' Nevis loved sniffing out scandal almost as much as tracking down antique porcelain. 'You surely don't need extra-mural activities, not with a stunning wife like yours.'

Catriona could feel cold sweat crawling down her back, running in rivulets between the goose bumps. Ally was right—if she was going to play games with married men she would have to go to evening classes in adultery.

'My wife may be stunning, Queenie, but while Catriona is probably a Member of the Institute of Bankers, Linda has a doctorate in shopping,' said Hamish dryly, casting a meaningful glance down the table at his wife. 'I've suggested she should leave her wardrobe to the National Museum of Costume. I'm sure that in twenty years or so they'll be able to devote an entire gallery to it, as a comprehensive record of late twentieth-century fashion.'

'I don't think men should make sarcastic comments about their wives in their hearing, do you, Bruce?' asked Linda Melville in a clear, carrying voice. 'It undermines their confidence.'

'I don't think Hamish was undermining your confidence so much as boosting Catriona's,' observed Bruce in reply, raising a sly eyebrow at his other neighbour.

'Which doesn't need it, I'm perfectly certain.' Linda's crystal voice displayed ample evidence of the elocution lessons she had received as part of her teenage modelling prize.

From the other end of the table Felicity Finlay eyed her husband curiously. Bruce would be thoroughly enjoying himself, positioned between two such beautiful women, she thought. Ever since she had first met Catriona Stewart, Felicity had speculated about the effect of her appointment on the bank. She was such a vivid, gorgeous creature to be working among all those grey suits, like a sparkling gemstone thrown into a pool lined with dull grey pebbles. What ripples was she causing on the surface of Bruce's pond?

The next course began to arrive, making conversation temporarily impossible around the

112

plump, ducking bosoms of the Irish butler's two assistant waitresses.

'Linda says that you'll manage to persuade me to let the people from *Introductions* take over my house for a photo-feature,' Hamish remarked to Lady Nevis as they picked up their fish forks. 'I can't believe for an instant that you will, but—'

'Why not?' cried his hostess gaily. 'They're all quite lovely people! They never say anything nasty about one, and the photographs they take are absolutely marvellous. They made our house look like a palace.'

'My dear Queenie, your house *is* a palace,' interjected Hamish. 'I just don't know what possessed you in this instance not to treat it as a castle and pull up the drawbridge.'

Lady Nevis considered this while she took a mouthful of trout terrine. 'I suppose it was pride,' she confessed at last. 'Sinful pride. I was just flattered that they thought people would find my unpretentious house and its rather dull inhabitants interesting.'

Hamish looked at Queenie Nevis's sumptuous table, at her glamorous gold-lace dinner dress, at the heirloom amethyst choker which clasped her long, aristocratic neck, and the noble and refined jut of her jaw and nose, and shook his head despairingly, turning to draw Catriona into the discussion. 'What do you think, Catriona? Dull? Unpretentious?'

Catriona shook her head, smiling. 'I might say incredible,' she put in, 'or fantastic.'

'There you are, Queenie. We agree that you

113

are exceptional,' concluded Hamish. 'Which means that no one else can possibly emulate you—so I can't do the *Introductions* feature.'

'Can't, or won't?' teased Catriona and then smothered a small gasp as she felt Hamish run his hand swiftly up her thigh, bunching the silk chiffon of her dress. It was a gesture of retaliation but also of possession, asserting both male dominance and sexual innuendo and Catriona's immediate reaction was complete astonishment. She had not expected it of him.

'Oh Hamish, you can be a notorious flatterer with one breath and an awkward cuss with the next,' Queenie Nevis declared indulgently, oblivious to her neighbour's lascivious sleight of hand beneath the table.

Catriona was prevented even from giving Hamish a dirty look because milli-seconds after she had smoothed her skirt down, Bruce turned to speak to her. 'I don't want to talk shop for long, but how did you get on with the Carruthers?' he asked.

Putting Hamish's handiwork firmly out of her mind, Catriona began to tell Bruce about the restaurant project and her tacit approval of a business start-up loan. 'It looks an eminently viable scheme. The Carruthers are experienced restaurateurs and they should make good profits, especially in the summer months.'

'But are you sure theirs is a prestige development?' insisted Bruce. 'Steuart's doesn't want to become associated with anything too down-market. Where is this steading?' He took a forkful of terrine.

114

'At Glendoran, on the Mallaig road. Do you know it?'

Bruce had his mouth full but gave a grunt and a positive jerk of his head. Before he could speak, however, he was forestalled by Lady Nevis, who interrupted from the end of the table.

'Did I head you mention Glendoran, my dear?' she asked.

'Glendoran is Lord Nevis's family estate,' Hamish intervened. 'Did your clients buy their property from the Earl of Lochaber, by any chance?'

'I must admit I haven't inspected the deeds that closely yet,' Catriona replied.

'Lochaber is my father-in-law,' Lady Nevis explained.

'Yes, I do know that,' Catriona asssured her. 'But I wasn't aware that his estates were in that part of the country. I suppose I should've been. After all, Ben Nevis is in Lochaber District, isn't it? And so is Glendoran. I just never put two and two together.'

'I should warn you, if you do become involved with him, that George's father is not a great fan of Steuart and Company,' continued Lady Nevis. 'He thinks that owning land conveys an unavoidable duty, rather like being king of a country, and that George should be using his talents for the good of the estate, not frittering them away in some bank.'

'But surely he realises that the money George makes will be ploughed back into the estate?' Hamish expostulated. 'Market forces dictate that you make money where you can, for use where you choose.'

Lady Nevis gave a tinkling laugh. 'I don't think market forces go down very well with my father-in-law. He's a bit of a socialist and a nationalist and a very awkward customer.'

'He doesn't sound like your average establishment aristocrat,' remarked Hamish with amusement.

'Far from it. I'm afraid poor George suffers from his father,' Lady Nevis said without much evident regret. 'They're like a pair of bulls in the same pasture: you have to keep them apart or they charge. That's why we hardly ever go to Glendoran. The boys visit their grandfather but we tend to steer clear.'

'The boys?' enquired Hamish. 'Oh yes. You have two sons, don't you, Queenie?'

'Not that I see a lot of them,' she agreed airily. 'One works in London and the other is all over the place—mentally as well as physically. A wild boy.'

Catriona turned back to Bruce to ask quietly, 'Do you think I'd better re-think the Carruthers' loan?'

But Bruce's attention had been diverted by Linda Melville, who was regaling him with a funny story from the Paris salons.

'It sounds as if you'd better be wary of the old Earl,' murmured Hamish, who *had* heard Catriona's question.

'Why? Do you think he might grope me under the table?' she murmured accusingly and witnessed his brief but unrepentant smile.

Lady Nevis was still holding forth about her father-in-law. 'He's a funny old stick really,' she continued. 'Goes about looking like a tractor-driver in awful old blue overalls. And he's a wood-turner, you know. Self-taught, of course, because he always complained that they never learned anything useful like that at Eton.'

Catriona was intrigued by the story of the Earl and the carpentry. 'What sort of things does he make?' she asked.

'Oh, chairs, small tables, bowls—the sort of thing you buy at craft fairs. Some of it is lovely. He uses wood from trees which have fallen on the estate. Says they speak to him and tell him what to make.'

Dinner progressed through a main course of collops of venison in damson sauce, and the dessert was a passionfruit mousse with feather-light shortbread wafers in exquisite Venetian glass dishes. Throughout both courses the wine flowed freely and the mood became ever more lively.

'Let's play the truth game!' cried Felicity Finlay when platters of cheese were laid out and the port decanter began to circulate. Her cheeks were already flushed rosily and would no doubt glow even more warmly when the rich fortified wine percolated into her bloodstream. 'May we, Queenie? It was such fun last time.'

'Well, of course we can, dear,' Lady Nevis smiled benignly down the table. 'As long as everyone promises to lie through their teeth. I dislike fascinating revelations at this stage of the evening because I may not remember them.'

'Oh, but the questions are usually more revealing than the answers,' trilled Felicity. 'Who's going first? You, George!' She laid a flirtatious hand on her host's arm.

Lord Nevis's usually smooth grey sweep of hair had drooped forward over his eyes so that he looked more like a naughty schoolboy than a distinguished banker. He cast his twinkling glance around the table from one lady to another and finally lit upon Linda Melville. 'Linda!' he called loudly. 'What colour are your knickers?'

Catriona couldn't believe her ears. The dinner party was developing in a way she could never have imagined. She had been mildly surprised that there had been no general female exodus on the arrival of the port. She had thought women's lib would have failed to penetrate the salons of the aristocracy but it seemed she was wrong. And now naughty games! Was this really how the rich liked to enjoy themselves?

Linda had played the game before—had probably even been asked the same question. 'I haven't any on,' she announced without hint of a blush.

Catriona recalled the floating panels of chiffon which were such a feature of Linda's gown. They were semi-transparent and, when she walked, revealed the shadow of her shapely legs beneath. Her statement was therefore doubly interesting, if true.

'But when she did have, they were black!' announced Bruce triumphantly, producing a miniscule item of lingerie from his dinner-jacket pocket and waving it around his head. Gales of surprised laughter rippled round the table.

'Did he bring those with him?' Catriona couldn't help asking Hamish in a whisper, wondering whether he liked his wife being singled out, however harmless the game.

'If he did they're not Felicity's,' came the cool reply. 'Not nearly serviceable enough.' Hamish showed no sign of discomposure.

The rest of the company were clamouring for more. 'Linda's turn!' came the shout.

A mischievous frown puckered Linda Melville's smooth brow. 'I'll get those back later,' she admonished Bruce, wagging her finger in comic reproof. 'And for that, you can tell us when you last bought your wife a bra, and what size it was.'

'Foul,' declared Felicity, laughing helplessly. 'You're not allowed to ask incriminating questions between couples.'

'Are you implying that I don't know the answer?' demanded her husband indignantly. 'I remember the occasion vividly. It was in nineteen seventy-two on our honeymoon in Ibiza, when your bikini top snapped and you wouldn't come out of the water until I bought you another one. It was size eighty-eight.'

Tears of mirth were beginning to stream down Felicity's red cheeks. 'You beast!' she shrieked. 'That's in centimetres!'

'Well, I was lying anyway,' Bruce grinned. 'I'm not allowed to tell the truth, remember. You don't want everyone to know it was really size ninety-two, do you?'

'It's all rubbish anyway,' Felicity gasped

merrily. 'It was a topless beach. Bruce insisted. My turn.' She glanced round the table, considering her prey, but interest in the game was waning as the party began to change its character.

Beside Bruce, Linda Melville stood up to leave the table. 'Excuse me, back soon,' she murmured to Lady Nevis as she passed behind her chair. One or two others followed suit, including Bruce, and some diners took the opportunity to swap places so that they could talk to other guests. Several conversations were underway by the time the waitresses came in with coffee, and amidst all the coming and going the gathering became rather diffuse. At his hostess's invitation, Hamish rose to cross to the display cabinet and view one of Lady Nevis's new pieces of Sèvres. At the same time Catriona, finding herself rather disconcertingly without company, murmured that she, too, would powder her nose.

'Of course, dear,' said Queenie Nevis over her shoulder, taking Hamish's arm. 'It's just up the stairs on the left.'

When Catriona mounted the staircase she found several doors in the passage to the left of the landing, all of them closed. Taking a wild guess she opened one, but saw instantly that it was not an empty bathroom—it was a bedroom and it was well and truly occupied.

A couple were sitting on the bed in close embrace, the woman astride the man's lap, her flowing dark skirts obscuring their joint activity but the rhythmic bouncing of the mattress making the nature of that activity abundantly clear. The man's hands were pumping the woman's buttocks urgently, the distinctive jewelled bodice of her dress was unbuttoned and his face was hidden from view as he nuzzled between her breasts, while her dark head was arched back, her mouth open and gasping in the throes of a building climax.

Catriona retreated hastily but not before she had recognised the woman as Linda Melville, despite the distortion of her face by approaching orgasm, and she did not need to have seen the man's face to know that it was Bruce Finlay. But to see him at full thrust with the exquisite Linda was a bewildering surprise.

When she eventually found the bathroom after cautiously opening two further doors, she sat on the loo for several minutes considering what she had seen. She was disturbed by her reaction to it. The island girl in her had been shocked, for the coupling had been so blatant, a fast fuck undertaken beneath the very noses of spouses, friends and colleagues. Catriona found the idea at the same time disgusting and wickedly titillating, like a pornographic movie. There was a carnal, libidinous side to her nature which couldn't entirely condemn it, the side which had launched her into her own affair.

Her head spun with questions. Did she need any more to feel guilty about her liaison with Hamish, when his wife was gaily having it off with another man, and clearly not for the first time? There had been something practised about the style of their intercourse that told her that.

Did Hamish know about it? Would he like to know? Was Felicity aware of the situation? Was she also playing away? Was adultery perhaps contagious, like flu?

Conscious of time passing, Catriona moved to tidy her hair and apply some lipstick, turning from side to side to study her reflection in the mirror. She felt disoriented, uncomfortable in her own skin, as if she no longer knew herself. The chic, sophisticated woman who critically surveyed the effect of the floating layers of her dress seemed a world away from the gauche, ingenuous girl who had left the Isle of Skye ten years before. But the island girl was still there, deep down, however many layers of cynical experience obscured her from view, and she made life so complicated with her deep-seated loyalties and her simple, family values. In this strange metropolitan world of wealth and scandal and immorality, the real Catriona Stewart got in the way.

In the dining room Linda Melville was seated once more at the table, looking every bit as fresh and neat as when she had left, bodice carefully buttoned, hair immaculate and eyes only slightly glittering with the after-effects of orgasm. The soft folds of her silk-chiffon skirt showed no sign of creases. Only Catriona recognised the glitter for what it was. No one would dream the woman had been playing bedroom games only minutes ago, she thought with grudging admiration as she responded a little apprehensively to Linda's gestured invitation to take the seat next to hers.

'Come and have a cup of coffee with me,' the lady purred with a kittenish smile. 'I'm dying to know how you became a banker. You must be astonishingly clever!'

'I think it's more a case of being in the right place at the right time,' Catriona replied, sitting down and wondering with sudden panic whether Linda might have seen her ten minutes before when she had definitely been in the wrong place at the wrong time. Surely, though, Linda had been in no state to register anything but her own bodily sensations.

'It can't possibly be as simple as that,' Linda demurred, pouring Catriona a cup of coffee from a circulating cafetière. 'Nothing ever is.'

At this point Bruce sauntered into the room, bent over his not-long-separated lover with a casual smile, picked up his port glass and wandered off to the other end of the table to seat himself beside his host. He, too, appeared unruffled and unblushing, not a cuff-link nor a tie-end adrift.

'You must have an aptitude for figures,' Linda went on. 'Hamish says the only kind of figures I know anything about are the kind models have.'

'Well, you should do,' Catriona remarked in complimentary mode. 'You certainly have one yourself.'

'Do you think so? How kind.' Linda looked appropriately modest. 'It's seen better days, I assure you. Of course, the older one gets the more effort one has to make...'

'Do you still do any modelling?'

'A little—for charity shows. You must let me send you an invitation to my next fundraiser. If you won't demonstrate country dances at my ball you can at least watch the latest fashions in a good cause. I see you wear them.' She fingered the floating fabric of Catriona's dress. 'Caroline Charles, isn't it? She does some very nice off-the-peg clothes.'

Almost out of perversity, Catriona decided to be honest. 'Does she? I wouldn't know. I'm afraid. I borrowed this from a friend.'

Linda raised an incredulous eyebrow. 'Really? What a good friend you have. I wouldn't lend my dresses to anyone.'

'To be honest I don't think I would dare to wear yours,' said Catriona with a smile, indicating the other's exotic jewelled gown. 'Too much of a responsibility, if this one is anything to go by.'

'Oh, couture clothes are tougher than they look,' Linda informed her. 'They're terribly well-made. It's amazing what liberties you can take with them. People may let you down but couture never will.'

Catriona's eyes widened to meet Linda's challenging look. She did see me, she thought, swallowing hard on a large sip of coffee. And it bothers her!

At that moment Hamish came up behind them and leaned on the backs of their chairs. 'I'm sorry to break this party up,' he said smoothly, 'but we're going to have to leave, Linda.'

His wife gave a small sigh as if regretting

the interruption, but nodded readily enough. 'I suppose so. Can we give you a lift, Catriona? I'm driving home. I've been such a good girl tonight!'

Catriona wondered whether Linda had intended sarcasm by this last remark but was distracted by catching Hamish's eye and detecting a miniscule wink. She shook her head at Linda's offer. 'No, thanks. I have my car here and I've also been watching what I drink.'

'Sensible girl,' remarked Linda as she rose and shook out her cloud of skirts. 'Nothing worse than alcohol for the complexion. Look at Felicity Finlay.'

'Linda,' hissed Hamish warningly. 'Miaow!'

Ignoring this, his wife swept up the room to make her farewells to the selfsame Felicity and to Bruce, displaying not an ounce of discomposure as they each turned their cheeks for her kiss.

Catriona had been looking for a chance to say something to Hamish about the painting; she drew breath to do so but was left high and dry as he abruptly wished her good night and strode off to thank his host and hostess. During the entire evening his only acknowledgement of their fledgling relationship had been the extraordinary grope during dinner and the tiny wink at the end.

She felt a depressing sense of anti-climax and remonstrated with herself as she drove home. 'Ally would say "I told you so. You're not cut out for this!" And damn it—she may be right!'

Five

When the phone rang next morning it woke Catriona from a dream. She'd been back in her childhood, on the island, chasing her sister over the expanse of wet, black rocks exposed at low tide on the shore below the croft. They were both giggling because their feet kept slipping and they couldn't make much headway over the football-sized stones, scrabbling in the slime and seaweed, knowing they were late for something and were going to be in big trouble, but happy and carefree, laughing and shrieking at each other with joyful childish exuberance. Marie's giggling grew louder and shriller until it sounded like a klaxon and resolved into the strident squeal of a telephone... And it was then that Catriona realised it was the real telephone ringing on the bedside-table.

'Hello.' Struggling out of sleep, her voice cracked on the lump in her throat. She had been so sure she was back home, had been so happy to be there.

'Did I wake you?' It was Hamish. 'I'm sorry.'

'No, it's all right. Where are you?' She sat up, trying to shake off the miasma of the dream. Suddenly she preferred reality.

'In the car. I drive to the village to fetch the papers on Sunday morning. It's impossible to

126

get them delivered out here in the sticks.'

'I can't hear you very well.' Now that she was more alert he sounded as if he was speaking from alongside a spitting roast in a hot oven.

'It's not a good signal. But I'm coming into town late this afternoon. Will you be in?'

'Yes, I think so.' Her heart began to skip as it had in the dream. She felt ridiculously glad that he had phoned but unsure how to react, more like the giggling girl on the shore than an adult caught up in adultery. 'I haven't any particular plans,' she added lamely.

'Well, I have,' he declared unambiguously. '*Very* particular plans. I'll be there around five. Don't dress up.'

She was sure he could hear her blush. 'I'll just come as I am then,' she told him, pulling the duvet around her naked body.

'Mmm! I'd say I'll be thinking of you but we're having lunch with friends and it might become crucially apparent.'

'The line's terrible—did you say crucially?'

'Work it, out for yourself, Jezebel. Goodbye.' The hiss and crackle on the line was replaced by silence.

Catriona felt absurdly grateful for the call, for it had crossed her mind after last night that he might not contact her and she had found the prospect mortifying. At the dinner party he had been so distant, apart from running his hand up her leg which seemed, in retrospect, like a gesture of contempt, even dismissal—'I can have you if I want you but I don't!' Now she felt childishly reassured, as if someone had patted her head and told her everything would be all right.

It was only later, daydreaming through a series of tedious domestic chores, that she began to analyse her feelings more specifically. Why should she feel grateful? Gratitude was a feeble, restrictive emotion. She had never found herself burdened with it in any of her previous relationships with men. There was no need to be grateful for being wanted. Love meant never having to say thank you! Yet she found herself inwardly thanking Hamish for deigning to allow her an hour or two of his precious time. Perhaps it was just another negative aspect of the married-man scenario—Gratitude to add to the burden of Guilt. The two big Gs.

When he arrived it seemed the height of decadence to answer the doorbell on a Sunday afternoon to a man who was there for one reason and one reason only, especially to one whose Rolex wristwatch probably cost more than all her possessions put together—except the flat, of course, but then that was on a huge mortgage. With her hand on the lock she felt so unaccountably shy and nervous that she could hardly turn the knob.

'You're soaking wet!' she exclaimed, nerves fleeing the instant she saw him standing somewhat forlornly on the mat, his hair dripping and the shoulders of his cashmere jacket dark with moisture.

'It's raining,' he told her with a rueful grin, stepping inside, 'and I didn't want to park too close in case someone recognised my car.'

She pushed the door shut behind him. 'Oh yes, I suppose they might,' she acknowledged. Hamish's torpedo-shaped black Jaguar XJS bore the distinctive numberplate HM100. It was hardly a car in which to travel incognito.

The moment the lock clicked he pulled her into his arms and kissed her, a long, eager, exploratory kiss which banished any doubts she might have had about his appetite for her.

'You're dripping all over the hall,' she laughed shakily when she came up for air. Her face and the front of her cream silk shirt were damp from contact with him.

'Let's go and drip all over the bedroom then,' he suggested, hurriedly taking off his jacket. 'I couldn't trust myself to think about you, so instead I've been fantasising all day about your pristine white bed with its embroidered linen sheets.'

The bedroom lay directly off the hall. 'Well, you got the white bit right,' she said, leading the way, 'but let me introduce you to my friend Polly Ester.' Like a game-show hostess she struck an attitude beside the bed with its pretty broderie Anglaise duvet and lace-edged pillows. 'The working girl's non-iron answer to cool, white linen.'

He surveyed the room with a satisfied smile and jerked off his tie, dropping the expensive strip of Paco Rabanne silk carelessly on the floor. Then he reached eagerly forward and tugged her towards him by the edges of the distinctive, ethnic-knit waistcoat she wore loose over her shirt and jeans. 'Which particular

Womble was sacrificed to make this amazing garment?' he mocked. 'Orinoco?'

With a supple twist she wriggled her arms out of the waistcoat and slipped from his grasp. 'Please feel free to examine it in close detail,' she teased. 'I'll just make the cocoa.'

'Not so fast, scatty-Cat!'

She never got past him through the door. With joyous exclamations of intent he grabbed her, tumbled her unceremoniously backwards on to the bed and began to undo the buttons of her shirt. Within minutes the smooth white duvet resembled a ski-slope after a major pile-up, with struggling legs and arms and other bits of body protruding from under snowy heaps. They soon discarded it entirely, however, along with their inhibitions and it joined trousers and shirts and the Womble waistcoat on the green-carpeted floor, but when they eventually subsided into languorous lassitude Catriona bent down to retrieve it, pulling it back over their fast-cooling bodies.

'Brr,' she said, shivering against Hamish's shoulder. 'I should have turned up the heating. I'm not used to stripping off on a chilly Sunday afternoon.'

'I'm glad to hear it,' he said, folding his arm around her. 'I don't make a habit of it myself. Still, I like what it does to your nipples.'

Under the downy quilt he cupped his hand over her breast where the tip had budded hard on the goose-bumped mound of white flesh. Soon his mouth followed his hand and they were off again, exploring and stroking and kissing and coupling, with the duvet forming hollows and moguls like an Alpine black run.

'God, I never thanked you for the painting!' Catriona exclaimed with chagrin when the piste had become smooth and calm once more and she had settled her hips into the curve of his belly. She turned in the circle of his arms. 'It was a wonderful thought but I can't possibly keep it.'

'Why ever not?' He looked hurt and surprised. 'I thought it would remind you of home. I was looking forward to seeing it hanging in your sitting-room.'

'I'm sorry. It's still in the paper you delivered it in,' she confessed. 'It's much too expensive. I can't let you spend that kind of money. It makes me feel funny.'

'What do you mean, funny?'

Embarrassed, she shifted away from him. 'As if I'm being bought. I don't want anything in return for—for this...you know.' She made a vague gesture indicating both the bed and the activities that had gone on there.

His face darkened in anger and he, too, moved away. 'I'm not paying you for THIS!' he declared roundly. 'I bought the painting because I saw how much it meant to you. I didn't want anyone else to have it who wouldn't appreciate it. It's only a little present, a memento of our first meeting. You must keep it, otherwise it will never have any real value. It will just be someone's bit of worthless wall-decoration, like a Van Gogh print or a set of flying ducks!'

As his initial anger dissolved into comic

131

exaggeration it was persuasive. Catriona bit her lip. She didn't want to hurt his feelings but, on the other hand, she still hadn't reconciled her own. There were a few moments of fraught silence.

'Very well then, I'll keep it—as a memento, as you suggest,' she said at last, relenting. 'Thank you very much.'

So much for love meaning never having to say thank you, she thought wryly.

'You don't have to thank me,' he said, as if reading her mind. 'Just hang it somewhere and look at it now and then.' He reached out and gathered her back against him, waiting while she wiggled into a comfortable position before speaking again. 'And now I can ask what I really came to ask you.'

She stroked the hairs on his arm, dark against his white flesh. 'I thought we'd managed that without words,' she commented softly.

'I agree that the most urgent matter has been resolved,' he responded gravely, sounding a little as if he was following an agenda, 'but now to Any Other Business. I want you to come to London with me next Friday. We could have a night on the town, stay somewhere luxurious, maybe go to a show, a nightclub, whatever you want. What do you think?'

She was thrilled. The unsophisticated island girl was jumping up and down inside her. She had only been to London a couple of times, once on a school trip and once on a cheap weekend break with a few of her colleagues from the High Street bank. She'd seen *Les*

Misérables from the gods, been to a pizza-parlour in Piccadilly, a disco near Leicester Square and stayed in a cubicle-sized room with shower in a two-star hotel in the insalubrious Elephant and Castle district. Even if it gave her more to thank him for, the idea of doing London with Hamish was irresistible.

'Yes. Oh yes,' she said. 'I'd love to.' She snuggled down, pulling his arms tighter around her. 'You don't have to go yet, do you?' she said sleepily. 'Please say you don't have to go yet.'

'Not for a little while,' he murmured, his lips against her hair. He thought it smelled like autumn flowers, tangy and fresh but enriched by a whole summer's sunshine. She was warm and soft and ripe but somehow untouched like an orchard fruit still clinging to the tree and he wanted to be the one who picked her, took possession of her, relished her sweet flesh. She was a trophy, a prize, a golden apple—the one every man wanted but only he would have...

'Linda tells me it was you who walked in on us on Saturday night.' Bruce's expression displayed a combination of chagrin and accusation as he handed Catriona a gin and tonic.

Her hand shook slightly as she took it, spilling the sparkling liquid over her fingers. 'I...er, yes. Yes, it was.' She set the drink carefully down in an empty ashtray on his desk, not wishing to mark the polished surface, then licked her fingers with an apologetic smile. 'I'm sorry.' It was not clear whether she was apologising for the intrusion or the spill.

'We—that is, Linda and I—have...er, known each other for some time now,' Bruce went on awkwardly, sipping his own drink and sitting down behind his desk. The position gave him a sense of superiority, of which he felt in dire need in the circumstances. 'But obviously we don't meet very often. We have to grab our opportunities.' He grinned broadly, as if anxious to convey the impression that she was being admitted as a conspirator in a light-hearted, high-spirited escapade. 'It would be a shame if Hamish were to find out.'

Catriona picked up her glass and took a gulp. The cold, slightly bitter liquid fizzled on the roof of her mouth, tasting faintly of the lemon slice floating among the ice cubes on its surface. 'Yes, I suppose it would,' she said noncommittally.

Bruce leaned back in his chair, crossing one leg carefully over the other. 'In fact Linda is certain he would instantly divorce her if he knew.'

'I'm surprised she does it then,' observed Catriona casually. 'She has quite a lot to lose, after all.'

'Yes, she has.' A brief, conceited twitch of the lips signalled Bruce's awareness of what Linda's recklessness indicated about his own magnetic attraction. 'But of course he isn't going to find out, is he?'

'Well, not from me,' Catriona said suddenly. 'If that's what you're worried about.' She could see the relief in Bruce's eyes. 'Did you really think I would tell him? Why should I?'

'No, I didn't. But Linda did. She doesn't know you, you see.'

'Would she have told Felicity if our position had been reversed?' Catriona asked with slight acerbity. 'I'm sure she wouldn't.'

'No, but she is more worldly than you,' replied Bruce in a fatherly tone. 'Her ways are city ways.'

And I'm a country bumpkin, Catriona thought indignantly. 'And what about you?' she asked rather daringly. 'Do you have no qualms about deceiving Felicity?'

Bruce shrugged. 'No, not really. My relationship with Linda doesn't threaten my marriage.'

Catriona was dying to ask what his relationship with Linda did for him. Was it simply the thrill of bonking dangerously? Or did he get a kick out of cuckolding the richest man in Edinburgh?

Instead she changed the subject. 'Would it be inconvenient if I took Friday afternoon off?' she asked suddenly.

'Is this blackmail?' he demanded, brow furrowed in surprise.

She laughed at this and shook her head. 'I hadn't thought of it that way. But I *would* like a long weekend!'

'Dirty or clean?' he asked slyly.

'Discreet,' she retorted. 'I promise not to bring the bank's name into disrepute.'

'In that case, permission granted,' he responded, emptying his glass. 'I hope you have a good time.'

'Thank you. By the way, I'm glad you sanctioned the Carruthers' loan,' she added

135

evenly, 'despite the involvement of the Chairman's father.'

'You checked the conditions of sale, didn't you?'

'Oh yes. The only remaining few rights refer to mineral deposits, so unless gold or oil is discovered in Glendoran there shouldn't be any further communication with the Lochaber estate.'

'And planning permission is through?'

'Yes. Conversion starts straight away.'

'Good. Things seem to be going well. If they've got any sense they'll ask the old Earl down for a slap-up meal as soon as they open!'

'How can you tell if your husband is having an affair?' Felicity asked.

She and Elizabeth Nicholson were waiting at the twelfth tee for the preceding players to clear the green before driving off. Murrayfield Golf Club was busy with weekday golfers, mostly women, taking advantage of a spell of sunny spring weather. The close-cut fairway grass was still winter yellow but the rough was beginning to colour up with new growth and in the copse of silver birches at the back of the tee there was a faint emerald haze on the graceful magenta twigs. Primroses gleamed like gold nuggets on the dark banks of earth between their ghostly trunks.

Elizabeth's nose almost seemed to twitch with sudden interest. 'I can't remember, Flick. You tell me,' she replied with just enough sympathy in her voice to encourage further revelations. 'What makes you ask?'

'Oh, you can imagine. Bruce is behaving strangely.' Felicity wiped her ball a little too assiduously on the small blue towel which hung from her golf-bag. 'He kisses me as if his mind is on something else.'

Elizabeth emitted a staccato laugh, not unlike a dog barking. 'Don't most husbands do that?' she observed.

'Well, Bruce never has before.' Felicity looked dubious. 'Perhaps I'm being silly but we've always been quite—well, easy together. Now I feel definitely *uneasy*. Have you heard anything? You always have your finger on the pulse.'

Elizabeth pursed her lips and shrugged. She wasn't sure if she liked the implication that she was a nosy parker. 'No, I haven't. Whom do you suspect?'

'Well, I wondered about Catriona Stewart. You know the new manager he's hired. She is absolutely gorgeous to look at—bright, intelligent, sickening! In a way I wouldn't blame him if he *had* taken up with her.'

'It would be rather unprofessional, wouldn't it? Bruce always strikes me as being very proper about such things.'

'That's true,' Felicity agreed. 'But he's at a susceptible age—mid-life crisis, wondering if time is running out.'

'Yes. My husband always called it the men-o-pause. Unfortunately at the crucial age he didn't pause, he stopped completely!' Elizabeth caught Felicity's shocked look and barked again.

'Don't mind my jokes, Flick—it's just my way of coping. Back to Bruce—you must have more than just a hunch to go on.'

'Well, he produced a pair of scanty black panties from his pocket at the Nevis dinner party the other night and afterwards I rather wondered where he got them from,' confided Felicity. 'It was all a huge joke at the time and he pretended he'd taken them off Linda Melville but he hadn't of course, and they weren't mine. I never wear black underwear.'

'Don't you?' asked Elizabeth curiously. 'Gosh, I do! It's the only small thrill left, I find.'

Felicity giggled, regarding her friend with wide eyes. 'Elizabeth Nicholson—the black-lace widow,' she teased.

'Well, it's better than being Widow Twankey,' retorted the other. 'Anyway, where do you think Bruce got them?'

Felicity sobered down. 'I've no idea. I'm not sure which I dislike most—the idea of him taking them off some nubile redhaired subordinate, or walking into a ladies' underwear shop and actually buying them.'

'It might be neither. He might have got them out of a cracker at Christmas.'

'And kept them in his dinner-jacket pocket on the off-chance of an opportunity to produce them?' cried Felicity incredulously. 'It's hardly likely, is it!'

'Stranger things have happened,' observed Elizabeth reasonably. 'Why don't you just ask him? And better still, why don't you ask this gorgeous young redhead to dinner and see how they behave together. That should give you a few clues.' She screwed up her eyes and peered down the fairway. 'They've sunk the last putt. Is it my honour or yours? I can't remember.'

'Mine,' said Felicity firmly and strode on to the tee.

After their weekly squash game, Alison and Catriona had their usual drink at the sports club. There were few others about so they sat on high stools at the bar in cosy intimacy, speaking in low tones with their heads close together.

'When is your appointment at the clinic?' Catriona asked.

'Friday. I'm as nervous as hell and John is like a grumpy grizzly. Will you come for supper that night and let us tell you all about it? We'll need someone to talk to.'

'I'm really sorry, Ally, but I can't, not on Friday.' Catriona felt genuinely regretful, for she knew how much was riding on this event.

Alison immediately pounced. 'Aha! What's up? A hot date?'

'I'm going to London.'

'On a Friday night? It can't be work.'

'No, I cannot tell a lie. It isn't work.'

The dark girl's eyes narrowed. 'It's Hamish, isn't it? That's why you're being so mysterious. You think I won't approve—and you're right, I don't.'

Catriona returned her slitty-eyed look with interest and then gave a sunny smile. Even her friend's outright opposition couldn't quench her eager anticipation of the excursion with Hamish.

'I wonder if John knows he's married to an old mother hen?' she began teasingly—and could have instantly bitten her tongue out.

'He knows he's married to someone who would dearly *love* to be an old mother hen,' retorted Alison indignantly. 'I'm just sorry my best friend won't be among the first to know whether I'm ever destined to become one, because instead she'll be gathering no moss with a rich, randy, rolling stone.'

Deeply contrite, Catriona tried to make amends. 'I'm sorry, Ally. Truly I am. Sorry I said that, sorry I can't come on Friday and sorry you don't like my choice of playmate. But I'm not sorry I'm going to London and I'm not sorry that I'm a happy little banker.'

Alison's air of recrimination dissolved on a snigger. 'Are you sure you mean banker and not something with an 'O' in it, you wicked wench?'

Catriona shrugged and grinned. 'Well, whatever,' she murmured. 'Anyway, I'm only going away for one night. How about getting together later in the weekend? Naturally I want to know exactly what the baby-doctors say about all your tubes and twiddly bits.'

'They'll probably advise me to stop worrying and keep a sharper lookout for low-flying storks,' groaned Alison. 'But there's just a chance they may have something a bit more positive to offer. OK, come on Saturday night then, Cat, and we'll compare notes. You can tell me all about *in flagrante* and I'll fill you in on *in vitro*. And let's hope neither of us regrets any of it!'

'There are times when I can definitely see the advantage of money being no object,' Catriona said happily two nights later, settling back against the blond leather upholstery of the chauffeur-driven Rolls-Royce which Hamish had hired to ferry them around London. They had seen *Sunset Boulevard* in front circle seats which had doubtless cost hundreds on the black market since it had been booked up for months, and were now on their way to dine at Quaglino's, a restaurant which demanded cash and kudos to jump the reservation queue. The distance between the Adelphi Theatre and the restaurant was eminently walkable but it seemed the height of luxury to avoid the chill night air by taking the car, since it was, with its driver and the contents of its built-in refrigerator, entirely at their disposal. 'It's a shame one can't live like this all the time,' Catriona added, watching Hamish climb in beside her and noting the dull, satisfying clunk of the coach-built door as he closed it without effort.

'That would mean foregoing the pleasure of stolen Sunday afternoons warming your tiny frozen hand in your tiny frozen garret,' teased Hamish, who had made a point of adjusting the thermostat on her apartment's heating system before he left the previous Sunday.

'I want to put on record that my tiny hand was not the only thing you attempted to warm,' protested Catriona, making a swift visual check that the sliding glass panel between them and the uniformed chauffeur was fully shut. 'And that I am not prepared to defrost your not-so-tiny hand at this precise moment.'

This last exclamation was in response to his exploratory advances under the flap of her wrap-around purple silk skirt and on to the bare flesh of her inner thigh, exposed above the stockings which she had elected to wear in preference to tights. 'It has become obvious to me in the time that I have known you, Hamish Melville, that you are an unpardonable groper.' Trying to look shocked, Catriona firmly removed his hand from its intimate resting place. 'Perhaps these frigid fingers could attend to the rest of the contents of that nice cold green bottle we opened on the way here?'

'If that's what you prefer...' With an injured expression Hamish leaned forward to open the fridge door and they both dissolved into laughter as he failed to aim the champagne into two narrow cut-glass flûtes whilst the Rolls surged powerfully away down Shaftsbury Avenue.

Being thus occupied they also failed to notice two particular pedestrians on the pavement. A tall man with curly brown hair and a pleasant, open face was trying to hail a cab, but his older female companion, defying the anti-fur lobby and wrapped unashamedly in a mink jacket, had noticed Hamish and Catriona enter the Rolls and observed the dumbshow of their laughing exchange, although salient aspects of Hamish's handiwork had been obscured below the level of the car's windows. 'Queenie' Nevis was on a theatre outing in the company of her elder son.

'Did you see that, Rob?' she asked, bubbling over with excitement when the young man finally managed to lure a cab to her side. 'Did you see who that was in the Rolls-Royce?'

Rob Galbraith was accustomed to his mother's penchant for scandal. 'Princess Di canoodling with Michael Winner?' he guessed wildly, handing her into the cab. He informed the driver of their intended destination and stepped in to sit beside her. 'Or Fergie on yet another will-they-won't-they-get-together-again outing with Prince Andrew?'

'Neither,' sniffed Lady Nevis dismissively. 'Something much more interesting. Hamish Melville looking as if he would like to kiss the toes off Catriona Stewart.'

'Really, Mother!' exclaimed Rob. 'Where do you get these lurid notions from? And who on earth is Catriona Stewart?'

'As to the toes, it was you who mentioned Fergie,' retorted his mother. 'And Catriona Stewart is one of your father's employees. A very able Manager of Private Banking, I believe, but altogether too beautiful for such a position.'

'I don't believe what I'm hearing,' said Rob, clutching at his hair in mock despair. 'Are you implying that where there's beauty there can be no discretion? A man who said that would be called a sexist pig—and quite right, too.'

Lady Nevis was unrepentant. 'I'm just saying that she's too tempting to be let loose among the randier element of Steuart's clientèle. You know what these rich rovers can be like. When they want something they tend to take it for granted they can have it, and Catriona, for all that she looks like a woman of the world, actually comes from a croft on Skye via Paisley High Street. She has no experience of such amorality. She came to my dinner party last Saturday and a more engaging girl you couldn't hope to meet, but much too field-fresh. Tch!' Lady Nevis made as if to smack her own wrist. 'It's my fault for seating her next to Hamish Melville. Although, to be fair, I didn't notice anything going on between them at dinner, but I don't like seeing them together this evening. Too sinister.'

Rob gazed at his mother with a bewildered expression and shook his head. 'I don't know how you can say you don't like it, Ma,' he expostulated. 'You know perfectly well that something like this is grist to your gossipmongering mill. I just feel rather sorry for—what was her name?—Catriona Stewart. By all accounts Hamish Melville is a tricky customer.'

Lady Nevis gave her son an old-fashioned look. 'I do not "gossipmonger"! But why do lovely single men like you let randy married rams like Hamish lure away all the nice girls, that's what I want to know?'

'If the girls are so nice, what are they doing being lured away? Had you thought of that?' he asked slyly.

His mother smiled knowingly. 'Of course I had. Niceness doesn't always go hand in hand with sense, thank goodness. If you weren't so nice you'd have the sense to be taking a beautiful young thing out on the town—not your raddled old mother. And then where would I be?'

'I'll remember that next time you ring up and say you're coming to London for the day,' he retorted. 'I'll just let you fend for yourself.'

At Laverockbank Linda was holding a supper-meeting of her charity ball committee. The five ladies present had consumed smoked salmon, poached chicken with asparagus and, accompanied by a chorus of protest about the effect on their waistlines, a large bowl of tiramisu. They had dealt with everything on their agenda except Any Other Business.

'I'll tell you what, Minto,' Linda said to the rather solemn, beetle-browed butler who had been serving them, 'bring that bottle of Vieille Curé with the coffee, would you? We deserve a sticky after all our hard work.'

'I think Mr Melville intended that for the Fife Point-to-Point, madam,' murmured Minto deferentially.

'Never mind. You can get another one before then, and Mr Melville will never know, will he?' Linda told him firmly, turning to add gaily to Felicity Finlay who sat on her left, 'And if Mr Melville chooses to spend a Friday night in London doing God-knows-what with God-knows-whom I think one bottle of French liqueur is a small price to pay, don't you?'

'You mean he hasn't told you what he's doing?' asked Felicity with astonishment.

'Oh, he's *told* me that he's attending some

145

City dinner—investment bankers or something, but I don't believe him for an instant.' Linda looked carelessly unconcerned about this state of affairs. 'As long as he meets me off the plane at Gatwick tomorrow morning. We're going to visit our son at school in Surrey.'

Felicity looked troubled. She had still failed to solve the puzzle of the black panties and would have loved to consult Linda on the subject but couldn't quite bring herself to do so. 'I don't think I'd like if it I thought Bruce was lying to me,' she said in a tight voice.

'You mean you believe everything he tells you?' scoffed Victoria Moncreiffe who was sitting opposite. She had clung to her membership of the ball committee despite the fact that she felt almost like a charity case herself, still battling the Hon. Charlie for every withdrawal from the bank. 'I don't even believe my solicitor these days and he's paid to be on my side. All men are lying toads.'

'Well, I don't blame you for that, you've had a rotten time,' responded Felicity sympathetically. 'But I've never suspected Bruce of cheating on me. He's too cautious, apart from anything else.' Secretly she wished these words still rang true to her own ear.

'OK, so what's he doing tonight?' Linda asked innocently, nodding at Minto as he broke the seal on the disputed bottle of liqueur, an expression of resignation on his lugubrious face. 'Or what did he *say* he was doing?'

'He's at home with the children,' replied Felicity triumphantly. 'He couldn't lie about that, could he? Not without involving Iona and Gus and I'm sure he wouldn't do that. Anyway, he made an awful fuss about this meeting being on a Friday evening. Said it was interfering with family life.'

'Oh dear,' cooed Linda sweetly. 'I must remember in future to call meetings so that they don't upset poor Bruce's home comforts.'

Felicity laughed. 'Definitely! But I'll bear in mind what you say, Victoria, about the toad factor. Perhaps I'm too complacent about Bruce. They say it's the quiet ones you have to watch.'

'Well, I wouldn't call Bruce quiet exactly,' observed Linda pertinently, watching the butler pour fragrant, honey-coloured liquid into the last liqueur glass and raising hers to salute the company with dancing eyes. 'Close your ears Minto,' she ordered, 'I'm going to make a toast to the laddies. Whatever you're up to, boys, you'd better remember that what's sauce for the gander is also sauce for the goose!'

After dinner the Rolls suddenly seemed very grand and formal. Effervescent after two bottles of vintage Krug, Catriona slid across the seat and snuggled into Hamish. 'Let's not go to Annabel's,' she whispered.

He gave her a welcoming squeeze and a raffish smile. 'What else did you have in mind?' he enquired.

'We have a lovely hotel room,' she pointed out wickedly. 'It seems a shame not to spend some time in it.'

'You wanton woman! Are you sure? You won't feel you've been cheated?'

'I do hope not,' she exclaimed. 'I don't expect to...' Her hand was inside his jacket, feeling the sensual smoothness of his silk-shirted chest. She felt reckless, uninhibited, as if nothing was off-limits.

Without further hesitation, Hamish leaned forward and tapped the glass panel. 'We've changed our minds,' he told the chauffeur as it slid down a few inches. 'We'll go straight to the hotel.' Not by so much as a flicker of his eye did the driver betray his opinion of this instruction. Beneath the Rolls-Royce hat-badge was a mind drilled in Rolls-Royce etiquette.

The Duke's Court had been Catriona's choice because she had read about it in a travel magazine where it had been cited as the most exclusive and luxurious small hotel in London. Within minutes the Rolls drew up outside the arched portico of an imposing red-brick and Portland-stone mansion tucked discreetly away in a narrow street off Pall Mall. In the lobby the décor was dark mahogany, gold-fringed crimson velvet and elegant plasterwork. Ferns and pot-lilies stood in huge brass planters in the landings and passages, imparting an air of heavy, scented opulence. It was redolent of an age of monocles and moustaches, cocktails and gaspers—an age of heedless hedonism and Gay Young Things.

In their green-papered room with its carved four-poster bed and drifting white voile hangings they removed each other's overcoat. 'Have I permission to grope now, please?' Hamish murmured, gathering Catriona into his arms and rumpling her silk skirt over her buttocks. 'I've wanted to do this all evening!'

'God, I'm glad you waited,' she said, squirming under his invasive fingering. 'I'd have been flashing my stocking tops at the whole world.'

'That's the only reason I didn't,' he declared, his roving hands finding the soft warmth at the top of her thighs. 'I want to keep all this to myself.' He stood back to undo the two-button fastening at her waist. Her skirt fell silently to the floor and he gazed raptly at the expanse of leg revealed, suspenders black against the white columns of her thighs. 'Your skin here reminds me of full-cream milk,' he said in awe, stroking the soft, sensitive inner flesh. 'The kind you used to get in a can straight from the farm.'

'In Motherwell?' she exclaimed in disbelief, shivering at the touch of his fingers.

'My uncle worked on a farm,' he revealed, his caresses becoming more intimate. 'We used to go there for holidays.'

'You obviously learned a great deal,' she moaned, feeling her knees beginning to give way. 'I hope you can hold me up.'

'No problem,' he said, taking her weight on his shoulder and giving her a fireman's lift to the bed. 'I used to hump bales of hay as well.' He dropped her unceremoniously on the sprung mattress and began to remove his trousers.

'Well, that makes me feel like a million dollars,' she giggled, wriggling out of her blouse and watching him undress.

'I thought every girl wanted to be swept off her feet,' he said, pulling off his shirt.

'Maybe, but "let me compare thee to a bale of hay!" is hardly Shakespeare, is it?'

Hamish paused in his own disrobing to observe Catriona lying on the bed, removing her stockings and suspenders, and so, tantalisingly, she mimed a striptease for him, pointing her toes and rolling the fine black hose slowly, one at a time, over her upraised legs. Grinning hugely he hummed a bump and grind accompaniment.

Her suspender belt zinged into a corner. 'If you could have your ideal evening's entertainment, any time, any place, what would it be?' she asked suddenly.

'Apart from what I've just witnessed?' he teased, but considered the question as he removed his shoes and socks. 'Domingo singing Verdi at the Paris Opéra, followed by dinner at Maxim's...and then the Hotel George V with my Catriona.' He shot her the same raffish grin he had delivered across the back seat of the Rolls, his blue eyes hooded and lascivious. 'Come to think of it, forget Verdi and Maxim's.'

'What was wrong with Andrew Lloyd-Webber?' she enquired. 'Not stirring enough for you?'

'He doesn't strike quite the same chord as Verdi, in my opinion.'

'So what would happen now then, if we were high on Verdi?' she taunted.

He crossed to the bedside to pick up the telephone. 'Let's find out,' he said. 'After all, this is supposed to be a first-class hotel...' He dialled room service and, turning his back, spoke quietly into the mouthpiece so she could not hear.

'What have you done?' she asked, intrigued.

'Wait and see,' he replied mysteriously, sitting down beside her on the bed and tracing the line of her shoulder with his finger, slipping off the strap of her camisole. 'If you can wait, that is?'

'Huh!' She sat up indignantly and returned the strap to the correct position. 'I can if you can,' she declared, crossing her legs and folding her arms over her breasts.

Less than a minute later there was a discreet scratching sound at the door. In his blue silk boxer shorts Hamish crossed to open it a crack and receive the small portable tape deck which was handed anonymously through. Almost before the door had closed the sound of a mellifluous tenor voice could be heard in the room.

'There you are—*Il Trovatore!*' declared Hamish triumphantly, placing the little machine on the table by the bed. 'Full marks to the night porter.'

'Domingo?' enquired Catriona, arching an eyebrow.

Hamish listened attentively, then shook his head as he eased himself down beside her on the bed. 'Carreras. But he'll do.' He reached for her hungrily, pulling off the camisole and covering her small, rose-nippled breasts with kisses.

'You're right,' she gasped, as his love-making

increased in intensity to match the swelling ardour of Manrico's aria. 'Carreras will do nicely.'

But instead of reaching the higher realms of ecstasy, which she had come to expect as Hamish's partner, her pleasure this time was muted. Somehow she could not lose herself in the thrill of it. Perhaps it was the Verdi, perhaps she had drunk too much champagne or perhaps the infernal big G was getting in the way again, she thought, busy analysing when she should have been fantasising. Gratitude was causing her to try too hard when she had formerly let herself go heedlessly down the road to Elysium.

Hamish did not seem to notice. If anything her relative passivity drove him to more violent passion and his relentless pounding at her unresponsive body was not only unrewarding but uncomfortable. She wanted to tell him to stop and once or twice she tried to twist away but found herself spreadeagled and pinned beneath his powerful strength until his climax almost hammered the breath from her lungs. Afterwards he lay panting with exertion, incoherent with post-coital pleasure, while she wondered what had gone wrong, drawing up her knees to curl herself around the unaroused core of her sex.

This time it was a perfect night for sabotage. Snow threatened but had not yet started to fall, the clouds were massed thick over the moon and the darkness was almost palpable. There was little traffic on the road, only a very occasional passing car flickering its headlights past the trunks of the silver birches clustered around the Glendoran steading.

An unlit four-wheel-drive vehicle rumbled over the bridge, pulled off the tarmac and lurched over a pile of rubble invisible in the shadowless gloom to take cover behind the dark hump of the low stone byre. The driver was alone, an amorphous black figure emerging bent under the weight of a heavy bag, almost invisible against the dark wall, but the letters which flowed from the nozzle of the spray-can were highly visible, luminous green and glowing menacingly on the gable-end, spelling out their spiteful message: ENG LISH OUT. SFS.

A yellow beam of torchlight danced, there was a click and a flash, followed by a crash and *whoosh* as bottle-glass shattered and petrol-fuelled flames burst through door and window, illuminating the bleak scene and the sinister, hooded figure which stooped again to select, light and hurl another missile.

This time the fire-bombs did not fizzle out. The old wooden stalls quickly caught and burned fiercely, igniting the roof timbers so that the glow of the flames lit the sky long after the anonymous, androgynous fire-raiser had climbed back behind the wheel and driven off, scattering loose stones and whooping and laughing in xenophobic glee. The snow began to fall in fat, silent flakes but they were neither moist enough nor numerous enough to have any effect on the fire which raged on unchecked.

'What did you tell Linda?' Catriona asked

Hamish the question over breakfast which had been served to them in their room.

'What did I tell Linda about what?' he enquired through a mouthful of croissant.

'About what you were doing in London, where you were staying, that sort of thing.'

'I told her I was at a bankers' dinner and staying here. The truth is always best,' he replied, smiling, 'just in case she might need to get in touch.'

He had slept solidly and tidily beside her all night, and the reason Catriona knew this was because she had not. 'So I could have answered the phone to her—still could if she rings!' Disbelief and a touch of indignation coloured her voice.

Hamish shook his head. 'No you couldn't, because I paid the girl on the switchboard to monitor all calls and tell us who was on the line before putting them through.'

'Anyone would think you'd done this before.' Catriona felt dizzy and tired and therefore spoke with uncharacteristic sarcasm.

He laughed, seeming not to notice. 'No, sweetheart—think about it. There might have been some change of arrangements. You never know.'

'What arrangements?'

'Our arrangements to meet.'

'You're meeting Linda in London—today?'

'At Gatwick, yes. We're going to visit our son.'

'Your *son!*' Catriona almost squeaked with shock.

'He's at prep school near Guildford. We're taking him out for the day.'

'I didn't know you had a son.' The croissant which Catriona had started to eat suddenly tasted like extruded polystyrene. She returned the morsel to her plate with a trembling hand.

Hamish frowned at her, puzzled. 'Didn't you? Good Lord! Max is nine. He's a nice wee chap.' He glanced at his watch and hurriedly picked up his napkin to wipe his mouth. 'I must get going. The Rolls will be here any minute. Eat up, darling. If you're ready in time I can drop you at Departures before I pick Linda up.'

She stared at him, amazed at his coolness, staggered by the sudden revelation of his fatherhood. 'Don't worry,' she gulped, shaking her head. 'I'll take the train. I'd like to do some shopping before I leave London.'

'Oh, right, good idea. Might as well make the most of the trip.' He stood up and brushed crumbs off his shirt, bending to give her a swift kiss on the mouth. 'I wish I had time to come with you. I'd love to buy you something sleek and sexy.'

She forced a smile. 'It's just as well you can't then,' she said as robustly as she could. 'You know how I feel about you buying me things.'

He straightened and shrugged. 'I thought we'd settled all that,' he said blithely, zipping up his suit-carrier which lay on the bed already packed. 'But if we haven't, we will next time we meet. I'll be in touch very soon.'

'Have a good day with, er...Max,' Catriona murmured, standing to return his farewell kiss.

I deserve an Oscar, she thought with grim humour, watching him leave. Or perhaps a BAFTA would be more appropriate—a Brave About Facing the Truth Award!

Six

Like hundreds of professional Edinburgh families the Home-Muirs lived in the infamously refined suburb of Morningside, in a two-storey terraced house situated on a quiet, tree-lined street. In summer a riot of roses clambered up the front wall and around the long sash windows overlooking the garden, but with spring still struggling out of winter only a few clumps of snowdrops and crocuses brought a hint of new life, shivering around the trunk of a solitary purple-budding cherry tree.

'You'll never guess what, Cat,' Alison chortled, taking her friend by the hand and pulling her straight through the house to the cosy, untidy, pine-and-terrazzo-tile kitchen at the back. 'Honestly you won't, not in a million years.'

The passage they passed down was a gallery of modern prints: Hamiltons, Hockneys, Wiznewskis—a medley of American, English and Scottish artists bearing witness to Alison's off-duty artistic leanings. In the kitchen itself, on the wall opposite the Aga, hung an enormous gilt-framed canvas of sheep grazing in rolling, wooded farmland. John's conservative taste in art.

'Hi, Cat. Here,' John greeted her with a grin, a kiss and a glass of red wine, 'sit down.' He pulled out one of the sturdy kitchen chairs grouped round a central table which was already laid for supper. A cheesy, meaty smell from the oven complemented the tangy aroma of Chianti.

Catriona frowned at Alison who sat down beside her. 'What won't I guess?' she asked curiously. 'You're both looking very mysterious.'

'I'm having a baby,' exclaimed her friend with the air of a magician producing a flock of white doves from a canary's cage. 'Yes I am, really. I'm three months pregnant!'

Catriona was momentarily speechless. Her eyes swivelled from Alison to John and back again several times before she found her tongue. 'Really? But how—why didn't you know? God, that's marvellous! Are you sure?'

Alison clapped her hands in delight. 'Isn't it amazing? No, I'm not at all sure. Like you I can't believe it—but a nice man called Dr Forbes and his scanner and stethoscope assure me I am.'

John swung one long leg over a chair and sat down opposite Catriona. 'Some place, that infertility clinic. Talk about speedy service. Within half an hour of walking in there we were expecting a baby.' His wide, grey-green eyes were dancing with glee under his wayward brows. 'I didn't even have to wank into a jar.'

'John's more peeved about that than anything,'

complained Alison, leaning over playfully to cuff her husband's head. 'He missed his big chance to slaver over a porny magazine without feeling guilty.'

'Is that what you have to do?' Catriona asked, innocently intrigued. 'But why didn't you know you were pregnant, Ally? You've been drawing up fertility charts for months. It's incredible!'

'It was all a plot to get me bonking to order,' grumbled John, winking at his wife. 'Ally's way of keeping me on the straight and narrow—too exhausted to stray. And now the secret is out. She's been pregnant for ages. I could have been sleeping at night!'

Alison blushed. 'Don't tease. I know it's daft, but in rare cases it seems that bleeding every month doesn't necessarily mean no baby. Do you want chapter and verse?'

'Well yes, of course, I shall want every gynaecological detail, complete with illustrations,' Catriona grinned. 'But tell me the important things first—like when is it due? Did you say you've had a scan? Do you know if it's a boy or a girl?'

'Um...September, yes and no.' Alison ticked off the answers meticulously on her fingers. 'This is Twenty Questions—you have seventeen more.'

'Well, I don't need to ask if you're pleased, do I?'

'Absolutely not,' confirmed John, leaning over to pat his wife's tummy. 'And you probably don't need to be told that we're also exceedingly glad that we didn't need any help. It's all our own work. Not even a cold shower, let alone a test tube.'

'Not that any help wouldn't have been gratefully received,' said Alison hastily. 'John was more squeamish about that than I was.'

'How you can be squeamish about medical matters when you've watched men tearing bits off each other on the rugby field for years I don't understand,' observed Catriona, shaking her head.

'Actually I was worried that the odd kick in the crutch might be the cause of our problem,' said John, serious for an instant but unable to wipe the smile off his face for long. 'Then Alison would have blamed rugby and I'd never have got her to watch a match again.'

'As it is we'll probably call the baby after the entire Scotland team,' chuckled Alison happily.

'Well, that'll be nice, especially if it's a girl,' joked Catriona. 'God, I'm so pleased for you both! John—you'll have to open an account for it at Steuart's on Monday morning.'

'Is there such a thing as a foetal account?' he wondered.

'And I'll buy it an Old Master at Wentworth's,' put in Alison immediately. 'This child is going to have an eye for figures in a landscape as well as figures on a balance sheet.'

'And for a ball,' insisted her husband. 'But *not* a round one.'

'Let's drink to Home-Muir Junior,' Catriona suggested. 'An artistic, financial, sporting genius and an absolute marvel!'

'Perhaps we shouldn't count our egg before

it's hatched,' warned Alison, sipping solemnly at her mineral water. 'There might be something wrong with it.'

'Quite,' nodded John with a twinkle in his eye. 'It might like soccer!'

When their meal was on the table—garlic bread, Marks & Spencer Lasagne and Home-Muir tossed salad—Alison fixed Catriona with an enquiring glance. 'Your turn now, Cat. How did it go? Fill us in on the Hamish factor.'

Catriona put down her fork and picked up her glass to take a large steadying gulp. Confiding in Ally was one thing, but she felt uneasy talking about Hamish in front of John. 'Oh, you don't want to hear about that,' she said diffidently. 'We just went to see *Sunset Boulevard* and then out to dinner. It was very nice.'

'Very nice,' Alison mimicked her rather prim tone. ' "Very nice" spending a naughty night in London with the richest man in Edinburgh. I suppose you travelled on the tube, ate at McDonald's and stayed in a B & B! Come on, Cat, we want every luxurious detail; we're all ears.'

Catriona looked at John for help and he shook his head warningly at his wife. 'I don't think Cat wants to tell us,' he said. 'And perhaps she's right. It is her affair.'

'Affair being the operative word,' observed Alison. 'Is that right, Cat? Are you embarrassed? Guilty conscience got you at last?'

'Yes—no!' Catriona's voice rose indignantly. 'I am embarrassed but I don't feel guilty.'

'Oh, Catriona Stewart—may you be forgiven!'

Alison took a bite out of a portion of garlic bread and stared accusingly at her friend, adding with her mouth full, 'The man is married. He has a nine-year-old son.'

'Yes, I know,' returned Catriona, avoiding Alison's eye. 'I know all that.' She thought grimly, Pity you didn't tell me about the son before, Ally.

There was an awkward silence.

John broke in gently, 'I don't think it's very fair to invite Cat round for supper, Ally, and then harangue her over the lasagne. She can hardly throw our own salad bowl at us, can she?'

Alison looked mutinous for a moment, then gave a small laugh. 'No, I suppose she can't. Sorry, Cat. I was a bit out of line. Put it down to hormones.'

Catriona raised her glass again, forcing a smile. 'Here's to hormones, eh, Ally? We wouldn't be celebrating if it weren't for them. Let's talk about the baby. Will it be a land birth or a water birth?'

'Help! I haven't thought about anything like that.' The atmosphere lightened considerably as Alison made a comical grimace. 'I'm not a very good swimmer...'

'If you want me to hold your hand I think I'd rather you stayed on dry land,' remarked John wryly. 'If you ask me, birthing pools are natural childbirth for whales, not women.'

'I'll probably look like a whale before too long,' moaned Alison. 'All blubbery and bloated.'

'You'll be the Princess of Whales,' John responded loyally.

'Well, don't you go getting any ideas about being the Prince,' his wife warned. 'He's not exactly my choice of husband role model.'

Catriona listened to this exchange with quiet relief. She was glad to have weathered the Hamish storm without too many bruised feelings. It was inevitable that Alison should have told her husband about the affair but it was also to be regretted. She and John had to share an office and Catriona felt certain that, although he wouldn't say so, he disapproved of her 'carrying on' with a client.

After drinking half of Alison's share of the Chianti as well as her own she went home fairly well-oiled and found she couldn't sleep, which was unfortunate because she would rather have dropped blissfully into oblivion than be burdened with the consequent thinking time. Over and above the matter of Hamish's son, which had blighted her day, Alison's pregnancy now struck poisonously at the core of her being. She had been completely unprepared for her reaction but there was no mistaking it—she was jealous.

It was a horrible sensation! Like maggots squirming in her guts! And why? She had happily been made an aunt twice by her sister and had never experienced a single twinge and now, all at once, she was eaten up with envy of Alison's great expectations. What was more, behind the niggling, wriggling worms of jealousy she could hear the loud and persistent ticking of her own biological clock.

She was thirty-two and for the first time she stared down the tunnel of time and found it empty. No jolly, bouncing bundle of joy in plastic Pampers kicking its way into her heart but piles of pounds and pence with cold, flat faces and mean, milled edges. Perhaps there were no outward signs as yet but lying there in bed she imagined she could feel the tendrils of decay creeping through her body, twining around her reproductive organs and shrivelling them up into dry, useless lumps of gristle.

'Damn!' she yelled aloud to the uncaring wall. 'Damn, damn, damn!'

The sound of the telephone filtered through to Catriona in the shower as she was trying to wash away the gritty residue of a sleepless night and an over-active mind. It was not Hamish, it was Bruce and he made no apology for the nine-thirty call.

'I'm glad you're there, Catriona. I thought you might still be away. Have you seen the Sunday papers yet?'

She had to confess that she had not, wondering privately why these married men all leapt out of bed so early on Sunday mornings.

'There's a front-page story about another attack by the SFS. They've burned out a place in Glendoran but it doesn't say who owns the property. Do you think it could be the Carruthers' steading? It looks a complete wreck in the photographs.'

'Oh God, yes it could be, although they've

hardly started work. When does it say it happened?'

'Friday night. Have you got a contact number for them? Perhaps you'd better ring and check. I hope they're insured.'

'Yes, they are. I saw to that when the bank took over the deeds. Leave it with me. I'll let you know what I find out.'

'Yes, do that. Sorry to interrupt your weekend. I trust you're having a good time?' There was a suggestive note in Bruce's disembodied voice and Catriona could almost hear his sly grin. So could Felicity, who just happened to be passing her husband's study at this point in the conversation.

'Fine, thanks, or I was until you phoned. The poor Carruthers—I hope it's not their place.'

'Don't worry about it too much. We'll discuss it later—oh, but don't ring between now and one-thirty because I'll be on the golf course, OK?'

'Yes, right. Goodbye.'

'Goodbye.' Bruce put the phone down.

Felicity moved forward into the room. 'And whom don't you want to ring while you're out?' she asked in a teasing voice, although she knew quite well.

Bruce laughed. 'Oh, it's only Catriona,' he said airily. 'Some bank business.'

Catriona sprinted down the road for the papers as soon as she was dressed. There was no mistaking the identity of the burned-out buildings in the press photo because the

164

mountains of Moidart stood out wild and snow-covered beyond the loch. Her self-absorption of the night before was submerged in sympathy for the Carruthers. All their hopes and plans lay charred and blackened in the ruins of that steading. She tried their number in Kent but got no reply. Bad news travels fast, she thought. Probably they were already on their way to view for themselves the wrecking of their Highland ambitions.

'I think I'll drive up to Glendoran,' she told Bruce later, on his return from the golf course. 'I feel terribly sorry for the Carruthers and besides, they'll need all the financial help they can get now.'

'You mustn't become too personally involved with the clients, you know, Catriona,' he warned sternly. 'You want to watch that.'

'Yes, I know,' she replied dryly, recognising a certain element of the pot calling the kettle black. 'But I'll just go up this afternoon and be back after lunch tomorrow.'

'Well, if you must. Go carefully, won't you? I'll see you tomorrow.'

'Yes, goodbye,' she said, unaware that at the other end of the line Felicity's suspicions were growing by the minute.

Sue Carruthers' cheeks were smudged with cinders and streaked with tears and her husband's jaw appeared set in stone, as if his whole face would crack if he moved it more than a millimetre.

'Oh God, Nick, what a mess!' exclaimed

165

Catriona as the apparently shell-shocked restaurateur opened the door of her car on her
arrival at the steading.

It was dusk, but an eerie opalescent light
was reflected off the thin crust of snow which
covered all but the grim black husk of the
burned-out building. The snow had finished
falling before the heat of the last flames died
so none had settled on it and the ruin stood out
dark and stark against its white surroundings.

Nick could not trust himself to speak but
Sue hugged Catriona like a drowning swimmer,
the tears brimming again in her reddened eyes.
'How fantastic of you to come!' she sniffed,
applying an already-sodden handkerchief to her
noise. 'We only got here half an hour ago and
we've just been standing and staring. Doesn't
it look awful?'

'How did you find out?' Catriona asked,
digging her hands into her pockets. The dying
of the day had brought a drop in temperature
and the snow was beginning to crackle under
their feet. The sharp tang of smoke still clung
to the chill air.

'The police had our number. They were
supposed to be keeping an eye on the place.
We asked them to after what you told us about
the SFS,' Sue told her. 'They rang us yesterday
but we had to make arrangements for the boys
so we only managed to start out from Kent at
crack of dawn today.'

'Who *are* these people?' asked Nick, speaking
at last through clenched teeth. He bent down
to pick up a lump of churned-up snow and

hurl it violently, at the scorched wall where the luminous letters were still clearly visible, SFS. 'Bastards!'

'I know it's no consolation but I don't think there are many of them,' Catriona said sympathetically. 'It's just that the few there are seem to have got a bit desperate and you're unfortunately the ones to suffer.'

'I'll make them suffer if I ever get my hands on them!' seethed Nick, kicking angrily against an icy rut. 'They've destroyed all the old panelling, the beams, the stalls—all the character of the place has gone up in smoke.'

'Yes, it's a terrible shame. How about the walls, though? They seem to be standing all right.' Catriona was groping around for any crumb of comfort.

'We won't know until we get a structural engineer to take a look.'

'The bank can help you there—one of our clients, who would give you priority, I'm sure.'

'It's just the thought of everything going backwards,' snarled Nick furiously. 'Our schedule was tight but we were on track to open in peak season. Now a few crackpot nationalists have put us right up shit creek! And God knows how long the insurance will take to pay up. The police have already asked us some pretty searching questions. I wouldn't be surprised if they suspect us of setting fire to it ourselves.'

'They couldn't!' cried Sue in anguish. 'Why would we do a thing like that? This place is our whole future. Well, it was!' Her voice broke on a sob.

'Look,' said Catriona hurriedly, seeing the hysteria building up in Sue and the paranoia in her husband, and feeling the cold beginning to creep through the soles of her feet even in the fleece-lined boots she had pulled on before leaving home, 'there's a pub a few miles down the road. Why don't we go there and get warm? I bet you haven't eaten properly today either. A bit of food and warmth is what you need.'

The bar of the Inverailort Hotel was small and hot and they found seats round an upright barrel-table at one side of the fireplace, where glowing coals in a small cast-iron grate no bigger than a shopping basket emitted more than enough heat to warm the pint-sized room. From his kiosk of a bar a cheery balding barman took their order for toasted sandwiches, and dispensed large tots of whisky together with continuous prattle about the weather and the latest shinty results.

Nick's set jaw began to loosen in the convivial atmosphere and his complexion lost its grey stony pallor. Sue's nose was as red as a cherry to match her inflamed eyes and her hair emerged flat and bedraggled from under the woolly pull-on hat she'd been wearing to keep out the cold. Neither looked their sartorial best but at least they no longer resembled two frozen fish fingers, Catriona thought as she sipped her whisky, and Nick had even raised his glass in a half-hearted salute before swigging back a large part of his dram in one gulp.

'That is a good deal better,' he declared

168

solemnly. 'A couple more of those and I might even be able to smile again.'

'Do you realise,' muttered Sue in an undertone, gazing at the folk sitting and standing around the bar, 'that the people who burned our place could be here, right now, having a drink.'

'They could,' agreed Catriona, a little worried by such obsessiveness. 'But they could equally well be propping up a bar in Inverness or Auchtermuchty. There's no particular reason to suspect that they're local. According to the newspapers, SFS recruits its members from all over Scotland.'

'But hardly anyone knew about us,' Sue pointed out. 'We'd only just started the conversion work. We've had no publicity and only a few locals knew anything about our plans.'

'You got planning permission from Lochaber District Council,' Catriona reminded her. 'And your plans had to be available for inspection for several weeks beforehand. Anyone could have taken a look at them, discovered your English background.'

'I suppose so,' said Sue doubtfully. 'I must say that I don't want to think that the person who burned us out might be living down the road.' She shivered, despite the heat of the fire. 'I'm not sure I'd want to stay in Glendoran if I thought that.'

'You're not thinking of giving up?' asked Catriona anxiously.

'Definitely not,' declared Nick stoutly. 'Who- ever chucked a fire-bomb in my window is going to bloody well see that window reglazed, the walls re-built and the restaurant flourishing despite all his best endeavours. If the Scots think the English give up as easily as that then they'd better have another think coming!' He downed the rest of his dram with a flourish. 'Anyway, the steading as it stands is worth nothing. We certainly wouldn't get our money back without the planned investment, and as far as I'm concerned that investment goes ahead as soon as possible and to hell with the SFS and all who rant and rail in her.'

'Well said!' exclaimed Catriona, picking up his glass. 'That deserves another drink—and I think our toasties are ready.'

Two young men were sitting at the bar when she went up to buy the drinks and Catriona was swift to notice that one of them was devastatingly good-looking in a wild, dark, Heathcliffe sort of way. When she returned to pick up two of the three plates of sandwiches to carry them over to the table he deftly swept up the extra one and smiled a fifty-megawatt smile.

'I'll help you with this,' he said, sliding easily off his stool. 'Save you another trip.'

'Thanks very much,' she said, returning about thirty megawatts. 'We're just over there.'

'Oh, don't worry, I've already noticed where you're sitting,' he assured her. 'Couldn't miss that fiery crowning glory!'

At the table Catriona put down her two plates. 'I'm not sure which are which,' she said, dimpling at her assistant. 'I'm afraid the staff may have muddled up the order.'

'Not at all,' retorted the volunteer waiter, unperturbed. 'This is the one with pickle—the other two are mustard.' He plonked his burden down and made a small mocking tug at his forelock, of which there was plenty since he had a shock of tousled dark brown curls which looked as if they hadn't seen a comb for several days.

'Thank you,' said Sue, perking up at the sight of him. 'Pickle is for me.'

'It's my pleasure,' he said, repeating the super-trouper smile for her benefit. 'All part of the Highland service.'

'You don't sound Highland,' remarked Catriona, sliding into her seat. 'You sound more Harrow to me.'

His hand dug into the tousled curls even deeper. 'Definitely not Harrow!' he cried, his eyes rolling in horror. 'Consonants clipped at Gordonstoun—vowels rounded at RADA!'

'Oh, an actor,' murmured Sue, who was looking distinctly less miserable. 'No wonder you play the waiter so well.'

Nick leaned over to offer his hand. Even he managed a tight smile. 'Wellington and hotel school,' he announced, determinedly entering into the spirit. 'Nick Carruthers and this is my wife Sue. Have a drink.'

'Andro Lindsay,' replied the actor. 'Yes, I will, thanks. I'll have the same as you.'

'And what about your friend?' enquired Nick, standing to move to the bar.

'Fergus? Oh, don't worry about him. He's not

171

very sociable,' replied Andro, pulling up another chair. The small, sharp-faced man with whom he had been sitting earlier had buried his face behind the *Sunday Mail* and didn't look at all approachable. Andro turned to Catriona. 'But you're not from England, surely? Not with a voice like yours and that Celtic colouring.'

Catriona laughed. 'No, I'm from Skye. Catriona Stewart.' His hand was dry and warm in hers and lingered just a shade beyond normal civility.

'Ciamar a tha, thu?' he said softly in Gaelic.

'Tha gu math,' she responded automatically.

'What language is that?' asked Sue with interest.

'It's Gaelic,' Andro told her. 'Catriona speaks it like a native no doubt, whereas I can only say how-d'you-do.'

'Do you speak it fluently, Catriona?' Sue enquired further.

Blushing slightly Catriona nodded. 'Yes, I do. Almost everyone does where I come from.'

'I hadn't realised. I thought it was dying out.'

'Far from it. It's on the increase if anything.'

'One large whisky,' said Nick, placing a glass in front of Andro. 'Do you take water or soda?'

'A little water thanks,' Andro responded, topping up his glass from the jug on the table. 'I don't know a Scot who takes soda in whisky. Lemonade perhaps, but not soda.'

'So, are you a local?' Nick asked, sitting down and picking up his toastie to take a bite.

172

'I stay up the road,' replied Andro vaguely. 'What are you doing up here in the frozen north, so far from home? It's hardly the tourist season.'

Catriona saw Nick and Sue exchange glances as if checking each other's willingness to reveal their ownership of the Glendoran steading. Then Sue finished her mouthful and told their story, briefly and succinctly.

Andro listened without speaking, his dark eyes hooded and expressionless, then asked, 'What will you do now?'

'Start again, of course,' said Nick firmly.

'What if they do it again?' Andro's fine, dark brows rose in his high, pale forehead.

'They won't,' growled Nick. 'Because they'll have to get past me next time and I'm not easily frightened. But if they did then we'd just start all over again. People shouldn't think they can get away with terrorist tactics.'

'Brave words,' murmured Andro.

Catriona slowly ate her sandwich during this exchange. She admired Nick for rallying as he had from the shattered individual she'd found stony-faced at the steading, and was aware that two large whiskies had only a little to do with it. Mostly it was pure defiance and she knew that the Glendoran steading would not remain a ruin long.

'Where are you going to stay?' Catriona asked Sue. 'They have rooms here.'

'No, we'd better get into Fort William this evening,' said Sue. 'I'll have to catch an early train tomorrow to get back to the boys and Nick has to make a statement at police headquarters.'

'I'll be back in Glendoran by ten-thirty though because I'm meeting the loss adjuster,' added Nick, glancing at his watch. 'Perhaps we should be getting off, darling. It's after seven and we have to find a hotel.'

'What are you going to do, Catriona?' asked Sue with concern.

'Well, I could drive home but I think I'll stay here if there's a room,' she replied. She was tired and the prospect of another spell on the road did not appeal. 'I could meet you at the steading in the morning Nick, before I drive back to Edinburgh. You may have a better idea then of how things are moving.'

Nick grimaced. 'At zimmer pace I should think, but that's fine.' He stood up. 'OK, Sue?'

Both women rose together. 'I'll come and see you off,' said Catriona. 'And I can ask about the room at the same time.'

Andro held out his hand. 'Well, goodbye Sue—Nick. Thanks for the drink. Perhaps we'll meet again.'

'More than likely,' agreed Nick, shaking on it. 'We're here to stay, SFS or no SFS.'

'Goodbye Andro,' smiled Sue. 'Come and try our bar when we're open.'

Andro grinned and nodded. 'Don't forget lemonade for the whisky,' he reminded her, then inclined his head in Catriona's direction. 'If you're taking a room perhaps we needn't say goodbye yet?' he murmured.

Before getting into the car Sue kissed Catriona

warmly on the cheek. 'You've been so kind,' she said. 'I keep having to remind myself that you're our bank manager.'

'Don't,' Catriona urged, laughing. 'I like to think I'm also a friend.'

'Definitely, and I hope one day you'll see us up and running and we can return your kindness.'

'I have every confidence that I will. Safe journey. Goodbye, Nick. See you tomorrow.' She waved them off making a mental note to recommend any reasonable level of borrowing they required. People as resilient as the Carruthers deserved all the support they could get. Opening the hatchback of the Golf she removed her overnight bag and carried it into the hotel.

'I got you another whisky,' said Andro when she returned to the bar after taking possession of a plain, clean single room over the entrance. He was back on his stool but his former companion was no longer beside him.

Catriona sat on the other stool. 'Thank you,' she said with a rueful smile. 'Although if I have too many more of these I'll be falling off this.' Raising the glass and indicating the stool at the same time almost made her suit the action to the word.

'Whoa!' Andro reached out to steady her. 'We won't have too far to carry you to bed, fortunately,' he grinned. 'I take it you got a room?' At her nod he withdrew his hand and continued, 'I've been sitting here trying to work out the relationship between you and the other

175

two. But I came to no very useful conclusion.'

'Well, you haven't very much to go on,' she observed.

'So?' He cocked his head on one side.

'It's professional,' she said briefly, deliberately unhelpful.

'Let me guess. You're the interior designer come to incorporate burnt beams into the décor.'

'What a tasteless notion,' she exclaimed, amused nevertheless. 'Wrong.'

'You're a race-relations adviser, helping the arrogant English to integrate with the savage Scots.' This suggestion brought the actor to the fore as his voice acquired a thick Highland accent and, riding his stool like a pony, he assumed the air of a wild, claymore-wielding chieftain.

She laughed merrily. 'Sounds a tough job. Too rough for me. Try something more mundane.'

'Brain surgeon? Supermodel? Astronaut?' He was acting desperation now.

She took pity on him. 'Bank manager. I'm their bank manager.'

It was his turn to nearly fall off his stool. 'You're a bank manager? I don't believe it. Bank managers wear grey suits and glasses and have no sense of humour—and they're men, by definition!'

'Not this one,' she told him firmly. 'I have humour *and* hormones. But then I don't work for your average pay-up-and-shut-up bank.'

'Aha!' Andro's dark eyes suddenly narrowed. 'You work for Steuart's—the bank that likes to say "Absolutely, darling!" ' He waved a languid hand and chameleoned into an upper-class twit.

Her eyes rounded in surprise. 'You know it!' she exclaimed. 'I don't think we're quite as bad as that, though.'

Andro subsided back into an untidy thespian, shaking his head in amazement. 'Imagine you being a bank manager—and working for Steuart's. You must know every millionaire north of Newcastle.'

'Give or take the odd one or two,' she agreed nonchalantly. 'Not all of them nice, I might add.'

'Anyone with money is nice,' he declared cynically. 'Especially in the eyes of an impoverished actor.'

She stared at him curiously. 'It's hard to tell from that crumpled shirt and those holey jeans whether you're poor or just unkempt, but I suspect the latter.'

He gave her the benefit of his atom-splitting smile again and dug his hands in his pockets, turning them inside-out to demonstrate their emptiness. 'It's your turn to be wrong. And to prove it I'll let you buy the next round.'

Catriona pursued her lips doubtfully. 'If I have much more whisky I'll need another toastie to soak it up,' she said.

'OK, you can buy me a toastie as well,' he responded blithely. 'And we can set the world to rights!'

She had no idea where Andro Lindsay slept

that night. When she staggered up to bed she was beyond worrying about breathalysers and blood-alcohol levels and rather suspected that he was too. The next morning she only knew that she had drunk far too much and had probably said things she ought to regret if only she could remember what they were!

But it had been fun—mad, irresponsible, unregrettable fun and she hadn't thought of the SFS, Hamish, his son or Alison's baby all evening. She couldn't remember the last time she had let her hair down in quite that way, and Andro had been the perfect drinking partner—amusing, light-hearted, good-looking and easygoing. They had met as strangers and parted like long lost friends. The only unpleasant part of the whole procedure was the hangover!

A bowl of porridge proved good blotting paper but the sight of the huge fried breakfast then placed before her by the shy, smiling teenage waitress was too much. Wordlessly she shook her head and handed back the plate. 'Coffee,' she murmured. 'Just coffee, please.' And paracetamol, she thought groggily, reaching for her shoulder bag.

Despite his woes, Nick Carruthers looked rather more lively than Catriona when they met at the blackened steading. It was his first opportunity to inspect it in full daylight.

'Well, it's bad but it's not disastrous,' he concluded bravely. 'I'm no expert but the walls look pretty solid even though the beams have fallen. I just hope I can get the builders back here pronto before the frost does any more damage.'

'Well, don't worry about signing cheques,' Catriona told him, bleakly wondering when the paracetamol would begin to work. 'I'm going to authorise an overdraft of up to twenty thousand without consultation. And as soon as I get back to Edinburgh I'll stir up that structural engineer I told you about and get him up here. Will you be staying on for a few days?'

'I'll stay as long as I need to,' Nick assured her. 'The police want me on the spot and I'm going to get the cottage habitable in time for Sue and the boys to join me when the Easter holidays start. Then we'll all have to work like demons.'

'Have the police stopped regarding you as suspect number one?'

'More or less, though I still have the insurance company to convince,' said Nick resignedly.

'Let me have your number as soon as the phone's connected and keep in touch meanwhile,' urged Catriona, watching a red Ford Sierra turn off the road and bounce over the rubble-strewn area in front of the steading. 'This looks like the loss adjuster. Do you want me to stay?'

Nick shook his head. 'No, you get off. I'll ring you at the bank later and let you know what he says.'

The village of Glendoran consisted of a few houses, a school, a kirk and a phone box scattered along the main road where the Doran Burn ran into Loch Eilt. Glen Doran itself was a hidden valley which nestled above the village in the shoulder of a mountain range. Catriona had studied the map and now knew that a hundred yards beyond the steading there was a turning which led up the brae into the Lochaber estate. Instead of heading straight for Edinburgh she turned her car up this narrow road, intent on discovering more about Lord Nevis's heritage and clearing her head at the same time. After half a mile the gradient slackened and she found herself driving along an undulating valley, Glen Doran itself, 'the valley of the otter' to translate it literally from the Gaelic. Towards its widest point the map showed there was a house of the same name, Glen Doran House, the Highland home of the Earl of Lochaber, chief of Clan Galbraith.

It stood in a sheltered hollow at the edge of a small loch, a surprisingly modest dwelling by the usual standards of Scottish baronial residences. No magnificent embellishments disfigured its clean, straight, grey-granite lines, only several tall and rather elegant chimneys breaking the stark outline of the slate roof which was finished with a carved parapet above a simple pedimented entrance reached by a sweeping stone staircase.

Catriona received her first glimpses of it from outside the shoulder-high enclosing wall which gathered the house and its various outbuildings into an intimate domestic policy, protected by a plantation of lofty winter-bare trees which, judging by their size, had probably stood there for as long as the house itself, nearly three hundred years. The wrought-iron gate at the main entrance stood invitingly open, leading into a wide sweep of gravel drive. Boldly, she decided to enter.

There was no evidence of human habitation—no car parked on the gravel, no movement behind the square-paned windows. Tentatively she wandered round the back, under a curved tunnel-arch which led into a courtyard containing garages, stables and workshops. The whirring sound of machinery echoed off the enclosing walls.

Drawn by the noise she peered through an open door. Under an Anglepoise lamp a weird figure wearing what looked like a space-age helmet was hunched over a spinning lathe. Scattered all around him were rough logs, tree-stumps with their roots still attached, planks and small branches, clearly the raw materials of his craft. Along the walls ran shelves containing rows of finished articles—wooden bowls, goblets, platters, small stools and even tiny fruit and vegetable shapes, apples, pears and mushrooms. So fierce was the turner's concentration and so loudly did his lathe shriek that he was oblivious to Catriona standing behind him and she was able to watch for several minutes as the length of wood attached to the lathe became a rounded and elegant chair-leg under his skilled application of the chisel. A pile of pale and fragrant shavings grew at his feet.

When he finally looked up and raised his protective visor she saw that he was old, with a lean, lined face and white wisps of hair emerging from the confines of his helmet. He peered at her with rather watery blue eyes over a pair of smeared horn-rimmed spectacles riding well down on his nose. He wore the kind of work-stained blue overall familiar to her as the habitual garb of the crofter. When he pressed a switch the spinning lathe whined to a halt.

'Excuse me,' she began timidly. 'I was looking for someone to ask for permission to walk round the loch. Would it be possible? It looks so lovely in the sunshine.'

The old man removed his helmet, laid it on the bench and walked towards her. He was quite spry on his feet despite his age. 'It is lovely in any weather,' he said, giving a throat-clearing cough into his hand. 'Ahem! Wood dust. I'll just come outside for a breather.'

His refined voice surprised her, a relic of the 'old-school', somewhat reminiscent of Wodehouse's Bertie Wooster without the silly affectations. Not a crofter this, or even any ordinary carpenter. She gave a hesitant laugh and on an impulse asked, 'Are you the Earl of Lochaber, by any chance?'

'Indeed I am,' he agreed, ushering her through the door and back into the courtyard. He blinked in the sunshine. 'Now I can see that you're as pretty as your silhouette. Who are you, may I ask, since you have the advantage of me?' He was tall, despite a pronounced stoop exacerbated by his habitual stance at the lathe.

'Catriona Stewart,' she responded, extending her hand. 'How do you do? I know your son, Lord Nevis, because I work at his bank.'

She was astonished by Lochaber's snort of

derision. 'Steuart's!' he exclaimed as if he was expelling phlegm. 'How disappointin'. No one as charmin' as you should be workin' in such a nest of vipers. It's a crime.' His hand in hers was rough and calloused, a worker's hand.

She smiled disarmingly. 'I'm one of the managers; it's a very good job.'

His laugh was like leaves rustling in the wind. 'I'm sure it is—for a pop-eyed pen-pusher. But you look like someone with nobler potential, in art perhaps, or music.'

'I'm afraid not. Banking is all I'm good at. I don't have clever fingers, like you.' She spread her hands, the fingers long and tapering, the nails smooth and pink; pretty, impractical hands.

'You need more than strong hands to work with wood,' the old Earl told her, flexing one of his own gnarled and scarred appendages. 'You need instinct and sensitivity to bring the character out of the grain.'

'What sort do you work with?' she asked curiously.

'Only native woods. Beech, oak, cherry, ash, elm, pine, birch, sycamore, rowan—there are so many! All the people on the estate know to tell me if a tree falls or they're clearin' bushes and undergrowth.' He looked more closely at Catriona. 'Where do you live?'

'In Edinburgh.'

His disappointment was obvious. 'Yes, I suppose you would, workin' in that bank. But you don't look like a city girl.'

'No, well, I'm from Skye originally,' she confessed.

'I knew it!' he declared, then glowered at her. 'Why did you leave?' he growled.

His vehemence made Catriona jump. 'I—I was posted to the mainland—by the bank,' she stuttered nervously.

'Bah!' he exclaimed. 'You shouldn't have left the island.'

'It was promotion,' she explained.

'It was forced exile,' he retorted. 'Foolin' you into thinkin' that the only worthwhile place to live and work is on the mainland, in the city. Poppycock! You should remain loyal to your roots.'

'I am loyal to them,' she protested, wondering how she had got into this conversation and how she was going to get out of it. 'I often go back to Skye. My family are there.'

'And what about makin' a family of your own?' The old Earl folded his arms across his chest and spoke in clarion tones like a judge passing sentence. 'You should be havin' children as bright and beautiful as yourself and bringin' them up to put Skye on the map, not fritterin' your life away countin' other people's money.' He shook his head sorrowfully, his voice trailing into a mumble. 'But it's the same everywhere these days. Ambition is everythin', Mammon is God. No one wants to pay back to the land what they've taken from it.'

'Is that why you work with wood?' she asked gently.

He gazed at her, head on one side, as if

trying to decide whether she was friend or foe, then he turned and strode back into the workshop and began rummaging around on the shelves, muttering to himself. Catriona hovered uncertainly outside, wondering whether she should stay or leave, whether she had offended him in some way or if he was simply old and eccentric and couldn't be bothered to talk to her any more.

She was on the verge of slipping unobtrusively away when he re-emerged clutching a round, flat, wooden object.

'Somethin' I'd like you to have,' he said unexpectedly.

It was a clock, made from a plate-sized disc of some beautifully grained wood, pale buff at its outer edge, darkening to deep red at its heart, carved with circular ridges and undulations to lend subtle lights and shades. The hours were carved out of some darker wood, as were the arrow-shaped hands and it was showing the correct time—eleven o'clock.

'It's lovely!' she exclaimed. 'But I can't possibly take it.' Shades of Hamish and the Uig painting, she thought crazily. But I haven't done *anything* to deserve this!

A wily smile transformed the Earl's age-lined face and lent it an echo of the handsome youth he had once been. He smoothed the clock gently with his fingers.

'This is wood from the rowan tree which used to grow here, beside the house. It was blown over in a gale and I planted another one immediately, of course. As an islander you'll know that rowans give protection against witchcraft.'

His voice grew bardic, its intonations more Gaelic than English, and to Catriona he suddenly resembled an ancient seer, a teller of tales and future fortunes. 'The rowan is the World Tree, with its roots in Hell and its branches in Heaven, for they all point skywards as they grow. It's a powerful symbol for all wild northlanders.'

Fixing his eyes on her to indicate that he numbered her among them, he went on, 'I want you to take the rowan clock back to wherever you live and hang it on the wall, and when you look at it, remember that time in this world is passin' and precious. And when you understand what it is you should do with the rest of your little allowance of it, you can bring the clock back to me, because you won't need it any more. So you see, it's only a loan.'

Catriona frowned uneasily, for his words had plunged her straight back down the dark tunnel of insomnia inspired by Alison's baby. The old man thrust the clock into her hands and she took it like one clutching at a straw.

'Well, yes,' she said without conviction. 'But I don't think...'

'*Don't* think,' he interrupted gruffly. 'Go for your walk and enjoy the scenery and leave me to get on with my work. Just take the clock and come back and see me when you've got the message.'

He cocked one bushy white brow at her and the image of the seer faded into that of an elderly sheepdog confronting a wayward lamb.

Then he turned and shuffled back into the dark workshop and the whine of the lathe began again, excluding her from his presence.

Catriona looked at the rowan clock briefly and then tucked it under her arm with a smile of resignation. Why not? she thought. Its value was more symbolic than real and it gave her an excuse to come back...

At this altitude the snow had already melted and the thaw had left deep puddles in the ruts of the track which ran round the loch. She was glad she had changed her leather boots for Wellingtons. The surrounding landscape reminded her of old sepia photographs of the Highlands, with white snow-capped mountains rising out of inky-black swathes of heather, scattered with patches of pale-buff winter grass and the glinting silver silicate of protruding rocks. In the distance, where there was forestry, bare brown larches were faintly tinted with spring viridian amongst the sinister dark green predominance of Sitka spruce. In the brilliant sunshine the horizon seemed to flutter like a tattered flag against an azure sky. March was supplying another of its violent weather variations, providing a few hours of hot sunshine to steam-dry the black peatbogs and melt the white fingers of the frozen waterfalls.

Loch Doran was a haven for waterbirds, and she spotted several species of duck patrolling the shallows among posses of busy little divers and scurrying dab-chicks, and watched for several minutes the determined, motionless vigil of a tall grey heron at the edge of a patch of dead reeds before it flapped off indignantly on detecting her presence. High in the sky overhead another big bird soared effortlessly on a thermal updraught, too high for her to identify. It could have been a buzzard but instinctively she felt it must be a rare golden eagle.

As she returned her dazzled gaze to earth she was surprised by the sight of a man approaching around the loch from the opposite direction. It was Andro Lindsay, his dark locks lifting in the breeze and a beaming smile on his secretive, handsome face. 'Well, met, Titania!' he cried from several yards distance. 'Rumour had spread that you favoured this blasted heath.' His stride was long and springy, spurning the spiky tussocks of heather which attempted to clutch at his ankles.

'I think you should brush up your Shakespeare,' Catriona suggested, returning the smile. 'The blasted heath was Lear's, wasn't it? I'm sure Titania favoured a forest glade. How did you know I'd be here?'

'I followed a silken trail,' he told her solemnly. 'Your discarded cobwebs are everywhere.'

'Phew, I should think they are,' she conceded, ruefully rubbing her eyes. 'You're an evil influence.'

'Huh! Who led who astray?' He fell into step as she moved off once more, leaving her to splash down the puddled ruts in her Wellingtons while his Caterpillar boots tracked through the grass and heather. 'I woke at seven with a crick in the neck. That sofa in the hotel lounge isn't long enough.'

'Is that where you slept?' she giggled then added on an accusing note, 'No one knew I was coming here.'

'It is impossible for a flame-haired siren like yourself to do anything in Glendoran without the whole community knowing,' he informed her. 'Dougie the Ditch saw you at the road-end as you turned up the glen.'

'Oh yes, I did see someone clearing a culvert somewhere down there,' she remarked, enlightened. 'Is he really called Dougie the Ditch? Poor man. All these assiduous enquiries, though. Do I owe you a drink or something?'

Andro glanced at his watch. 'Come to think of it, a hair of the dog might not go amiss,' he said, eyes dancing at her expression of distaste. 'But you don't owe me anything. I just thought you had made a fatal error last night and you might like to rectify it, that's all.'

'What error was that?' she asked doubtfully.

'You failed to take my telephone number in case you should want to ring and ask me for a date.' Even a ragged growth of dark stubble didn't diminish his unquestionable beauty. Andro was Apollo after a hard night!

'Well, that doesn't sound like the kind of mistake I would usually make,' she replied solemnly.

'That what I thought,' he said with Olympian confidence. 'So I've written it down for you.' He waved a yellow square of paper. 'Look, it's a Post-it. You can stick it wherever you like.'

'Don't tempt me!' she chuckled, taking it from him.

189

'If you don't use it I shall haunt Steuart's doorway like a pestilential poltergeist. I'm sure they won't want a hairy actor in grubby jeans and boots sullying their elegant entrance, will they?'

'Only if he's a client,' she grinned.

They had reached the end of the path where his battered green Suzuki was parked off the narrow roadway. He climbed aboard and wound down the window.

'I might even be willing to become one,' he declared, 'so that you can handle my overdraft. Bye!'

It was an actor's exit. There was a sucking squelch as four tyres dug into soaked peat and he accelerated away, leaving Catriona smiling and waving the yellow square of paper—hangover, Hamish and Alison's baby all forgotten.

Seven

Hamish Melville was not the type to be forgotten. 'Where on earth have you been?' he demanded somewhat tetchily when she answered her telephone to him at home that evening. 'I've been trying to ring you.'

'I had to go away unexpectedly,' Catriona replied, surprised by his carping tone. Having driven fast from Glendoran she had worked at the bank until seven catching up with her work and was feeling tired and still a little hungover.

'Who with?' he asked curtly. He had been unprepared for how much her unexplained absence would affect him, and frustrated by the impossibility of finding out where she was. She did not manage his accounts so he could hardly ring the bank to enquire.

Catriona frowned. Surely that was the wrong question. 'Where did you go?' or, 'Did you have a good time?' maybe, but—'Who did you go with?' She didn't feel inclined to answer that one.

'Catriona? Are you still there?' he persisted.

'Yes, I am. How are you?' She spoke with her usual warmth but she noticed that several crucial sensations were missing. Where was the wildly bounding heart, the sweet surge of hot blood at the sound of his voice, the leap of gratitude for his call?

'I'm fine. Why didn't you answer my question?' Hamish sounded puzzled, bewildered even, yet she couldn't remember him ever being anything but super-confident.

'Which question was that?'

'Oh, never mind.' Perplexity had given way to irritation. 'You got back all right anyway.'

'Yes, but only this afternoon... Oh, you mean from London! Yes, I did. It was a wonderful trip—fantastic. Thank you very much.'

Her thanks were balm to his petulance. He dropped his voice to an intimate murmur. 'Next time we'll go to Paris,' he suggested. 'The Opéra, dinner at Maxim's, the George V, exactly as promised.'

'Mmm. I can't wait.' What was wrong with

191

her? Where was the excitement, the high-octane, super-charged thrill of simply speaking to him?

He continued ardently, unaware of her distraction: 'I'm aching for you right now, but I've got a dinner at the New Club. It shouldn't go on too late, though. I could come round afterwards. I'm staying in town...'

'No.' The refusal was out before she could control it. 'I mean—of course, normally that would be great, Hamish, but right now I'm absolutely exhausted. I'll probably be asleep by nine.'

'Leave the key under the mat—I'll wake you up. Do you want me to tell you how?'

'I can imagine,' she exclaimed. 'But I really don't think I'd be much good.'

'You could never be anything else,' he said cajolingly. 'I can suffer dinner with any number of dull old New Clubbers if I know my Catriona is for dessert.'

'An *old* New Clubber doesn't sound quite right somehow,' she observed with amusement.

'Well, it may be called New but this particular gentlemen's club is actually quite ancient and so are its members, with the odd exception.'

'Meaning you?'

'Of course meaning me! So what do you say? Shall I abandon them to their brandies and bath-chairs and jog up the hill to your place after dinner?' He sounded boyishly eager.

'Oh Hamish, honestly I'm just too tired. Can we leave it for tonight?' Catriona hoped she sounded genuinely regretful. After all, she was telling nothing but the truth.

'Sure. Don't worry about it.' His umbrage was audible. 'Unfortunately I can't manage any other night this week.'

'Oh, I see.' She didn't know what to say. Part of her wanted him—the wild impulsive part which had been responsible for her falling into his arms in the first place, but another part of her was retreating from him—the part that felt guilty about his son and saw the relationship progressing down a dark tunnel into an arid future. 'Well, we'll just have to wait until next week then,' she sighed after a pause.

'Catriona!' he exclaimed with disbelief. 'What's happened to you? I thought we had something going. We had such a ball in London! You've been with someone else, haven't you? You were away with someone!' He sounded harsh and indignant, not like the suave, self-contained, charming Hamish she was accustomed to.

'No, of course I wasn't,' she declared. 'Why are you being so cross?'

He subsided with a little laugh. 'I'm not cross, darling. Just frustrated. I confess I hate the idea of you being with someone else—with another man. Do you blame me?'

'No. No, I suppose not.' But she thought she did, rather. After all, he hadn't exactly declared Linda a no go area.

'Listen, it's the Fife Point-to-Point on Saturday. Will you be there?' The old, confident Hamish seemed to have returned.

'Yes. There's a few of us going from the bank.'

'We'll be dispensing champagne and lobster

193

near the final fence. Come and join in the party and then I'll arrange a rendezvous somewhere private. Meanwhile, think about our little foreign jaunt. I know I said Paris but you might prefer Florence, or Venice—a night or two at the Danielli, a walk along the Lido and dinner at La Capanna...'

She couldn't help smiling. He saw life in such splendiferous terms! 'You make it all sound irresistible. I promise to think about it. See you on Saturday then. I'll look out for a lobster waving its claw, shall I?'

'Yes. From a dark blue Range Rover. By the way, I've just been made a Trustee of the National Galleries of Scotland. Who would turn you on next, after Picasso? Titian? Tintoretto? Rembrandt? You can have your pick of artists now.'

'Congratulations! That's quite an honour, isn't it? But I thought you didn't like to think of me with another man—even an Old Master.'

'Cheeky! Are you sure you won't change your mind about tonight? You don't sound very tired.'

'Believe me, I am. Don't they have cold showers at the New Club?'

'No, but I've always suspected that they put Temazepam in the coffee. That's why everyone falls asleep after dinner.'

'Have two cups!'

'I'll need more than that, with you only half a mile away. I'll see you on Saturday, you bright and beautiful banker. I'd like to compare you with that bale of hay we talked about in London. I'll work on it. Goodbye.'

'Sounds fragrant—but itchy! Bye.'

Almost as soon as she put the phone down it rang again, making her jump. 'Hello Catriona, this is Felicity Finlay—Bruce's wife. I can't believe you've been at Steuart's nearly three months and we haven't yet invited you to dinner with us. I feel awful. I wondered if you might be free this Friday?'

Catriona was pleased, detecting no ulterior motive in the invitation. 'Yes, I'm sure I am. Thank you. I'd love to come.'

'Good. Nothing formal. Just a few friends— some from the bank, some not. About eight o'clock.'

'Right. Thanks very much.' Catriona wondered whether Bruce knew she'd been asked and how much he would relish having her at his table knowing what she knew about him and Linda. Such were the perils of playing away from home!

After the phone calls she occupied herself by making some soup with a few carrots, an onion, lentils and a handful of parsley and then sat musing in the kitchen while it simmered cosily on the hob, filling the flat with an appetising aroma and reminding her of home. It evoked a deep yearning for the relative simplicity of life on the croft, so thirled to weather and season and so unaffected by low morality or high finance. Her present life seemed unpredictable and her situation problematic. What did she really feel for Hamish? Why did the existence of Max make her so uneasy? And why should she be so jealous of Alison?

For a few hours the plight of the Carruthers had driven all these imponderables to the back of her mind and then the interlude with Andro had lifted her spirits back to full buoyancy. But Andro was another conundrum. He'd just appeared and reappeared with his stun-grenade smile, rather like the Cheshire Cat. Should she endow him with any more significance than Alice had given to her feline fantasy in Wonderland? Certainly they had shared an instant rapport but she knew almost nothing about him, not even what kind of acting he did. During the course of their convivial encounter the conversation had been more philosophical than personal, righting the wrongs of the world and Scotland in particular. He had evinced a burning sense of national pride and she had responded to it. Probably it had been the whisky talking. Still, he'd given her his number. Why shouldn't she use it? She'd stuck the yellow Post-it paper on the door of the fridge. The cordless phone was by her elbow. Impulsively she picked it up and dialled.

It rang four times and then a recorded female voice answered: 'This is Precipitous City Productions. There's no one to take your call at present but if you leave your name and number we'll get back to you as soon as possible.'

Catriona heard the high-pitched tone which indicated that the answerphone was ready to record her message. She thought it over for a few seconds and then pressed the Off switch without speaking. She'd assumed he had given her his home number. Who was the woman and what was Precipitous City Productions?

The rowan clock was lying on the hall table where she'd dumped it when she unloaded the car. She dug in a drawer for a hammer and a nail and carried them all through to the sitting room. Glancing around for a place to hang the clock, she caught sight of the little landscape of Uig Bay which she'd put just to the left of the mantelpiece. There was a similar space to the right and it seemed appropriate to position the two items either side of the fireplace—unlooked-for gifts with strings attached and both providing an insidious notion of time passing, as if going up in smoke!

As she hung it she inspected it closely. The clock was fashioned out of two semi-circles of wood cut from the same side of the tree-trunk and glued together into a round face. A hazy memory of school woodwork classes surfaced to remind her that a single slice across a trunk would warp and twist whereas two halves of the same side, glued together across the diameter, remained true and straight, the one half countering the distorting effect of the other. It was like a good marriage, she thought, conjuring her parents' longstanding union, bound together by love and law and yet successfully allowing for each other's individual faults and foibles. What had she ever achieved in her own life to equal that?

At the thought of her parents she was assailed by a dreary, maudlin feeling which she could only properly describe with a Scots word sometimes used by her mother. She felt *wersh*—feeble. What she needed was a good old-fashioned dose of maternal chat.

Sheena Stewart was not one to beat about the bush. 'What's up, dear?' she asked on hearing her daughter's voice. 'Have you lost a pound and found a penny?'

'Is that how I sound?' Catriona attempted a bright laugh. 'Sorry!'

'You can't fool me, love. I may not have set eyes on you for far too long but I can still tell when my Cat's eating grass. It's not like you to be down. What is it?'

They spoke in English for, having been brought up on the Clyde, Gaelic was not Sheena's native language, but the low, steady, musical voice, even over a phone line, was enough to spirit Catriona straight back into girlhood again. Tears of self-pity stung her eyes. 'I'm not really down, Mum, just a bit hemmed in. I think I've got city-itis.'

Her mother gave a sharp inward hiss. 'Ouch! Painful. But it's more likely to be Island Deficiency Syndrome.' Her intonation gave it capital letters. 'I get it after only a few hours on the mainland and you've been there ten years now.'

Catriona laughed despite her jaded mood. 'You and your IDS! I've never believed you when you've said that before but this time I think you may be right.'

'Well Cat, there's only one cure. You'll have to come home for a few days. Couldn't you, *eudail?* I'm longing to see you, Dad's pining for you and those little girls of Marie's are hardly aware they've got an aunt.'

Catriona could picture her mother, probably sitting as she was herself, in the kitchen, writing her diary or assembling one of her dried-grass pictures on the well-worn scrubbed deal table. They sold well in the local shop, especially to the summer tourists, as vivid souvenirs of the wild, spacious beauty of Skye. Her father would be down at the Ferry Inn where he went every evening for an hour or so after dinner, along with the majority of Uig males over the age of eighteen.

'I'm coming at Easter. It's only three weeks away.'

'Hmm. Your IDS could be terminal by then.' Sheena was not entirely joking. Melancholic yearning for home was a recognised condition among Highland exiles, often passed down through generations. Hence the tradition of clan gatherings in places as far away as Nova Scotia and New Zealand.

'Tell me what's happening around the Bay.' Catriona just wanted to hear her mother talk about everyday matters. It would be like a sticking plaster on a severed artery but at least it was first-aid of a sort.

'Well, the schoolteacher was seen buying a bottle of Blue Nun in the Co-op and the following Sunday the minister preached on a text from St Paul's letter to the Ephesians—"Be not drunk with wine".'

Catriona giggled. 'Did he? And went straight

round to the Ferry Inn afterwards, no doubt.'

'Oh no, dear. Not on a Sunday.'

'Speaking of the teacher, how's her romance with Donnie J.?' The J was always added to differentiate this Donnie from the four others in Uig, one of whom, Donnie B, was married to Catriona's sister, Marie.

'Much the same. Still blowing hot and cold like the farrier's fire. Any romance on your horizon, by the way?' Sheena asked the question casually but Catriona knew only too well her mother's strong dissatisfaction on that score.

'Oh, you know, Mum. The usual orderly queue forming at the door.'

'Any princes among the puddocks?'

'No, but then I'm no princess.'

'Don't tell your Dad that. He thinks you are.'

'Is he OK?'

'Fine. Same as ever. Nothing much changes here.'

'Except the tide.'

'And the weather—about every five minutes at present. Talk about mad March winds!'

As the conversation drifted into the island climate and the state of the croft, Catriona began to feel better. Normality still lurked abroad. It put all the city shifting and swapping into perspective. She realised that there might be some sense in what the old Earl had said. Perhaps she was a grass snake in a nest of vipers, appearing similar but with a fundamentally different nature.

When the rowan clock said ten o'clock she

ate her lentil soup and went to bed, leaving no key under the doormat.

The East Neuk of Fife is a glorious secret, jealously guarded by those fortunate enough to have discovered it. Oil industrialists jet over it to Aberdeen, foreign tourists drive straight on past it, aiming for the salmon rivers and whisky distilleries of Speyside, and eager golfers skirt it, making direct for the Royal and Ancient shrine of St Andrews. Little do they know that they are missing out on one of Scotland's most charming localities.

As its name implies, the East Neuk is a nook, a small friendly corner lying behind the eastern headland of Fife Ness and consisting of a series of quaint stone-walled fishing harbours ringed by white houses with crow-stepped gables and red-tiled roofs, linked by a string of long sandy beaches, spectacular rocky coves and rich rolling farmland. Despite the lure of Greece and Spain, in summer the area is still a Mecca for wealthy families from Scotland's central belt seeking safe and sunny bucket-and-spade holidays. For, by a climatic freak, the East Neuk often basks under hot sunshine whilst the rest of the east coast languishes under cloud. Its beaches are crowded with children, while their parents play tennis and golf and entertain each other to barbecues sizzling with rare steaks and pink champagne.

In spring the same families drive their status-symbol four-wheel-drive vehicles to an inland farm called Balcormo, bumping and bouncing through furrow and stubble on a rare excursion over the kind of rough terrain for which the vehicles were designed, to park in orderly rows alongside the three-mile course of brushwood jumps set up by the Fife Hunt for their annual point-to-points.

'Why is it called a point-to-point?' Catriona asked Donald, having met up with the Steuart's contingent at an agreed rendezvous by the parade ring. Catriona had brought her own car, wanting to be free to leave when she chose, but her secretary Moira had given Gillian and Donald Cameron a lift for which he was duly grateful because it meant he could 'swill down a few' and not drive home. Like Catriona they had parked in the five-pound car park and walked the quarter-mile to the course. To put a car on the rails cost twenty-five pounds and a position near the winning post demanded membership of the hunt.

'I'm not sure really,' Donald admitted in answer to Catriona's question, his florid cheeks darkening to pale puce in the sharp wind. 'I think it sprang from a wager that one hunter was faster and nimbler than another, put to the test from Point A to Point B over hunt country. It's like a steeplechase, only the entries have to be horses which are actually ridden to hounds. It used to be entirely amateur but nowadays the edges—or should that be the points?—are a bit blurred.'

'There aren't any spectator stands,' observed Catriona with surprise, surveying the sparse scattering of tents and portaloos around the parade ground. Her knowledge of horse racing was almost entirely gleaned from television coverage of the Grand National and the Derby. At Balcormo a first-aid station, a beer tent, a hamburger stall, an ice-cream van and a bouncy castle summed up the level of sophistication. Rows of motorised horseboxes stood in for racetrack stables.

Donald laughed. 'It always amuses me that people *sit* in a stand! Seasoned point-to-pointers tend to climb on their cars to get a good view of the course. In fact, the more battered the vehicle the more useful it is because you can stand on the bonnet without bothering about the paintwork.'

Moira had been consulting with Gillian over the race card they'd bought. 'There's lots of time before the first race,' she said. 'Let's go to the posh car park. We're bound to know someone we can cadge a drink off.'

Without a doubt, thought Catriona, smiling to herself. She had not told the others of Hamish's invitation. She would evince complete surprise when they encountered his lobster-laden Range Rover!

'Well, the bank dishes out enough hospitality so I think its employees might justifiably claim some of it back,' declared Donald, tucking his race card into his coat pocket and rubbing his hands briskly together from both chill and expectation. 'This place will be hooching with clients and I'm always prepared to do a bit of boot-crawling.'

'Boot-licking, you mean,' declared Moira mischievously.

'I certainly do not.' Donald looked offended. 'I mean boot-crawling—as in pub-crawling, only here drinks are dispensed from car boots.'

'Oh, I see,' giggled Moira. 'Free-loading.'

'No, free-booting!' quipped Catriona.

Laughing companionably they all set out in a bunch but soon split up when Moira, detecting the sound of high, rounded vowels, dragged Gillian off towards a noisy group standing behind the open hatchback of a big grey Volvo. 'That's Colonel Buchanan, from Daddy's regiment,' she trilled.

Catriona and Donald heard the braying laughs issuing from the regimental group and caught each other's eye with a mutual shake of the head. 'We'll catch up with you later, girls,' said Donald cheerfully. 'You carry on!'

Although it was not actually raining the clouds were low and heavy over the surrounding hills, distinctive with their treeless, grassy summits and steep escarpments plunging into the wide pastured hollow, or 'howe' as it was termed locally, in which the point-to-point was located. Lunchtime refreshments were in full swing, fanned by a cold wind whipping down out of the north-east, causing alcohol levels in bottle and hip-flask to plummet. Among the stalwart racegoers rosy cheeks and noses were as common as binoculars and tweed caps.

'Will you look at that!' cried Donald impulsively, clutching at Catriona's arm.

In prime position, exactly halfway between the final fence and the finishing-post was the polished navy Melville Range Rover, its hatch-back raised and a crowd of chattering individuals grouped around two tables at its rear. These were spread with white cloths and amply laden with bottles and platters, presided over by an impeccable butler whose attire made no concession to the *al fresco* and sporting nature of the occasion. He wore a black tailcoat over a wing-collared shirt, black bow tie and striped waistcoat, and his snow-white gloves were an undoubted part of the uniform rather than buffers against the icy wind. With dignified gait Minto moved amongst a milling crowd of Melville 'hangers-on', dispensing champagne with lugubrious mien.

Hamish held court at one side of the group, his round face genial and smiling, his body encased in a beige, belted, fleece-lined mac and his head in a brown felt Fedora. With occasional nods and deft flicks of his hand he conducted the dispensing of drinks by his manservant.

Linda Melville was entirely swathed in winter-white cashmere, layers and layers of it, clinging to her long coltish legs, wrapped around her willowy waist and wound around her head and shoulders in the form of a soft chaperon hat with a long mink-trimmed scarf. With her perfect teeth, dark, flashing eyes and wide-legged model stance she reminded Catriona of a Russian Cossack princeling, even down to the highly polished black knee-boots which looked as if they should be sprouting a gilded spur at each heel.

Dressed as she was in a plain grey duffel coat and Donegal tweed trousers Catriona felt like a dowdy beetle compared with Linda's exotic moth. Only her stylish green pull-on felt hat gave her any sense of individual chic. 'I don't think Linda Melville is here for the horses,' she murmured to Donald as they paused to watch, fascinated.

'And she certainly isn't here for the beer,' he replied on an undertone. 'I wonder what she *is* here for?'

As he spoke Bruce and Felicity Finlay approached from the opposite direction and were summoned into the Melville circle with enthusiastic greetings, easily audible over a fifty-yard radius.

'I may have a clue,' Catriona observed cynically. 'Come on Donald, let's go and drink a health unto Their Majesties.' The number plate of the Range Rover was HM 200. When she drove it about town there was no doubting whose consort Linda Melville was.

'Ah—Steuart's here in force, I see!' called Hamish, sighting them and waving them forward, whilst in the midst of ensuring that Bruce and Felicity were furnished with drinks. 'You're Donald Cameron, aren't you?' he observed as they came within earshot. 'We've met at the bank. Come and have a drink.' He shook Donald's hand briefly and turned solicitously to his companion. 'Catriona, you look frozen. You'd better have something more warming than champagne.'

'No, champagne would be lovely,' Catriona assured him, returning his social kiss and receiving a quick and meaningful squeeze on her upper arm. Smiling her thanks, she lifted the proffered glass from Minto's silver salver.

Felicity Finlay came bustling up to Catriona. 'Hello. I hope you enjoyed last night. I thought it might have been a little dull for you.' Behind her she didn't notice Bruce greeting Linda Melville with barely-restrained enthusiasm.

'Not at all, it was a lovely evening,' Catriona responded with genuine warmth. 'I especially enjoyed meeting your friend Elizabeth—er, Nicholson was it?' She and the ebullient Elizabeth had spent much of the Finlay dinner party devising sporting ways of raising money for the children's hospice appeal, a charity and a fundraising method which had greatly intrigued Catriona.

Felicity nodded. 'Yes. She rang me this morning. She was thrilled with your ideas, especially the celebrity pitch and putt. She's been looking for a way of charging the public money to watch celebrities play golf. She says the pro-am formula is fraught with difficulties. So you made a great hit!'

Nor had Elizabeth been Catriona's only conquest. Having been on tenterhooks to catch her husband showing any kind of partiality towards his beautiful subordinate, Felicity had been disconcerted to discover that although Bruce was on suspiciously friendly terms with Catriona, she herself also felt positively disposed towards the girl. The situation left her wanting her suspicions to be wrong but still unable to discount them altogether.

'Do I gather that you were entertaining

Catriona last night, Felicity?' enquired Hamish, teasing. 'What have the poor Melvilles done to deserve exclusion from such a feast of fun and games?'

'There is absolutely nothing poor about you, Hamish,' declared Felicity frankly and unrepentantly. 'And you were at Finlay Mansions only three weeks ago, as I recall. However, I fear we regaled you with nothing to compare with *this* gastronomic extravaganza.' She swept her arm in an arc to encompass the sumptuous spread displayed on the nearest table. 'There must be more caviar here than is loaded on to the QE2 for an entire Caribbean cruise!'

There was indeed, an enormous cut-glass bowl nestling on a bed of crushed ice and piled high with the twenty-pounds-an-ounce little black fish-eggs, for all the world as if the company were gathered on the famous cruise liner rather than a windswept Fife howe. Alongside stood a magnificent platter of giant prawns and cracked lobster claws, and an ashet bearing a huge rib of cold roast beef, partly carved into succulent pink slices running with meat juices.

'I think I see a lobster claw waving personally at me,' murmured Catriona, flashing a sideways smile at Hamish.

'Doesn't it look scrumptious,' Felicity said. 'You spoil us, Hamish. I can't remember when I last had lobster.'

'How did you manage to park so close to the post?' asked Donald after a sizeable swig of champagne. 'This is absolutely *the* prime position. Are you a member of the hunt?'

'No, I'm not,' Hamish demurred. 'I prefer my horses in a frame, preferably painted by Stubbs or Munnings. But Minto's a member. He rides to hounds regularly, don't you, Minto?'

'Indeed, sir,' agreed the crow-like butler, never far from his employer's shoulder. 'When duty permits.'

'He keeps two hunters at livery,' explained Hamish. 'Shows how well I pay him.'

'Yes, sir. Excuse me,' muttered the butler on a small apologetic cough and departed to attend to a summons from Linda.

'I hear you've been appointed a Trustee of the National Galleries, Hamish,' remarked Felicity. 'Bruce is green with envy. He's only made it to the Fine Arts Trust.'

'I fear it probably has more to do with how far up your back you're prepared to have your arm twisted, rather than any great level of artistic expertise,' drawled Hamish with uncharacteristic self-deprecation.

'Have they twisted yours then?' she enquired curiously.

'To the most exquisite pitch of pain,' he admitted. 'My coffers are full of cobwebs.'

'That I find hard to believe,' retorted Felicity, chuckling.

'Well, let's just say that now that I'm on the Board I may develop fine-art fatigue. I'm going to diversify—invest in other art forms.'

'Give someone else a chance to buy their way into the fine-art Mafia, you mean?' suggested Donald with amusement.

'Precisely.' Hamish grinned unashamedly.

'What other art forms?' asked Catriona with interest.

'I haven't decided yet. Anything from a fiddle orchestra to a feature film. I just think paintings and sculpture get more than their fair share of the cake. Something Scottish, though.'

'Gosh. You'll have queues forming down the street,' Felicity said. 'Every potter and poet will be after your pennies.'

'Tough then,' returned Hamish unabashed. 'I'm an investor, not a patron. I expect many happy returns on my money.'

At this point Linda came up under full sail, her cashmere billowing, her mood effusive. 'I've told Minto to start the buffet,' she declared. 'The first race is in forty minutes and Bruce says he's starving.'

Catriona thought she had never seen anyone attach themselves to another person in quite the obvious way that Bruce trailed behind Linda. She wondered that Felicity didn't notice.

At this point Minto put down his bottle, cleared his throat and announced in ringing tones that luncheon was served.

Moira and Gillian appeared as if on cue. 'Aha,' Donald laughed, putting a comradely arm around each girl's shoulders. 'The locusts have descended on the lobster.'

'How do you eat a slice of roast beef with a fork?' Felicity Finlay asked plaintively, being first to emerge with a full plate from among the jostling crowd around the buffet.

The implement in question swiftly rapped

Donald over the knuckles as he reached out and snaffled a slice of her succulent beef and popped it into his mouth. 'Like that,' he said indistinctly, trying to grin and chew at the same time.

'Naughty thief,' remonstrated Felicity, following his example with a second slice and then wielding her prongs again to defend her plate against any further embezzlement on his part. 'Unhand my lobster, sir!'

Catriona had by now acquired a plateful of large prawns and lobster claws, a dollop of mayonnaise and a spoonful of caviar, thinking that by strategic fingering and dipping she could combine all the flavours together in a single great taste sensation. She relished half of her plateful in this way and one of the prawns had just conveyed a substantial amount of caviar to her mouth when a voice at her elbow took her by surprise.

'Enjoying yourself?' it said.

In her astonishment she spluttered and only narrowly avoided spraying little black eggs all over Linda's glorious white cashmere. She swung round to verify the lean, handsome face and wild shock of gleaming curls that went with the voice. 'Andro!' she marvelled. 'What on earth are you doing here?'

'Following up a hunch.' The actor's eyes twinkled with amusement as Catriona thrust her plate into his hands in order to brush mayonnaise and caviar off her coat with the embroidered linen napkin issued by Minto to each guest. Andro immediately selected a giant

211

lobster claw and began to suck at it. 'Slumming it a bit, aren't you?' he mocked.

Making no concessions to the 'country' look, Andro was dressed more or less as he had been in Glen Doran—in jeans, a long hand-knitted scarf double-wrapped round his neck and a baggy black leather jacket—more Spotlight than Horse and Hound. Since he disdained headgear, his tousled hair was blown into an exceptional state of dishevelment by the mischievous, nipping wind and Catriona increasingly suspected that his ever-present dark stubble was achieved by design rather than disinclination to shave.

'You finish them,' she said shaking her head, as he offered to hand back the plate. 'I've had enough.'

He raised a speculative eyebrow, dunking a giant prawn in mayonnaise. 'Yes, you look quite well-fed today,' he commented frankly, 'or is it thermal undies?'

She shivered and nodded ruefully. 'Layers of them! I'm beginning to wonder why I came.'

'Because instinct told you I'd be here,' he responded glibly, gobbling the prawn and making a face. 'Ugh, there's caviar in this mayonnaise. I can't stand caviar!' He took her glass from her and sipped champagne to wash it down.

'Show off,' she giggled, gratefully thrusting her freezing hands, thus freed, into her pockets. 'That was the first I've ever had and you made me spit it out.'

'Just as well. You can't have liked it,' he told her. 'No one with real taste does.'

212

'How *did* you know I was here?' she persisted.

'I didn't. It's serendipity,' he replied serenely. 'Or kismet if you prefer.' He waved the now-empty plate. 'By the way, to whom am I beholden for this largesse?'

At that moment Hamish strolled up to them, a smile stretching his lips but failing to reach his eyes. 'Well, well, a newcomer. A friend of yours, Catriona?'

She could hear the ice frosting his words. 'Andro Lindsay,' she said nervously. 'Andro, this is my host, Hamish Melville.'

'Forgive me not shaking hands,' said Hamish, indicating his glass and plate. Spotting the half-full glass in Andro's hand and Catriona's lack of one he put two and two together and added, 'You don't have to give him yours, Catriona. Minto!' His imperious call instantly summoned the butler to his side. 'A drink for Mr Lindsay. What would you like?'

Whatever Andro chose to drink it was obvious that he, Hamish, would have liked it laced with hemlock. Seeing the beautiful young actor exchanging laughing banter with Catriona had fired an explosion of malevolence in the entrepreneur which was almost frightening in its intensity. He found himself filled with the furious aggression of a rampant lion confronting an upstart contender for his pride.

Andro shook his head. His antennae had detected threatening undercurrents and his instincts were to beat a judicious retreat. 'No, really, don't worry. I was only passing on my way to the bookies. I'll see you again,

213

Catriona.' He thrust the glass and plate back into her hands and turned to leave.

But Catriona had no intention of letting Hamish control her friendships. Smiling brightly she knocked back the rest of the champagne and placed it and the empty plate on the startled butler's silver salver. 'Great! If you're going to the bookies Andro, I'll come with you,' she said firmly. 'I've never bet on a horse before and I need someone to show me the ropes.'

'Ah well, you've come to the right person,' exclaimed Andro, gamely playing to Catriona's hand. 'Harry the Horse and I are like *that.*' He linked his two forefingers together and grinned.

'Excellent,' declared Catriona, meeting Hamish's disapproving glare with wide defiant eyes. 'Thanks for a fabulous lunch, Hamish. I'll come back and let you know how the betting goes.'

'Right,' said Hamish, watching her go and only with difficulty controlling his urgent desire to drag her bodily back. It had been a week since he'd touched her and his arms ached for her!

'But don't bother to bring your friend,' he added in an undertone.

Eight

'Harry the Horse' turned out to be Harry Dean, one of a dozen independent bookies lined up in the designated area near the parade ring. Under a garish purple and yellow umbrella he presided

214

over his blackboard, chalking up the odds for each race. For the first, a novice cup, they varied from two to one up to six to one.

'You giving it away today then, Harry?' said Andro when he and Catriona sauntered up.

'Well, if it isna the Lindsay laddie hisself!' exclaimed the bookie, a small cheerful man in a grey overcoat which had seen better days, a frayed tartan scarf tightly wrapped around his throat and a battered bowler hat.

'That's a new hat, Harry,' observed Andro. 'You weren't wearing it at Perth races.'

'Aye, well it's no' exactly new. I got it at the Oxfam shop. Thought it would improve ma image.' Harry raised the bowler to Catriona. 'Guid day to you, ma'am. I hope you'll no' be takin' this loon's advice on the bettin'. I took a hundred off him at Perth last year and I never did gie any o' it back!'

Catriona laughed. 'I should have thought you'd be wanting him to encourage me then,' she said.

Harry shook his head in mock despair. 'It's like takin' bawbees off a bairn, ma'am. I wouldna want such a fine lassie as yoursel' to be misled.'

'I'll tell you what,' suggested Catriona. 'I won't put my money on the same horse as him. That way we have two chances of winning.'

Harry winked. *'He's* got nae chance, but you—well, you look lucky to me. Just dinna listen to his advice.'

Andro heard this exchange with an expression of growing indignation. 'Right!' he announced.

'I'll make you eat that damn bowler, Harry. I'll have five pounds on Blue Wonder to win. You've got it down at four to one and I fully expect to take twenty pounds off you.' Andro proffered the blue note defiantly.

'Blue Wonder,' the bookie sniffed disparagingly. 'Into the blue yonder—that's where that one will go, wi'oot its rider.'

'Nothing—he knows nothing!' cried Andro blithely. 'The rider just happens to be a friend of mine.'

'It wouldna matter if it wiz Peter Scudamore,' muttered Harry to Catriona behind his hand. 'Now, are you havin' a flutter, lassie?'

But Catriona smiled and shook her head. 'Not yet. I want to look at the horses first.'

'Oh aye?' The bookie looked pained. 'One of them as thinks they can spot the winner by the shine on its rump.'

'Something like that,' she agreed. 'I like the red ones. We share a hair colour, see.' She removed her soft-brimmed hat and let her hair spill out like molten metal.

'Chestnut!' breathed the bookie, eyes widening in surprise'.

Andro tutted. 'Down, Harry. You're a terrible one for the fillies. Come on, Catriona, let's go and see if there are any old chestnuts for you to back.'

They spent a happy half hour watching the runners parade, putting Catriona's fiver on a rangy horse called Red Gorton to win, and jumping up and down on the rails hemmed in by cheering crowds as it galloped in second.

216

Andro's Blue Wonder, a pretty dappled grey, did indeed shed its rider by falling at the sixth and then disappeared down the back straight, though not quite into the blue yonder since it was successfully caught by a steward with no harm done.

'Oh well,' mused Andro philosophically, 'at least Harry doesn't have to eat his hat, and maybe he'll have made enough to buy a new overcoat.'

'I should think he's secretly as rich as Hamish,' Catriona grumbled, tearing her betting slip in half and throwing it in a waste-bin. 'He may buy his racetrack clothes at Oxfam but I reckon he really dresses at Austin Reed and drives a Jaguar.'

'Bet it's a BMW,' Andro cried then added, 'On second thoughts perhaps I won't bet—not with my track record. What is it with you and Hamish Melville anyway?' he asked curiously. 'He eyed me like something that crawled out from under a stone. Have you got something going with him?'

Catriona made a face. 'When you're as rich as he is it's easy to think you can have whatever you want,' she said evasively.

'Including you?' asked Andro.

'Now why would he want me? An insignificant bank manager!'

Andro grinned. 'Hardly insignificant. Harry the Horse would describe you as a chestnut filly with classic potential. That kind attracts big money.'

'I don't think Hamish is a betting man,' she

responded. 'He tends to see money in terms of investment.'

Andro looked interested. 'Really? What sort of things does he invest in?'

'Companies mainly, but he also buys paintings. Although he says he's going to branch out into other art forms.'

'Such as?' Andro looked decidedly calculating.

Catriona glanced at him sharply. 'Why do you ask? Are you looking for an angel?'

He flashed her a wily grin. 'In my business it's always a good idea to cultivate the money men.'

'What exactly is your business?' she demanded suddenly. 'And who, or what is Precipitous City Productions?'

'You rang!' cried Andro delightedly. 'I knew you would.'

'Did you now? Yes I did, but only once. Answerphones put me off.'

'Shame,' he said mournfully. 'You didn't even leave a message.'

'I wasn't sure I had the right number,' she protested. 'It didn't sound like you.'

'Oh, that's just Isabel. We share a flat—it helps to pay the rent,' Andro said and changed the subject, 'If you want to bet on the next race we'd better wander over to the parade ring and inspect the ponies.'

In the third race—the most prestigious with the greatest number of runners and the longest odds—Catriona's horse came in first at three to one. Jubilantly she danced up to Harry's stand and presented her betting slip. 'Sorry, Harry.

You've got to give it all back to me. Fifteen pounds, please!'

Harry shrugged. 'And the five you put on—makes it twenty. I said you had a lucky look about you.' He handed the money over readily enough and winked at Andro. 'Still got *your* dollars though, ain't I lovey?'

' 'Fraid so, Harry.' Andro shrugged and winked at Catriona. 'I might have to tap your friend Hamish for a loan,' he muttered.

'Dream on, boy,' she laughed and looked down to stow her winnings in her purse. She looked up again—straight into Hamish's face.

'Hello Catriona,' he said. 'Someone's winning anyway.'

It's extraordinary, she thought, how Hamish can smile with his mouth and do something else entirely with the rest of his face. 'Yes,' she said, patting her purse with satisfaction. 'I've banked a few pounds.'

'Perhaps you could show me how to do it, now that you've discovered the trick.' He thrust his race card at her. 'What about the next race, for instance? What do you recommend?'

'Oh no,' she grinned. 'I can only pick a horse if I see them all in the flesh.'

His hand was under her elbow in a flash. 'Come to the parade ring with me then and choose. You don't mind, do you?'

This last was flung at Andro who gallantly stepped aside, mumbling under his breath, 'Don't mind me. Just don't lose too much of that lovely money.'

Catriona cast an apologetic glance back at

him, as if to say, 'Sorry, I'll have to go,' and allowed herself to be led away.

'At last I've got you alone,' groaned Hamish as soon as Andro was out of earshot. He sounded as if he had drunk a great deal of his own Dom Perignon. 'Just who is that guy?' he enquired with a distinctly curled lip.

'I told you. He's Andro Lindsay—a friend.' Catriona smiled at Hamish with a brightness she did not feel. 'You didn't mind him joining us, I hope?'

'Yes, I did as a matter of fact,' Hamish responded truculently. 'He definitely comes under the heading of people I don't like to think of you being with. Fill me in. Where did you meet him? What does he do? Why is he here?'

'Which school did he go to? Who is his father? What size shirt does he wear?' Catriona continued the list on an amused crescendo. 'Honestly, Hamish, you should hear yourself. I told you, he's just a friend.'

'You don't act like he's "just a friend". You flirt with him.' Hamish was now walking doggedly past the parade ring but Catriona didn't ask him where he was going. He seemed like a man with a definite destination in mind so she strode along beside him curiously.

'Your wife flirts with Bruce and you don't seem to mind,' she said daringly.

'We're talking about you, not Linda,' Hamish growled. 'Linda flirts with everyone, you don't.'

'Well, I'll tell you something—I'm certainly not going to flirt with a grumpy grouch like you,' Catriona stated, trying to jolly him along. 'Where are we going, by the way? I think you have to wear a special badge to get into this area.'

They were approaching the line of parked horse-boxes, most of them with their ramps down and busy with the people, animals and paraphernalia of the horsey end of a race-meeting. Hamish mutely displayed a yellow cardboard shield which was attached to his coat-button by a string. Catriona noticed that it resembled the identity tags visible on all the people who were coming and going around the boxes. Clearly they weren't heading anywhere on spec. Wherever they were going Hamish had checked it out but he was giving no clues.

With a deep sigh he said, 'Look, I'm not normally like this as you know. You seem to bring out the caveman in me, darling.'

'Well, I hope you're not going to hit me over the head with a club or anything,' she returned with an exaggerated shiver. 'This looks like white-slave recruitment territory to me.' She was trying to preserve a note of humour, finding his brooding intensity rather intimidating.

They were now alongside one of the boxes. Although its ramp was down there was no evidence of any activity either inside or out.

'I need to talk to you properly,' Hamish said urgently 'In private. We can go in here.' He took her hand and marched swiftly up the ramp into the dim interior. It was partitioned to hold three horses but only the inner stall showed signs of occupation, with an abandoned head-collar, a recent heap of horse-droppings and a half-full haynet.

Catriona began to laugh nervously. 'So this is what you meant by finding a bale of hay. Who does it belong to?'

'A trainer friend of Minto's,' Hamish grudgingly revealed, leading her further into the depths of the vehicle. 'But we don't need to get too involved with the hay. Through here.'

A narrow door led into the cab of the lorry which, behind the usual driving accommodation, was kitted out like a campervan with plush red banquette seating. Hamish turned in the confined space, immediately crushed Catriona in a fervent embrace and kissed her hard. She had been expecting it but his fierce ardour still took her breath away. In a matter of moments he had pushed her down on to the red plush and his hands were tugging impatiently at her clothing.

'Christ! I want you so much I don't know how I've managed to get here,' he gasped, his urgency such that he was totally unaware of her non-cooperation.

'Hamish, whoa. Hang on a minute. Stop!' Catriona shouted almost at the top of her voice and fought to pull his hands off her.

He raised his head in bewilderment. His fairly advanced state of inebriation had turned his usually bright blue eyes hazy and bloodshot. 'What is it? You don't have to worry, no one will come. Their horse is running in the next race and they're all away. Minto fixed it.' He pushed her duffel coat off her shoulders and then paused to flash her a lascivious grin. 'But perhaps I'm spoiling the fun. Maybe you'd like to do another of your celebrated stripteases? Only make it quick, darling, or I'll explode.'

Catriona summoned all her strength and shoved him off. 'Stop it! I don't want to do any striptease, Hamish! I don't want to do *anything* in here.'

She shrank away, pulled her coat back on and drew her knees up, wrapping her arms defensively around them as a deterrent to any further advances, knowing she was being absurdly prim, knowing she had walked into the situation and had only herself to blame but adamant nevertheless.

'This is not my idea of making love. This is a furtive fumble—a quick bonk while the coast is clear.' She suddenly remembered Alison's words of warning in the wine-bar when she had first told her about Hamish. *A quick bonk when His Majesty can ditch the wife.*

'What's wrong with that?' Hamish demanded, looking offended. 'I thought you'd find it rather exotic. You've been pretty turned on by unusual circumstances in the past. Remember Picasso?'

'Yes, of course I do. But that was different. We'd been out to dinner, it was romantic, it was warm and you were charming—irresistible, in fact. The circumstances are hardly comparable.' She shivered eloquently. 'This place is sleazy and freezing and you are being far from charming.'

She felt bad that she could not respond to him but she also felt a frisson of fear. She couldn't help remembering how oblivious he had been to her lack of response in London and how bruised she had felt in both mind and body as a result. And now also, in the back of her mind, there lurked the uncomfortable spectre of a nine-year-old boy called Max.

She could see that Hamish was struggling to come down from his sexual high. He sat a little apart from her, breathing deep and hard. But after several seconds he regained control and gave her a comic sideways look.

'Now who's being grumpy?' he asked slyly. He reached out and took her hand. It was not an advance but a placatory gesture. 'I'm sorry, I pounced a bit, didn't I? But I've missed you—been wanting you like hell. It's not easy to find opportunities to meet, you know, darling. We can't always be nipping off for fun weekends in luxury hotels.'

She nodded instant reassurance on this point. 'I know that. You mustn't think that I only want the lap of luxury. But I just can't do it here! I don't know why. Perhaps I'm a prude at heart. Perhaps Alison was right and I'm not cut out for this kind of relationship.'

'Alison? What do you mean, Alison? Does she know about us? Did you tell her?' In his present mercurial mood anger built as fast as passion and he turned and grabbed her by her upper arm, his fingers digging in painfully. 'I told you not to tell anyone. Christ, I suppose that means John Home-Muir knows as well. It'll be all over the bloody bank!'

Catriona bit her tongue as he shook her. 'No—it won't—I swear it. Hamish, please!

224

Ouch!' She could taste blood and recoiled.

He let her go, suddenly apologetic. 'I'm sorry, Catriona. I didn't mean to hurt you. I wouldn't hurt you for anything. I was just angry for a moment.' He tried to wrap his arms around her but in the curled-up position she maintained it was impossible and he drew back, shaking his head bemusedly. 'I just can't get you out of my mind these days. You're there all the time, when I'm trying to work, when I'm with Linda; even when we took Max out for the day I kept wondering what you were doing, how you were feeling. It's ridiculous!' He gave a shaky laugh. 'I think you've bewitched me.'

She didn't know what to say. It all seemed so fearfully improbable. Here they were, in a horse-box in the middle of a race-meeting, with the wind blowing cold off the hills and this man, who commanded companies worth millions and held the jobs and livelihoods of thousands in his control, was talking about being bewitched.

'What *can* you mean?' she asked with exaggerated astonishment, trying to lighten things up. 'Spells and love potions and black cats and broomsticks?'

'It's not a joke,' he said gruffly. 'You are a very beautiful girl, Catriona.'

'Thank you,' she said flatly, summoning the courage to drop her knees and place her feet firmly on the floor. 'You make me wonder if that is such a desirable thing to be. I'm sorry if I'm not as wildly sexy as you'd like, Hamish, but one thing is certain—I am not a witch.' She stood up.

'What are you doing? You're not going?'

She decided it must be the drink which made him seem suddenly so inept. He, who was always in control, so manipulative and powerful, was weakened and deflated by his own excesses. She bent and gave him a swift, friendly peck on the cheek.

'I think I will go, Hamish, if you don't mind. I'm sorry this wasn't the romp you expected.'

'But we haven't talked about when we'll next meet,' he said, rallying. 'Linda has a fashion show on Friday evening. If you don't like strange places, how about me coming to your flat?'

'I'm supposed to go to that show,' Catriona told him apologetically. 'Linda sent me an invitation.'

'Oh, for God's sake! You can cry off, surely? Be ill or called away.'

She hesitated. After this episode she didn't know how she felt about seeing him again at all. 'I'll have to let you know,' she said. 'Where can I ring you? It's all a bit one way, this ringing business.'

They could hear the noise of the crowd cheering the fourth race to its conclusion. Hamish stood up and shook himself. He pulled what appeared to be a used envelope out of his inside pocket and scribbled on it with a pen.

'This is my mobile phone number,' he said, seeming to sober up a little. 'I'm usually in the car between seven-thirty and eight in the morning, and at lunchtime and sometimes in the evening. If anyone answers other than me,

226

don't speak. They won't suspect anything. There are always wrong connections on these cellnet circuits.'

'Such cloak and dagger stuff,' Catriona remarked, watching him push the envelope into her duffel-coat pocket, glad to be making her escape. 'I'll be in touch then.'

'Just be at home on Friday,' urged Hamish vehemently. 'Or I won't be responsible.'

'Are you coming now?' she asked. 'The runners will be out soon for the next race.'

He shook his head, put an arm around her neck and gave her a kiss on the lips which prompted an echo of their first fine careless ardour. 'You go on,' he said huskily. 'I'll see you back at the Range Rover. And I don't want to see that "friend" of yours!'

'I expect he's got that message,' Catriona said dryly. 'If I'm not there when you come though, don't worry. I won't have gone off with him. I'll have gone home. I'm frozen.'

Outside, she peered cautiously around before descending the ramp. There were grooms and jockeys wandering about and one or two gave her a curious stare but there was no sign of anybody approaching the box she was leaving. She hurried away, half-running over rough grass and rutted track, heading not for the members' enclosure but for her own car. She was a little angry with herself for leaving, berating herself as a coward, but the hemmed-in feeling she had complained about to her mother had worsened almost to phobia. She didn't want any more champagne or any more rich food, she didn't want to see the jealous fire in Hamish's eyes or the seductive smile in Andro's and she couldn't face Linda's flirting or Bruce's silent lust. Of all the people who would be there, under Minto's beetle-browed eye, only Felicity seemed genuinely to be what she appeared—straightforward, kind and warm, but one among so many was not enough.

'Mum's right,' she murmured to herself as she turned the key in the ignition. 'I've got IDS in a big, bad way.'

She drove back to Edinburgh fast and hard, encountering little traffic even at the Forth Road Bridge tollgate. Back in her flat she took off her duffel coat and went to hang it up. As she did so she remembered the phone number Hamish had written down and felt in the pocket for the envelope. Sure enough there was the number, but the envelope was not empty. It was sealed down and she ripped it open to inspect the contents.

'Dear God!' she breathed as a flashing, sparkling river of fire slithered out into the palm of her hand. It was a diamond bracelet such as she had rarely seen and certainly never worn, fabulous stones set into swirling wreaths of platinum and twisted together into a rope of burning ice. The mere touch of it made her jump as if stung. Nothing had been said and nothing, other than the carphone number, had been written on the envelope but there was no mistaking the intention of the gift. Hamish wanted to hold on to her and his name was invisibly written over every facet of every diamond in the whole dazzling confection.

Initially she was thrilled and amazed. She felt the cold, hard stones against her skin and marvelled at the way light pulsated from each gem in a coloured rainbow as if generated by some inner energy source. But after a few moments wonder gave way to anger. Why had Hamish slipped such a magnificent piece of jewellery into her pocket without saying anything? If he wanted to give it to her, why hadn't he done so openly? She knew the answers to these questions and that was what made her angry. He'd used subterfuge to give her the bracelet because he knew she wouldn't have accepted it from him face to face. This way he had achieved the purpose of giving it and, if she wilfully chose not to keep it, landed her with the awkward task of giving it back.

The man was impossible! Impossibly generous, impossibly rich and impossibly determined to get his own way. He wanted her and he wanted to bind her to him with glittering bonds. He did not realise that, far from capturing her heart, the bracelet assumed the guise of a glittering handcuff.

As she gazed at it some of the old guilt returned, not over Linda or even little Max but over Hamish himself. She had let him make love to her, let him give her the Uig painting and let him take her to London and therefore led him to think she might accept the bracelet, let him believe that she loved him when in truth what she felt for him had never been love and was no longer even lust. Alison had been right all along—it was his money that had turned her head. If he hadn't been mega-rich she would never have ignored her conscience and his family situation. It wasn't a pleasant conclusion to come to, that she had become just the sort of money-loving, pleasure-seeking, heedless hedonist she abhorred.

The thought of Alison added to her sense of self-loathing. Unforgivably, she had hardly spoken to her friend since learning about the baby and she knew it was because she couldn't bear the fact that Alison was everything she was not—wise, successful, happily married and pregnant!

For a time she fiddled about in the kitchen making herself a boiled egg for supper, assailed by a deep and poignant longing for Skye. Self-pity welled in her like the yolk around the strip of toast which she dipped ruminatively into the egg and then left untasted. Her life was a mess. Her affair with Hamish was regrettable, her secret hankering for Andro pathetic, and her green-eyed envy of Alison reprehensible. She added up to a feeble character—light years removed from the self-sufficient, liberated career-girl she affected to be. In control of her own life? Pah! Far from being Wonder-Woman—there was no other word for it—she was *Wersh*-Woman!

'Where are you, Andro?' exclaimed Rob, banging on the telephone receiver with his hand as if that would dispel the deep-fry crackle in his ear. 'This is a terrible line!'

'I'm in a phone box in Fife. The back end of nowhere, to put it in a nutshell.'

'What the hell are you doing there?' Rob sounded impatient and with good reason. It was early evening, he was in the middle of dressing for a film-première and was standing with his black tie half-knotted, knowing he was already running late.

'I've been doing a little spade-work on a scheme I have for raising that million pounds. I just rang to find out how much time we've still got.'

'I told you, until the turn of the financial year. Not long in other words.' Rob tucked the receiver under his chin and tried to attend to the complicated business of his bow tie. It was a losing battle. 'Damn!' he swore as he dropped the phone and lost track of the bow.

'Are you still there, Rob?'

'Yes, just about. Tell me more about this scheme of yours.'

'I can't go into detail now, I only put fifty pence in the slot. I'll know in about ten days or so if it's going to work.'

Rob thought Andro sounded a little shifty. 'Make sure it's legal, won't you? And keep me posted.'

'Who do you think I am—Robert Maxwell? Of course, it's—' The line went dead.

Rob replaced the receiver and moved back to the mirror to wrestle once more with his tie. He thought about the unexpected call and wondered just what Andro was up to. One could never be absolutely certain what went on in the actor's

231

devious mind but Rob was willing to bet on two things—it wouldn't be straightforward and it would probably involve a woman.

'I'm definitely going to get one of those ready-tied bows,' he exclaimed staring ruefully at his final effort. Although he didn't appreciate it himself, its lopsided tilt lent an endearing dishevelment to his otherwise immaculate appearance. 'They may be naff but at least they're neat!'

Catriona rang the Finlay's number at about the time she estimated they would have returned from the Fife Point-to-Point. She had come to the conclusion that the sorry state of her life was mainly due to galloping IDS as her mother had said and would respond to one treatment only. A treatment which she intended to get, even if it meant telling a few white lies.

Felicity answered the telephone. 'Catriona! Where did you get to this afternoon? I was hoping to talk to you. Are you all right?'

'Yes, I'm fine thanks, Felicity. And thank you so much once more for dinner.'

'You must come again, maybe just for family supper one evening, then I might get a chance to talk to you myself.' It occurred to Felicity that only two days ago she would have bristled at the sound of Catriona's voice.

'I'd love that, yes. Any time. Do you think I could have a quick word with Bruce now, please?' Catriona found that her heart was pumping fast as the adrenaline built up to lubricate the lie she was about to tell. She wasn't good at it, didn't like to do it, but felt impelled to do so.

'Hello, Catriona. What is it? Are you OK?' asked Bruce brusquely. He'd had an unsatisfactory day, having failed to get Linda to himself and had been quite glad when, after the fifth race, Hamish had growled that he'd had enough and told Minto to pack up the Range Rover. Bruce couldn't know that the catalyst for Hamish's darkening mood had been Catriona's failure to reappear.

'Yes, I'm fine but my mother isn't. I was wondering if it would be possible for me to take a few days off to go to Skye.'

'I don't see why not. Is she very ill?'

'To be honest I'm not sure but I am worried. I'd like to drive up tomorrow and see for myself. Can I take an extra couple of days?'

'Take as long as necessary. Perhaps things aren't as bad as they seem from this distance.'

'I hope you're right. Thanks, Bruce. I'll be in touch as soon as I know what's what.'

'Very well. I'll warn John and Donald to handle your accounts meanwhile.'

That will mean Alison will know I've gone away, thought Catriona guiltily, and she'll wonder why I haven't told her. Well, it can't be helped. I'll have to sort things out with Alison later.

It took her ages to decide what to do about Hamish. In the end she decided she couldn't just go away without a word and since she also wanted to return the bracelet she wrote a brief note to go with it. *'Thanks very much*

233

but no thanks. I know they're a girl's best friend and they're quite lovely but I truly can't accept them. Sorry. I'll phone about Friday. C.'

She folded the note around the bracelet and pushed them both into an envelope on which she had printed Hamish's name. Before she hit the road tomorrow she would post it through the letterbox of his Moray Place flat. The mere thought of heading for Skye lifted her depression by several millibars. She could almost smell the tangle o' the isles!

Nine

Sheena Stewart had just finished clearing the débris from Sunday lunch when the telephone rang.

'Hello, Mum. Guess where I am?'

With a mother's instinct Sheena immediately suspected the worst. 'Cat! You sound...funny. Are you ill?'

'No, Mum.' A hint of irony crept into her voice. 'It's you who's ill, actually. I'll explain later. I'm on the island—just off the ferry at Kyleakin. I'm coming home, if that's all right.' The inhabitants of Skye hardly ever called it by its name. It was always 'the island'.

'Well of course it's all right, dear. I'm thrilled! But you haven't got the sack or anything, have you?'

'No no, nothing like that. It's IDS. You know, you diagnosed it.'

'Ah, so I did. You just get yourself along here but take care on the road now, you hear me?'

'I hear you. I will. Bye.' Catriona smiled to herself. It was one of her mother's endearing foibles that she always believed members of her family were going to suffer grievous accidents when driving to or from wherever she herself was. At other times they could be on any road, day or night, driving thousands and thousands of miles of which she was not aware, but as soon as she knew they were anywhere near home she began to worry.

Sheena Stewart had started life as plain Jane Clark. For the first twenty-one years of her life, home had been a first-floor tenement flat up a close in Clydebank. Her chief interests had been boys, the Beatles, fashion and 'fillums', in that order. Then she had met Jamie Stewart, better-looking (she thought) than his Hollywood namesake, witty as John Lennon and with the added attraction of being a romantic Highlander who spoke Gaelic and had heather in his soul. He was a bright, handsome, redheaded crofter's son come down from Skye to be an apprentice on the Northern Lightships and, when he was not at sea, he had occasionally lodged with the Clarks, because Jane's mother was a war widow who let rooms to make ends meet.

Following his marriage, promotion came quickly for Jamie and he was well into his training for his master's certificate when the snapped hawser whipped away his left eye, a large chunk of his skull and half his good looks. Only by a miracle did he keep his life, his sense of humour and most of his brain-power. After a long, tedious recovery he donned a raffish black eye-patch, invested his substantial compensation cheque in an annuity and took his wife and two young daughters back with him to the family croft at Uig.

So, at the age of twenty-eight, Jane Stewart experienced a complete change of lifestyle, began cooking on a peat-fired kitchen range, taking water from a well and persuading the local, Gaelic-speaking community to accept her. As part of this process she had not minded when her name was altered from Jane to Sheena, although when they wrote it down, if they ever did, the Gaels spelt it *Sine*.

The people of Uig lived off the land and the sea. Thirty-two crofts, each of approximately six acres, were arranged in a single row around the bay so that each possessed a stretch of foreshore, some flattish garden-ground around the house, a gently sloping field for hay and seed-crops, and a steep patch of rough pasture at the back where the ground rose suddenly into the surrounding hills. Above the fences, in the high glens, there were other smaller crofting communities and the communal grazings and peat-beds where they all herded their stock in summer and cut their fuel for winter.

Every man, woman and child in Uig shared in the working of the crofts, clearing, ploughing, planting, harvesting, peat-cutting, sheep-shearing, lambing, dipping, gathering and fishing, for most families also owned a small boat and a few crab and lobster pots. Almost everyone in Uig—the local publican, the doctor, the postie, the builder, the teacher and even the minister, also owned or part-owned a croft and worked it. After a time Jamie himself landed the job of harbour master and so much of the croftwork devolved on his wife and daughters.

This then was the community which had nurtured Catriona from a child of four. People who were kind-hearted, hard-working, churchgoing, caring, handy and shrewd, who liked a dram and a joke and who looked after their own. And it was to this cradle of sanity and self-reliance that she had now turned for an injection of old-fashioned values, a transfusion of basic moral fibre.

'My dear girl, you look tired out,' said Sheena, standing back from the warm embrace with which she had welcomed her elder daughter. Over the years mains water and electricity had come to the croft and, being handy with a tool-kit and a brickie's trowel, Jamie Stewart had made various additions and alterations to the house, one of which was a roomy lean-to lobby with a big wide window where he and his wife could sit and catch the sun on winter days and watch the comings and goings of boats and ferries in the bay.

Catriona forced a wan smile, grateful almost beyond words for the genuine love and concern expressed by the hug and those few words of her mother's.

'It's lovely to be home, Mum,' she declared

237

on a deep sigh, pulling off her jacket and hanging it on the familiar hooks behind the front door. She bent to pick up her baggage.

'Don't bother with that now,' her mother told her, taking her hand. 'You look starved as well as tired. Come and have something to eat. Your father will get that later.'

'Where is Dad?' Catriona asked, happily following Sheena through into the kitchen.

'At the Ferry Inn, dear, where do you think?' There was no element of censure in Sheena's voice. 'He'd just gone down there when you rang. He'll be home soon. Meanwhile, it gives us a chance for a chat. Sit you down.'

There was a place laid at the kitchen table and Catriona obediently sat whilst her mother busied herself ladling something into a bowl from a simmering pan.

'Chicken soup,' Catriona sniffed appreciatively. 'I could guzzle a gallon of it!'

Sheena put the bowl on the table and produced a warm brown bread-roll from the range's bottom oven. 'You look as if you need it, Cat,' she remarked critically. 'Haven't you been eating properly?'

Catriona laughed and began to spread her roll. Butter oozed wickedly into the coarse, wheaten dough. 'Of course I have, Mum. Better than properly some might say. Yesterday I had caviar for lunch.' Was it only yesterday she had spluttered over the little black fish-eggs in surprise at Andro's arrival? In the comforting security of the family kitchen it seemed like an incident from fantasy.

Sheena raised her eyebrows. 'Caviar? Jings, what does it taste like?' Even after twenty-five years her slang speech still harked back to her Clydeside youth.

'Not bad but I'd rather have herring roe if the truth be known.' There was a pause while Catriona took several spoonfuls of soup. 'This is ambrosia, Mum. Nectar of the gods!'

'Well, you enjoy it dear,' said her mother contentedly. 'But don't wait too long to tell me exactly why you're here.' Sheena took a bottle of Bell's from a cupboard and put it on the table. 'Marie will be glad to hear you're home. We'll give her a ring later and tell her.'

'Mm, and get the kids round,' said Catriona with her mouth full. 'Katie Mac must be walking by now.'

'Not quite. She's a lazy wee thing but so bonny and smiley. She reminds me of you when you were a bairn.'

'Why, because she's lazy?'

'No, because she's so sunny. She sits and smiles at you and your heart melts.'

'Daft old granny,' teased Catriona. 'So you spoil her rotten?'

'I do not!' Sheena was indignant. 'I treat both children the same.'

'Marie's lucky to have you around. I bet she takes advantage of you.'

'Well, there's nowhere for them to play much at the shop. They're desperate to get a house now.'

'Why now particularly?'

Sheena blushed. 'I'm probably not supposed

to tell you. Marie will want to do that herself.'

'She's not having another?' Catriona shook her head disbelievingly. 'Don't they know what causes it yet?' she asked in amazement. 'That'll be three under five!'

'Well, and why not?' demanded Sheena, rallying to her younger daughter's defence. 'That's what we need in the island—lots of children and young people. There are too many grey heads in the kirk.'

Catriona laughed. 'I don't think Marie is doing it for demographical reasons, Mum. She just likes having babies.'

Sheena opened her mouth to say something in response to this but thought better of it. Her remark would have made an invidious comparison between her two daughters and she avoided doing this at all costs. Instead she reached for the whisky bottle and poured two measures into glasses already laid out for the purpose, adding an equal amount of water from a jug. In repose her face was beautiful, although the fierce winds and icy rains of Skye had weathered her once-fine skin into a complex tracery of lines and broken veins. Her short, thick, curly hair, which had once been bright honey-blond was now faded to ash-grey but her eyes were still as blue as meadow cornflowers, as bright as when she'd ringed them with black eye-liner, put on a mini-skirt and bopped to Beatles records in the Clydebank Pavilion on a Saturday night.

She handed one glass to Catriona and raised her own in salute. '*Slainthe!*' they said in unison and both took a good gulp, waiting for the shudder of recognition as the fiery liquid hit their stomachs.

Sheena leaned her elbows on the table and fixed her daughter with a commanding stare. 'Now, Catriona Stewart, just you tell me what's up.'

Catriona found it hard to meet her mother's eyes. 'It's hard to explain,' she began evasively. 'I've just been feeling a bit lost lately. As if I've turned a corner and no longer recognise the road.'

'And who was standing on this corner?' asked Sheena pertinently.

'Several people really, but one in particular, I suppose.' Catriona fiddled with her tumbler, running her finger around the rim but finding that toughened glass didn't produce any eerie sounds. She felt suddenly shy about discussing Hamish with her mother, fearful that Sheena, whom she had always found eminently practical and almost shockingly unshockable, might have her blind spot, especially when it came to adultery. Supposing she was utterly disgusted and appalled by her daughter's behaviour? Part of Catriona wanted her mother to berate her for immoral behaviour and lewd practices, to punish her with fierce reproaches and dire warnings of hellfire, but she didn't want her to disown her or to judge her beyond redemption.

'And would that one have been a married man, by any chance?' asked Sheena, coming straight to the point.

'How did you guess?' Catriona expected her

241

mother to be intuitive but was nevertheless surprised by the instant accuracy of her intuition.

Sheena shrugged. 'It's true, even on a remote island, Cat, that when a single woman gets to a certain age the world is full of married men.'

Catriona shuddered. 'I never thought of myself as being of "a certain age" before!'

'That's because you've always been bright, always ahead of your peers,' Sheena told her. 'You were the youngest in your class and the top scholar, the fastest runner, the best dancer, the prettiest student, the fastest-promoted in the bank, the youngest Branch Manager. You excelled in everything and you still do, dear. But you can't go on for ever being the youngest and prettiest. Sooner or later you have to suffer younger and prettier girls coming up behind.'

'You make me sound like a prize prig, Mum. A horrible, smug prima donna who can't take competition or criticism.' Catriona looked horrified. 'I wasn't like that, was I? Am I now?'

'No, of course not. You're a lovely and beautiful person but you're not a girl any more, you're a woman—with a past as well as a future.' Sheena took a measured gulp of her whisky. 'I take it this affair is now in the past.'

Catriona gave her an uncertain look. 'Well, I think it is but he doesn't, if that makes sense.'

'It does, but it sounds complicated. Did love come into it at all?'

'I'm not sure—no, I don't think you'd call it love. Not like you love Dad.'

Sheena smiled. 'How do you know how I love Dad?' she asked slyly. 'There are lots of ways of loving, and your father and I have experienced most of them.'

'But your love is strong and steady and built on rock. I never loved Hamish like that. I've never loved anyone like that.' A wistful expression clouded Catriona's eyes as she said this.

'Ah, but love doesn't come with its own ready-made rock. You have to build it. It's DIY foundation-laying! It's taken Jamie and me years, and I don't suppose we've finished ours yet. How did yours start?'

'A bit like an outboard motor really. A couple of tugs and then—*vroom*—full speed ahead!' Catriona gave a hollow laugh. 'But we hit a few snags and the engine sort of conked out.'

'Compared with that, your father and I are like an old puffer. What were the snags?'

'His wife, his young son, his money,' Catriona began ruefully.

'The first two are certainly major snags—but money?' Sheena queried.

'It's just that he's mega-rich and tends to think he can buy anything he wants.'

'What did he buy you with?' Sheena was intrigued. Wealthy people did not abound in her experience.

'Oh—presents, dinners, outings.' Catriona's expression darkened. 'He was generous but not always kind, do you know what I mean?'

'He expected something in return? Something you weren't prepared to give?' Sheena spoke quietly but ominously.

'Yes, but not what you think.' Catriona blushed suddenly. 'I suppose you could say that I gave him *that* for nothing, right at the beginning. He is terribly attractive...' Her voice trailed away to a hesitant whisper. 'Are you very shocked?'

Sheena smiled again and shook her head. 'No, I'm not shocked. Why should I be? Sex can be a terrific bond at a very early stage. Look at Donnie and Marie, for goodness sake! They were tumbling in hayricks as sixteen-year-olds and claiming they couldn't help themselves! Is that what you meant by the *vroom?*'

'Yes. I know exactly what Donnie and Marie meant now. It's a bit like lighting a blue touch paper. Explosive—and very exciting.'

'But very shortlived,' observed Sheena pertinently. 'You might remember that in future. So you've run away from him.'

Catriona thought of Andro and Alison and the contribution they, too, had made to her departure but chose not to mention them. 'Yes, I suppose I have. But he'll still be there when I go back. I know I have to face him. I just need a bit of island reinforcement in order to sort it all out.'

Sheena gazed for several minutes at Catriona, wondering if she should say what was in her mind. An uncomplicated individual, straight-thinking, decent and caring, Sheena hated to see anyone deluding themselves or letting themselves down and she considered her daughter was doing both. She believed that Catriona had a very compassionate nature and a great well of love to share, the surface of which she had as yet hardly skimmed, but in Sheena's opinion Catriona consistently denied this side of herself in order to further the progress of the ferocious intellect which she also possessed. If this intellect was allowed to have full rein, there would come a time when it would stifle the rest of her character, leaving her sterile and unfulfilled.

'I think you need to stop thinking and start feeling, darling,' she said at length. 'You want to stop asking yourself if what you are doing is right and start asking if you feel comfortable doing it. Your instincts are atrophying in the big city.'

Tears sprang to Catriona's eyes. 'That's almost exactly what the old Earl said to me, Mum,' she told her. 'He said I should never have left Skye and I should be living here and having babies and giving something back to the land of my birth. But that's rubbish. I want to do more with my life than that.'

'Like what, dear?' asked Sheena gently, who had raised children and tended a croft and never felt inadequate for doing it. 'Like sleeping with a married man and jeopardising the security of a little boy? That doesn't sound like overachieving to me. And what is worse, it doesn't sound like you.'

'I do a bit of banking, as well you know,' protested Catriona tearfully. 'People need banks as well as babies. You make it sound as if I set out to be a homebreaker but there's never been any question of that. Hamish's wife is just as guilty in that direction as anyone.'

'Two wrongs don't make a right,' Sheena reminded her firmly. 'But that's not my main point. The most important thing to remember is that you have to square things with your own conscience and I think you've been muzzling yours.'

'It's not a perfect world here either,' retorted Catriona, rallying her defences. 'People have affairs in Uig, too. Remember when the wife of the landlord of the Ferry Inn ran off with a crofter from Staffin?'

'No good came of it, though,' Sheena pointed out. 'The crofter's now a hopeless drunk and the children ended up with the social workers. So much for careless rapture.'

'I'm not looking for careless rapture, I'm looking for—oh, I don't know what I'm looking for! It's all such a muddle, Mum.' Catriona pulled a paper towel from the kitchen roll on the wall and blew her nose noisily.

'Let's have another drink,' said Sheena kindly, unscrewing the top of the bottle. 'And you can tell me what this Hamish looks like and where you met him. I'd like to hear more about the man who's succeeded in bowling my level-headed daughter over.'

When Jamie Stewart strolled in from the pub an hour later he was astonished to find that his wife and daughter had consumed half a bottle of whisky. Not that he begrudged them a drink, or even several. Sheena did not often choose to share his excursions to the Ferry Inn but that did not mean she abstained from alcohol. Like most crofters, male and female, she enjoyed a drop of the *usige beatha* now and again. Jamie's surprise stemmed not only from the fact that Catriona was there at all, but that both women had obviously been crying.

'You're as damp as new-cut peat,' he said in alarm. 'Has somebody died?'

'No, Dad,' Catriona smiled sheepishly. 'Mum and I have just been talking.' She stood up to receive her father's bear-hug of welcome and the tears welled again.

'About what, for the Lord's sake, to make you greet all over each other?' Jamie's scarred face puckered further with concern and he ran his hand through his thin, fading, topaz-coloured hair. Catriona had only to look at her father to know that her striking, polished-brass locks would not stay that way for ever, at least not without help.

'About life, love and the pursuit of happiness,' Sheena told him mysteriously. 'In other words— girl-talk.'

'And is it just the need for a bit of girl-talk that's brought you home out of the blue like this?' asked Jamie. 'Or might a mere father be put in the picture?'

'Don't worry, Dad,' Catriona said hastily, 'I'm not on drugs or pregnant or out of a job or anything. I just needed to come home for a few days.'

'This wouldn't have anything to do with a

man, would it?' Jamie persisted, worried and threatened by what seemed to him a female conspiracy to evade explanations.

'Well, yes, it is something like that but it's finished now.'

Catriona looked pleadingly at her father, willing him not to probe further. He could be like a terrier when he got going and she already felt wrung out and exhausted by the outpouring of emotion prompted by her mother's sympathetic ear. Besides, she knew that when it came to morals, Jamie's views were stricter than Sheena's. He would definitely not understand the terrible lure of sex and money the way that Sheena, surprisingly, had. 'Can I tell you about it another time?'

He shrugged and nodded but continued to look worried. Jamie was inordinately proud of his bank-manager daughter, whilst remaining perpetually puzzled as to where and how she had acquired the mental powers sufficient for such a career. Neither he nor Sheena had ever displayed any financial aptitude and Catriona's growing academic success had been a constant source of pleasure to him throughout her schooldays. Of course he had battled with her as a teenager, when she and her sister had wanted to attend every ceilidh and disco within reach, wearing outrageous clothes and far too much make-up, in his opinion. He had been a fierce father in those days but this had not prevented Marie from breaking out into a perilously early marriage. Catriona however had justified his care, eventually abandoning her wild cavortings and concentrating on forging a brilliant future in a way which had outstripped his wildest hopes for her.

'All right, *a nighinn,*' he said reluctantly, using the paternal Gaelic vocative, 'O daughter'. 'I'll get the story from your mother. I daresay you won't need to be telling it twice. If that's your suitcase in the hall I'll take it upstairs for you.'

He made to leave the kitchen but Catriona jumped up. She had heard the hurt in his voice and seen the clouding of his one good eye. As a child it had always been to him she had run with her problems. She felt bad cutting him out now.

'I'll come with you, Dad, and unpack my jeans. Then maybe we could walk along the shore together, if you feel like it.'

'Aye, that'd be fine,' agreed her father, brightening at the prospect.

'Nothing's changed in your room,' Sheena said, firmly putting the whisky bottle back in the cupboard. 'There's even a pair of your old boots in the cupboard, if you're going out.'

Like most crofthouses in the island the Stewarts' was basically two up and two down with a lean-to kitchen at the back, but soon after installing his family, Jamie had extended the kitchen outbuilding upwards to incorporate a bathroom and a third bedroom. This had eventually become Catriona's because its position meant it was warm throughout the winter due to the ever-burning kitchen range below, and she could retire there to study, away from the bustle of the rest of the house. After reading the appropriate classic Greek saga she used to jokingly describe herself as an Aganaught, and returning to the room now, with its pretty flowered curtains and her old collection of stuffed toys, she felt as if she had discovered the Golden Fleece.

'No, no, Niall. Don't pull Katie's hair! That's unkind.' Marie Macdonald née Stewart swooped down on her two-and-a-half-year-old son and lifted him off his little sister whom he threatened to render bald before her copper curls had even reached her ears. The baby's face creased into the beginning of a yell. 'There, look what you've done. You've made her cry. Bad boy.'

Under his mother's arm the small boy looked mutinous. 'Niall want Catty!' he declared. 'Want play with Catty.'

Catriona, who had been cuddling her niece when the hair-pulling offence occurred, quickly rubbed away the pain and planted a kiss on the little creature's fluffy head. Then she put her down on the floor and watched her pick up a toy and begin to wave it, beaming amiably and showing her four baby teeth. 'All right, Niall,' his aunt said, turning to the little boy and holding out her arms. 'What do you want to play? Horsey-ride?'

Marie relinquished her son to her sister and laughed as Catriona began to bounce him up and down on her knee, reciting an ancient bit of nursery doggerel—'*This is the way the farmer rides, gallop-a, gallop-a, gallop.*'

'I'm so glad he remembered you, Cat,' Marie said. She was smaller and plumper than Catriona, fair-haired like her mother and pretty in a natural, unsophisticated way whereas her sister's beauty was in a more classic mould. She wore leggings and an outsize sweater which did not quite conceal her already swelling belly. 'Even if Katie Mac didn't.'

'Well, she was only just starting to crawl when I last saw her,' observed Catriona, pausing in her recital to tickle Niall's tummy, much to his chortling delight. 'I mustn't leave it so long next time or you'll have another one who won't know me.'

Marie went a little pink. 'I suppose you think I'm mad having another?' she probed tentatively.

Catriona shrugged and smiled at her sister. 'Well, it is a bit mad really, isn't it?' she said gently. 'Especially when your flat is so small.' Marie's husband, Donnie Macdonald, ran the Uig Cooperative, and the family lived in a two-bedroomed flat above the store.

'I know. I didn't really mean to fall again so soon but I got in a muddle with the pill. I'm not very good at remembering,' Marie admitted. She dangled a toy in front of Katie for a few seconds and then let her grab it, waiting while Catriona gave Niall another boisterous horsey-ride. Then she went on wistfully, 'We'd so love to have a proper home—a croft like this one. But there just aren't any available.'

Catriona nodded. 'I know. It's such a shame that all the houses that come on the market

251

seem to go for holiday homes these days.'

'The prices they fetch are just too high for us,' grumbled Marie. 'We can't afford the mortgage, not on what Donnie earns.' She ducked down to retrieve a plastic brick which Katie had thrown under the sofa. When she came up she looked even pinker but it was from indignation rather than exertion. 'Do you know there's a croft up in Sheader that we thought we might be able to acquire. The house is a complete ruin but Donnie could rebuild it and I know Dad would help him. Only we can't borrow the money because the building societies say they want the work done *before* they'll advance the loan! Isn't that stupid? How do they expect us to finance the place *and* the building materials before we get the loan? We wouldn't need the loan if we could do that.'

Catriona said nothing. She was very familiar with the need for securities when advancing capital, and one tumbledown croft and the good intentions of a potential buyer wouldn't be good enough collateral, not on Donnie's relatively meagre salary.

'I bet some solicitor from Slough will get the place,' went on Marie, warming to her theme. 'And he'll bring his family up for three weeks a year and leave it empty for the rest, while we stay crammed in four rooms above the shop. It's not fair!'

'No, it's not,' Catriona agreed but her next words were drowned out by Niall's noisy demands for more 'gallop-a-gallop-a'!

It was the day after her arrival and the first

time the children had seen her. The previous evening they'd already been put to bed and were sleeping soundly when she'd popped in to see Donnie and Marie after her walk with Jamie. Her father had diplomatically avoided the subject of her sudden return home and the two of them had enjoyed one of their favourite conversations about island politics and the position of the Trotternish Peninsula in the world scheme of things.

Ostensibly preoccupied with making pastry, Sheena surreptitiously observed her daughters through the glass door of the kitchen. They had cleared back the furniture in the living room to make more play-space for the children and were sitting on the floor in front of the carefully guarded fire. She watched Catriona dandling little Niall and frowned. Sheena was certain that, at thirty-two, her elder daughter must already be facing the prospect of living her life without children and couldn't believe she would be content to do so.

Sheena had never wholeheartedly applauded Catriona's successful career. In her book, beauty and material success didn't always add up to happiness and fulfilment. Watching Catriona with Marie's children, it concerned Sheena greatly that the older girl might have suppressed her natural instincts to her own disadvantage. For although Catriona's description of her guilty liaison with the millionaire businessman had been a sketchy one, her narrative had contained enough innuendo to confirm her mother's worst fears. Why would a healthy, balanced island girl like Catriona suddenly succumb to adulterous, lustful urges if it were not from a dreadful fear that life was passing her by? Smart city society seemed to Sheena to be no golden object of odyssey if these were the values it imparted. Not for the first time her mother fervently wished that Catriona would find a nice, kind, unattached man and settle down.

After lunch they were waving Marie off, she wheeling the children home in a double buggy for their afternoon nap, when they noticed a green four-wheel-drive vehicle slow down in the narrow road to let them pass safety. Only five crofts were reached by the road, the Stewarts' being the last in the line and as the boxy little vehicle bounced inexorably past the other four Catriona's heart began to race. With gradual certainty she realised who was at the wheel.

'Mum, this is a friend of mine, Andro Lindsay—Andro, my mother, Sheena Stewart.'

With lithe agility Andro leaped down from the driving seat. 'How are you, Mrs Stewart. I must say, you look a lot better than I had been led to expect.' Andro shook Sheena's hand and grinned slyly at Catriona's guilty flush.

'How do you do,' said Sheena with a puzzled frown. The name Andro Lindsay meant nothing to her. What did he mean to Catriona?

'You must have contacted the bank,' Catriona accused him. 'Did they tell you where I was?'

'Not exactly. They just said you'd rushed to your mother's sickbed and I remembered you said you came from Uig. A very nice man at the store told me where to find you.'

'My brother-in-law,' nodded Catriona, then grinned a little sheepishly. 'My mother made a miraculous recovery, didn't you, Mum?'

Sheena had been appraised of her daughter's excuse for being absent from work and, while not entirely approving, had agreed not to answer the phone for the time being in case the call was from Steuart's. However, she could hardly pretend to be ill in the flesh when her rosy cheeks and robust appearance declared otherwise.

'Overnight,' she agreed with a wry smile. 'You must be thirsty after your drive, Andro. Will you come in and have a drink?'

'Thank you,' said Andro gratefully. 'I must admit my throat feels like a blacksmith's rasp. A cup of tea would be great.'

Sheena glanced at the young man's handsome profile as he stood back to let her precede him into the house. Where does this gorgeous creature fit into Catriona's life? she wondered curiously. She hasn't so much as mentioned him and yet they are clearly friends.

Catriona's silence on the subject of Andro spoke volumes to Sheena. No girl as hot-blooded as Catriona had recently revealed herself to be could remain unresponsive to such a perfect male specimen! Unless of course he was indifferent to women—but Sheena considered this highly unlikely.

In the kitchen she busied herself with the kettle, lifting the Aga cover and placing it on the hotplate. 'You don't work at Steuart's yourself, Andro?' she asked.

255

'No. Too long of hair and short of tooth,' he protested.

'Huh—thanks very much!' exclaimed Catriona indignantly. 'We're not all sere and grey with short back and sides.' She wasn't certain how she felt about Andro's sudden appearance. To her he was uncannily like the fire surrounding the frying pan.

Sheena dashed four spoonfuls of tea into the pot and set it to warm. 'Are you hungry, Andro? There's plenty of home-made bread and a bit of ham. Would you like a sandwich?'

'Yes, please. A ham sandwich with home-made bread sounds terrific.' Andro hovered helpfully. 'Can I do it myself?'

'No, let Catriona. She knows where everything is. You sit down and tell me what it is you *do* do, if you don't work at the bank.' Sheena suddenly herself using a light, flirtatious tone. Surprising what a good-looking young man can do for me, she thought with amusement. What must he be doing for Catriona? 'Now that I look at you properly,' she added, eyeing him with her head on one side, 'I suppose I should never have mistaken you for a banker.'

He accepted the compliment with a graceful inclination of his own dark head. 'I'm an actor,' he told her gravely. 'At present a resting actor, though I hope not for long.'

'I've seen you on the television!' cried Sheena in delight. 'Would that be right? In something exceptionally good—a classic serial. Now what was it?'

'I was in an adaptation of *Mansfield Park* a

256

few years ago,' he suggested. 'Could that have been it?'

'It was,' she agreed through a cloud of steam as the boiling water hit the teapot. 'You played Edmund Bertram and you were heartbreakingly romantic.'

'Ah, but I was younger then,' he demurred. 'How flattering of you to remember me.'

Catriona, busy with the bread and butter, smiled to herself and kept to one side, content to let her mother vet the young man whom she probably thought 'heartbreakingly romantic' in real life as well, having pursued her daughter to Skye.

Sheena brought teapot and mugs to the table and sat down. 'I love theatre and films,' she confided. 'When I was young I was never out of the cinema but now I never get to go. I have to make do with the television.'

'What sort of films do you like?' enquired Andro. 'A good weepy love story?'

'Not too weepy,' objected Sheena. 'I like something to think about.' She poured milk into a mug, followed it with fragrant brown liquid from the tea pot and pushed it towards him. 'I hope you're an MIF person,' she said.

'Milk In First!' he translated gleefully. 'My mother says that, too. And I am, thanks.'

There was a pause, as if no one knew whether or of what to speak.

'Tell me, do you like Robert Louis Stevenson?' asked Andro, eventually breaking the silence.

'*Treasure Island?* Oh yes. And *Kidnapped*—I saw the film of that. But that was made quite a bit before your time, I should think.'

'I'm involved with a project to make a film of the sequel to that—*Catriona.*' Andro leaned forward earnestly, stirring his tea.

Across the kitchen Catriona glanced up at the sound of her name, not having heard the preamble. 'Yes?' she said.

Andro laughed. 'Not you, dear girl. The Robert Louis Stevenson novel *Catriona.* We're going to make a film of it.'

'It's a lovely book,' enthused Sheena, who read avidly during the winter months when the croft was quiet. 'Stevenson's only real love story. Are you going to play David Balfour?'

'I'm afraid not.' Andro shook his head. 'Now that I *am* a bit too sere and withered for the part. He's no more than a bashful boy, really. A Whig Romeo to Catriona's Jacobite Juliet.'

'So what is your involvement then?' asked the modern Catriona, bringing the completed sandwich over to Andro and sitting down at the table opposite her mother.

'Well, I wrote the first treatment—the one which persuaded the American producers to back it—but of course they've put their own writers on it since.' He sank his teeth fiercely into the sandwich as if he wished it were a Hollywood mogul.

'What a shame!' exclaimed Sheena. 'So it won't have your name on it?'

'Only in the cast list. I'm due to play Alan Breck, a swashbuckling outlaw with a price on his head.'

'And will you get to swash and buckle much?'

asked Catriona with a twinkle.

'Yes, quite a lot. We've dressed the part up a bit to add some action to the film.' Andro spoke with his mouth full, relishing the ham and bread. 'That's if it ever gets made,' he added indistinctly.

'Why shouldn't it?' Sheena sipped her tea with a frown.

'Well, it's intended to mark the centenary of Stevenson's death. So we must make it this summer if it's to be ready in time.'

'And what's to stop you?'

'Money,' replied Andro simply. 'We're a million pounds short.'

'A million!' echoed Sheena, clattering her cup into the saucer. 'How much will it cost altogether, for heaven's sake?'

'Films are expensive to make, Mrs Stewart. Gil Munro has agreed to appear for a reduced fee because he's a Stevenson fan, but even so the total budget is eleven million.'

'I simply can't conceive of that much money,' Sheena whispered, her eyes like saucers.

'But if you've already got ten why can't you raise the other one?' Catriona was less impressed by millions. 'It ought to be relatively easy.'

Andro looked aggrieved. 'Because we've only just discovered that we need it and we don't have enough time.'

'Did you say Gil Munro?' asked Sheena, still breathing in gasps. '*The* Gil Munro?'

'*The* very one,' grinned Andro, amused by the older woman's awe. 'He'd be mighty angry if someone else started using his name.'

'But he's a movie star—a real Hollywood movie star.' Sheena clutched her head in distraction. 'I can't think how many films I've seen him in.'

'Well, he's knocking on a bit now but he's agreed to play the Lord Advocate who befriends David Balfour against his better judgment. It's a great character part and Gil Munro's name will put bums on seats as they say.' Andro took a last gulp of tea and sat back in his chair. 'Mm, that was just the ticket. I feel a new man.'

'Do you know lots of famous actors?' asked Sheena eagerly, then blushed. 'But I expect you get bored talking about them.'

'Not at all,' said Andro gallantly. 'It's my favourite subject. Pour me another cup of tea, Mrs Stewart, and I'll tell you all I know.'

'Of course I will.' Sheena suited the action to the word and then suddenly looked guilty. 'Oh, but I can't sit around chatting all afternoon. I promised I'd help Cairistiona with the costumes for the pageant. She's the teacher at the village school,' she added for Andro's benefit. 'She lives in the next croft but one.'

'What pageant?' enquired Andro with genuine interest.

'It's based on the Uig disaster of 1887. We've had our dramatic moments out here in the sticks, I can tell you!'

'I'd like to hear more about that,' said Andro. 'Perhaps we can postpone our chat until later?'

'Of course, if you're not in any hurry to leave. I'm sure my husband would love to hear your stories as well.' Sheena glanced uncertainly at her daughter. 'Why don't you ask Andro if he can stay overnight, dear? Then we could make a real party of it.'

'Would you like to, Andro?' Catriona raised an eyebrow at him. 'There's a spare room and there'll be a new toothbrush at the Cop-op if you haven't brought yours.'

'How can I resist?' cried the young man happily. 'Invitation accepted—but only if you let me get in some wine. Does the Co-op have an off-licence?'

'All kinds of licence,' Catriona assured him. 'Off-licence, TV licence, dog licence, driving licence, marriage licence—you name it, they license it.'

'Do they have a licence to print money?' he asked eagerly. 'Then all our troubles would be over!'

Ten

Smart city restaurateurs called them *langoustines* and charged two-figure sums for the three or four of them served with a lemon wedge and a few shreds of lettuce, but islanders simply called them prawns, caught them in the Minch and ate them by the kilo around the kitchen table. Donnie's father had a fishing boat and landed a good catch of them in the late afternoon, so after Sheena had boiled a huge panful and Andro had helped Catriona to peel them with much joking about shell-suits and prawn crackers, they sat round the table and dunked them in a variety of sauces—garlic, tomato, lemon and pimento—all made and mixed by Sheena. There was crusty brown bread and butter and a colourful dish of crunchy raw vegetable sticks—cauliflower, carrot, celery, cucumber and sweet peppers.

'And the French think their cuisine is the best,' scoffed Andro, enthusiastically spearing another prawn with his fork. 'I can categorically say that I have never eaten such a delicious meal in all my life.'

Sheena looked gratified but shook her head modestly. 'It's simple fare,' she said. 'No fancy frills here, I'm afraid. I'm always telling Donnie that the Co-op should send him on a gastronomic adventure training course, aren't I, Bristle?' She smiled fondly at her son-in-law whose nickname came from a children's song heard on the radio about a train with a 'guard from Donibristle'. Not to be done out of a party, Marie had prevailed on her mother-in-law to babysit so that she and her husband could join in the prawn feast and share in Andro's tales of stage and screen.

Donnie 'Bristle' Macdonald was the youngest of three sons, a pleasant, mild-mannered, pink-faced man who'd never taken to fishing like his father and brothers and never stopped counting himself lucky for marrying Marie, the flighty girl he'd followed doggedly from classroom to ceilidh throughout their teens and finally won by perseverance and because they kept going too far in haystacks and she ended up pregnant. Sadly they'd lost that baby but happily the marriage, made in what turned out to be unnecessary haste, ended up being enjoyed at leisure. Although he was never going to set the heather alight, Sheena was extremely fond of her loyal, steady, unambitious son-in-law but she still tended to tease him for the very qualities which made him lovable.

'Aye, you are,' he acknowledged ruefully. 'But most Co-op members couldna tell Parma ham from heart of palm if I stocked them, and what they dinna know they wilna eat. I did OK last time the wine-waggon called though, I reckon.' He raised his stemmed glass and sniffed at the pale, greenish liquid it contained. 'I canna pronounce the name of this one but it tastes good.'

'Niersteiner,' articulated Andro obligingly. 'And it was a pleasant surprise to find it on your shelves, Donnie. In the local store where I come from you're lucky if you can find a bottle of Bristol Cream.'

Donnie looked sheepishly pleased at this professional compliment. 'It goes well with the prawns anyway,' he said with a slight blush. 'Better than a can o' lager.'

'Where are you from, Andro?' asked Marie shyly, a little in awe of this posh-talking actor.

'Oh, it's a small place near Fort William,' Andro replied vaguely. 'You won't have heard of it.'

'But we don't want to talk about that,' protested Sheena. 'We want to hear about Gil Munro and all the other stars you've acted with. Have you met Kenneth Branagh? He's my pin-up! I went to Portree to see Henry V last winter. He looks just like Jamie used to before his accident!'

Jamie held a table napkin over the damaged half of his face and declared, ' *"Once more unto the breach, dear friends, once more; Or close the wall up with our English dead!"* I've always rather liked that quote—especially the bit about the English dead.' He grinned. 'It's the Wallace in me.'

Andro laughed delightedly and turned to Sheena. 'I like your politics—and I see what you mean about the likeness.'

Sheena gazed lovingly at her husband's face. 'Only a few years and a few scars difference,' she said softly.

'Wheest woman,' Jamie flashed her a twisted smile and blushed modestly. 'You're embarrassing me and anyway I'm much more interested in Emma Thompson than Kenneth Branagh.'

'Ah, now she sprang to fame in *Tutti-Frutti* on TV,' said Andro. 'Before my time but it was a Scottish production and I've heard lots of tales about that one.'

As the conversation took a thespian turn Catriona observed Andro weave a spell over her enthralled parents and, with time and wine, the spell extended to bind them all, herself included. The lights were out and the candles on the table wrapped them in an intimate theatrical nimbus and Andro's fine-boned face expressed every nuance of emotion through each story that he told, some funny, some sad, some utterly scandalous, of the arcane world of stage and screen, so familiar to him and so alien to the rest.

Catriona sensed the attraction she already felt towards the actor strengthen and tighten into a secret knot of longing, tied ever sweeter and tighter by the enjoyment of her family in his company. Hamish became an alien being, her affair with him an unfortunate episode which she fervently wished was well in the past instead of hovering threateningly on the edge of her conscience. Soon she would have to make contact with him and resolve things between them. He was not a problem which could be left untackled for long. But meanwhile Andro was here—warm, worldly and unattached.

Lying in her narrow bed that night, she felt as if his presence filled the house. In wishing her good night he had scarcely touched her hand but the caress of his fingers and the penetration of his mellow brown eyes had triggered a profound reaction. Despite the bedroom wall dividing them, every nerve in her body seemed to tingle with the nearness of him. His beam beckoned like a harbour light.

'Tell me about the Uig disaster,' said Andro as they walked along the road which ran between the tawny fields and the dark, rocky shore. The spring day was sapphire and gold, with a clear blue sky reflected in the calm waters of the bay and the sun gleaming on yellow winter grasses. 'The one the pageant is about.'

'I can do better than that,' Catriona said,

pointing ahead. 'It happened over there. A big house stood at the mouth of the river which flows into the bay, a hunting lodge with parkland and shrubberies where a rich landowner used to entertain his friends.'

'I don't suppose that went down too well with the crofters,' remarked Andro.

'No, it didn't. His name was Major Fraser and he bought most of the Trottemish Peninsula from one of the island chiefs then he immediately cleared hundreds of crofters off the land in order to bring in sheep and extend the deer herd. There were demonstrations which he called riots and rent strikes which he called bad debts.'

'I think I detect whose side you're on,' smiled Andro.

'One of my ancestors was jailed for leading a protest,' Catriona responded hotly.

'So, what about the flood?' Andro prompted her, stopping to view the small trickle which flowed among rocks and boulders down into the waters of the bay. 'You call this a river but it doesn't look much more than a burn. Hardly big enough to cause a disaster!'

'You'd be surprised. There was a cloudburst. We can get amazing deluges of rain here in the island but this was apparently freakish even by Skye standards. They reckon seven inches fell in one day! It was Friday the thirteenth of October.'

'An ominous date,' commented Andro with relish. 'I sense the Force of Destiny.'

'Actually it was the force of tons of water which streamed off the hills and backed up

266

behind a rockfall in the ravine.' She pointed up the brae, through a brake of tall sycamores. 'When it finally gave way it was like a dam bursting and huge boulders thundered straight down the ravine into the house.'

'Where I trust the landlord was entertaining a dozen of his despicable friends,' cried Andro, carried away by the justice of it all.

'History doesn't relate,' continued Catriona. 'The real crack of doom occurred because the Uig burial-ground was also inundated and coffins were washed out of their graves. Legend has it that they found the corpse of one of his evicted tenants lying festering in Major Fraser's study.'

'Ain't legend wonderful,' declared Andro gleefully. 'I bet the kids love acting that bit.' He stared through the trees. There was no visible evidence of a dwelling-place. 'What happened to the house?'

'It was demolished and the stones were used to build new croft-houses. Major Fraser fled as if the devil was at his heels and subsequently died in the fleshpots of London.'

'What a very tidy moral tale,' said Andro with satisfaction. 'Worthy of a Hollywood horror movie. *Nightmare on Uig Bay!* Where are we going, incidentally?'

They had turned their backs on the scene of the disaster and were climbing the main road which curved down the hill and around the bay. 'I want to have a look at this ruined croft that Marie and Donnie are so keen to buy,' Catriona told him. 'It's above the Conan ravine in a small enclosed glen. On the map it's called Sheader but we call it the Fairy Glen.'

'Why? Is it full of little people?'

'It's not very full at all any more but its few inhabitants are no wee-er than anyone else.' Catriona lifted her sweat-soaked hair off her neck. The sun was beating down on their backs, warming them as they climbed. 'Phew! I can't believe it's not yet April. We're so lucky to have weather like this. It's rare that the wind moves into the east but it always means clear skies.'

'I hope you've put some drink in this picnic,' remarked Andro, shedding the straps of the small back-pack he was carrying in order to pull off the lightweight cagoule he'd borrowed from Sheena.

'There are a couple of cans of lager. And there's a bottle of water if you want a swig now,' said Catriona, removing her own jacket and using the sleeves to tie it around her waist. Shirt and sweater proved warm enough in the shelter of the narrow glen road.

At the top of the brae the lane plunged between high banks on which wildflowers had begun to bloom profusely, yellow aconites and white wood anemones peeped up from the shade beneath a hedge of straggling hawthorn, while across the road, the sun burnished the petals of scattered violets and clumps of blue spring squill. A gaggle of cackling geese heralded the appearance of the first croft, a well-kept white house with red corrugated-iron outhouses and a copse of tall larches sheltering its windward side, their branches tipped with spring viridian.

The geese proved to be friendly.

'This reminds me of a James Guthrie painting I saw once,' Andro mused dreamily.

'Who was James Guthrie?' Catriona asked.

'One of a group of artists called the Glasgow Boys. They used to paint farmyards with real mud and hens scratching in the dirt. Toffee-nosed Victorian critics scorned it as "kailyard art" but now it fetches five-figure sums. I'm trying to remember where I saw it. It might have been at a Wentworth's sale.'

'Do you often go to Wentworth's sales?'

'To the viewings, not the sales. I can't afford to buy but I like to look.'

They had resumed their leisurely walk. 'I have a friend who works at Wentworth's,' said Catriona. 'She's having a baby.'

Andro glanced at her in surprise but made no verbal response and they strolled on in silence for several minutes. 'I don't know why I told you that,' Catriona added at last in a puzzled tone.

'Perhaps because it's important to you,' said Andro. 'Is she a very good friend?'

'Yes, very. And I do know why I told you, actually. It's because I'm jealous. Isn't that awful?'

'Jealousy drives people as much as ambition. It was envy of my brother that pushed me into acting. I wanted to do something wild and different—everything he wasn't. Are you jealous of Marie's babies?'

'No.' She frowned, mulling over her instant denial. 'I didn't mind Marie having babies

269

because I had my career,' she said slowly. 'But this friend of mine has a career as well.'

'And now you want it all, too—just like her?'

She glanced sideways at him. Their faces were dappled now in the shadow of some budding trees and she could not read his thoughts. 'This glen must harbour some bitter memories,' she said, changing the subject. 'Sometimes in the evening you can hear weeping.'

'The fairies?'

'No, the spirits of the crofters who were evicted.' She pointed to a field scattered with rocks, rather like large hailstone. 'Look, that was a house once. The landlord threw out the people, tore off the roof and let the sheep clamber all over the walls. I'm not sure I'd like to live here. There must be ghosts everywhere.'

'It's certainly weird,' observed Andro, halting on a sudden intake of breath.

They had turned a tight bend in the road and all at once were hemmed in by steep hillocks. An extraordinary range of miniature mountains rose sharply from the peaty floor of the glen, treeless but horizontally ridged and striated by the erosive feet of grazing sheep. Even in the bright sunlight they seemed to loom intimidatingly over the tumbled walls of several ruined crofts huddled around a muddy lochan.

'It's like walking into a giant egg box!' exclaimed Andro. 'What strange hills. I've never seen anything like them.'

'Dozens of people lived here once,' Catriona

said sadly. 'The place was full of children laughing and shrieking, each of these hillocks had a name. Chickens and geese and cows grazed them, not sheep, and the lochan was alive with flapping moorhens and quacking ducks. It must have been dirty and smelly and a bit insanitary, but human and sociable and full of life and death. A bit like your kailyard.' She began to climb over one of the tumbled walls. 'I think this is the croft Marie and Donnie want to rebuild.'

'Rather them than me,' Andro remarked doubtfully, scrambling after her into a ruined enclosure which had once been a two-roomed house. 'There's not much to work on.'

The ground which had formed the packed-earth floor was grassy now, overgrown with brambles and teazel and scattered with fallen masonry. One stone gable-end still stood and what remained of the rest of the walls was covered with moss and lichen. Several bushy trees grew close by, without trunks, their branches ascending in a bunch directly from the roots and extending numerous twigs with papery, grey bark bursting with pale green shoots.

'What strange trees,' Andro said, rubbing a twig experimentally between his fingers. 'Do you know what they are?'

'They're hazels. When I was a child I remember the whole family coming up here in the autumn to collect the nuts. The original crofters must have planted them as an additional food supply.'

'Speaking of food,' remarked Andro, heaving the back-pack off his shoulders and dropping it on a flat, fallen stone, 'my stomach is beginning to think my throat has been cut. Would this be an appropriate place to have our picnic!'

'It is the very place I had in mind,' Catriona said, prowling around the perimeter and looking for the dryest patch of ground. 'Just here, I think, in the corner. The sun is quite hot if you get down out of the wind.' She squatted under the lee of the wall and nodded. 'Perfect. And it's out of sight of the road, not that it's Princes Street exactly—we're probably the first people along here this week. There's a groundsheet in there somewhere.'

Andro began to remove articles from the pack, among them a folded blue waterproof sheet. 'Just like the one I had for my Duke of Edinburgh Award scheme,' he observed, shaking it out.

'I bet you got a gold medal,' she teased. 'Quite the Queen's Scout!'

'Certainly I did,' he boasted, laughing. 'I suppose you did *your* gold medals at the Gaelic Mod, wobbling your tonsils and twinkling your toes.'

'Do you mind!' she exclaimed indignantly. 'Definitely not. The Mod was not cool.'

'Not even the boys doing the Highland Fling?' he demanded disbelievingly. 'They always struck me as the ultimate in chic.'

'Bare chic, if their kilts flew up too high,' she giggled, taking the other end of the groundsheet and helping him lay it out on the grass.

272

They sat down side by side. Catriona felt happy and relaxed with Andro in a way she couldn't ever remember feeling with Hamish. There was no sign of guilt or gratitude, just the warm sun and the prospect of food and drink. She tore off a ring-pull and handed him a lager can. 'It's a bit warm but it's wet,' she said.

He poured some of the lager down his throat. 'Phew! That put a fire out,' he said on an exhalation of breath. 'Did I see a mutton pie in amongst the goodies there? It's one of my failings, mutton pie.'

She picked up the other can of lager and a plastic bag containing two pies, handed him one and sat down beside him with the other. 'Here's to pie in Skye,' she said as they each sank their teeth in and smiled at each other with their mouths full.

'You've got grease on your nose,' Andro observed after an interval of contented chewing, relishing his last morsel.

'Thanks,' she said without concern, stretching out in the sunshine. 'Look, there's a primrose growing out of a crevice in that gable-end, right up at the top. You'd think the wind would wither it up there.'

'It's on the sheltered side,' said Andro, squinting upwards. 'There are several, actually.'

'The spring is sprung, The grass is green, The bird is on the wing...' she murmured dreamily.

'But that's absurd, I always heard The wing was on the bird,' he finished merrily.

'I've never heard that bit before. Did you

make it up?' she asked curiously, blinking up at him through the bright glare of the sunshine.

He laughed with delight and shook his head. Her copious red-gold hair was tousled and shining, her eyes half-closed. She looked inviting, intoxicating, limned with a luminous brush. He leaned over and touched her mouth with his, once, then again and a third time, running his tongue over her parted lips in a motion that felt to her like a ring of fire. She let the fire lap at her, not fighting it, letting it warm her and relax her and lead her gently into the heat of passion. She wanted no declarations of bewitchment, no extravagant gestures or cries of ecstasy, she just wanted uncomplicated ardour, unfettered, uninhibited and unhindered by any need for caution or subterfuge.

She had felt something building between them ever since Andro had arrived at the croft. She did not ask herself if it was wise, enmeshed as she still was with Hamish, because this time it felt so different. With Hamish there had been a violent urgency driving each encounter. The needle of the sexual barometer had spun to storm force at the first touch of their lips. But with Andro these first kisses felt like a gentle overture preceding a symphony. He was an actor, an artist who could portray every subtlety of mood. He was in no hurry. Long, long minutes passed while his hands stroked her hair and his fingers entwined themselves deep in its luxuriant growth, making her flesh tighten and tingle from her scalp to the soles of her feet. She responded by shyly feeling the muscles of his back through the thin wool and cotton that he wore. They were hard and strong and supple and the bones of his spine undulated smoothly under her fingers.

'You taste of mutton pie,' he told her, breaking away at last to regard her with teasing brown eyes.

'You said you liked mutton pie,' she said throatily.

'Yes, I do,' he murmured, leaning forward to kiss the spot where her voice had come from, where the top buttons of her shirt were open. 'Would you like to make love? Here, in the Fairy Glen?'

The directness of the question startled her. She hadn't expected to be asked, had more or less assumed they would, that they had already begun.

When she didn't respond immediately he let his gaze wander from her face to the sky and the budding canopy of hazel twigs and swept his hand above them in a wide arc. 'It would just be marvellous, wouldn't it? Out here in the spring sunshine with the primroses blooming and the birds singing. It would be an experience not to be missed, don't you agree?'

'Yes,' she said softly. 'Yes, I think it would.'

'Wonderful!' he exclaimed, kissing and embracing her and laughing exultantly. 'It will be fantastic—you'll see.'

Physically they were well-matched, these two tall willowy people. Their long legs and bodies entwined easily and gracefully, moving from one position to another like dancers in a horizontal *pas de deux* on the floor of the ruined croft, a place which had almost certainly seen many a similar human merger during the years of its habitation. But those had been furtive couplings in the smoky dark, in a houseful of people and animals, awkwardly achieved under dank and fetid covers. This was free and unfettered, a melding of two bodies—beautiful under the kissing sun, a performance before the abundant promise of nature.

What followed this overture was like an intoxicating holiday musical. For two more days the Trotternish Peninsula was their love-nest as the wind stayed in the east and the sun shone on and they found numerous secret and sheltered places for a series of lovers' trysts. They took Andro's Suzuki bouncing down a remote track to a deserted cove where they exclaimed over a family of tiny brown weasel-kits gambolling among the stones on the beach and held their own revels in a quiet, sandy hollow above the tide-line. They tramped a windswept path along a northern headland to ruined Duntulm Castle where the Macdonalds had violently repulsed the Macleods in the sixteenth century but where, in a vaulted undercroft, Stewart did not repulse Lindsay in the twentieth. And, on the last afternoon, they climbed into the Quiraing, a dramatic terrace of basalt rock, shattered and weathered into rugged spires and needles between which were inviting grassy gulfs, as echoing and mysterious as cathedrals. It was no god however, that they worshipped in these secret temples, it was flesh and blood, and they celebrated not with hymns and psalms but with sighs and cries of exultation as they discovered ever subtler and more glorious ways of bringing each other to joyful, quivering climax.

But although they explored each other's bodies with a wild and wonderful intensity they did not probe each other's minds. Afterwards, with a surge of shame, Catriona realised that she knew little more of Andro's thoughts and beliefs than she had discovered on that first, rather drunken evening in the Invereilort Hotel bar. She knew where she must kiss him to make him groan with pleasure, and how she could caress him into extraordinary heights of ecstasy, but she did not know whether he believed in God or how he regarded love and truth. If such serious matters ever impinged on their obsessive love-making he was adept at side-stepping the issue and diverting her attention, so adept that at the time she did not notice.

She was just absurdly, thoughtlessly and fantastically happy, existing for three magic days in a state of enchantment, a contentment which she believed had wiped the memory of Hamish from her mind for ever. She might have known it was a fool's paradise but, like many another caught in a whirlpool of delight, she did not.

On the last day, as the shadows lengthened across the Quiraing, they helped each other to dress, briskly rubbing their arms to dispel the sudden chill of the late afternoon.

'Will you see Hamish Melville when you go back to Edinburgh?' Andro asked casually, shrugging on his leather jacket.

The question took Catriona by surprise. 'I—I don't know,' she stuttered. 'Why?'

'I just thought you might have some unfinished business with him, that's all.' He helped her with her duffel coat and put his arm around her shoulders as they began to wander over the grass towards the car. 'He is a friend of yours, isn't he?'

'Yes. Yes, I suppose he is,' she admitted, unwilling to be drawn further, not wanting the magic of the past days to be shattered by the spectre of Hamish. It was Thursday. She would have to ring him about their putative date the following night.

'I'd like you to meet a friend of mine when we get back,' Andro went on. 'My partner in the film company.'

'Ah. The lady on the answerphone.' Catriona tried to keep her voice even. She felt as if the ground beneath her feet was becoming treacherous, although the thick, tussocky grass was firm enough.

'Isabel, yes. I think you'd like her.'

'Well, fine. I'll meet her,' she said. 'Any particular reason?'

He laughed airily. 'No. Should there be? If you come to my flat I guess you're bound to meet her anyway.'

'You're inviting me then?'

'Try and keep away!' He bent and kissed her lingeringly on the lips.

'Not a hope!' she murmured happily.

'What is there between you and Andro, Cat?' asked Jamie flatly, to his daughter's consternation. They were in the field behind the crofthouse checking the ewes before nightfall. There were ten of them, all heavily pregnant with the time fast approaching when they would drop their lambs.

Catriona shot her father a look of alarm. 'How do you mean?' she asked, dreading his answer.

'Well, you go about like a pair of moon-calves but I thought you were only just getting over some affair with a married man. You want to watch yourself, Cat. There's such a thing as jumping out of the frying pan and into the fire.' Jamie spoke gruffly, embarrassed at having broached the subject but driven by concern for the daughter who was his secret favourite.

'Oh Dad, don't worry. Andro's OK. He's not married and he's very nice. You like him, don't you?'

'Oh aye, I like him well enough. He's an entertaining fellow to have around. But he's an actor.' Jamie said the word as if it tasted bad.

'What's wrong with actors?' Catriona asked indignantly. 'They're just like anyone else. They live, breathe, eat, sleep—and love.'

'So they do,' agreed her father. 'But not just like anyone else. Andro reminds me of a sailor I once knew when I was on the ships. He was a right charmer—sang, danced, told stories, kept the lads amused for hours at sea. But he also had a girl in every port. Well, we didn't go to many ports but there was always a different girl

279

seeing him off every time we went to sea.'

'So? Why does Andro remind you of him?' Catriona sounded peeved, hurt that her father seemed to refuse to be happy for her.

'He's a rolling stone. I can tell.' Jamie leaned on his shepherd's crook and rested his chin on his clasped hands. His scarred face looked more macabre than ever in the mother-of-pearl gloaming of the spring evening.

'Look Dad, I know you only worry because you care about me but you don't have to. Anyway Andro and I haven't known each other for long. Who's to say there's anything serious about it?'

'When you live on an island I think relationships are easier,' remarked Jamie pensively as if he had not heard her question. 'You know exactly what you're dealing with when you know the mother and father and all the relations. You don't know anything about Andro's family.'

'Yes, I do!' retorted Catriona hotly. 'I know they come from Glendoran and he has a brother and I know that he doesn't get on very well with his father.'

'Why doesn't he?' enquired Jamie tersely.

'Well, I don't know that, Dad. But it's not a crime, is it? Not everyone can relate to their father.'

'I don't see why not. Strikes me that if you can't get on with your father then there's something lacking.'

'With the father or the child?' she demanded, glaring at him accusingly.

He shook his head a little wearily. 'I don't want to argue with you, Cat. You and I have always understood each other so don't pretend we haven't. I'm just pointing out that you seem to have rushed things a bit with Andro, especially so soon after the other one. You should always clear the decks before trying to load another cargo.'

Catriona felt a sudden rush of affection for her father. He was narrow-minded and uncompromising but he was also sensible and kind. She knew it could not have been easy for him to have lost his looks so early in life but she had never heard him bemoan his luck or rail against fate. He was a fighter and a stickler for the truth and she loved him.

'I wish there were a few more cargoes like you around, Dad,' she said, giving him a hug. 'I'd clear my decks pronto.'

Jamie coughed to dispel the sudden lump in his throat. Then he gestured in the direction of an ungainly, lumbering ewe, laboriously easing herself down behind one of the specially provided straw-bales to rest for the night. 'I wouldn't be surprised if she didn't lamb before morning,' he said hoarsely. 'Be good if they all did while the fine weather lasts.'

'I hope Andro likes cloutie dumpling,' Sheena remarked to Catriona as they walked back from the Ferry Inn along the Bay road. Because it was Andro's last night they had all been to the pub for a farewell drink and now the

281

women were on their way to put dinner on the table.

'Have you made cloutie dumpling?' asked Catriona, amazed. Cooking the delicious traditional fruit and suet pudding was a long, slow process demanding hours of boiling and it was usually only prepared at Christmas or for special celebrations. 'Are you sure you aren't just a wee bit taken with Andro, Mum? Cloutie dumpling indeed!'

It was Sheena's turn to blush but she denied any favour to Andro. 'It's for you I cooked it, you ninny. You need feeding up and you're leaving tomorrow.'

'Ah, how sweet of you,' responded Catriona, visibly moved. 'I promise to do it justice.' They walked on in companionable silence for several minutes, watching the sinking sun colour the sea flaming orange. 'I've been thinking about Marie and Donnie,' she remarked thoughtfully.

'You mean about the Sheader croft?' asked Sheena curiously. 'Do you think Donnie could rebuild it? And if he could, should he? It's such a weird place. Sometimes I wonder how they can even think of living there.'

Catriona smiled to herself, remembering her initial feelings of apprehension in the ghost-ridden 'Fairy Glen' and her subsequent change of heart. After she and Andro had made love in the deserted croft, it was as if the generations of others who had loved in that very place had welcomed them into a magic circle. Sheader had become a crowded spirit-place, redolent with group memory.

'I think it's time there were children playing again up there by the lochan, Mum, and I have an idea to help Marie and Donnie buy the croft,' she said.

'Are you sure?' asked Sheena doubtfully. 'They tried all the building societies and even the banks. Surely your bank won't lend to them? They only deal with rich people, don't they?'

'They may not lend to Marie and Donnie but they'll lend to me,' said Catriona. 'I can take out a preferred loan for a year or eighteen months to give them a chance to do the work and then they can borrow from the building society and pay me back. What do you think?'

'It would be wonderful, dear, if you think it would work,' Sheena agreed doubtfully. 'I was seriously beginning to consider whether Jamie and I should let them have our croft and retire into a flat in Portree or something.'

'Oh no, Mum, you mustn't do that! That's your home—our home. I can't imagine you and Dad anywhere else.' Catriona looked stricken. 'Sometimes in the city it's what keeps me sane, thinking of you in the croft, on the island, where you belong.'

'Perhaps it's where you belong, too, Catriona,' suggested Sheena gently. 'You don't have to lend your money to Marie. You could buy the croft for yourself.'

'No, it must go to Marie and Donnie and the children. Sheader needs children again. I have to be in Edinburgh and I don't want a second

283

home when some people can't even manage to get a first.'

'And of course Andro is in Edinburgh, isn't he?' Sheena observed solemnly, hiding a smile. 'I can see the attractions of the capital.'

Catriona picked up a stone and threw it as far as she could out into the bay. The splash of its landing flashed silver and pink above the beaten-brass sheen of the water and ripples radiated into wide, glinting circles.

'The city can be a treacherous place,' she observed grimly. 'People there think money can buy them everything. I couldn't stay there if I didn't know better.'

'And what do you know that's better?' asked Sheena.

Catriona let her gaze wander round the bay, from the tip of Ru Idrigill, the steep northern headland glowing proudly in the last of the evening sun, along the black rim of the shore, past the intrusive barrier of the jetty, over the line of crofthouses nestling domestically in the midst of their fenced fields, up to the white church perched high on the darkling brae and on as far as the indigo hump of Ru Chorachan at the far end of the bay's western arm. On the horizon the irregular shapes of the Ascrib Isles showed faintly purple in the sunset haze. It was quiet, but for the occasional mewing cry of a gull and the slow, regular slap of waves on the rocky beach.

Catriona turned away from the gentle, cradling bay to regard her mother solemnly. 'This,' she said. 'This is what I know.'

Eleven

The ballroom at the Caledonian Hotel was stuffy and hot. On one side of the dance floor Felicity Finlay flopped into a chair at a round table laden with half-empty glasses and abandoned coffee cups and gasped to the magnificently kilted man who dropped down beside her, 'I'm absolutely wacked, Donald. An Eightsome, a Foursome and *then* Strip the Willow. It's torture by country dancing!'

'I thought all that golf kept you fit, Felicity,' admonished Donald Cameron, picking up a pint mug and proceeding to pour its remaining contents down his throat. Displaying the characteristic flexibility of most Scottish Country Dance bands, the musicians had diminuendoed into a slow cheek-to-cheek number.

Felicity drank thirstily from a glass of white wine and soda water. Her face shone more ruddy than rosy, the result of exertion and alcohol. She grimaced and put down her glass. 'Look at Alison Home-Muir. She isn't even warm.'

Alison and John were on the dance floor, closely entwined, Alison's dark head resting conveniently in the hollow of her large husband's shoulder.

'That's because they've only just stood up,' remarked Donald. 'Alison is preserving her

285

strength. John says she's usually asleep by nine-thirty these days, so this must be a bit late for her.'

'Oh yes, of course, the baby. Isn't it lovely for them?' said Felicity, stretching her neck to peer over other tables. 'By the way, have you seen Bruce? I haven't laid eyes on him for ages.'

'No, I haven't. Ah, hello Gillian, I thought I'd lost you for good.' Donald sounded rather relieved as his partner for the evening was returned to the table by a politely smiling Hamish Melville, who thanked her for the dance and swiftly retreated towards the bar.

Gillian looked glamorous but rather severe in a tight-fitting ruby-red ruched-taffeta gown, her blond hair piled into a chignon to show off a pair of exotic glass and jet 'fabulous-fake' earrings. 'It's dead hard to reel in this dress,' she complained. 'I'd no idea it was that kind of hall.'

'Cheer up, I'll order some more champagne,' Donald said breezily. 'You'd like some, wouldn't you, Felicity?'

Felicity stood up suddenly. 'Maybe later, thanks Donald,' she said abruptly, easing her billowing, blue and green silk-tartan skirt between the chairs. 'I think I'll just go and get some air.' The velvet bodice of her gown was uncomfortable because it was too tight, making her irritable and aware that Bruce was neglecting her. She made her way towards the glass doors which led into the atrium at the centre of the hotel. This was open to the sky and its fuchsias and tubbed conifers stirred invitingly in a light breeze, cooling to flushed cheeks.

At the last moment Hamish veered away from the bar. It would be full of people he preferred to avoid. Two days before, he'd been forced to close several branches of a large and ailing chain of domestic-appliance stores which he had recently taken over, rendering him vulnerable to charges of asset-stripping. This charity ball had come at an unfortunate time for his public image, and he was tempted to blame Linda for forcing him to attend such a high-profile event, positively crawling with Round Tablers and Chamber of Commerce members who expected information and explanations which Hamish was not prepared to give.

He and Felicity took parallel routes to the atrium, each pausing to stand, unseen by the other, in adjacent doorways. Sounds of escalating merriment began to issue from the ballroom where the band was now playing an old Beatles number, 'Money Can't Buy Me Love'. Hamish tapped his foot to it as he lit a cigar and blew smoke into the variegated leaves of a tall *ficus* tree. Perversely it made him think of Catriona and metaphorically grind his teeth. After he'd waited most of the previous week for her call she had finally contacted him on Thursday evening as he was driving home from work. There had been little objection he could make to her maternal mercy mission to Skye but his end of the line had crackled with anger nonetheless. With wife and business both giving him aggravation he had been looking forward to a morale-boosting

287

session in Catriona's white bed to restore his bruised ego and was therefore doubly frustrated by her absence. He could forgive her a lot but not being continually unavailable. It began to look suspiciously as if she was avoiding him, and no one did that to Hamish Melville!

The ash on his cigar was an inch long before he became aware that the atrium was also the scene of a more active form of recreation than his slow, ruminative smoking. From behind a central and particularly dense bank of brushes came voices raised in flirtatious intercourse and Hamish gradually realised that he was able to identify at least one of them.

Felicity stood half-in and half-out of her doorway appreciating the cool air. It was dark in the atrium apart from a few yellowish lamps scattered among the greenery which cast a rather sinister pattern of moving shadows and deterred her from venturing any further alone. Behind her the Beatles tune thrummed and she hummed it tunelessly under her breath, pondering the lyrics. Money may not buy love, she thought cynically but love could very frequently buy money, and plenty of penniless beauties knew it. Did Catriona know it, Felicity wondered, still nervous about Bruce's feelings towards his young female subordinate, despite, or perhaps because of, her own liking for the girl. After all, if she herself felt drawn to Catriona, why should not Bruce feel the same attraction? At least she was not here tonight. Then suddenly Felicity was also alerted by the voices coming from beyond the bushes. One of them was surely familiar?

As she stepped from her doorway, suspicion banishing all fear of the shadows, she saw Hamish begin to cross the atrium from a similar arch not ten yards away, cigar in hand. She let him go ahead, following swiftly and silently in his wake and saw him stop short as he rounded the central greenery. She heard his voice snap out like a nut cracking.

'Look at that! The Chairman of the ball and the Managing Director of the bank in very private conference!'

'Hamish!' and 'Christ Almighty!' said Linda and Bruce together and Felicity was just in time to see them spring apart, hastily adjusting themselves, and rise awkwardly from the bench on which they had been surprised in close embrace.

'I have been known to answer to both,' commented Hamish icily.

'Bruce! What's been going on?' screeched Felicity, her face as red with fury as her husband's was with embarrassment.

Linda was still rearranging the top of her ball-dress, a skimpy jewel-encrusted bodice which covered only the essentials when it was properly in place but had, until a few seconds before, been putting up little resistance to Bruce's thorough body-search.

'That's right, Linda, you'd better *wear* your Dior dress while you can still afford it,' Hamish drawled, observing her efforts.

'Very little has been "going on" as you put

289

it, Flick,' said Bruce uncomfortably, wiping his hand across his mouth as a precaution, although any lipstick which Linda might have transferred to him had long since been worn off in the course of their activities. 'Linda just got a little carried away after all the excitement of the reels, that's all.'

'Very gallant, Bruce,' Linda retorted indignantly. 'It wasn't *me* who was Stripping the Willow!'

'Omigod!' Felicity croaked, her face suddenly ashen. 'It's been *you* all the time, Linda, and I've been thinking it was Catriona!'

'Thinking what was Catriona?' demanded Bruce, blustering madly. 'She's not even here. Anyway, there's been nothing to think. This was just a bit of...' he searched for a way to describe it. '...interval entertainment. Just a one-off kiss and cuddle. Nothing serious. Linda will tell you.'

'Yes, tell us, Linda,' said Hamish laconically, drawing deeply on his cigar and blowing smoke insultingly in his wife's direction.

'For God's sake, Hamish!' snapped Linda, refusing to be cowed. 'Stop trying to turn this into a boardroom confrontation. Of course it's only a bit of fun.' She turned on Bruce with a scowl which banished all earlier tenderness between them. 'Although I think you could claim *some* of the initiative. You weren't exactly backward in coming forward.'

Felicity sat down abruptly on the bench, her wide, accusing gaze still fixed on Bruce. 'I knew there was someone,' she whispered, 'but

I thought it was Catriona. How awful.' At this moment of emotional turmoil she seemed more concerned that she had suspected the wrong woman than with her husband's infidelity.

Bruce sat down awkwardly beside her. 'Of course I wouldn't be seeing Catriona, Flick. I work with the girl.' He attempted to put an arm consolingly around his wife. 'Look, darling—it's no big deal, you know.'

Felicity made a rude noise and furiously rejected his advance.

'Oh, well that's fine, isn't it?' declared Hamish sarcastically. 'The man takes my wife behind the potted palms and says it's no big deal. Well, I happen to think it's a very big deal indeed and I can assure you this won't be the last you hear of it.' His blue eyes had greened to the colour of melt-water, freezing the atmosphere.

Felicity looked up, her face flaming. 'No, it certainly won't, Hamish, don't you worry about that. You deal with your wife and leave Bruce to me. I'll handle him!' All at once she appeared much less the distraught wife and more the vengeful dragon. Any man other than Hamish might have felt a twinge of pity for Bruce.

'Well, well. It seems I'm not the only one with marriage problems.'

To add to the sense of farce, a new character had arrived on stage—Victoria Moncreiffe, glowing with intrigue and gratification. In the sulphurous yellow light her high-collared red and black ballgown made her look rather like a gloating member of the Spanish Inquisition.

'Victoria! What are you doing here?' demanded Linda with a fierce frown, assuming instant authority as Chairman over a mere member of the ball committee. 'Is there a problem?'

'I've been looking for you everywhere,' cooed Victoria, who was not in the least deceived by Linda's business-as-usual bluster. 'It's nearly midnight and you're due to draw the raffle prizes. But if you're involved in something, I daresay I could do it.' Her gaze wandered slyly from Linda to the other three stony faces.

Linda glanced at the diamond Rolex on her wrist. She had already used the appropriate items from her evening bag to tidy her hair swiftly and re-apply her lip-gloss. 'No. It's nothing that won't wait,' she said firmly, tucking the beaded bag under her arm. 'We can sort all this out tomorrow—*if* there is anything to sort out. The raffle is more important. Are you coming, Hamish?'

'I think not,' Hamish informed her acidly. 'The charms of the casino seem infinitely more attractive than any here.' From the outside world the chimes of a church clock drifted faintly into the atrium. Glancing at his own Rolex, which gave the date as well as the time, he added grimly, 'How very appropriate. It's just turned April the First.'

In a dormer-windowed bedroom in an Edinburgh mews house, Andro was throwing clothes into piles. 'What the hell are you doing?' demanded Isabel, who had just completed a gruelling Sunday of videotape-editing in the studio in the converted garage on the ground floor. She had heard Andro arrive back half an hour before but stayed below to finish cutting a sequence.

'Hi, darling,' Andro shot her a wide grin from over an armful of sweaters and T-shirts. 'What does it look like? I'm moving out.'

Isabel did not return the smile but stood impassively in the doorway and watched his exertions. It was impossible to read the expression in her dark, deep-sunk eyes. 'So— things went according to plan?' she enquired after a few moments.

'Like clockwork,' he agreed with satisfaction. 'What did you expect?'

'Well, of course you were always reliable in such matters,' she observed, moving across to pick a hairbrush off the dressing table. 'Don't forget this,' she said, tossing it on to the bed. 'Not that you ever use it.' Leaning towards him, hands on the brass end-rails, she declared indignantly, 'You might have made the odd phone call, just to let me know how things were going.'

Andro shrugged. 'I was too tied up. I can only concentrate on one thing at once.'

'I spoke to Rob last night. He asked if there was any news on the million.'

'I'll ring him tomorrow evening. I should have something positive to tell him then. By the way, we have a lunch-date tomorrow. There's someone I want you to meet.'

Isabel raised an eyebrow but made no verbal

reaction to this. 'I'm going to have a bath,' she said wearily, stretching her arms above her head and moving towards the door. 'Then we'll go to Umberto's. You owe me a decent night out.'

He grimaced comically. 'I'd rather have a decent night in,' he said with feeling. 'But—I suppose it's your call. Umberto's it is.'

'You'll be back this afternoon, won't you?' Linda prompted Hamish as he sorted out his briefcase prior to leaving for the office on Monday morning.

'Why? Will you be putting on another performance of *Caught in the Act?*' he demanded sarcastically, snapping the locks shut and more or less snatching the overcoat she held ready for him in a perfect-wifely way.

Linda smiled sweetly. She appeared at her most alluring, in a sheer white silk wrap, belted tightly enough to reveal every curve and ridge of her bulgeless body. The body which he had studiously ignored since Saturday night. 'Perhaps you'd like to join in next time?' she asked with a little pout.

'Next time I'll kill you,' he muttered grimly. 'This time I'll let you off with a divorce.'

'But not before the people from *Introductions* have been, surely?' She brushed a non-existent hair off the shoulder of his coat and stroked his sleeve.

He snorted derisively. 'Christ, woman, you can cancel them! I never wanted to let them in anyway but there's no question of it now.'

Linda tilted an eyebrow. 'It's your first

appearance on the National Galleries Board tomorrow, isn't it? What will they say if there are lurid headlines about a messy divorce?'

'Why should there be, unless you tell the press?' snapped Hamish.

'Well, I'll have to tell the press won't I, if I'm going to cancel the *Introductions* photo shoot?' she pointed out in a maddeningly reasonable voice. 'They won't keep quiet about it. Then of course Max will get teased at school, poor wee boy.' Tears were visible, glinting in her caramel eyes.

'I'll tell the school to keep the papers from him. What the hell are you playing at, Linda?' Hamish stared at her briefly then stooped, picked up his briefcase and strode to the front door. 'Whatever it is, stop it. It's going nowhere.'

'I'm not playing at anything. I'm just pointing out that Max need never know that his mother or his father have strayed from the straight and narrow if we both play our cards right. But he will, of course, if we cancel our appearance in *Introductions!*'

Hamish stared at her calculatingly. Could she possibly know about his affair with Catriona? Or with any of those who had come before? He'd been so careful. But it was true that *Introductions* would be bound to be suspicious of any cancellation and that would set the terriers of the gutter press sniffing about, and once they got their teeth into a story... God knows how many top politicians they'd toppled recently. What hope did a mere entrepreneur have?

'So what do you suggest?' he enquired through gritted teeth. 'An "I'll-stand-by-my-errant-wife" photocall?'

'No, darling,' she purred, reaching up to kiss him on the lips and ignoring his lack of response. 'A "Still-crazy-for-each-other-after-all-these-years" feature in *Introductions*. That'll sort them out!' She slipped past him to open the front door. 'They're coming at three. I'll press your linen suit,' she said brightly. 'It always makes you look coolly sexy.'

'You'd better lay out the strait-jacket while you're at it,' he muttered darkly and left.

'How's your mother?' Bruce asked Catriona, stopping at her desk as she worked on her morning refer list.

'Much better, thank goodness,' she replied sunnily. 'Out on the croft, gambolling with the newborn lambs. You look awful though, if you don't mind my saying so. Have you been ill?'

Bruce did indeed look as if he'd been through the mill which, in a way he had, since Felicity had spent the whole of Sunday being reproachful and demanding. Why? she had wanted to know. How often? Where? What had she done wrong? How had they gone wrong? How could they go on? Fortunately Iona had disappeared to the stables where she kept her pony at livery and Gus had gone mountain-biking with a friend. Bruce had wished fervently that he, too, could take to the hills.

'No,' he said tersely. 'I want to see you, in my office.'

'Now?'

When he nodded she stood up and followed him through to the front of the building where his Adam-style sanctum overlooked the square. The elm trees, level with his windows, were still bare of leaves and a squall of rain was hurling diamond drops at the panes. Office-workers could be seen scuttling along the wet pavements with umbrellas at fixed-bayonet charge. It was, for Bruce particularly, a *dreich* Monday.

'Is something wrong?' Catriona asked.

He groaned. 'Don't you start asking questions too. I've had it up to here with questions.' His finger made slicing motions at his throat as he sat down at his desk and indicated the chair opposite. Catriona took it in silence, waiting. He stared at her and gave a sharp, self-deprecating laugh. 'I'm sorry,' he sighed. 'Things are a bit sticky at home at present. And that's partly why I want to talk to you. I want you to take over Hamish Melville's accounts.'

A small gasp of astonishment burst from Catriona before she could control it. Able to think of nothing more profound to say, the murmured, 'That's a big portfolio.'

Bruce nodded. 'One of the biggest we have. And we don't want to lose it.'

She leaned forward, frowning. 'Is there some chance that we will? Yes, I know that's a question but some just have to be asked.'

Bruce looked uncomfortable. His collar appeared to be too tight and his cheeks began to glow. 'There's every chance if I continue to handle it, I'm afraid,' he confessed.

'He found out about you and Linda.' She spread her hands. 'It's a statement, not a question.'

'Yes,' he agreed, 'you needn't ask but I'd better tell you. There was an embarrassing scene at the charity ball on Saturday night. We were only kissing behind a potted palm but Hamish and Felicity read *everything* into it.' Bruce toyed with the idea of telling Catriona of Felicity's suspicions about her but decided against it in the interests of preserving their working relationship.

'The thing is though,' he went on, 'Hamish is not going to want me to handle his banking affairs now. He always seems very impressed with you, so if we tell him you're taking over he may not move his business. I think we should hand him a *fait accompli* rather than wait for him to make the first move.'

Catriona made no immediate reaction. Privately she was asking herself whether she could successfully tell Hamish with one breath that their affair was over and with the next that she was his new bank manager. This reorganisation really couldn't have come at a worse time for her but she couldn't tell Bruce that. 'Wouldn't John or Donald do it better?' she suggested at length.

'I don't think so, no. It's not like you to hesitate over such an opportunity, Catriona. Is there something I should know?' demanded Bruce suspiciously.

Catriona shook her head firmly and squared her shoulders. The sojourn on Skye and the

298

affair with Andro had filled her with renewed energy and confidence. 'No, nothing. Of course I'd be glad to handle Mr Melville's accounts. Thank you. You place a very flattering level of trust in me.'

'I'm sure you're equal to it,' Bruce told her. 'But Melville is a tricky customer. He doesn't always play straight.'

'I'll watch him, don't worry,' Catriona assured him. 'Incidentally, have you heard anything about the Carruthers' insurance claim while I've been away? I promised to chase it up for them.'

Bruce passed his hand across his forehead distractedly. 'No, there's no news. Oh, and Catriona—I've told no one else here about the—er—incident at the ball. I can rely on you to keep it that way, can't I?'

'Of course,' she said, rising. Suddenly she couldn't think how she had ever remotely fancied Bruce or why the sophisticated Linda Melville had jeopardised her marriage to have a fling with him. Today he looked like a hunted creature, his habitual bonhomie reduced to barely preserved civility. 'Thank you so much for the time off, by the way,' she added with a grateful smile. 'It was much appreciated.'

He grunted. 'Good.' It was curt dismissal.

While Bruce frowned gloomily at his pile of morning mail, Catriona left his office with a sprightly step. She had only to settle the end of the affair with Hamish and then life would be almost totally wonderful. She was seeing Andro for lunch!

'This is Isabel,' said Andro after greeting Catriona with a kiss. 'Isabel Carlisle—Catriona Stewart.'

Extending her hand, Catriona saw a dark girl in a droopy khaki jacket and skirt, her straight brown hair as long and lank as her clothes. She wore round, metal-rimmed spectacles which should have been ugly but were somehow the opposite. She had an 'I-know-what-suits-me-whether-you-like-it-or-not' arrogance which Catriona did not immediately take to.

'It's kind of you to meet me at such short notice,' said Isabel in a pleasant contralto. 'As soon as Andro told me you might be able to help I begged him to fix it immediately.' Her eyes were an unusual deep violet blue, heavily made-up behind the prim-looking spectacles and they regarded Catriona calculatingly.

They were in a popular New Town pub-restaurant called The Drum and Monkey, and the lunch-time crowd was rapidly filling the numerous polished mahogany tables. 'Let's grab somewhere to sit quickly,' suggested Andro, avoiding Catriona's eye.

What has he told her I might be able to do? Catriona wondered warily, parking herself behind a table in a crimson button-backed chair. This breezy, businesslike Andro seemed a rather different animal from the ardent, tactile lover she had embraced all over Skye.

'Shall we order?' suggested Andro, aware of Catriona's puzzled frown. He picked up a menu and glanced down its contents. 'They have

300

warm chicken-liver salad—how about that?'

'Fine,' agreed Isabel. 'And some Aqua Libra.'

Catriona was familiar with the menu. 'I'll have roasted peppers with anchovies and a bottle of Perrier,' she said, and added with an enquiring look at Andro, 'and more information.'

Andro caught a passing waiter, gave him the order and turned back to the table with one of his most devastating smiles. 'I know you'll probably think I'm dropping you in it, Cat,' he began—he had picked up her family's habit of using the shortened form of her name—'but needs must when Hollywood drives!'

'Perhaps it would help if I introduce myself properly,' put in Isabel swiftly. 'Andro and I are both directors of Precipitous City Productions, which is a film company we started in order to try and get a particular project off the ground.'

'*Catriona*. Yes, I know,' said she of the same name. 'Andro told me about it.'

'So you are aware that we've hit a large financial snag?' Isabel went on.

'Yes. But I told Andro that Steuart's never invests in such high-risk ventures. It's not in our clients' interests.' Catriona couldn't prevent her voice from sharpening. Had she been a real cat, she would have been prowling around Isabel with her tail waving danger signals. What exactly *was* this female's relationship with Andro?

'Yes, you did tell me,' agreed Andro soothingly. 'But we were thinking that perhaps an individual client might be interested in

301

making an investment, if he was properly introduced to it and given the right encouragement.'

'Such as who?' enquired Catriona, although she had a sinking feeling she knew exactly who Andro meant.

'Such as Hamish Melville. You know him well, you could make the initial moves,' suggested Andro earnestly, leaning forward to press her hand with his. 'Darling Cat, you know you could.'

'No!' cried Catriona so forcefully that she startled the waiter who was about to place her roasted peppers in front of her, almost causing them to become flying peppers. 'Sorry,' she added more circumspectly. 'That looks great, thanks.'

'Well, *I* can't make the proposal,' Andro pointed out sullenly, 'because he treated me like an earthworm when I barged in on his picnic, whereas he looked as if he would eat out of your hand.'

'Neither of you need make the proposal,' Isabel interposed with a baleful glare at Andro and a slight shake of the head, indicating that he should back off. 'I'll do that. All I need is a quick introduction. It could take ages to go through official channels and we just don't have ages. I had another chat with our Completion Bond broker last night and he said we only have a week to tie up the budget or the new financial year will throw all the calculations out. We would be forever in your debt if you set up a meeting with Mr Melville, Catriona, but it would need to be tomorrow, or Wednesday at the latest.'

Catriona stared at Isabel. The other girl was certainly fervent enough to be persuasive but she had an abruptness about her which was not endearing. She seemed ill at ease, as if she was doing something necessary but uncomfortable. Isabel struck her as the kind of female who did not make bosom friends with her own sex.

'I will shower you with kisses, throw myself on your neck and anoint your feet with tears of gratitude if you will only agree!' declared Andro extravagantly, clasping his hands and assuming his most appealing, mendicant expression, dark eyes wide, brow deeply furrowed.

There was a tense pause. Catriona took a mouthful of her meal and chewed pensively, glancing from Andro to Isabel. Partners in a film company and in what else? she wondered apprehensively.

'Mr Melville *had* indicated that he might be interested in backing a new Scottish arts project,' she admitted. 'He even mentioned a film as a possibility.'

'I told you!' Andro raised his glass of white wine triumphantly to Isabel. 'I'm certain we can sell him *Catriona.*' He winked. 'The film, I mean, not the girl—who is *not* for sale.'

The look he gave her then dissolved many of Catriona's doubts. It made her guts turn over and her body yearn for him. She wanted to keep him, not lose him. How could she reveal that she had an unfinished affair with Hamish which might prejudice their chances, when telling might jeopardise her own with Andro?

'I'll need to know much more about the film,' she insisted. 'I'm his bank manager. I can't recommend anything about which I'm not completely confident myself. A banker without a nose for a dud deal is professionally dead.'

'Come to our production office and we'll show you all the figures,' Isabel urged instantly, her impatience acute. 'It's not far away. Come now!'

Catriona glanced at her watch and shook her head. 'No, I haven't time. It'll have to be this evening, after work.'

'OK, I'll pick you up at the bank,' Andro offered eagerly. 'Five-thirty?'

'All right, five-thirty,' agreed Catriona, sipping her Perrier thoughtfully. Uncertainty still nagged like a dull ache.

'I hear you're my new bank manager,' Hamish said gruffly in her ear. Catriona nearly dropped the receiver in surprise. Although his secretary had told her where he was to be found she had not expected him to answer personally when she rang the number and she had not expected the news to have been imparted so soon.

'That's right,' she agreed, with her heart in her mouth. 'I hope that's agreeable.'

'It's fine with me,' he muttered. 'Excellent, in fact. Mind you, anything's better than dealing with that reptile Finlay, *even* what I'm doing at this present moment.'

'What's that?' she couldn't help asking.

'Standing in the conservatory alongside my

dear wife, looking like a pair of prize aspidistras,' complained Hamish. He noticed that the rather Sloane-Rangerish lady-photographer from *Introductions* was clicking away at him while he was using his mobile telephone and ducked angrily behind a large Swiss cheese plant.

'Are you still there?' demanded Catriona, puzzled by the resulting line crackle.

'Yes,' replied Hamish. 'I'm afraid Linda has arranged for us to be in that appalling magazine which makes out that everyone lives on candy-floss and uses dental-floss. *Introductions* they call it and apparently it sells like hot-cakes, though I personally would introduce every copy to the shredder.'

Catriona wondered whether this meant Hamish had decided to overlook Linda's transgression with Bruce but naturally did not mention it. Instead she asked, 'Is it a bad time to discuss your money-market account then?'

'Definitely. We'll lunch tomorrow.'

'A lunch isn't necessary. It will only take a few minutes.'

'Lunch,' he persisted, 'or I remove the account.'

Feeling obliged to fulfil her promise to introduce Isabel to Hamish before she could untangle her own relationship with him, lunch seemed safe enough. 'Very well, if you insist,' she said with a smile in her voice.

'I do. The Courtyard, one o'clock.' Hamish pressed the line-clear button and dropped the telephone into his pocket.

Catriona replaced her receiver and turned her

attention to other matters. Concerned about the continuing lack of his insurance clearance, she decided to ring Nick Carruthers. He needed urgently to go ahead with his restaurant reconstruction and a loan of working capital was only a small gamble for the bank to take. In fact it might pay dividends if he was able to take advantage of at least some of the rapidly advancing tourist season. She would authorise an extension of his overdraft.

'Let's hope the SFS have flown on to fresh threats and targets new,' he joked with gratitude and relief when she told him. 'I'm sure lightning doesn't strike twice.'

'Keep me informed on progress,' Catriona reminded him. 'And send me an invitation to the opening. You're very important to me—my first solo investment project for Steuart's.'

'Of course we will. But come up and see us before that, won't you? Sue and the boys arrive on Thursday. I promise you'll get the red carpet and a fatted calf.'

'That's sweet of you but I know you're only camping in the cottage. Red wine and a fat sausage would be fine.'

A brass plate beside the entryphone declared the white-painted mews house to be the headquarters of Precipitous City Productions. In the hundred and fifty years since it had been built, the ground floor had progressed from providing stabling for a team of six carriage-horses to its present incarnation as a film and video studio. The flat above served as both home and office.

'But we only share it, we don't live together,' Andro explained carefully to Catriona as he drove her there from the bank, negotiating the corners with one-handed élan while his other hand held hers.

'You mean the house isn't called Sin,' joked Catriona with a lightheartedness she did not entirely feel.

He smiled in response. 'Isabel and I share a front door, a kitchen and a production company.' Andro was at his most appealingly persuasive and his hand squeezed reassurance.

'And a friendship,' Catriona added, studying his face.

He was watching the traffic, having halted to make a right turn off the main road. He nodded. 'Yes, of course a friendship.' At that moment he had to use both hands to spin the wheel. Her own suddenly seemed sadly empty.

Within seconds they were turning down the mews. As soon as he had secured the handbrake he turned to kiss her and she drew strength from his encircling arms. Strength which she chastised herself for needing in order to face Isabel. Nevertheless the need was there.

'I tend to handle the financial and technical side of the business,' said Isabel as she led Catriona up the steep stairs on which the front door opened directly. 'And Andro does the artistic bit.' She had changed into casual black flares, topped with various layers and shades of grey. Isabel was into sophisticated grunge. 'I've got all the costings and schedules ready for you.'

Also waiting for them in the cluttered office-cum-sitting room above was another man who was introduced to Catriona as the potential cameraman for the film. Alex Duncan was of middle height, aged around forty with a high, domed forehead, and wore a three-piece tailored suit with immaculate shirt and tie. He looked more like a lawyer than a film technician and he shook Catriona's hand with the grave assurance of a high court judge.

'You're Scottish, judging by your name,' she observed after being introduced, sitting down at the table Isabel indicated, which was strewn with papers and files ready for her perusal. 'Yet I thought American film producers always insisted on choosing their own key technical personnel.'

'Well, I am Minerva's first choice, as it happens,' drawled Alex in an accent that owed more to Los Angeles than Alloa. 'I've just finished shooting in Spain so I hopped over here to see my folks and to check on progress with Isabel, but I live in LA and I have to fly back there on Friday. My agent has several irons in the fire.'

'What Alex is saying is that, like ours, his deadline is also looming,' put in Isabel.

'Yes, I have that message loud and clear,' said Catriona, smiling ruefully. 'I intend to work on it into the small hours.'

'Right then—I'll let you get started,' the cameraman said, making for the door. 'God, I hope you can wave the magic wand, Catriona. It would be nice to be able to work in brilliant, dazzling all-Scottish light. I'll hope to see you again very soon.'

Catriona spent ten minutes glancing through the pile of files, extracting those she considered merited further study. Clearly it would take more than an hour or so's work to familiarise herself with all the details necessary to make an informed decision on whether to recommend the project to Hamish.

'May I take all this home?' she said suddenly, sweeping the chosen documents together. 'I have a computer there and I can run the figures through it.'

'You mean you won't be able to tell us yes or no tonight?' protested Isabel.

'No, I'm afraid not,' Catriona told her firmly. 'But I could do with a lift home, Andro. And perhaps some brow-mopping?' She felt a yearning to have him to herself. Three was a crowd, especially when the third was Isabel.

'Andro can't help you much with the financial break-down,' Isabel pointed out a little sulkily.

'But I can glean all that from your excellent reports,' Catriona replied smoothly. 'What I need are the artistic arguments which lift the project into the irresistible.'

'Right,' declared Andro, gathering up an armful of files. 'If that's what you need, that's what you shall have.'

'I hope you don't mind, Isabel,' said Catriona, picking up the remaining documentation. 'I'll work a lot better in my own space.'

'Not at all.' But despite her words Isabel did not look exactly happy.

On the way to Catriona's flat Andro said casually, 'I get the feeling that you don't like Isabel much.'

Catriona bit her lip. 'It's not that I don't like her,' she said hesitantly. 'It's just that I feel threatened by her.'

'Why, because she's intense and serious? She has to be, really. Being a film producer is a tense business.'

'I can imagine. No, I don't think it's that. She just seems to be watching me all the time, as if she's ready to pounce on any adverse remark I might make. It makes me feel uncomfortable.'

'Well, she does have a bit of a chip on her shoulder about the film,' Andro said thoughtfully. 'Perhaps she feels defensive. It is a good project, you know, Cat. Gil Munro wouldn't have agreed to a dud. I don't think he needed cold towels and midnight oil to decide it was a winner.'

'No, but I bet he read the script fairly carefully,' Catriona retorted. 'I have a good feeling about this film, Andro, but I can't rely on instinct and gut-reaction. We're not up the Fairy Glen now. This is big money we're dealing with and Hamish will want some sound arguments even to consider a meeting.'

'Yes, I know. And I'll make sure you have them at your fingertips, don't worry.' Andro revved the Suzuki up Castle Wynd. 'But you can't blame Isabel for feeling a bit left out.'

Catriona did not comment any further on Isabel. 'You can park on the Esplanade,' she told him, indicating the gated entrance to

Edinburgh Castle where a soldier stood on duty. 'I'll tell the guard.'

'Not bad, eh? Your own personal sentry.' Andro was impressed. 'Does he count us in and count us out?'

'Definitely!' she laughed. 'A girl's got to keep her reputation somehow.'

Residents of the flats which bordered the wide sweep of the Esplanade were permitted to park there when it wasn't being used for military purposes such as the famous Edinburgh Tattoo. Living alone as she did, Catriona found it reassuring that there was always a serviceman within hailing distance.

They carted all the film bumph up the three flights of stairs and soon had them spread all over the floor of the living room. Catriona tapped figures into her computer and began to make calculations which had Andro mystified within ten minutes.

'Tell you what,' she suggested. 'I'll finish feeding Mac here and you go and get some pizzas to feed us. There's a place in the High Street.'

By the time he returned she had a good idea of how the film budget would be allocated and had started to read the script. She was familiar with Robert Louis Stevenson's novel *Catriona,* but this version of the story ignored a good deal of the rather turgid political background to his tale and concentrated on the good old-fashioned love-story buried within it. It read to the twentieth-century Catriona rather like *West Side Story comes to Auld Reekie* but she could

311

see that it did have some wonderful characters and a compelling romantic charge to it which, coupled with glorious Jacobite costumes and evocative eighteenth-century locations, would surely attract audiences of wide variety.

'I'm beginning to get excited about this,' she announced to Andro as he plonked pizza and red wine down on the floor beside her. 'I really think I can honestly recommend it to Hamish Melville. Of course, I can't guarantee that he'll share my enthusiasm but it certainly presents a viable and exciting way for him to vary his investment in the arts.'

'So, you'd go and see it, if it was showing in a cinema near you?' asked Andro, taking a large bite of pizza.

'I would, especially if it has Scotland's answer to Hugh Grant playing the swashbuckling Alan Breck.' She leaned over to kiss him, happy that she felt she could reconcile both her professional reputation and her emotional desire to please Andro. The question of how to juggle her own side of the Hamish problem she would face the next day.

'There's just one thing you could help me with though,' she added, supporting herself against his shoulder as she drank her wine.

'Your wish is my command,' he responded eagerly, trying to keep his voice steady. He could sense the winning post and his heart was beginning to pound with excitement.

'These figures all appear to balance out beautifully and yet the—what do you call it?—the Completion Bond chap didn't like them. My client will need chapter and verse on where his money will be used. I need to hear from the Bond man exactly why another million is needed.'

'There is a breakdown of that somewhere, isn't there?' Andro began to rifle through the papers around them.

'Yes, but it doesn't explain how the film will benefit artistically and that's what Hamish Melville will be most interested in. Don't forget he's not a Hollywood mogul simply trying to make millions. He has a reputation to consider. When and if he makes his first venture into film he can't afford to be seen backing a shoddy production. The artistic merit of the project is almost more important than the profits, although he'll want to see those as well.'

'He doesn't want much, does he, this Hamish Melville of yours!' exclaimed Andro.

'I wouldn't call him mine exactly,' Catriona said hastily. 'But you can see that if his million-pound investment is portrayed as turning a potentially average film into an artistic triumph then he will be much readier to advance the money.'

Andro raised his hands in submission. 'Yes, I see that. I'll put you in touch with the Completion Bond broker. His name is Rob Galbraith.'

'Another Scot!' she exclaimed. 'It certainly is a Scottish film, despite the American money—that's very much in its favour from the Melville point of view.'

'He is a Scot but he's based in London.'

Andro had picked up the telephone.

'No, don't you ring him. I'd rather do it myself. When you're not here. Will he mind a call at home?' she asked. 'Some of these City types are a bit sticky about such things.'

'If he doesn't like it, he can complain to me,' Andro said grimly. 'Do I take that as meaning you'd rather I made myself scarce?'

'Absolutely,' murmured Catriona, giving every indication of meaning the opposite. 'But not just yet.'

Andro moved a half-full wine glass carefully out of the way before pulling her down beside him. The energy of their kisses began to rustle the strewn papers on the floor. 'One more question before you liquidise my mind,' he breathed, pushing them aside.

'Yes?' She could feel her pulses racing Skye-high.

'When will you speak to Hamish Melville?'

She jolted back to earth, but only momentarily. 'I'm having lunch with him tomorrow. I should be able to give you yes or no by the afternoon.'

Twelve

'Hello, this is Rob Galbraith.' The voice on the line had a smooth, easy flow with a faint Scottish flavour clinging to the vowels. The sort of accent, Catriona thought whimsically, that crabby old Dr Johnson might have described as 'not offensive'.

Since Andro had not made himself scarce until after midnight she had decided on an early morning call to the Completion Bond broker. 'I'm so sorry to ring you at home on a business matter, Mr Galbraith. I hope you don't mind,' she began tentatively.

'That depends on the business matter,' was the guarded reply. 'I won't discuss Julia Roberts's contract, if that's what you're after.'

Was he joking? Catriona wondered. He did not sound ironic. In fact he sounded genuine in every way. Perhaps people in his profession discussed such glamorous names on a regular basis! 'As far as I know it has nothing to do with Julia Roberts,' she assured him. 'I believe you're handling the Completion Bond for the Precipitous City film, *Catriona.*'

'Yes, that's right.' There was a sudden sharpening of the disembodied voice, a quickening of interest.

'My name is Catriona Stewart. Andro Lindsay gave me your home number because, as you know, they are urgently seeking extra finance for their project and it is possible that I may be able to help.'

'Do you have a spare million then?' enquired Rob Galbraith pertinently.

'Not personally, no, but I represent someone who might. However, first I need to know exactly why top-funding is required.'

'Haven't they shown you our report?'

'Yes, but it merely indicates there's a shortfall

315

on salaries and production costs. My client won't be interested if he thinks he's putting in money simply to boost the producers' profits.'

'No, I can understand that. Mind you, producers have to make profits now and then or there'd never be any films made.'

'So what are these production costs?' Catriona insisted.

'Mostly costumes. They've skimped too much, trying to bring it in under the ten million mark. Costumes are a very important element of an historical feature.'

'Yes, I'm sure they are. So that would definitely come under the heading of improving the artistic standard. And the salaries?'

'Well, they've budgeted for two relative unknowns to play the young lovers, hoping that Gil Munro and a couple of other famous faces will carry the film—a bit like Zeffirelli did with his *Romeo and Juliet*—but we've recommended that they use experienced young British actors, otherwise American equity might insist on using their nationals—and I have yet to hear a Yank speak Highland Scots successfully.'

Catriona shivered. This man clearly understood the subtle nuances of preserving the film's artistic credibility. 'Yes, I know what you mean. Shades of *Brigadoon!*'

'Exactly.' She could hear the amusement in his voice and was glad to have made him laugh. 'But whoever plays the parts will still need plenty of voice-coaching, and they haven't budgeted for that either. The extra million is really just to add the essential finishing touches

316

that make an average movie into a good one.'

'That's more or less what I wanted to hear. So you're impressed by its chances?'

There was a pause before Rob Galbraith went on in measured tones, choosing his words carefully as if he were addressing a court of law or a press conference: 'Everyone concerned with the British film industry would like to see it made. There is no other major feature film scheduled to celebrate the Robert Louis Stevenson centenary so it has a large potential audience base. Whether the investors recoup or not is another matter. A Completion Bond does not guarantee success, it only protects the workers, so to speak.'

She understood his professional reticence but felt he sounded human enough to push for a more gut-level reaction. 'Can I ask you what chance you think my client may have of seeing a reasonable return on his million?'

'Strictly speaking, no, you can't ask me,' replied Rob Galbraith, still resisting any commitment. 'But the American backers wouldn't have put up their ten million if they didn't think it was a goer. On the other hand they are also involved in movies budgeted at two and three times that sum, investments which they must be far more worried about losing.'

'So *Catriona* is pretty small fry?'

'Yes, it is. But that doesn't mean it might not make big money if they get it right. Look what happened with *Four Weddings and a Funeral*.'

'Yes. That kind of profit would appeal to any investor,' she laughed.

317

'Are you going to tell me who this angel is?' he asked. He was attracted by the sound of her voice, would have liked to put a face to it.

'No. Sorry. Not yet.'

'Oh well. Let's hope he comes good. I'd like to see the film made.' Despite his professional fence-sitting he sounded definite about that, a fact which further disposed Catriona towards him and towards the project. If credibility could be gleaned from a voice, then Rob Galbraith must be deemed trustworthy.

'Thanks for talking to me. It's helped a lot,' she told him warmly.

'I hope we speak again. I'm sorry, I didn't really take in your name at the start. What did you say it was?'

'Catriona Stewart. I work for Steuart and Company, a private bank in Edinburgh. You've probably never heard of it.'

'Oh, but I have,' Rob contradicted her, his mind spinning back to the evening he'd spent with his mother at *Sunset Boulevard*. He knew the bank, all right. And now he knew just what the girl he was speaking to looked like, and, recalling her companion of that evening, he thought he knew who her potential investor was. But he said nothing of this. 'Let me know how it goes. Do you have my office number?' He gave it to her. 'I'm in Edinburgh from time to time,' he added. 'Perhaps we'll meet.'

'Yes, perhaps we will,' she said. 'Goodbye.'

'I feel guilty about Catriona,' Felicity said to Bruce suddenly over breakfast.

'What do you mean?' he asked, lowering his paper. In the present marital climate he found it politic to pay attention to what his wife said.

'I feel I've maligned her,' Felicity went on, pouring herself more coffee from the cafetière. There was a loud banging from the scullery next to the kitchen and she called out irritably, 'For goodness sake Iona, what are you doing?'

'Just getting the mud off my hockey boots!' her daughter shouted. 'We've got PE today.'

'Well, don't leave a mess all over the floor. Do it outside,' her mother urged shrilly.

'How have you maligned her?' demanded Bruce.

Felicity lowered her voice from screaming-at-the-kids pitch. 'I told you, I thought it was her. It never occurred to me it would be Linda Melville.' Her face clouded as she spoke. The emotional wound caused by her discovery of her husband's affair was still raw and painful.

Bruce coughed slightly. 'I think you should try and stop brooding over it, Flick,' he suggested tentatively, not wanting to spark another row. 'I've told you it won't happen again.'

'Huh.' Felicity's dismissive grunt revealed how much faith she had in his words of reassurance. 'That's not the point. I feel awful that I suspected Catriona. I ought to make it up to her somehow.'

Bruce tried to hide his impatience with what he saw as needless female angst. 'Why, for heaven's sake?'

'Because I made her name mud at the golf club and I feel responsible if Catriona has

319

acquired a reputation she doesn't deserve. And so should you.'

'Me?' Bruce looked indignant. '*I* wasn't accusing Catriona. It's got nothing to do with me!'

'Yes, it has. If you hadn't been doing the dirty on me in the first place I wouldn't have had any suspicions.'

Bruce subsided, knowing when he was outmanoeuvred. 'Well, I shouldn't worry,' he said soothingly. 'A girl like Catriona is bound to be the subject of gossip, whether or not she deserves it.' He picked up his coffee cup and drained it.

His wife was still glaring daggers at him. 'Why should she be?'

'Because she's beautiful. Don't pretend that isn't why you suspected her. If she'd been plain and mousy you wouldn't have given her a moment's thought. Anyway, I don't suppose she is entirely above suspicion. I'm sure Hamish has made moves in that direction and it can't be easy for a girl to resist him when he pulls out the chequebook.'

'*Hamish*, Bruce, he wouldn't, would he! God, Catriona would really find him more than she could handle.'

Once again Bruce didn't see this. 'Why? She must have quite a lot of experience in that sort of thing, I should think. I mean, she works with men all the time. She can't always be crying sexual harassment every time they wink at her.'

'But Hamish is in a different league, you

know that. You were terrified when he found out about you and Linda—admit it! You began to worry that he might start throwing his weight around, and Hamish and his money together, put to determined use, are daunting opponents.'

'But he's not going to be an opponent of Catriona's, is he? She's his bank manager now. They have to work together and if she's any good at her job she'll find a way of doing it, even if she does have to drop her drawers.'

'Bruce! Shut up!' Felicity was furious, not just with her husband's appalling callousness and demonstrable misanthropy but also his paternal carelessness. 'Iona's only next door.'

As if on cue Iona burst in from the scullery, brown hair flying, sports bag swinging and obviously in a tearing hurry. 'Can you give me a lift, Dad?' she pleaded, dumping her bag on the floor and hastily buttering a piece of toast. 'I'm going to be dead late!' She crunched her toast noisily, with a sound akin to that of running feet on new gravel. Felicity looked pained. At fourteen her otherwise presentable daughter had still not perfected the art of eating with her mouth closed.

Bruce rose and folded the *Scotsman*. 'I'll take you if you come now. Otherwise I'll be late myself. Bye, Flick. Don't forget I've got a Sports Council meeting this evening. If you're so worried about Catriona why don't you take her out to lunch or something?'

'I can't today, I'm having lunch with Elizabeth. Bye, darling. Have a good day.' This

321

last was to Iona, accompanied by a kiss. Bruce received no such salutation. He had not earned enough forgiveness to merit good wishes, kiss or endearment. Still, reflected Felicity, hearing the front door slam, at least she knew the meeting of the Sports Council was *bona fide* because one of her golfing cronies was also on it.

In high summer the Courtyard Restaurant was one of the few in Edinburgh which placed tables outside, amongst the flowering clumps of fuchsia and escallonia which grew in the picturesque, stone-flagged enclosure after which it was named. But the early April weather proved too chilly to allow this so Catriona strode through the arched entrance and across the deserted flags to an outside staircase which led up to the winter quarters, a long casemented gallery overlooking the yard. Behind a large flower arrangement, at a damask-covered window table, sat Hamish Melville.

Under the pretext of studying the menu, he had observed Catriona's approach, thinking how seductively elegant she looked in her long tailored sea-green tweed jacket and short navy skirt and stockings, with her eye-catching burnished mane bouncing freely on her shoulders as she walked. Even in high heels and over an uneven surface she seemed to glide rather than stride, head high and with an easy fluidity, casting scarcely a downward glance at the treacherous ankle-twisting pavement under her feet. He was assailed with such a surge of desire for her that his arms and fingers began to tingle.

'You look wonderful, as usual,' he said, standing up to greet her formally with a shake of the hand but also with a more intimate kiss on the cheek. A kiss that was keenly observed from another table further down the room where Felicity Finlay and Elizabeth Nicholson were already into their *antipasto,* heads together and tongues wagging.

Catriona felt far from wonderful, having had little sleep. After Andro had finally left, taking the film files and his high hopes with him, she had tossed and turned in bed, wondering whether she would be doing the right thing in recommending the Precipitous City film to Hamish. She was conscious that she would be guilty of double deception, firstly in making the investment suggestion before she had made it clear that she wished her future relationship with Hamish to be a purely professional one, and secondly in concealing Andro's involvement both with the project and with herself. But she had persuaded herself that it was only a matter of timing. If Hamish was interested in the film then she would square her relationship with him as soon as the investment had been settled. Surely it was unfair to jeopardise a potentially good film simply because she had an unfinished affair with its possible saviour! If she had not been certain, both on the basis of her own researches and her early morning conversation with Rob Galbraith, that the film was a viable proposition and a worthwhile investment she

323

would not have contemplated doing what she was about to do. Nor was she totally confident that she could carry it off.

Hamish seemed more like the charming, authoritative man she had first met rather than the somewhat inebriated, ineffectual individual she had abandoned at the racecourse. 'Well, I must say Edinburgh has been much duller since you took off for the Hebrides,' he told her. 'But it's brightened considerably now that we are to be working together.'

'In line with Steuart's policy, I have every intention of providing the best financial services available,' she assured him earnestly. 'I'm sure you would expect no less.'

'Correct,' he responded with a smile. 'But that doesn't mean that we can't continue to be friends. As I hope we will—very close friends.'

She returned his artful smile with a guileless one and launched straight into business. 'I've only had time for a brief survey of your accounts but I do have some observations to make, if you'd like to hear them.'

'Not right now. Let's order first, shall we?' he suggested. 'They have good fish here I know, though I think not Dover sole...' His blue eyes twinkled with amusement at this reference to their first meal alone together, with all its ramifications.

Catriona felt a twinge of alarm but covered it with an enthusiastic reference to mussels and her intention to have them cooked according to the restaurant's special recipe, with tomatoes, basil and red wine. 'And when you've eaten the mussels you end up with a soup that's delicious to mop up with focaccia bread,' she added.

Hamish regarded her affectionately and shook his head. 'You talk so enthusiastically about food and yet I know that you'll eat only about half the shellfish and dip maybe two pieces of bread in the soup. Still—I suppose that's the price you pay for having a figure like yours.'

'I eat masses,' she objected. 'You should have seen me tuck into my mother's cloutie dumpling last weekend.'

He laughed. 'I don't know about cloutie dumpling but I do know you order a lot and eat very little. Fortunately, one of the great advantages of having money is not having to worry about wastage and spillage.'

'Well, even if I don't eat every morsel it buys, at least you can be very certain that I will do my utmost to ensure that your money remains in safe hands,' she retorted.

'I'm sure you will,' he said, adding out of the blue, 'I think I owe you an apology.'

'What for?' she asked with surprise.

'For slipping that bracelet into your pocket. I wanted so badly to give it to you that I resorted to subterfuge but I should have been more upfront.'

'Well, the result would have been the same. I couldn't accept it. I hope you understand,' said Catriona apologetically.

'No, not entirely,' he replied frankly. 'I confess I can't see the objection to a few presents. It's not as if I can't afford them and it makes me feel better for not being able to be with you very often.'

The conversation was not going the way Catriona wanted. She was anxious to steer clear of references to their romantic involvement before she had clinched his agreement to meet Isabel Carlisle. 'The gift of the painting was generous enough,' she told him firmly. 'I love it but I'll have to give that back as well if you keep showering me with diamonds. I honestly meant what I said—thanks very much but no thanks!'

'They look as if they're having a bit of an argument,' Elizabeth remarked to Felicity over their pasta. 'And a not entirely professional one at that.'

'Do you think Bruce could be right?' asked Felicity. 'Has she started an affair with him?'

'Not enough evidence yet,' responded Elizabeth briskly. 'But I must say that when I met her at your dinner party she didn't strike me as the type to be a mistress, even to a millionaire. She has too lively a conscience. Look at the way she sympathised with the children's hospice project.'

Felicity looked doubtful. 'But look how I suspected her of being involved with Bruce. He says someone as beautiful as she is, is bound to be faced with more temptation than others and is more likely therefore to give in.'

'I don't follow that logic,' scoffed Elizabeth. 'Women have affairs to bolster their egos, to make them feel attractive. Catriona doesn't look as if she needs that kind of reassurance.'

'We don't know that. She may be a mass of insecurities under that beautiful, calm exterior.'

'Well, I'm going to find out,' Elizabeth declared. 'I want to get her on to our sports fund-raising committee—co-opt her to investigate the possibilities of her pitch and putt idea. You discover lots of things about the people you work with on projects like that.'

'I wonder if she'll agree?' mused Felicity. 'Still, I think she does need more social activities than she has at present. She shouldn't rely entirely on the bank for meeting people.'

'Not if it means consorting with wily customers like that!' Elizabeth gestured towards Hamish, who now displayed a distinctly calculating expression.

Catriona had complied with his suggestion that they move on from differing about presents by launching into her film spiel. 'I have a project to put to you as a possible investment, Hamish,' she began determinedly. 'You mentioned that you might be interested in diversifying your artistic interests. Through clients of the bank' (only a small white lie) 'it has come to my notice that a Scottish film company are desperately in need of some additional finance for their mainly American-funded feature.'

There was a pause while the waiter brought their mussels and focaccia bread which Hamish had also decided to order, on her recommendation. When wine had been poured and pepper screwed with the usual waiterly flourishes she sampled her first mussel and then raised her eyebrows enquiringly over the large, earthen-ware bowl in which they were served.

'Shall I go on?'

He nodded. 'Why not? Just how Scottish is this film company, by the way?'

'Completely Scottish-based; only the finance so far is American—but then there is so little film money available in the UK. You know that.'

'Yes, that was part of my reason for considering supplying some,' he agreed. 'Tell me more.'

'The company is called Precipitous City Productions, after Robert Louis Stevenson's description of old Edinburgh with its steep wynds and closes. The film is to mark the Stevenson centenary.'

To her slight surprise he appeared to know a great deal about the preparations for celebrating this particular anniversary, including a general regret that no film project had yet made production. She could see from the rapt way he ate one mussel after another that he was tasting little of them but absorbing much of what she said. His genuine interest encouraged her to reveal her own personal belief in the viability of the film and to provide chapter and verse about the script, the casting and the financial backing.

'Except that their funding is a million pounds short,' she added finally.

'Just that?' he asked. 'A mere million!'

She gave a small laugh. 'It sounds a great deal for an individual to invest, I know, but I assure you I wouldn't recommend it if it weren't a very worthwhile project and one which would fit well with your public profile. Its launch next year would provide some very positive PR. Why not meet with one of the producers?'

'Is he a Scot?'

'*She* is a Scot. Her name is Isabel Carlisle.'

'Is she pretty?'

'What does that have to do with it?' Catriona was amused and exasperated at the same time.

'I swear that when you're angry sparks fly out of your hair,' he told her with delight. 'It's true what they say about redheads!'

'My hair is not red! Rubies are red, and roses. Not hair.'

'So what colour would you call it then?' Hamish teased, reaching out to finger one of the waves that framed her face.

'You're trying to change to subject,' she admonished lightly, pulling her head back. 'Will you meet her?'

A few tables away Elizabeth had a better view than Felicity. 'He's touching her hair,' she hissed to her friend. 'Surely he wouldn't do that if they were talking about bank balances.'

'No, he wouldn't,' agreed Felicity with a grimace. 'He is definitely not to be trusted and she's not being too clever.'

'Time for a little motherly advice?' suggested Elizabeth, grinning at her friend.

'Hardly motherly,' objected Felicity indignantly. 'Sisterly perhaps...'

'I'll tell her to ring you, shall I?' persisted Catriona, still trying to keep Hamish's mind on the film 'Or shall we make a date now?'

Hamish shook his head. 'I don't want to meet her,' he said abruptly. 'You handle it for me. You've obviously done your homework, you believe in the project, you're my bank manager. I'll take your advice.'

Catriona started in surprise, not only because of his sudden agreement *(had* he actually agreed?) but also because under the table his silk-clad foot was rubbing her leg, creeping with insidious determination up to her thigh. He had slipped off his shoe and was skilfully demonstrating that the table was small enough for some intimate sole-searching.

'Do you really mean that?' she said, anxious not to mistake his verbal meaning even though the meaning of his footwork beneath the cloth was unmistakable. Reaching down she used her hand to push his foot away, adding in a hiss, 'What are you doing, Hamish? Please don't! Someone will notice.'

'No they won't,' he grinned unrepentantly, returning his foot to its hot, secret burrowing. 'You said once that I was an unpardonable groper and I'm only living up to my reputation. No one will notice if you don't move. And yes, I do mean it.'

At that moment the waiter wheeled up the dessert trolley and Catriona was forced to sit and wait while Hamish deliberately took ages deciding between chocolate parfait and passion-fruit torte, wriggling his toes in a highly disconcerting fashion in a place to which she seemed unable to deny him access without actually standing up. 'I think the passion-fruit, don't you?' he finally announced, lounging back in his chair and appearing to relax expansively, purely in order to be able to push his foot a little further on its mischievous legation.

Catriona recognised that his behaviour was merely that which he still had every right to think she might welcome. He knew nothing as yet of her withdrawal from him, of her unwillingness to continue their affair—nor, indeed, of her embarkation on another with Andro. Of course, if he did know he would almost certainly abandon any intention of investing in the film. She was torn between natural honesty and wanting to steer him into what she genuinely believed was an interesting and exciting investment project. And there was also the matter of pleasing Andro. She liked to think that this was a secondary consideration because, after all, her affair with the actor was only recent and could hardly be described yet as rock-solid. She was juggling on a precipice, hoping to keep all the balls in the air without falling off. If she managed it she reckoned she could never again be described as inexperienced.

With relief she felt his foot slide away as he leaned forward over his dessert. But in her present circumstances his whispered words brought no ease of mind. 'I would like to make love to you right now, on that trolley,' he murmured, his head very close and his eyes holding hers. 'Do you realise it is more than two weeks since London? I know your mother couldn't help being ill, but what are the chances of you getting away this Friday? Linda is hardly in a position to question me too closely about what I'm doing at present. We could fly to Paris as we planned.'

'I don't know, Hamish,' Catriona said hesitantly. 'I've had so much time off lately, I couldn't get away early on Friday. I have an awful lot of work to catch up on.'

'Well, let's just go somewhere in Scotland then,' he persisted. 'There are any number of hideaway hotels within an hour or so's drive just waiting for people like us to make use of them. I'll book one and surprise you.'

Catriona bit her lip. She didn't want to have to lie any more than necessary and she did want Hamish to concentrate on the film investment.

'If you like,' she said vaguely. 'Perhaps it could be a celebration for clinching the film deal.'

'Why? Does it have to be done as soon as that?' he asked in surprise.

'Oh yes, Hamish,' she said urgently. 'That's the whole point. There's a London lawyer who's what they call a Completion Bond broker and he says the money must be raised by the financial year-end or all the estimates will have to be revised. He's the one who insisted on the extra million pounds.'

'It sounds as if I should meet the Completion Bond character rather than the lady producer,' said Hamish.

'Well, I'm sure that could be arranged.'

'Right, you arrange it and the contract and the money transfer, and get it all organised for

Thursday evening at my office. Then, on Friday we can celebrate.' Hamish grinned and made an extra deep thrust with his foot so that she jumped to her feet, scarlet with embarrassment.

'I—I'll be back in a minute,' she stammered in confusion and bolted for the Ladies to give herself time to recover and to think. She seemed to have sealed the film deal but into what hot water had she plunged as a result?

'She's very red in the face, isn't she?' murmured Elizabeth pruriently. 'Do you think he was making an indecent proposal?'

'It does look that way, doesn't it?' agreed Felicity in troubled tones. 'Bruce actually said he wanted her to make sure Hamish Melville was happy even if it meant dropping her drawers.'

'He didn't, did he?' Elizabeth looked both amused and askance. 'He's a bit of a bastard isn't he, your Bruce?'

'Well, he didn't say it to Catriona of course, only to me,' Felicity hastened to assure her. 'And I think he was joking really.'

'I wouldn't be too sure,' murmured Elizabeth into her coffee cup.

When Catriona returned she sat sideways to the table with her legs deliberately turned away from the concealing cloth.

'Coffee?' asked Hamish, with a knowing glance at her prim position.

She shook her head, looking at her watch. 'I really haven't time. Are you sure you're happy with your decision about the film? I don't want

333

you to feel I've talked you into something you may regret.'

'You haven't talked me into anything,' he said. 'I think *Catriona* is a girl with great potential, just what I am looking for to balance my reputation for ruthlessness, and I am more than happy to invest a few spare bawbees in her.'

'As long as they *are* spare,' she put in, acutely aware of his *double entendre*. 'There is the outside chance that *Catriona* will flop, you know.'

He spread his hands expressively. 'What else should I spend them on—diamond bracelets?' He laughed at her grimace. 'A film is a much better investment. And besides, it will give me a chance to meet Gil Munro. He might even play a round of golf with me!'

A flash of amusement lifted Catriona's dubious expression. 'It's an expensive round of golf,' she remarked, standing up. 'I'll try and fix everything for Thursday and let you know. Thanks for lunch. It was very eventful.'

'Well!' breathed Felicity, sipping her *sambuca* and watching Catriona walk out of the restaurant. 'They haven't left together. What does that mean?'

'Discretion. After all, Hamish Melville wouldn't want to give his wife any grounds for divorcing *him*,' observed Elizabeth, pensively swirling the liquid in her brandy balloon. 'I should think he likes to be in control.'

'So, does Bruce, I suppose,' murmured Felicity. 'He's just not quite so clever.'

'You hope!' retorted Elizabeth.

'Cat! You're back then?' crowed Alison on answering Catriona's afternoon telephone call. 'Great to hear from you. I was beginning to think one of us had died!'

'But surely John told you I'd gone to Skye?' enquired Catriona with concern. For some days she had been screwing up her courage to contact Alison, conscious that she had hardly spoken to her since learning about the baby, and acutely aware that the lack of communication had been deliberate on her part. The first agonising surge of jealousy over her friend's condition had passed but she was still disturbed by occasional ignoble pangs of envy.

'Oh yes, he did of course. But I thought you might have rung me from there. Was your mother very ill?'

Alison sounded justifiably peeved, Catriona thought. 'No, not really,' she said, knowing she was being deliberately evasive and Alison couldn't have failed to notice it.

'Still, you must have been worried. I know I argue like mad with my mother but I'd be devastated if she became really ill.'

'You're not arguing at present though? Not now that there's a baby on the way. She must be thrilled.'

'Yes, she is. But she also wants me to stop work and put my feet up all day. She hasn't a clue about career mums.'

'Oh dear!' Catriona chuckled softly. 'I'm sure my Mum would be the same. I rang to see if we're OK for squash, or has your mother told you to stop playing that as well?'

'No, not my mother but my doctor. It wipes me out and he says it's not worth the risk. Sorry. Shall we meet anyway and have a drink at the club? I want to talk to you, hear all your news.'

'Just when I might have a chance of beating you, you duck out on me,' Catriona complained ruefully. She realised that she did want to see Alison, had missed her sensible, down-to-earth attitude and genuine affection. 'All right. The club at six tomorrow. I might drag you out for a walk first.'

'Fair enough. I think I can still manage that.'

Isabel watched Andro's face as he answered the telephone in their flat. He looked almost instantly jubilant. 'Well done, Catriona! Darling, that's brilliant! And he doesn't want even to see us or talk to us or anything?'

A deep frown creased Isabel's brow. She was both disappointed and ecstatic as the meaning of the last query became clear. Disappointed at missing the chance of meeting Hamish Melville and ecstatic about his million pounds.

'Sure. Will you ring Rob or shall I? OK, you do it. I can't believe you've done this all by yourself. You clever girl—he must really fancy you! All right, all right, you're just a good financial adviser, I know. Isn't there anything we can do? Oh yes, we'll do that all right. Come round after work and we'll open a bottle of bubbly. Alex will be here and we

336

can all drink to the film's success. What do you mean, you're not part of the company! There wouldn't even be a film without you. Good, see you later.'

Disconnecting the call he put down the telephone and turned slowly to look at Isabel. 'It worked,' he said fervently, watching her long face shorten in a gloating, secretive smile. 'Great galloping gobstoppers, Izzy. IT WORKED!'

Andro gambolled up to her like an overgrown puppy, emitting a strange, lilting whoop like a clan war-cry, and tumbled her excitedly over on to the sofa. 'She's got us the money,' he declared proudly. 'So you can produce your film and I can swash my buckle all over the cinema screen. It's pure dead brilliant.' He stared down at her for a few moments, then slowly removed her spectacles and placed them on the arm of the sofa.

She gazed up at him with the myopic look of the very short-sighted. 'We're not very nice people though, are we?' she remarked slowly but not very solemnly, her face without its normal owlish frames resembling that of a dark Botticelli angel. Then she arched her back to reach his mouth with her lips. They kissed like long-lost lovers re-united, as indeed, after a fashion, they were. 'Will you move your toothbrush back into my bathroom now?' she asked, when she could speak.

'Maybe not just yet,' he told her, undoing the buttons on her long black over-dress and slipping his hands under the white T-shirt beneath. 'But soon—very soon.'

337

Thirteen

The terminal building at Edinburgh Airport was at its busiest, bustling with commuters returning on evening flights from meetings all over Europe. Catriona stood at the foot of the staircase which led directly from the London shuttle lounge among a jostling group of people waiting to meet relatives, and agents holding up cards bearing the names of otherwise unknown arrivees. She wondered whether she, too, should have a card with the name GALBRAITH printed on it.

Alison had said she would know him by his London broker's scowl. 'You've seen them in the financial reports on the telly. They all look the same—as if they have a telephone in each pocket, a fax machine in the car and a laptop in their briefcase—so high-powered they don't need plugging in.'

Catriona had laughed but protested, 'He didn't *sound* like that at all.'

The evenings were beginning to lengthen and the two friends had met at the club and taken a sunset walk in place of their usual game of squash. The Sports Club was situated on the banks of the Water of Leith, along which a leafy river walkway had recently been constructed by an environment-conscious council. Pedestrian bridges, earth-and-plank steps and gravel paths made a pleasant promenade for jaded citizens, meandering for several miles along the northern edge of the city centre between high tree-strewn banks choked with glorious untamed ivy, and along quiet grassy backwaters alive with water-birds.

'How's your mother now?' asked Alison as they skirted an estate of new townhouses built close together under a steep section of riverbank.

'To tell you the truth, she's absolutely fine,' Catriona replied sheepishly. 'Always was.'

Alison glanced sharply at her friend. 'Why the fib to the bank then?' she asked.

Catriona shrugged. Her desire to confide further in Alison was swamped by a sense of her own shortcomings and the presence of a third party which seemed to loom between them, tiny yet but ever-growing, so that Catriona felt they could no longer relate as two equal and kindred spirits. 'I needed to get away,' she said diffidently. 'A case of Island Deficiency Syndrome as my mother calls it. Her being sick was the best excuse I could find.'

'You're not usually irresponsible like that, Cat—and you normally keep in touch. I haven't heard a peep from you for over two weeks.' Alison sounded aggrieved—and with good reason, Catriona thought. 'Being with you this evening is like being with someone else. You're all touchy and glum, not the sunny, light-hearted Cat we all know and love.'

'Cat on a hot tin roof,' Catriona prevaricated. Her dubious juggling act was impossible to explain. The situation was too complicated and

339

however she mentally analysed it, she appeared to herself in a very poor light. Confiding these feelings of inadequacy to the perfect career-girl and mother-to-be was a dismal prospect.

'Yes, exactly. Just like that.' Catriona had not stopped walking and Alison had to break into a jog to catch her up. 'It's that bloody man Hamish, isn't it? Was it him who made you run away? Is he messing you around? For God's sake Cat, tell me! I'm your friend. I want to help.' Alison was almost skipping alongside Catriona now because of the other girl's agitated speed as she marched on determinedly with head down and hands in pockets.

Exasperated, Alison grabbed her arm. 'Stop! Just stop for a minute, Cat.'

Catriona stopped. They were on a deserted, enclosed stretch of river where a crack willow grew at a crazy angle from the bank, trailing its branches in the water. One of them made a thigh-high seat just wide enough for two people. 'Let's sit down here and talk,' Alison urged, pulling her friend off the path. 'Look, there's no one around, it's lovely and quiet and you can hear the river chuckling merrily along.'

Catriona gave a mirthless snort. 'Huh! It's probably having a good old laugh at me,' she declared.

'Why should it be laughing at you of all people?' asked Alison, wriggling into position beside her friend. 'What's wrong with you? And what have I done wrong that you won't talk to me about it?'

Catriona gave Alison's arm a rueful squeeze.

There was nothing wrong with Alison Home-Muir and there was everything wrong with Catriona Stewart! She gave a sigh and shook her head. 'You've done nothing at all, Ally. Nothing.'

'Well, don't tell me it's not Hamish because I won't believe you. I know I warned you against him but that doesn't mean I'm not on your side.'

Catriona took a significant breath. 'Well, it's not really him. Actually he is causing a problem but only because I've cooled off and he hasn't. It's all my fault in that sense.'

'Well, I'm glad to hear you have seen sense,' said Alison approvingly. 'What made you cool off?'

Catriona wrung her hands awkwardly. 'I suppose it was his son, really. I didn't know he had one at first, you see—and then he told me.' (She would have liked to add, 'And you told me you were pregnant at about the same time and I began to recognise the value of family life.') But instead she went on, 'And that seemed to coincide with me realising that the whole affair was going nowhere and that all the advantage was on his side.'

'Dead right. Ten out of ten for being a clever Cat.' Alison put her arm round Catriona and hugged her. 'John will be delighted.'

Catriona gave a sharp laugh. 'Well, that's a relief,' she remarked ironically.

Alison flushed a little at her tone. 'Well, I suppose you think that is funny but I've been defending you to John like mad. He

341

just couldn't understand you getting involved with a client. I know he seems easygoing but underneath he's terribly proper about these things.'

'Yes, well, I suppose he's right. The problem is, Ally, that I've made everything more complicated by being too cowardly to tell Hamish how I feel. Consequently he still thinks there's something between us.'

'Oh Cat—just tell him. It can't be too difficult. It isn't as if you've professed undying love or anything, have you?' For a moment Alison looked worried.

'No, of course not! But he did give me a painting and he tried to give me a bracelet and I feel guilty about him.' Catriona saw Alison's incredulous expression and added almost under her breath, 'Besides, I've met someone else.'

'Ye gods! You don't waste time, do you?' her friend cried. 'Who?'

Catriona had relaxed a little by now. The baby no longer seemed to hover between them like an admonitory cherub. 'A man called Andro Lindsay. He's an actor.'

'Should I have heard of him?'

'No, but then you hardly ever watch telly. He's done a lot of it and a few films. He's quite well-known.'

'How well do you know him?' Alison asked curiously.

'Quite well—OK, very well.'

'In the Biblical sense? Old testament stuff—and Jacob knew his wife and lo she brought forth another son—that sort of know?'

'God, you're so nosy!' Catriona protested. 'Yes, all right, that sort of know—though without the bringing forth bit.'

'Why have I not had an inkling of this wild affair?' enquired Alison rather huffily. 'I thought we were friends.'

'It all happened rather suddenly.'

Alison gave her an old-fashioned look. 'Hmm. You're a bit prone to it all happening rather suddenly, it seems to me.'

'No, I'm not. It's just coincidence. You know very well that I hadn't been near a man for ages until recently.' Indignation carried Catriona's voice into a high treble. 'I was beginning to think celibacy might be a permanent state. It might be preferable even now.'

'Oh yes?' Alison sounded cynical. 'And what about this actor? After Hamish go straight to Andro—do not pass Go, do not collect two hundred pounds. Not too much sign of celibacy there.'

'You make me seem like some sort of *femme fatale*,' cried Catriona, half-vexed, half-amused. 'It wasn't like that, honestly. Hamish was over. I'd made up my mind. It's just that I hadn't told him yet.' Now that she'd started, the whole process of telling Alison had become easier.

'And then you ran away to Skye. So where did Andro materialise from?'

'I'd met him the week before, in Glendoran when I went to set up a loan. His folks live there and he was in the pub I stayed at. We just got talking. Then he turned up at the Fife Point-to-point and finally he followed me to

343

Skye. It all seemed rather flattering and he's so different from Hamish, not rich or possessive.'

'Tell me,' prompted Alison shrewdly, 'is he a bit dishy?'

Catriona grinned and blushed. 'Knock-out, drop-dead dishy,' she confirmed. 'Eat-your-heart-out-Hugh-Grant dishy.'

'And he's definitely dish of the day?'

'Yes, and hopefully for a good deal longer—but it's all much more complicated than that,' wailed Catriona, suddenly rather glad she had confided in Alison. Perhaps if she explained her dilemma to her friend she might begin to come to grips with it herself.

Alison shivered and jumped down off the branch. 'Let's walk again, Cat. I'm frozen. If there are complications I think I'll have to take them on the move.'

Round the next bend the river flowed over a weir into a dell of some width, site of the ancient village of Dean where, before steam and electricity, industries had been powered by the fast-running steam; first flour mills and then bakers sending bread in cartloads up to the walled city of Edinburgh, and then tanneries and dyeworks supplying leather and cloth for the growing population. Nowadays however, Dean village was a hidden residential corner favoured by artists, students and Bohemians.

Where the glen narrowed, a famous Telford bridge spanned the gorge on hundred-foot-high arches which still carried traffic on the main route north. Rather than continuing along the river-path under the bridge, the two girls began to thread their way through the closes and courtyards of the village where it clung to the side of the valley.

'It seems to me that your first move should be to tell Hamish the bitter truth—and the sooner the better.' Alison's tone did not imply that she considered it bitter at all but exceedingly sweet.

Catriona shook her head. 'That's where the complication lies,' she said unhappily, and she began to tell Alison all about Precipitous City Productions and the film and Hamish's agreement to top up the funding.

'Rollicking Rembrandts!' exclaimed Alison when the tale was told. 'You don't do things by halves, do you, Cat? When you drop yourself in the mire you do it to the tune of a million pounds. Some style!'

'I hope I'm not in the mire,' returned Catriona stiffly. 'I've only got to get through this rather awkward meeting tomorrow and then I can talk to Hamish and tell him exactly how I feel. But if I do it before that he's likely to back out of the film deal, which apart from anything else, I believe is a thumpingly good one.'

'It's all a bit turgid though, Cat, isn't it?' observed Alison. 'Why on earth did you have to get personally involved in the film at all? You could have just flung Andro and Hamish together and let them get on with it.'

'Well, I know it looks that way but Hamish took against Andro as soon as he met him at the point-to-point and that was because of me. I want to help Andro—why shouldn't I? But I also

345

genuinely believe that this is a perfect investment for Hamish and I am his bank manager now. I'm involved up to my neck from every angle and somehow I've got to play all sides to the middle without cocking it up.' They had reached the steep cobbled lane which led up the brae to the main road and they bent to the hill, hands in pockets.

'You're taking a lot on your shoulders,' Alison warned, puffing slightly. 'Supposing the film's a complete flop?'

'I haven't deceived Hamish about that possibility. He's aware of all the risks. The only thing he doesn't know about is Andro's involvement both with the film and with me. And I'm going to tell him on Friday, honestly.'

Alison looked long and hard at her friend and shook her head. 'I wouldn't be in your shoes then, my girl. I think you've grabbed a tiger by the tail.'

Catriona turned troubled silver eyes on her friend. 'What else could I do? The deadline for the film was the end of this week. A lot of hopes and careers ride on it—and Hamish was the one chance they had. I couldn't let it go, could I?'

'I don't know, Cat. It sounds to me as if your own career could be on the line if things go wrong. John would have a fit if he knew what was going on.'

'Well, this time you're not to tell him anything, Ally,' said Catriona urgently. 'Not until next week, anyway.'

'OK, OK. I just hope this Andro guy

346

appreciates what you've done, that's all,' added Alison. 'And who's this character coming up from London with the contract?'

'A man called Rob Galbraith. I've never met him but I've spoken to him on the phone. He's a kind of specialist lawyer-accountant who works for a Completion Bond company.'

'What on earth is that? Don't tell me!' Alison giggled suddenly and put on a drawl and a swagger. 'My name's Bond—Completion Bond.'

Catriona laughed delightedly. 'Oh Alison, you're a tonic!' she cried, giving a little skip. 'I don't know why I didn't talk to you about all this before.' They emerged from the lane into the rush of traffic converging on the bridge. 'Brr! I'm absolutely frozen. Can we get a taxi back to the club?'

In the airport concourse Catriona smiled to herself as she remembered this riverside conversation. It had restored a little of her own self-belief and her affection for Alison, pregnant or not. Envy still lurked but without the accompanying antagonism.

The public address system gave its customary double-bong and broke in on her reverie. 'Would Miss Catriona Stewart please go to the Information Desk. Miss Catriona Stewart to the Information Desk, please!'

With a guilty start she glanced up at the flight indicator over her head. The Heathrow shuttle had landed ten minutes before. She had been in a daze and Rob Galbraith must have walked straight past her.

He was standing in the main concourse, a small black overnight bag at his feet. A man of some height—over six foot, broad-shouldered and with a straight back which gave him a slightly military bearing despite the civilian-conservative nature of his clothes—an impeccably cut charcoal-grey suit with a barely discernible pinstripe and a cream shirt with a discreetly figured tie in dark blue and red. His hair was the colour of ripe barley, a warm golden brown, thick and wavy, the waves flaxen-tipped as if he had been in the sun. His face, however, was not tanned but pale and smooth-shaven, the eyes candid and grey-blue, fringed with thick, dark lashes. An uncompromisingly straight nose dominated his features, balanced by a strong square chin and a mouth which held the hint of a smile even in repose. He looked what he was, a well-heeled city professional with access to a good tailor, a good barber and a good old-school network. Had her mind not been elsewhere when he passed her she would have recognised him easily.

He watched her as she almost ran to greet him, pale buff trenchcoat flying, revealing long black-stockinged legs stretching the kick-pleat of a short, tailored camel-hair skirt and a black tunic-sweater. Her burnished hair was dishevelled from her windy walk from the car park and she looked endearingly flustered, eyes huge and penitent, her even white teeth set wide in a contrite smile which made his heart miss a beat.

'I'm so sorry I missed you,' she said, shaking

his hand. 'I was waiting at the shuttle steps.'

'I noticed you there,' he told her, smiling in return. 'But you looked—unapproachable somehow. As if whoever it was you were meeting, it certainly wasn't me.'

She put her hand to her mouth in a gesture of remorse. 'Did I? Oh dear, I'm really terribly sorry. I'm not usually so vague but I've had a lot on my mind lately. Still, we've got together now so all's well. That was a good idea.'

He picked up his bag and looked at her quizzically. 'What was?'

'Going to the Information Desk. Perhaps we should have arranged it anyway. My car's in the short-term car park. It's not far to walk but you can't stop at the door here any more even for five minutes. Security, I suppose. Did you have a good flight?' She had a notion that she was gabbling but couldn't stop herself.

He strode beside her, bending politely in her direction to catch her words. 'Fine, thanks. The usual cocktail-run crush, but OK.'

'Did you have one?'

'What? Oh, a cocktail. No. I thought I'd leave that until after our meeting.'

She looked at her watch as the automatic doors opened to let them out of the long airport building and on to the pavement that led to the car park. 'We've plenty of time. The meeting isn't until eight and it should only take twenty minutes to get into town.'

'Might take a bit longer, as it's Thursday.'

'Of course, late-night shopping. How did you know?'

'Isn't it the same everywhere on Thursdays? But I'm often in Edinburgh, as I told you. As a matter of fact, my parents live here.'

'I see. So you'll be able to stay with them tonight?' They had reached the car and Catriona operated the central-locking device.

He opened the hatchback and put his bag inside before climbing into the passenger seat. 'No, not tonight,' he said smoothly. 'I've booked in at the George. It's only a flying visit and I won't have time to see them properly. I'll be up again next week anyway, for Easter.'

'Well, I'll take you to check in at the George first, then. It's not far from where our meeting is.' Catriona drove out of the car park into the silver gloom of the April twilight. The road surface was wet but the shower of rain had passed leaving only a haze of wheel-spray to necessitate the use of the intermittent windscreen wipe. The sound of it punctuated their conversation, lending it a flow it would not otherwise have possessed.

'You still haven't told me where that is—but let me guess.' Rob turned his head to look at her. 'How about a penthouse office on Queen Street?'

A slight swerve of the Golf's wheels betrayed her surprise. 'Yes. Right first time. Have you been there before?'

'Once,' he told her. 'I was involved with an arts trust and went to a reception there. Hamish Melville, right?'

She gave a short laugh. 'Absolutely right. Ten out of ten for deduction.'

He grinned, not yet prepared to reveal his sources. 'Just a brilliant brain. How did you get involved with Hamish Melville?'

Catriona wished he had used a different turn of phrase but replied readily enough. 'I'm his bank manager.'

'Oh yes, you told me. Steuart and Company.'

'Do you know it?' she enquired.

'Only relatively speaking. My father is the Chairman.'

'What!?' This time the swerve was more pronounced. She straightened up rather shame-facedly and checked in her mirror. The following car was fortunately a good distance back. 'Sorry, I didn't mean to give you a fright. I'm just a bit amazed. I've never registered Lord Nevis's family name. It just says Viscount Nevis, KT on the bank's headed notepaper.'

He chuckled. 'KT for Killing Time.'

'I thought it was short for Knight of the Thistle—it's a great honour, isn't it?'

'Yes, it is, of course. It's a family joke that it stands for Killing Time—till he inherits the title, you know.'

'Then he'll be Earl of Lochaber?'

'He's just called Lochaber—chief of Clan Galbraith. We aim to confuse people in the weird and wonderful world of the aristocracy. We're all Galbraiths, but my father is Nevis and my grandfather is Lochaber. It's quite simple when you know how.'

'I've met your grandfather,' she revealed. 'I went to his workshop up at Glendoran.'

'Did you?' He looked pleased. 'I bet he liked

you. He's always had an eye for a pretty face.'

She frowned. 'He seemed more interested in my background than my face. Said I shouldn't have left Skye and ought to think about having babies and fulfilling my obligation to my homeland. He gave me a clock he'd made—or rather he lent it to me. It's of rowan wood and is supposed to have magic powers. I'm to give it back when I've learned how precious time is.'

A burst of laughter greeted this story. 'I'm sorry,' Rob said breathlessly, 'but he really is an old rogue. Did he say all that at first meeting?'

'All that and more. He has very fixed views about duty and loyalty, hasn't he?'

'Oh yes, he's quite a political animal in his own inimitable style. Still, at least he practises what he preaches.'

'He doesn't seem to have persuaded his family to follow suit though.'

Rob gave a little shrug. 'Removing our talents from our roots, you mean? Well, it may look that way, and certainly with my father it is that way but he hasn't lost all hope of me.'

'What, you mean you don't see yourself staying in London for ever?'

'God, no! I couldn't stand it.'

She smiled. 'You look pretty citified if you don't mind my saying so.'

'Do I? Of course, looks can be deceptive. Shall I tell you what I've observed about you?'

'That's turning the tables a bit, isn't it?' she objected. 'You hardly know me.' When he raised an eyebrow she had the grace to demur. 'OK. I started it. Go on then.'

'You're very nervous about this meeting.' He looked at her candidly but she kept her eyes on the road. The windscreen wiper squeaked over dry glass and she switched it off mechanically.

She was not sure how to respond. 'Not at all,' she contradicted him unconvincingly. 'It's only a formality.'

He nodded. 'Yes, it should be, but for some reason you're twitchy about it and I think, since I'm going with you, I ought to know why.' He deliberately withheld the fact that he had seen her with Hamish in London and that he suspected their relationship was more than purely business. He wondered if she would tell him.

She turned left off the main road, taking a back route through the city centre. Tall, imposing Edwardian tenements hemmed them in, some with lighted windows where people had settled down at home for the evening, others, converted to offices, dark and empty.

'It's nothing sinister,' she told him cautiously. 'I've just never handled a deal quite like it, that's all. You're probably used to mega-movie budgets but they're a novelty to me, and to Mr Melville. I just want it all to go smoothly.'

They halted at a junction. Straight ahead, the floodlit façade of St Mary's Episcopal Cathedral passed silent moral judgment on her half-truths.

'I see,' Rob commented flatly.

'You have yet to see the view from my office,

Catriona,' remarked Hamish after he'd been introduced to Rob and the three of them were seated around a table.

Picasso's blue Columbine gazed down the room with her black, knowing eyes which Catriona found she could not meet. She felt highly uncomfortable in this location, seeing it for the first time under full illumination. It was airy and spacious, the grand expanse of thick, cream carpet seeming to mock her, shouting of her first crazy coitus with Hamish and magnifying an overall impression of aesthetic opulence. The furniture was modern and minimal, making much use of glass, chrome and pale, champagne-coloured leather and there was an apparent absence of electronic business aids, but Catriona guessed that a series of blond polished-wood panels beside the limed-oak desk concealed every possible high-tech invention indispensable to the modern entrepreneur.

'There is quite a spectacular view from here,' Hamish went on to explain to Rob, 'across to Fife.'

'Remarkable though the outlook may be,' replied Rob politely, gesturing towards the picture on the wall above them, 'it surely wouldn't divert one's attention from that.'

'My Columbine,' nodded Hamish with satisfaction. 'She is quite special, isn't she? I must say she brings me great pleasure.' Despite her best efforts Catriona found herself blushing at his double meaning. 'But you've seen it before, haven't you?' For a nerve-racking moment she thought Hamish was addressing her and glanced at him in alarm but he was still looking at Rob, a slight frown creasing his brow. 'I seldom forget a face but I can't quite recall the occasion...'

Rob nodded approvingly. 'You have a good memory, Mr Melville. It was about three years ago. You held a reception for the Trustees of the Caledonian Gallery. I was on the board at the time—a very junior member.'

'Ah yes, I remember. So you're an art-lover, Mr Galbraith?' Hamish glanced at Catriona. 'We all have something in common then. Perhaps we could dispense with the formality and get on to first-name terms? Catriona and I achieved that very quickly, didn't we?'

She nodded and smiled obligingly but said nothing. Regrettably there was so much that was unspoken between herself and Hamish.

'Please, call me Rob,' agreed he of that name.

'And I am Hamish. Is your name short for Robert, like the Bruce?'

'No. It's Robaidh. It's Gaelic and it looks much more formal than it sounds.' He spelled it out. 'But when it's spoken it sounds like Robbie, which in London is a bit heathery. So I stick to Rob.' He unzipped the leather document-holder he had laid on the table in front of him, withdrew several sheets of thick cream paper and glanced up. 'Shall we get down to business?'

'By all means,' agreed Hamish.

Ten minutes later he had read through the contract which Rob had prepared and pulled a heavy gold pen from his inside jacket pocket.

'Do I sign each page or just the last one?'

'Each page please, where the pencil crosses are,' explained Rob. He turned to Catriona. 'I take it you have the money draft?'

From her briefcase she extracted a large parchment envelope bearing the red and gold Steuart & Company logo. On the enclosed pro-forma an impressive number of zeros was visible in the payment-box.

Hamish glanced briefly at the draft and then at Catriona. 'I am relying entirely on your judgment in this matter,' he murmured softly. 'I trust it lives up to expectations.' With a small, theatrical flourish he signed.

Rob handed Hamish his copy of the contract and tucked the money draft into his briefcase before offering his right hand to the tycoon. 'All parties hope for great things from the film,' he declared enthusiastically. 'But I'm sure Catriona has impressed on you the nature of the risk you have taken.'

Hamish shook the proffered hand briefly. 'Indeed she has,' he agreed, turning to Catriona. He held on to her hand for an appreciatively longer period and said enigmatically, 'You're fully aware of the nature of the deal, aren't you, Catriona?'

With sinking heart she withdrew her hand. 'I'm convinced the investment will be of advantage to both sides,' she said steadily, 'And I look forward to seeing the finished product.'

'Hear, hear!' declared Hamish, rising and striding to the deceptively blank wall beside his desk. 'This calls for champagne.' Pressure on a particular panel caused it to slide open, revealing a small fridge. From this he removed a distinctive green and gold bottle. 'I'm sorry that I have another dinner engagement, but at least we can drink to *Catriona's* success.'

'The girl or the film?' enquired Rob with a curious smile.

'Why not both?' offered Hamish as he popped the cork. 'As far as I'm concerned, they're both worth a million.'

The topaz liquid fizzed into the flutes and Rob raised an eyebrow at Catriona. Worth a million? Did he know half of what this girl had to hide? he wondered, and wished the slate could be clean.

They parted company in the office foyer, Hamish whispering to Catriona when Rob was sufficiently distant, 'I have a surprise, as promised. I'll be round at six-thirty tomorrow.'

Rob marked the communication though he could not hear the words. As the lift descended he asked mildly, 'You're not *just* his bank manager, are you?'

Catriona felt her stomach lurch violently, not entirely due to the sudden deceleration of the lift as it halted at the ground floor. 'It's a long story,' she said unhappily, stepping out into the main entrance hall of the building.

'Well, I don't necessarily expect to hear it but will you dine with me anyway?' He gazed at her appealingly. 'You'd be saving me from a lonely evening.'

'Well—all right. I'd love to. Thank you.' As

she said it she realised that she meant it. She liked his businesslike air and his kind smile and there was something attractive about spending time with someone who knew nothing of her self-inflicted problems.

Out on Queen Street she said suddenly, 'What about Isabel and Andro? We must tell them about the money. They'll be hanging over the telephone.'

'Yes, of course they will. But let's drop this draft into a night safe first,' Rob suggested, tapping his breast pocket. 'Then we'll go to the George and phone.'

The Clydesdale Bank on the corner of Hanover Street was closed and dark but they paused in the shelter of the pillared entrance while Rob filled in a deposit envelope and operated the night-safe chute with a satisfying clunk. The million-pound draft disappeared on the first stage of its journey into the electronic whirlpool which would eventually debit it from Hamish's funds and credit it to Precipitous City Productions. With her mind on tomorrow's date with Hamish, Catriona fervently wished she could post her personal life into a similar computerised sorting system.

Isabel toyed with a plate of lasagne and stared anxiously at Andro over the kitchen table. 'Do you really think the meeting's going OK?' she asked for the fourth time. 'I'm sure they should have rung by now.'

Andro was tucking blithely into his meal, apparently without nerves or worries. 'Don't fuss, Izzy darling. As I said, they're probably popping champagne corks and forgetting to put us out of our misery. Rob will have it all under control.'

'I wish I had your confidence,' Isabel said gloomily. 'God, Andro, if this falls apart that's it. We've no chance of ever making the film.'

Andro looked pained. 'Look—a fortnight ago we had no chance anyway. This was a last-ditch stand and it looks like it's going to pay off. We'd be twice as gloomy now if I hadn't gone up to Skye.'

'How do you feel about Catriona?' Isabel asked sharply. 'She's going to think you're a pretty big shit after this, you know.'

Andro's fork hovered in mid-air. 'Yes...I'll have to confess pretty soon, I suppose. It's not as if I declared undying love or anything.' He looked only mildly troubled about his perfidy, a bit like a guilty schoolboy caught smoking in the toilet, not regretting having done it but regretting being caught.

'She must think quite a lot of you though, or she wouldn't have approached Hamish Melville. I don't believe you feel even a twinge of remorse,' Isabel accused him indignantly. 'Perhaps you don't want to end it.'

A withering look greeted this sally. 'Don't be daft, Izzy! It's not like you to be jealous. You know what I am—no one knows better. That's why we're so good together.'

Isabel made a face. 'I hadn't expected her to be so beautiful. You *must* fancy her. Any man would.'

Andro chuckled. 'Well, of course I fancy her. I couldn't have done it at all if I didn't. What do you think I am—a stud?'

'You can give a pretty good impression of one,' Isabel sniffed. Her long face looked meltingly mournful, like a high-bred hound waiting for the scent. 'So you haven't fallen in love with her?'

'No.' Andro grinned sheepishly, put down his fork and reached out his hand to cover hers, so restless on the table. 'You're the one for me, Izzy. You know that—however much I stray. We're a pair, you and I, and we're going to make the most brilliant film to come out of Britain in years.'

Isabel allowed a small smile to illuminate her dark face briefly. 'You're all talk, Andro Lindsay. All cock and bull. No woman should ever trust you.'

At that moment the telephone rang. Andro was first to his feet to pluck the receiver from the wall-set. 'Rob? It's in the bag? Oh, in the bank. Even better! Good man. Yes, I'll tell Isabel. No, we've just eaten. You go ahead. We'll join you for a drink afterwards if you like. At the George, OK. About ten. Brother, you're a star! Give my love to Catriona.' He made a face at Isabel as he said this. 'We'll see you later.'

'Now for the third degree,' said Rob with determination, elbows on the table and brow creased enquiringly at her. 'What secret power does Hamish Melville have over his high-powered bank manager?' They were in the hotel restaurant, cosily ensconced at a corner table between two square, fluted pillars. Only four other tables were occupied.

'Excuse me?' she responded, softening her negative reaction with a smile. 'I feel bound to point out that this has nothing to do with you or with the contract.'

'You're right, I'm sorry,' he agreed amiably, smacking the back of his hand in self-chastisement. 'I'm unforgivably inquisitive. My mother always told me it would be my undoing.'

'I like your mother. She very kindly invited me to a splendid dinner party and we played party games.'

'Not that awful guessing game?' Rob sank his head in his hands. 'Sometimes I despair of my parents.' He raised his eyes to look at Catriona. 'She likes you too. She told me.'

'So you knew who I was all the time!' she cried indignantly.

'Yes, I'm afraid I did. And I have another confession.' Rob told her about seeing her in the Rolls with Hamish outside the Adelphi Theatre.

She bit her lip and stared at the tablecloth. 'What did your mother say about that?' she asked dully.

'She didn't seem too happy. Said it was all her fault for seating you next to Hamish Melville at dinner.'

'Did she?' Catriona was amazed. 'But she can't have approved.'

'No, she didn't—but not how you think,' he

grinned teasingly. 'For some reason she thought you were much too good for the likes of him.'

'What a broadminded mother you have,' she marvelled. 'Funnily enough mine expressed similar feelings—but then you expect it of your own mother somehow. And they've both got it wrong. It's me who's doing the dirty on Hamish, not the other way around.'

'How do you make that out?'

He seemed so sympathetic and approachable this stranger, sitting there, stalwart as the pillar against which his chair was placed, so she told him. She told him the whole story, about Hamish, about Andro and about the million-pound dilemma and she was astonished to see that he went quite pale as her story progressed. Not pale from anger or shock but pale like someone made nauseous by a nasty smell.

'So, there you are,' she concluded lamely, glad to have got it off her chest and thinking that whatever had caused him to look that way at least he could always go back to London and forget all about her. 'I know I sound like the most awful *femme fatale* but actually I'm more of a *femme stupide!*'

At this moment the waiter came to take their order and Rob, for one, was extremely grateful for the diversion. By the time they'd ordered the *hors d'oeuvre,* steaks and Burgundy his pallor had disappeared and he'd had time to consider his response. He hoped to God that she meant it when she said that the film seemed an excellent investment and that she hadn't only approached Hamish for Andro's sake, because if she had she was in even more of a mess than she knew. Bloody Andro. He was a liability in any woman's life, including that of the long-suffering Isabel.

'I wouldn't for a moment agree that you were stupid,' he contradicted her stoutly. 'I shouldn't think anyone is in a position to cast the first stone when it comes to affairs of the heart.'

'That's just it,' Catriona concurred. 'I don't think my heart ever really logged-in to the affair with Hamish.' She found herself blushing because of what this implied and hastened to add, 'Somehow relationships, however intense, don't seem worthwhile without some sort of cardiac involvement.'

'Well, I tend to think that way myself, but I've always been told I'm an old-fashioned sentimentalist,' remarked Rob somewhat sheepishly. 'By Andro in particular.'

'Andro? Why Andro?' she asked with surprise. 'Do you know him well?'

'Yes. I should do—he's my brother.' That much he could tell her, he thought. It might well be enough. She was intelligent; it wouldn't take her long to work it all out for herself.

'Your brother! How on earth...' Catriona clamped her lips shut as her voice rose inadvertently to a squawk.

If Rob hadn't been so concerned about that very brother's behaviour towards Catriona he might have found the situation quite funny. But during her telling of the story it had become dreadfully clear to him that his devil brother had deliberately deceived and seduced her in order to win his way to Hamish's million pounds. Andro was a villain but how could he, Rob, bear to reveal his brother's villainy to this gorgeous, gullible girl? She would end up hating both of them.

'Andro and I are so unalike that sometimes I have wondered if my beloved mother might possibly have strayed with a thespian,' he confided wryly. 'Although I suppose that's rather an unworthy thought for a son to have.'

'Yes, it is, very unworthy,' she commented, smiling. 'But I do see what you mean. You don't seem one iota alike.'

'Elaborate, please,' he demanded as their *hors d'oeuvre* arrived. Perhaps he could keep her mind from too much analysis of the past for the time being.

'Well, he is impulsive and carefree and vivid,' she began, carefully picking her words, 'and, from what I can tell, you are resourceful and thoughtful and calm.'

'For which also read cautious and boring and dull,' he grimaced. 'I get the message.'

'No. No, that's not what I said and it's certainly not what I meant,' she retorted, wagging an admonitory finger whilst trying to work the pepper-mill, which resulted in a violent fit of sneezing.

Rob laughed and poured her some water from a jug on the table. 'Here—have a drink.'

'There you are, you see,' she said when she could speak. 'Resourceful, thoughtful and calm.'

They tackled their food in silence for a few minutes.

'Andro obviously didn't tell you about me,' Rob remarked casually.

Catriona looked pensive. 'No, he didn't. But then I suppose there was really no reason why he should.'

But now, the more she thought about it, the more she realised that there was every reason why he should *not*. For if Rob was Andro's brother, that also made Andro Lord Nevis's son and Lochaber's grandson. So when they met in Glendoran he had been staying with his grandfather and he had deliberately deceived her about this from their very first meeting. But why? Surely through his family connections he had as much access to rich and influential people as she had? Nevertheless, for some reason which might not reflect well on his reputation with his own kind, he had needed an intermediary through whom to reach the wealthy clients of the bank. Finding her at the point-to-point with Hamish had revealed to him the identity of one client eminently suitable for his purposes. Had following her to Skye then simply been the next stage in a carefully orchestrated plan? A plan which had come to fruition this very evening when the banker's draft dropped into the night safe?

With growing uneasiness Rob watched her gradually stop eating as the cogs began to mesh. He was almost expecting the next question.

'Are Isabel and Andro really only friends?' she asked hoarsely. She could hardly get the words out, so dry was her throat. The unpalatable truth about Andro's pursuit of her had just dawned on her and the food she had consumed thus far suddenly sat like gall in her gullet.

'Well, yes, they are friends, and colleagues as well—but they also live together.' He gazed at her seriously, wishing he didn't have to tell her, feeling her distress. 'I mean, they share a pillow and a duvet and a tooth-mug, whatever else they may pretend.'

'Oh God. I've been such an idiot!' Catriona wailed aloud before clamping her hand over her mouth to stifle the sound, staring wide-eyed at Rob over her fingers. The entire structure of Andro's plan was now agonisingly clear. A man at the next table turned to see where the unexpected noise had come from and hastily turned back as he saw tears begin to slide down Catriona's cheeks. She flicked them away and stood up. 'Excuse me a moment, please,' she whispered and made a dash for the corner of the restaurant where the Ladies room was situated.

In its pastel-peach interior she felt her high hopes and ardent aspirations dissolve, not in tears of self-pity but in waves of remorse. True, she had been duped and deceived by Andro but it was no more than she deserved.

For in much the same way she, too, had duped and deceived Hamish. She was hoist with her own petard! No one would have any sympathy for a stupid fool who had gambolled into Andro's trap like a spring lamb to the slaughter, since at the same time she had

366

been using a similar bait herself. It was pure justice, she told herself miserably, using reams of loo-roll to mop and blow. But it was rough justice and God, did it hurt!

Rob sat unhappily at the table, nodding agreement when the waiter came to take away the remains of the *hors d'oeuvre* and suggesting that he wait until the lady returned before bringing the steaks. 'But you can pour the wine,' he told him, thinking that Catriona might need it. He would have liked to comfort her, to soothe away her misery, but he was not so foolish as to imagine that she would let any man through her guard again at this present juncture, especially Andro's brother!

Fourteen

The ubiquitous Minto was driving the Melvilles back from dinner in town. 'When are you fetching Max home?' asked Hamish sleepily. They'd had a less than exciting evening with the Chairman of one of Edinburgh's largest pension funds. Attendance had been a necessary but tedious chore and Hamish had drunk more than he usually did.

'Minto and I are driving south tomorrow and I'm flying back with Max from Gatwick. Minto will drive his trunk up on Saturday.'

Hamish was suddenly not so sleepy. 'I thought you were all driving back on Saturday,' he said.

'We were, but Max gets so car-sick these days, poor boy, I thought I'd just bring him up on a plane,' remarked Linda. 'Minto doesn't mind driving back alone, do you Minto? Anyway it will give us Saturday to do some shopping for Max's new skiing gear. Don't forget we're leaving on Sunday.' The Easter holiday would be spent in Zermatt, in the shadow of the Matterhorn. Skiing was a favourite with all three of them.

Hamish remained moodily silent for several minutes. 'What's the matter?' Linda asked at length. 'You won't be out tomorrow night, will you? You wouldn't disappoint Max on the first night of his holidays, surely?'

Hamish grunted with annoyance. 'No, I won't. But I may have to join you a bit later in Zermatt. Something has come up.'

Eyes narrowed, Linda leaned close so that Minto should not hear. 'Or perhaps something will be coming down,' she murmured with deliberate vulgarity. 'Like someone's knickers, for instance?' Since the incident at the ball she had, as yet, been unable to lure Hamish back to her side of the bed and knowing his voracious sexual appetite she assumed he must be getting it elsewhere—but with whom?

Hamish pushed her away angrily. Although he had rejected the idea of divorce he had not forgiven her for making him look a fool in front of others. 'I may be a bit late tomorrow, but I'll be home for dinner with the boy,' he said gruffly.

He disliked having to change his plans but

reasoned that from Sunday at least, with Linda and Max safely away in Zermatt, he and Catriona could party at their leisure. In his present state of inebriation, when he closed his eyes he could picture her slim, white body and leonine mane, her silver eyes gleaming and lustrous. It had been *so* long! He had this urgent, erotic desire to bonk her for days in some luxurious hotel room. That she might deny him never crossed his mind. He saw only a simple equation. If he had just slipped her a million pounds, their sex should be sensational!

In the dim light of her sitting-room lamp, Catriona stared mutinously at the rowan clock. 'I wish I'd never met you or any of your bloody family, my noble lord!' she swore at the timepiece, as if it were its maker.

In her jaundiced mood the clock seemed to represent the whole miserable midden her life had become, with Galbraiths cast as chief culprits. With the scorn of the deceived she saw them collectively as having no scruples, playing host to a foul-minded clique which revelled in crude party games and condoned nefarious deals and sordid affairs. And since joining Steuart's and moving into the Nevis orbit she had become just such a monster herself—no better than the eccentric Earl, the unprincipled Lord Chairman, his scandalmongering wife and the devious, scheming Andro. It was tempting to consider Rob an exception but when push came to shove he was likely to be just as bad as the rest. After all, it was he who had urged Andro to find the million pounds, by whatever means available. He must have known his perfidious, double-dealing brother would use unethical tactics. They both sprang from the same privileged, manipulative, immoral social set, without conscience or probity.

Nor did she excuse herself from this general moral castigation. She recognised that she had treated Hamish no better than Andro had treated her—used him blatantly and without compunction to achieve her own ends. All the money, charm and glamour in the world could not disguise the fact that she and the whole self-seeking circle in which she presently moved were a bunch of graceless, grasping, hedonistic barbarians—all tarred with the same brush and all a complete waste of time! Angrily she ripped the clock off the wall and shoved it into a drawer.

Ironically, she thought, it was Hamish who came out of all this smelling, if not actually of roses, of something rather more wholesome than the rest. At least when he did a deal he made no secret of being out for what he could get. Her only consolation was that now she could not be accused of partiality. Whatever shenanigans surrounded its financing she, as an informed outsider, believed the film to be an exciting investment and she could look Hamish in the eye and say so. It was no longer necessary to admit any relationship with Precipitous City Productions or any of its employees because there was none. She had successfully juggled her way through her dilemma, but at what cost to herself? And to everyone concerned?

The thought of Hamish exacerbated her sense of gloom. Her distress over finding Andro a rope of sand had not altered her feelings towards the entrepreneur. The little Uig landscape mocked her from the wall. 'You accepted me,' it told her, 'just as you accepted a million pounds on behalf of Precipitous City Productions.' It was reasonable to think that when Hamish came tomorrow he would expect something in return and this time she would have to face the music. There could be no running away to Skye...

'I knew you were a selfish bastard, Andro, but I never knew just how bloody unscrupulous you really are,' snarled Rob.

His brother and Isabel had strolled languidly into the bar of the George, a long, panelled room with dark mahogany tables and sober blue carpets and upholstery. It was a place where grey-suited executives met to whet their appetites with dry martinis. Andro's extrovert dishevelment and Isabel's studied grunge looked weirdly out of place in such surroundings.

'Where's Catriona?' asked Andro, sitting down and pretending to ignore his brother's forthright condemnation. Isabel took the chair opposite, saying nothing. The room was quiet at this hour. There were only a few couples seated at other tables and three men perched on stools around the mirrored bar.

'Catriona has put two and two together and made a very unpalatable four. But then she's a banker, she's good at sums,' replied Rob coldly.

371

'What the hell did you tell her?' asked Andro with a flash of anger.

'I merely told her that you were my brother and that you and Isabel were an item. And since she knew one or two salient facts about me, like who my father and grandfather are and therefore how closely connected you are to the bank and Glendoran, she didn't take very long to calculate just what a manipulative, conniving, deceiving bastard of a brother you are.'

Rob turned to the waiter who had approached the table with a bottle in an ice-bucket and three champagne glasses. 'Thank you,' he said politely, waiting until the man had popped the cork and poured two glassfuls before putting his hand over the third glass. 'No, I won't thanks. I'm not celebrating.'

The waiter replaced the bottle in the bucket and retired. Andro defiantly picked up the two full glasses and handed one to Isabel. 'Well, we're celebrating, aren't we, Izzy?' he declared. 'Here's to Precipitous City's first film—and to a long and prosperous cinematic future!'

As they chinked glasses and drank Rob observed dryly, 'I could agree with all that if the foundations of that future had not been built on such a load of shit.'

It was Isabel's turn to flare. 'For Christ's sake, Rob, don't be such a hypocrite. You told us we needed another million and Andro went out and got it. End of story.'

'It may be the end of your story, Isabel, but it's the start of disillusion and self-doubt for Catriona. You know Andro better than anyone.

He's the consummate conman. He could sell ice to an Eskimo. But he *could* have played this particular role with some compassion. He didn't have to go and make the poor girl fall in love with him.'

'Did she?' enquired Andro, preening slightly. 'The silly Cat! It was only a bit of a fling—the tangle o' the isle and all that.'

'Tangle? You made it a bloody labyrinth! You lied to her mother and father, you took their food and lodging and you trampled all over Catriona's roots. But the worst of it is that she not only believed in you, she believed in your project and pursued it on your behalf. And you let her!'

'Well, she shows great taste,' remarked Andro, taking another gulp of champagne. 'Look Rob, I know I hooked her on a worm instead of a fly but it was in a good cause. She'll get over it and meanwhile lots of excellent British actors and skilled technicians will see their talents put to good use as a result. I'm sorry but I can't grieve too much when there's so much to crow about.' He leaned over to pluck the bottle out of the bucket. 'Now calm down, brother, have a drink and come down off your high moral horse's arse.'

Rob scowled and stood up. 'No. Leave me out of it. I'm going to bed. I just wish you'd seen the misery in the face of the girl I saw off in a taxi only half an hour ago.' He withdrew a bulky envelope from his jacket pocket and threw it down on the table. 'Here's your Completion Bond. Relish it, for it's the last help you'll get out of me. And enjoy your drink—you're paying for it!'

As he swung on his heel and marched out of the bar he could still picture Catriona's tight, pinched face framed in the window of the taxi. He wondered what she was doing now.

'I really thought he cared for me, you know,' she had told Rob when she eventually emerged from the Ladies. 'I know he never said it in so many words, but we got on so well, I just assumed...I can't believe it was all acting.'

Rob had watched her struggle to consume a quarter of her steak before abandoning the attempt. 'It's no consolation, I'm sure, but you are not alone,' he told her kindly. 'Audiences in their millions have been convinced by my brother's performances. He may be a first-class bastard but he is also pretty good at his job.'

Hamish stormed into the bedroom clutching a glossy magazine. 'What the hell is this?' he yelled in white-heat rage, thrusting it under Linda's nose as she prepared to get into bed.

On the cover the word *Introductions* was printed in large white letters on a red banner, beneath which was a full-length photograph of himself and Linda standing rather self-consciously in their conservatory, a riotously flowering pink camellia between them and a caption across their feet which read *'Melville Marriage Flourishes as Tycoon Forgives and Forgets.'*

'How the fuck did they get that line?' he thundered, beginning to flick violently through the pages to find the inside story.

Linda sat stock-still on the edge of the bed. She had hoped to conceal the new edition of the magazine until Max was at home, thinking that Hamish might contain his anger if his son was in the house. But he must have had it specially delivered. Perhaps Minto...? Yes, that would be it. Minto must have got him a copy and left it in his study. She should have checked!

'Yes, quite the investigative journalists, aren't they?' she remarked as calmly as she could, although her heart was thudding with apprehension. 'They must have had a tip-off. Normally they couldn't dig out a story if it was buried under the editor's potted palm.'

'Who told them?' he insisted furiously.

'I rather think we need look no further than Victoria Moncreiffe,' continued his wife. 'This is the sort of thing that happens when a woman finds herself rejected and broke. For the right price she'll always kiss and tell.'

'Only in this case it was you who was doing the kissing!' Hamish's flinty blue eyes were flicking over the printed page with manic intensity. 'And I am cast as the "magnanimously merciful magnate". Jesus, this makes me look a complete nerd!'

'On the contrary, you emerge as the soul of compassion and Christian principle.'

'In my book that means a bloody doormat,' he growled darkly, unmollified. 'Christ, if any bastard thinks he's going to wipe his feet all over me as a result of this, just let him try!'

'If you read the story carefully you'll discover

375

that they haven't really revealed any facts,' Linda observed, settling cautiously back against the pillows. Hamish's tempers made her nervous. 'Just a bit of gossip which you have been generous enough to overlook. In fact, it's a dreadful speculative piece of rubbish over which we could sue for libel.'

'We don't have libel in Scotland, you ignorant bitch,' snarled Hamish rudely, still reading. 'It's all slander—and it's only defamatory if it's not true. Thanks to you, this is no slander.' As he perused the final paragraph he slapped the shiny page with a sound like a pistol-shot, his face congested and ugly. 'It's bloody shite! You stupid cow—you fucked it up completely, didn't you!'

As if something had exploded in his head Hamish lost control. He rolled up the magazine and, without warning, began to use it as a club to belabour Linda about the head and shoulders, shouting ever more violent expletives. As the blows fell she cowered down in the bed, burrowing under the pillows for protection and, due to their padded shelter and his rather inaccurate aim, she survived the onslaught without visible damage.

It was over pretty quickly. When his ire abated Hamish hurled the offending magazine at Linda's precious collection of porcelain cats which were arranged on a window-shelf, smashing a number of them into smithereens. Then he marched out of the room, slamming the door.

Like many a wife in similar circumstances,

Linda blamed herself for the outbreak of domestic violence. Not that she repented the affair with Bruce or the attentions of *Introductions* but she chided herself for having let Hamish find the offending article at a time when he was 'tired and emotional'.

She dragged herself over to the scene of feline destruction and silently gathered the fragments of shattered porcelain into a waste-bin, then stumbled to the bathroom to run cold water and bathe her face. Without make-up she looked small and pathetic, the usually bright caramel eyes puffy and smeared. Picking up the discarded magazine on the way back to bed she tried to reread the offending article but the print blurred on the page as she fought back tears of self-pity.

In truth it was hardly damaging. If it had not been for the suggestion of a recent impropriety on Linda's part it would have been quite acceptable, even welcome at a time when Hamish's professional image was seriously dented by accusations of asset-stripping and takeover tyranny. The photographs were flattering and glamorous, showing the house and its owners to their best advantage and the copy, in every aspect other than the one passage of adulterous innuendo, was bland and irreproachable. Linda was hardly made out to be a scarlet woman, more a pale shade of pink.

'Bloody Victoria Moncreiffe,' she muttered indistinctly, letting the magazine fall to the floor. 'And bloody Charlie for keeping her so short of funds that she has to rat on her friends to make ends meet!'

For Catriona the agony of Friday morning at the bank was partially relieved by a phone call from Sue Carruthers to tell her that the whole family was now officially in residence at Glendoran Steading.

'I just thought you might be going to Skye for Easter and could stop over for a meal with us on the way up or down,' she said. 'Of course, it's still absolute chaos here but Nick has done wonders with the cottage. Besides, I'd like you to meet the boys. You can fill them in on life at a Highland High school.'

'Heavens, I can't remember—it's years since I left school. But how kind of you to think of me, only I'm not sure what my plans are yet. Can I let you know?' Catriona felt tears sting her eyes and blinked them back. She had barely slept and in her present state of nervous exhaustion, any kindness could trigger an emotional reaction.

'Yes, of course. Are you all right?' queried Sue, hearing the catch in Catriona's voice. 'You sound a bit—what's that wonderful Scottish expression I've learned?—peelie-wallie. Yes, that's it. You sound peelie-wallie.'

Catriona had to laugh. 'And you sound like my mother,' she retorted. 'I'm fine. How's the money lasting?'

'Oh, we're OK, thanks to your overdraft. But the bloody insurance still hasn't paid up. How long can they take, for God's sake?'

'Till hell freezes over, probably. Let me know

if you want to extend the facility, won't you?'

'Yes, don't worry, we won't sign any huge cheques without consulting the oracle.'

'There was an SFS attack in Argyll last week. I saw it in the *West Highland Free Press*. No sign of fresh activity in your area, I hope?'

'No, all seems quiet here. Nick has bought a dog, a great big Alsatian who's as soft as butter really but his bark is terrifying. I don't think they'll come back.'

'That was a good idea.'

'Yes, isn't Nick a clever old thing? I think I'll stick with him a little bit longer—even though we're sleeping in the kitchen. Don't forget about Easter. I'll wait to hear from you.'

Sue sounded buoyant and happy and a few hours of her company would be heartening, but Catriona was in two minds about going to Glendoran at Easter. There was always the possibility that Andro would be visiting his grandfather, and running into him would be mortifying. Outwardly, especially at work, she kept her upper lip good and stiff but inside she felt as wobbly as a half-set jelly.

Moira came back from lunch clutching a copy of *Introductions*. 'Have you seen this?' she asked, putting it down on the desk. 'Apparently Queen Linda has been having naughties and King Hamish is being magnanimous about it. It doesn't sound like him, somehow.'

Catriona grabbed the magazine and opened it at the appropriate page. Hamish and Linda gazed at her from an antique sofa in their 'gracious Georgian drawing room'.

'Does it say who she's been naughty with?' she asked, although if it had, Moira would have been full of Bruce's guilt.

'No, worse luck. It's all innuendo rather than information. Honestly, it's the most dreadful rag! They're always ducking the issue, making everyone seem whiter than white and purer than pure.'

'Well, no one would ever agree to appear in it if they didn't,' Catriona pointed out.

'The Melvilles do look terrific though, don't they?' trilled Moira, peering over Catriona's shoulder. 'And their house is an absolute gem! Look at all those antiques. Mummy will love reading this.'

Hamish's piercing blue gaze shafted out of the glossy pages at Catriona and made her stomach turn over. What on earth was she going to say to him when he turned up this evening, expecting to whisk her off to a romantic hideaway? How would he react when she told him she didn't want to go—that she couldn't go on seeing him? She had toyed with the idea of begging Alison to be there but had come to the conclusion that asking her was not fair. Alison must be going through enough emotional turmoil herself with her hormones hopping about in pregnant frenzy. She didn't need to witness her best friend being slagged off by a justifiably angry jilted lover.

Nothing turned out as Catriona expected. As she fiddled about in the flat, nervously awaiting Hamish's arrival, Elizabeth Nicholson phoned and her brisk Morningside tones seemed like a smattering of sanity in a mad world.

'I hope you don't mind me ringing you, dear,' the lady began when she had identified herself. 'I got your number from Felicity because it was so interesting meeting you at her dinner party. Do you remember?'

For a moment Catriona was nonplussed, but the penny dropped when she cast her mind back to Felicity's table and to an animated conversation with the rather formidable widow opposite. 'Yes, we talked about your charity—the children's hospice appeal. I remember very well.'

'I'm so glad. You seemed very interested at the time so I'm going to risk believing that you genuinely were and ask you a favour.' Elizabeth went on to remind her about the 'Jolly Hockey Sticks' committee and some of the fundraising events they had in train. 'But I was so taken with your ideas, my dear, that I wondered if you'd like to join us on the committee to explore them further? I'm allowed to co-opt people to work on specific events, you know.'

'Well, it was only an off-the-cuff conversation. I haven't given them much thought,' Catriona confessed aloud whilst speculating silently that, far from being 'allowed' to do anything, a woman like Elizabeth Nicholson probably ruled the committee with despotic zeal, telling everyone else exactly what *they* could or could not do and doing precisely as she liked herself. In some ways Catriona envied such decisiveness.

'That's why I want you to come on the committee, dear, so that we can all give them some more thought. What do you say?' Elizabeth didn't waste time with unnecessary flannel.

'When is the next meeting?' asked Catriona, caught off-guard.

She proved easy prey for a practised campaigner. 'It's tomorrow afternoon. Three-thirty at my house in Hermitage Drive. Number Ten. Shall we see you there? Do say yes.'

The doorbell rang and Catriona's stomach did a somersault. 'Y-yes. Yes...all right,' she stuttered in panic, hardly knowing what she said.

'Excellent! I hear your doorbell,' cooed Elizabeth happily, 'so I'll let you go. See you tomorrow. Goodbye.'

To Catriona's surprise when she opened the front door she found Hamish looking sheepish and clutching a bunch of red roses and a bottle of wine. 'Not a present—a peace-offering,' he said hastily, enfolding her in a bear-hug before thrusting the flowers into her hands. 'Because we can't go away tonight. I am so sorry.'

The apology was so effusive and she was so relieved at his words that Catriona was rendered speechless, staring at the roses and sniffing them to steady herself while he put down the wine and pulled off his overcoat. He was still in his business suit, a well-tailored double-breasted grey worsted with his usual immaculate cream silk shirt and designer tie. He did not look like a man about to embark on a wild and dirty weekend.

'Max is coming home today instead of tomorrow and I must have dinner with him tonight. I brought this for us to drown our sorrows.' He showed her the wine. It was a bottle of Pouilly Fumé of the same year and label as the one they had shared at their first meal alone together. 'It is cold,' he assured her. 'Shall I open it?'

'Yes,' she smiled and nodded. 'Yes, please. There's a corkscrew in the kitchen.'

'I've never been in the kitchen in your flat,' he remarked as he followed her through. 'We usually seem to go straight to the bedroom.' She said nothing to this but opened a drawer and took out a corkscrew. 'Believe me,' he grinned, twisting it vigorously, 'I would like to do that this time, but I want to talk to you and sadly we haven't time for both.'

Catriona put two glasses on the central table and watched as he poured the wine. 'What do you want to talk about?' she asked apprehensively.

'Us of course,' he said, lifting both glasses and handing her one. *'Slainthe.'*

'Slainthe,' she echoed mechanically. They both drank, eyes locked, silver and blue. 'Shall we take the wine through?' she asked.

He shook his head. 'No, let's sit here with the table between us and then I won't be tempted to pounce.'

She shrugged. 'OK. If you like,' she said and pulled out a chair.

'You don't seem very upset about not going away,' he observed, taking another chair. 'I thought you'd be looking forward to it. I know I was.'

Catriona flushed at his words and held her glass against her cheek to cool her hot skin. 'To tell you the truth, Hamish, I wasn't going to come,' she said in a rush, as if frightened that she might halt in mid-sentence. 'I haven't even packed a bag.'

'Why not? What's happened?' Hamish looked stricken.

She took a fortifying sip of wine. It was crisp and frivolous, tasting of sunlight and flowers, in direct contrast with the sudden sourness in the atmosphere. 'Nothing new has happened,' she said faintly. 'I have felt this way for some time now but I haven't had the courage to tell you.'

'What way?' he repeated sharply. 'Felt what way?'

'That we couldn't go on—that *I* couldn't go on—having an affair with a married man who has a nine-year-old son,' she continued, her voice becoming firmer. 'When we went to London I didn't know about Max. Perhaps I should have but I didn't. When you told me it came like a bombshell.'

'I don't understand.' He looked genuinely bewildered. 'Why?'

Catriona stumbled on, feeling as if she was digging herself into a deeper and deeper hole. 'I'd felt guilty enough that you were married but then I discovered about Bruce and Linda and so it didn't seem so bad.'

'You *knew* about Bruce and Linda?' Hamish snarled.

'Yes. I happened to catch them, er...together,

at the Nevis dinner and I thought if she had a lover, why shouldn't you? And why shouldn't it be me?'

'Very logical, but you didn't bother telling me about them.' From high indignation his attitude had chilled to biting sarcasm.

'What purpose would that have served? Except to alienate you from Bruce.'

'Oh yes—and there was the small matter of bank loyalty, of course,' he muttered cynically. 'You wouldn't want to bite the hand that feeds you.'

'If you think about it, Bruce and Linda did you a favour,' Catriona said bravely. 'If you wanted us to become a regular fixture then their affair set the agenda nicely. Until you told me about Max.'

'I could hardly pretend he didn't exist,' exclaimed Hamish. 'I never guessed how you felt. Why didn't you say something?'

'There wasn't time. You let it slip when you were already late,' she reminded him. 'You were hurrying to take Max out. But in a way it was good, because it gave me a chance to think about it, and thinking made me realise that it's not just Max that comes between us, it's me—my character. You might say I'm too selfish or too self-centred, but I'm simply not cut out to be a second string. I can't stand the guilt or the uncertainty.'

Hamish balled his hand into a fist and banged the table, making the wine slop in the glasses. 'But that was two weeks ago! Two weeks, Catriona! Don't you think you might have said something about how you felt before this? Before I invested a million pounds in a dodgy film venture purely because you asked me to and because I love you!'

'It's not dodgy—it's perfectly sound...You *what?*' Catriona's voice faltered as she registered what he had said.

'I love you,' he repeated, his eyes searching her face. 'I have only come to realise it over the last few days. They say absence will do it, don't they? Well, I don't think I have ever felt about any woman the way I feel about you, Catriona. You fill my thoughts constantly, you distract me from my work and disturb me in my sleep. It is baffling and puzzling and entirely against my nature but I can't ignore it.' He ran his hand through his hair in agitation. 'And now you calmly tell me that two *weeks* ago you decided you wanted out.' His look of fierce accusation as he said this made Catriona gasp.

'I—I'm sorry,' she whispered hoarsely. 'It wasn't something I intended. It just happened.'

'But why didn't you tell me?' he insisted grimly. 'You have not played straight with me, Catriona, and I don't like that. I don't like it at all.' He had expected her to be flattered and charmed by his declaration, perhaps a little flustered but definitely pleased. Instead she was startled and dismayed, hunted, like a hind at bay.

She shook her head, tears welling in her eyes. 'I know I haven't been straight. I've behaved appallingly badly and I'm sorry. I just have to hope that you'll forgive me.'

God, she thought, supposing he finds out about Andro? Things could get much, much worse.

'I don't want to forgive you,' he snarled with frustration. 'I just want to love you and for you to love me. Can't you understand?'

Catriona flared at that. 'No. No, I don't understand. I think it's you now who is not playing fair. You want to keep your wife and your son and at the same time you want me to be some kind of permanent bit on the side. But I could never be that, even if I loved you the way you want me to, Hamish. I told you—I'm too selfish. I want to be the main item—a joint account, not a despised little deposit which receives only occasional credits and debits.' Catriona gulped at her wine and made a wry face. 'This stuff tastes much better when one's happy. It seems to go bitter when the mood does.'

'I thought we were going to be happy,' Hamish said. 'I have booked us in for Sunday night at an old castle hotel in the Borders and I was looking forward to taking you there and making love to you in the bed where Mary Queen of Scots once slept with Bothwell.'

Catriona shivered. 'Look what happened to them,' she joked feebly. 'I'm not sure we need to disturb such doomed spirits.'

'That's one way of looking at it,' Hamish conceded. 'The other is to see them as dauntless lovers, pursuing their mutual passion against the odds. I took the romantic approach.'

Catriona shook her head sorrowfully. 'I'm

sorry, Hamish. I tried passion against the odds but it didn't work.'

'It could, though,' he persisted. 'Now that we both know where we stand. You know that to me you are not merely "a bit on the side" as you put it, and I know that you feel anxious about threatening my boy's future. So both these things can be avoided. We can make it work, Catriona, I promise you! You will see that being the mistress of a rich man does not mean having to play second string. You can have everything you want. I'll even tell Linda about us. We'll go public. She'll get used to it—find her way of living with it. She's very adaptable is Linda, very realistic.'

During this speech Hamish stood up and came round the table to Catriona's side. Nervously she rose to meet him, wondering what he intended. Her head was whirling with objections to what he had said but the look on his face prevented her from voicing them. Nor could she refuse him when he took her in his arms and kissed her, a kiss that was neither demanding nor unpleasant but a firm, lingering statement of his feelings, filled with desire and promises.

'Think about it,' he said gently, his blue eyes softer than she had ever seen them. 'I have to go now, but don't desert me just because of Max. I'll never let him suffer. He's my son and very important to me. But so are you. And don't forget that we have a million pounds invested in a film. I see that as very much a joint venture: something we can share together.' He gave her a slow wink. 'I didn't go into it blindly. I know quite a lot about Precipitous City Productions, including who its directors are. Your gypsy actor-friend is more of a force than he looks. I'll come on Sunday about three. Don't worry, I'll see myself out. Goodbye, my darling—till Sunday.'

She heard the latch click on the front door as if from the middle of a centrifuge. What was happening? What did he mean? Did he know *all* about her and Andro? Did he know Andro was Lord Nevis's son? Was he aware of the whole, complicated, seemingly-insoluble jigsaw? Was he inextricably involved? Had she been mad to think she could simply tell him to go away?

Question after question went flashing through Catriona's brain, only to be repeated again and again until she felt dizzy. And she could answer none of them.

Fifteen

Andro and Isabel had not slept since getting their Completion Bond. After leaving the George, they had spent the early hours of Friday morning swapping transatlantic faxes—with their American backers, with mega-star Gil Munro's super-agent and with the less-super agents of other key members of the cast and crew. When Los Angeles went to bed there were British contracts to finalise, designs to confirm, lighting rigs and generators to hire, caterers, make-up artists and voice coaches to appoint, sets and locations to fix, and all the other minute details to organise which go towards getting a film into full production. With only six weeks to go before they planned to start shooting they could not afford to waste a single minute. Andro made arrangements to fly to London to meet the director at the casting agency, for there was the all-important matter of final screen-tests for the two central roles, those of the young lovers David and Catriona.

'But before you go you simply must see Catriona Stewart,' urged Isabel, looking up from her dog-eared copy of *Film Bang*—the Scottish 'bible' on technicians and facilities available to production companies.

Andro made a face. It was Saturday morning and they both looked drawn and tired, their eyes smudged with dark shadows. Beside them a Cona coffee machine hissed insidiously, surrounded by dirty mugs and open milk cartons. 'Why?' he demanded curtly. 'She knows what I did. What is there to say?'

'You could try "sorry", for a start,' snapped Isabel.

'What's the point?' Andro grumbled, surly and unwilling. 'Sorry isn't going to make it all go away.'

'But she isn't going to go away either,' retorted Isabel. 'Hamish Melville has invested a million pounds with us and she is his representative. We can't afford to have unhappy angels at this stage of the proceedings!'

'You come with me then,' suggested Andro plaintively. 'She can't scream at me if you're there.'

'Absolutely not,' Isabel said. 'You can grovel on your own. Tell her you never meant to deceive her but that she's so attractive you were unable to resist taking it all too far. A bit of flattery will get you everywhere.'

'Do you think so?' asked Andro dubiously. 'I'm not sure if Catriona is susceptible to flattery.'

'Well, she's pretty gullible,' Isabel pointed out, 'as you've already discovered. You fooled her once, you can probably fool her again.'

Andro shot her a sharp glance. 'You're a hard-hearted character Izzy, aren't you? Not much milk of human kindness in your little bosom.'

Isabel laughed. 'You leave the size of my bosom out of it,' she said. 'And go and practise your abject apology technique in front of the mirror. A little rehearsal never goes amiss.'

Andro caught Catriona on her doorstep, just as she was about to depart for Elizabeth's meeting. She nearly jumped out of her skin when, at the top of the tenement stair, she was confronted by an enormous bunch of lilies on legs and was even more shocked when they were shifted aside to reveal Andro's pale, heavy-eyed face.

'I know they can't make up for anything,' he said hurriedly, thrusting the lilies at her. 'But I couldn't think of any other way to apologise.'

Catriona firmly shut her front door behind

her. She didn't want Andro stepping over her threshold; in fact she wanted him to go away—as quickly as possible and as far as possible. It seemed incredible that only a few days before, they had been making love behind that very door and now she could hardly bear to look at him.

She held the lilies indifferently, flower-heads down, like a bag of shopping and said in a businesslike way, 'I see. Well, thank you. I'll take them in the car with me just now though, if you don't mind. I'm on my way to a meeting and I'm going to be late.'

'Does that mean you won't forgive me?' asked Andro plaintively, following her as she swept down the stairs.

Catriona endeavoured to treat the encounter as if she had bumped into an acquaintance at the supermarket, affecting an exchange-pleasantries-and-get-on-with-the-job-in-hand attitude. 'No, it means I'm going to be late,' she replied briskly.

'It wasn't entirely my fault, you know,' Andro continued, his unruly mop of hair blowing about in the force of the breeze she made whisking down the circular stairway. 'You have to take some of the blame, you and Skye.'

'Oh? How do you make that out?' queried Catriona, reaching the exit and beginning the short climb up the hill to the archway that led to the castle esplanade.

'Because Skye is so romantic and you are so beautiful. I didn't mean it all to go so far but I couldn't help myself.' Andro was trying to get ahead of her so that he could give her the benefit of his well-rehearsed expression of helpless admiration. 'You're a walking temptation you know, Catriona. Provocation on legs.'

Catriona stopped in her tracks. In thirty-six hours her attitude to Andro had suffered a sea-change, mainly because she didn't like what she had discovered about herself through knowing him. But she wasn't having him pass the buck.

'Oh please!' she snapped. 'Don't give me that line.' She adopted a stern, judgmental stance and fixed Andro with a steely eye. 'Under the Equal Opportunities Act I consider your plea for mitigation completely out of order. I'm ashamed to admit that you fooled me about love, Andro Lindsay, or Galbraith, or whatever your name is, but you can't fool me about lust. You weren't overcome by any overwhelming passion, you coldly and calculatingly set out to find me and seduce me in order to get your hands on Hamish's million and I would think a great deal more of you if you came clean and admitted as much, rather than tried to shift the blame on to some adolescent inability to control yourself. I suspect that you have more control over your emotions than almost anyone else I know. Certainly more than I have, or had, unfortunately! You can probably turn them on and off like a tap and I just hope you do so to devastating effect in the film, the saving of which is the only worthwhile aspect of the whole sorry episode!'

Andro was somewhat taken aback by this

outburst. It revealed an assertive side of Catriona which he had not witnessed before. 'So you won't be turning your back on the project then?' he asked tentatively.

Catriona began walking again, almost dragging his glorious long-stemmed lilies on the ground behind her. 'No I won't, because the stupidest part of the whole silly saga is the fact that I'm sure I would have considered the film a good investment for Hamish anyway. You could have put it to me as a straightforward business proposition. You didn't have to offer me your irresistible body first.' She paused and shrugged. 'Of course, to be fair. I didn't have to fall for it either. Morally, I don't know who comes out of this worst, the seducer or the seduced.'

By now Catriona had reached the place where her car was parked and she opened its rear door, throwing the flowers inside like an old coat. Then she got into the driving seat and slotted the key into the ignition but her hand was trembling so much it took her several attempts to achieve this successfully. Meanwhile Andro said, with his hand on the open door. 'OK, now that you've had your say, perhaps we could call it quits?'

At last Catriona managed to start the engine and put the car into gear. 'I wouldn't trust myself to call it anything,' she said with a rueful smile, pulled the door shut and accelerated away.

The 'Jolly Hockey Sticks' consisted of Elizabeth, Felicity and three other sportingly charitable ladies of varying ages, one a typical Young Mum called Jeanette who looked horribly fit in Catriona's eyes and the others a less athletically daunting and slightly older pair of chums called Cee and Fee (short for Celia and Fiona) who seemed to agree with each other all the time and never disagree with anyone else. In fact they were so busy fence-sitting that it was difficult to see how the committee would ever have come to any decisions if it had not been for Elizabeth more or less telling them all what to think and do. As it was, under her capable guidance, the day's business was swiftly completed—a vote of thanks to a local paper for sponsorship of a round-Edinburgh walk, progress reports on arrangements for a grand hot-air balloon rally beneath Arthur's Seat, a schools' swimathon at the Commonwealth Pool, an orienteering championship in the Pentlands, an end-of-season junior ski championship at Cairngorm, and a seven-a-side-soccer knockout competition in Glasgow. Under Any Other Business Elizabeth brought up the subject of Catriona's celebrity pitch and putt suggestion and successfully engineered her ad hoc election to the committee.

'If you have a few minutes afterwards you might stay on and we can toss around a few ideas together, Catriona. Strictly informally of course, since things are hardly at an action-this-day stage,' suggested Elizabeth.

Catriona agreed readily enough, was actually quite grateful for the distraction and, after Cee and Fee and Felicity and Jane had nattered their way through Elizabeth's tea and shortbread and down the path of Elizabeth's substantial detached stone-built house, she found herself furnished with a seriously strong gin and tonic and a cosy armchair in Elizabeth's so-called 'den', a small untidy sitting room at the back of the rambling house.

'I know that most women like me who find themselves on their own tend to sell the family home and buy a small flat but I never wanted to,' the widow confided. 'I rather like rattling around like the last pea in the pod. I sleep in what used to be the maid's room over the kitchen, which is lovely and warm, and I don't bother to heat the main rooms unless my daughters and their families are visiting.' Elizabeth took a restorative pull at her drink and smiled at her young companion. 'What kind of a place do you have yourself?'

'Oh, it's quite small, just one bedroom, but it has a great view of the Castle. That's the best thing about it,' Catriona told her, nursing her glass and still shuddering slightly at the alcoholic power of her first sip.

'So you don't live with anyone?' asked Elizabeth.

'No. I used to when I worked in Paisley. Three of us shared a house, but when I got the job at Steuart's I found I could afford to buy something on my own.'

'And you don't get lonely? You're not tempted to live with a boyfriend or anything?'

'No, I've never found a man I could live with. Too fussy, my mother says.' Catriona smiled, though her eyes avoided Elizabeth's.

The older woman made an expressive noise. 'Huh! Good men are not easy to find. I know because I only found one.'

At this Catriona risked a sympathetic glance. 'Your husband?'

'My late husband,' Elizabeth corrected her wistfully. 'Daft old fool! He left me much too soon.'

'So, forgive me if I ask you the same question you asked me,' said Catriona gently. 'Don't you get lonely?'

'Dreadfully. But I'm learning to live with it. I'm prepared to believe that not every woman needs a man about the house, but I did—still do, really—and I suspect you do too.'

Catriona raised an eyebrow. 'What makes you say that?'

'Intuition. Aren't I right?'

Catriona shrugged the question off. 'Maybe what you never had you don't miss,' she suggested, adding pertinently, 'This is not pitching and putting, by the way.'

'Bother pitch and putt. We can talk about that any time. Let's have another gin,' said Elizabeth, downing the remainder of her first and gesturing at Catriona to do the same. 'And then you can tell me why you were looking like a victim of trench-warfare when you arrived today.'

'Was I?' Catriona asked in amazement.

Elizabeth chuckled. 'Well, there were definite signs of shell-shock.'

'I suppose I *had* just been under fire, but I think I gave as good as I got.'

'That's what I like to hear.' Elizabeth was busy at a drinks' tray on a side-table. 'Don't let the bastards get you down.'

'I bet you don't,' exclaimed Catriona, but was surprised by her hostess's bleak look as she handed her a fresh drink.

'No one is shell-proof,' Elizabeth said. 'Not even an old battle-axe.'

'You're not a battle-axe,' contradicted Catriona, smiling acceptance of the gin and tonic. 'More like a pocket-battleship.'

'I like that description,' nodded Elizabeth, sitting down again. 'It makes me sound small, busy and effective.'

'Which you are.'

'Substitute bossy for busy and you might just about have it right,' commented Elizabeth, putting down her drink. 'And I will now prove it to you.' She made come-hither movements with her hands at Catriona. 'Come on. Give. Who was firing and what were the missiles?'

Catriona hesitated. She needed to talk to someone and on this occasion Alison was no good because of John's heavy disapproval of the situation. Elizabeth was an independent ear, existing completely outside what Catriona had come cynically to regard as the 'vicious circle'. Also she was unattached, would not immediately discuss what she heard with a partner, and she was older and more experienced and might just have some sound advice to offer. But could she be trusted, or would she inevitably use Catriona's confidences as gossip-fodder for her cronies at the golf club?

'Perhaps it would help if I tell you what I know,' said Elizabeth encouragingly. 'I know Bruce Finlay was having an affair with Linda Melville because Flick told me—Felicity, that is. What you may not know is that she suspected that it was you he was going with.'

'Me? Whatever made her think that?' asked Catriona indignantly.

'Perhaps because you are evidently unattached and yet you look like a girl who just *must* be involved with a man. Singular beauty such as yours attracts suspicion, especially from vulnerable middle-aged ladies like Felicity.'

'She's not middle-aged,' Catriona objected. 'She's only eight years older than me.'

'Yes, but her marriage is middle-aged and that's what makes her vulnerable. She's not sure she can still hold Bruce's attention when there are distractions like you in his orbit.'

'Well, she chose the wrong target for her suspicions, didn't she?' observed Catriona dryly. 'Anyway, Bruce was only doing it with Linda to prove he still can.'

'Quite. I advised lacy black underwear and a night or two away from the kids but Felicity thinks it's too late now.'

'Bruce should be grateful she cares at all.'

'Yes, she's quite a honey is our Flick. Meanwhile, however, with everyone's attention focused on Bruce and Linda, Hamish and Catriona were busy whipping up a little storm of their own, weren't they?' Elizabeth eyed her visitor over the dancing surface of her drink and then took a meaningful gulp, waiting.

'I don't think Hamish would like to hear you say that,' responded Catriona cautiously. 'Especially as it's only based on guesswork.'

Elizabeth shook her head. 'No, it's not. Queenie Nevis is a member of my club,' she said. 'Also she's a great gossip and she just happened to be at *Sunset Boulevard* on the same night as you.'

Catriona gave a big sigh and nodded. 'Yes, I know. Rob Galbraith told me.'

Elizabeth's eyebrows climbed under her grey fringe. 'Ah—Queenie's elusive son and heir! Where does he come into this?'

Catriona took the plunge. 'Look, can I trust you?' she asked baldly. 'I would like to talk to someone but I don't know you very well and I can't say I fancy my affairs becoming the subject of the next hen-session in the golf-club bar.' She made a placatory gesture. 'I'm sorry, I must sound very rude.'

'No. No, you sound very sensible. I can certainly promise you not to breathe a word of what you say to anyone, but of course you must make up your own mind whether to trust my promise.'

Catriona wondered, watching her, who Elizabeth reminded her of and then suddenly realised it was Julie Andrews. Not Julie Andrews singing and dancing all over the Austrian Alps in *The Sound of Music* but as she must be now that she was nearing sixty. It was the wholesome niceness of her that she recognised in Elizabeth, the reliability and the squeaky-clean integrity beneath the bossy, governessy exterior.

At school you maybe wouldn't have smoked behind the cycle shed with such a companion but you would have rushed to do your Duke of Edinburgh survival test with her.

'I warn you, it's rather a long and complicated story,' she began. 'Are you sure you can be bothered?'

'Try me,' Elizabeth suggested.

So Catriona did, and was amazed at how easy it was to tell this small, grey-brown owl of a woman all about Hamish and Andro and Rob and the million pounds and about her own self-disgust as a result of the whole unsavoury episode.

'And the net result is,' she concluded dolefully, 'that I would dearly like to duck out of the vicious circle, say goodbye to Steuart's and sail back over the sea to Skye.'

'Yes, well, I can see how all this might make you feel that way,' responded Elizabeth sympathetically. 'But you'd be wimping out a bit, wouldn't you?'

'Absolutely,' agreed Catriona unrepentantly. 'Being a complete wimp. Which I can't because, if nothing else, I've promised to help my sister buy a croft and I need to stay on at Steuart's to do so.'

'Well, maybe you can't do it immediately, but if you're seriously feeling like a fish out of water you could work towards changing your way of life,' Elizabeth suggested. 'For a start you can sort out the Hamish factor. That's the first thing—after another gin, of course.'

'God, if I have another of these I'll be squiffy!'

exclaimed Catriona.

'That's the idea. Get a bit squiffy and then ring Hamish.'

'I can't ring him—that's the whole trouble.'

'Rubbish! Just ring his home and if Linda answers simply ask to speak to him. Never apologise, never explain—that's the old Thatcher adage, isn't it? One of the few things she was right about in my opinion.'

'It'd probably be Minto who answered anyway,' Catriona smiled weakly.

'Minto? Oh yes, I've heard of him. He's the butler, isn't he?' Elizabeth chortled. 'Trust the Melvilles to have a butler! You could never get on with Hamish for long, believe me, dear. Not if he employs a butler.'

'I'd never thought of that before,' giggled Catriona. 'You're probably right.'

''Course I'm right,' sniffed Elizabeth. 'I told you. All you have to do is ring. Too bad if he gets cross.'

'You're forgetting the bank factor. Lord Nevis wouldn't appreciate Hamish defecting to another bank just because I told him to get out of my life.'

'Yes, I suppose there is that. Perhaps a little more subtlety is called for.' Elizabeth stood up. 'Well, planning a campaign definitely requires sustenance. One more gin!'

'No. If I have more alcohol I need food to go with it,' said Catriona firmly.

'Good idea. We'll go to the local Chinese restaurant and have crispy duck and rice wine.'

'Or green tea,' suggested Catriona hurriedly.

'But the duck sounds great.' She suddenly realised she was hungry, having had no appetite for days.

'Lovely,' cried Elizabeth. 'We'll nibble on ducky bits and work out how to wrap up the Hamish affair without any hard feelings. And then I want to hear more about this son and heir of Queenie Nevis's. She always makes him sound like one in a million, but I suppose that's just mother-talk. Still, they say that a man who's good to his mother makes good husband material.' She glanced slyly at Catriona as she said this, but her visitor ignored the innuendo and merely shuddered.

'Don't mention a million,' she said. 'It gives me the shivers!'

On the phone to his mother on Sunday evening, Rob confirmed that he would be up to visit his parents at Easter. 'And I want to see Grandfather, too,' he added. 'Are you going to Glen Doran House at all?'

'Your father's doing his annual tour of the estate on Easter Monday so I imagine we'll go up there on Sunday afternoon and have the usual picnic supper in the kitchen. You know what the old boy's like about any formality. Why do you ask, dear?' Lady Nevis had her mobile phone tucked under her chin and was busy arranging flowers as she spoke. Her husband dozed behind the *Sunday Telegraph* in another corner of their sitting room whilst a village choir sang Songs of Praise unheeded from the television set.

'I'd rather like to ask someone up there,' Rob told her. 'If that's alright.'

'Of course it's alright,' his mother assured him, immediately all ears. 'Who is this someone?'

'Just a girl. I think I'll ask her first before I tell you, if you don't mind,' Rob replied craftily. 'I'll let you know if she's coming.'

'Anyone we know?' Queenie asked curiously.

'I'm saying nothing. And don't tell Andro, for God's sake!' There was a distinctly hard edge to Rob's voice as he said this, causing Queenie to frown.

'Andro's not coming up at Easter, he's already told me,' she said. 'He's far too busy with his film. You know they got the money, don't you?'

'Of course I do, Mother. I did their Completion Bond, remember?'

'Did you, dear? I'd forgotten. Anyway he rang George at the bank, full of beans, to tell him the good news. George was thrilled. I think he thought Andro would never show any drive!'

'Oh, he's got drive all right,' said Rob. 'It's who he drives over that's the problem. To be honest, Ma, I'm delighted he's not coming. The less I see of him at present the better.'

'Oh dear,' moaned his mother. 'I hate it when you two fall out.'

'Well, at least we no longer resort to fisticuffs. Give Father my best. Tell him I'd love a round of golf on Saturday if he wants to book a tee.'

'Very well, dear. He's still sleeping off today's exertions at the nineteenth hole but I'll tell him. Goodbye.'

'Bye. See you soon.'

Rob put the phone down and wondered whether to ring Catriona immediately. He had been mulling over the idea of seeing her at Easter ever since returning to London but feared that his brother might have put her off his family for ever. Having been the one to nudge her into full realisation of Andro's duplicity, he felt rather like the man at the top of a bungy jump. He had pushed her off the platform but would it be wise to try and grab her as she bounced back? It had crossed his mind that perhaps he should let her find her equilibrium before asking her to embark on another jump, but he had a strong desire to mop up the milk Andro had spilt, especially as it was spilt over Catriona's tender heart and haunting beauty. Rob's hand hovered indecisively over the telephone...

Hamish drove straight from the airport to Catriona's flat. He had felt a twinge of guilt at Max's woebegone expression as he hugged him goodbye but promised to 'Race you down the Gornergrat in a day or so. You'd better put in some practice runs!'

In response to Linda's query as to exactly when he would join them in Zermatt he was more evasive. 'Wednesday or Thursday. I'll ring you when I know.'

After their last conversation he was vaguely apprehensive about confronting Catriona. The super-confident side of him could not believe she would dump him as she had insinuated. He had never been dumped in his life, not even when he was a sixteen-year-old schoolboy luring girls into dance-hall car parks with his glib chat and charming smile. Most had eventually succumbed to his innate seductive skills, laid back on the bonnet of a car or humped crudely against a brick wall. It was only when he learned that sex was infinitely better with a bit more female input that he began to look for longer-term relationships, but by then he'd started dealing in property, making money out of acquiring rundown Glasgow tenements and letting rooms at inflated rents to students made desperate by the sixties' shortage of college accommodation. By his late teens he had his own place to take his girls to and a car to take them in and his charm still worked a treat. None of them dreamed of dumping him in favour of his less enterprising peers; it was always he who made the break, thirsting for fresh flesh and pleasures new. Even when his first wife, Annie, whom he married in order to acquire a stake in her father's thriving retail business, went off with her American art dealer it had been a relief rather than the affront the dealer had thought it was, and the Picasso conscience gift had more than compensated for her departure.

It was only in a deep-buried, insecure corner of his mind that doubts arose concerning Catriona. She was not like any of his other women, not even Linda who had managed to inveigle him into marriage and fatherhood and even cuckoldry but nevertheless remained the subservient, submissive partner. Catriona alone was different, was assertive, had not wanted his presents and had even suggested that she might not want him if she could not have him all to herself.

Wasn't that what she had said, more or less? That she couldn't be a second string. Well, he would make her number one if that's what it took to keep her. Or at least, he reasoned, he would tell her that she was number one and, by the time she started demanding proof, he would have had enough of her and would be able, as usual, to be the one to do the dumping. As he parked the car Hamish smiled with satisfaction. His plan was made and he was sure it would work.

A blood-alcohol level boosted by several jugs of rice wine on top of the large gins she had drunk earlier had led Catriona to take a taxi home from the Chinese restaurant the previous night, dropping Elizabeth Nicholson at her house on the way and checking that her car was secure in the road outside it. Then at lunchtime on Sunday she had cleared her head with a brisk walk through Edinburgh's prosperous southern suburbs to collect it.

For what remained of the afternoon she had pondered the scheme that she and Elizabeth had hatched to handle Hamish. In daylight and sobriety it did not look such a good one as it had towards a well-oiled midnight.

'If you like him as much as you say you do and want to let him down lightly then your best plan is to go away with him for the night, but tell him this must be the last time,' Elizabeth had suggested. 'And whenever you actually *talk* you can discuss the film, make sure he realises that you genuinely think it is a good investment for him. You can tell him that you intend to nurse it all the way, to make sure that he gets all the perks of being an angel along with the risks—meeting the cast, watching the film, going to the première. He'll love all that, I'm sure, especially if there's good publicity to be had from it.'

At the time Catriona had agreed that this seemed the best course to follow but the more she thought about it, and the nearer she got to putting it into practice, the colder her feet became. *Could* she go blithely away with Hamish to some luxury Borders retreat and spend a night cavorting in Mary Queen of Scots' bed when they both knew that this would be their last romp? Wouldn't it be a bit like Mary and Bothwell bedding together with the prior knowledge that he was going to die a slow death in some Danish dungeon and she was going to have her head chopped off? Could a good time possibly be had by all with the axe poised over their heads?

Hamish breezed in just after six with an air of barely suppressed triumph. 'Everything's going to be fine,' he declared, flinging his arms around her and kissing her eagerly. 'No more skulking in shadows, no more going where no one knows us. It's all going to be upfront and you and I are officially about to become what is known as "an item"!'

Bewildered, Catriona pulled back in his arms to look at him. 'What do you mean? What about

Linda? What about Max? You haven't told him, have you?'

Hamish detected panic in her voice and hastened to reassure her. 'No, no. We're agreed that he isn't to be involved. Anyway they'll both be safely in Zermatt tonight and having a ball on the slopes tomorrow.'

'And when are you going to join them?' asked Catriona, wondering what he thought was so marvellously different from the way things had been before.

'In two days—or three. It doesn't matter,' Hamish replied, bending to kiss her again. He had an air of intense excitement about him that was infectious and his kisses were so deep and disturbing that Catriona could feel familiar melting sensations beginning. He had not lost the power to destabilise her, to block all thought and reason. Yet there was still a small voice inside her which whispered caution, tempering the hot flame that his kisses kindled.

'Let's do it now,' he said unexpectedly, his arms encircling her like cooper's bands. 'It's been so long, hasn't it? I can't wait until we get to the hotel. What is there to wait for?' He kissed her again, his hands beginning to roam over her body in eager exploration. Bemused, Catriona was in two minds and confused about which one to heed. He was still the same Hamish she had fallen for in the first place, charming, ardent and skilfully passionate. It would be perfectly possible simply to relax and go with the flow, follow his expert lead down the headlong stream to wild abandon. But in the waters lurked an unseen obstacle, something which only she knew was there and which might snag their progress, and that something was her own moral code. Could she really do as Elizabeth said—kiss and run?

Meanwhile he appeared not to notice her hesitation, driven by his own unambiguous desires. 'Where shall we do it?' he asked with a lascivious grin. 'The bedroom, the kitchen, the sitting room? Or shall we do it right here in the hall, on the floor, as if I could hardly wait to get across the threshold, which is true! Darling Catriona, I've wanted you for weeks but it seems like months or years. I've thought about you every day, I've kissed you in my dreams and lost you in my nightmares. I've seen you crossing the road and spotted you on buses passing in the street—but it's never you! I see you in my drink, in my food, in my newspaper, even on my windscreen when I'm driving along. You're in my fantasies, in my deepest, deepest longings. But fantasy is no substitute for the unique, beautiful, warm, real-life body of my lovely Catriona.'

All through this sensuous soliloquy he was undressing her. He removed her jacket, running his hands over her shoulders and down her arms, pushing it off at the wrists, and then he nuzzled her throat as he lowered her on to the rug and started on her soft, cream wool blouse, one button after another until only the two at the cuffs remained. Between fervent phrases he kissed her breasts through the thin silk of her camisole. She lay mesmerised by his voice, passive and yet troubled, wondering if this was really what she wanted or something she had simply not said no to. Above her head there was a patch of peeling paint on the ceiling.

'You have the most beautiful body I have ever seen,' Hamish said with the glimmer of a smile, staring at her hungrily as he began to undo his belt. 'And the prettiest, brightest, burningest bush in the whole, wide world!'

Then the telephone rang.

Sixteen

'Don't answer it,' urged Hamish. 'Let it ring.'

But the sound of the bell had dragged Catriona out of her trance. All her doubts rushed into focus as the double-trill broke into her thoughts and she rose to her knees, intent on answering it.

Hamish tried to stop her, grasping her hand. 'Catriona, don't. It'll stop ringing. Don't go!' His voice held a falsetto stridency, sharpened by the fear that if she moved away from him now he would never get her back. Inside his head his will clashed with hers with an almost infantile vehemence. He didn't *want* her to answer it. Couldn't she see that his body ached and throbbed for her? She was being deliberately aggravating, knowingly perverse. The violent streak in him almost surfaced, was only kept under by an unpredictable urge to please. He

411

was tempted, so tempted, simply to drag her back and hold her down until the infuriating, frustrating, blasted bloody ringing stopped!

'I've got to answer it. Hamish, let me go!' Catriona wrenched her hand from his, grabbed her blouse from the floor and loped through to the kitchen, snatching the cordless phone from the wall-unit. She pressed Receive. 'Hello,' she said breathlessly. 'Catriona Stewart.'

'Hello, Catriona. It's Rob Galbraith.'

'Oh! How are you?' Catriona was trying to steady her breathing and shrug on her blouse as she spoke, nearly dropping the phone in the process. 'Whoops! Sorry.'

There was a bang and crackle on the line. 'What's happening?' asked Rob, amused. 'You're not *that* surprised to hear from me, surely?'

In the hall Hamish sat on the floor with his head on his knees. I should be in the recovery position, he thought with furious irony. Send for the Crash Unit.

'Nothing,' Catriona assured Rob hastily, pulling her blouse around her. 'I'm all fingers and thumbs, that's all. I'm in the kitchen.' Well, that bit was true anyway. Let him make of it what he would.

'Cooking or cleaning?' he chuckled.

'Neither,' she replied. 'Just fiddling about. Did you want to talk about the film?'

'No. I wouldn't ring you at home on a Sunday evening to talk about the film. It's not one of my favourite subjects at present anyway.'

'Oh?' Catriona wondered why not, since he had originally been so enthusiastic about her acquiring the extra funding.

By now Hamish had recovered enough to listen to her end of the conversation. He heard her mention the film and speculated with extreme irritation whether it was that unkempt actor with the greasy smile who was on the line. Discovering Andro Lindsay's identity as a partner in Precipitous City Productions had given Hamish much pause for thought, but in the end he had decided that he would have more influence with Catriona as an investor than as one who had refused the privilege, and his other private investigations into the film's prospects had been encouraging. He could not deny that, despite his plentiful misgivings it was, as she had suggested, just the sort of project he favoured.

'I rang to ask you to Glen Doran House at Easter.' Rob's words came tumbling out in a rush as he hastened to amplify his invitation. 'I just thought you'd probably be going up to Skye to see your family and might like to stop off on your way back. I'll be there on Sunday afternoon and all of Monday if you can make it. It would be lovely to see you again.'

There was a silence on the line. Why didn't she speak? he asked himself disconsolately. Perhaps his fears were justified and Andro had put her off the entire Galbraith clan.

In a nutshell Catriona did not know what to say. To a disinterested party the whole situation might appear hugely comical, she thought. Here she was, caught in a state of undress with a man whom she didn't really want, being invited home by the brother of a man who hadn't really wanted her, and who himself probably wouldn't want her either if he could see her present circumstances, and all because of a miserable million pounds! In the process of mentally summarising this farcical chain of events Catriona suddenly knew what she must do, whatever the consequences.

'Er—would you think me very rude if I rang you back about this?' she asked, acutely aware that Hamish must be listening.

Rob was puzzled but relieved. At least he hadn't received an instant brush off. 'No, of course not. There's no rush.'

'OK. I won't leave it too long, I promise. Tomorrow evening at the latest. There's just something I have to do first. Goodbye.'

She pressed the Clear button and turned to find Hamish standing in the kitchen doorway, shirtless and glowering.

'What is the something you just have to do first?' he enquired in a sarcastic tone. 'Finish off the little job you started ten minutes ago by any chance?' He noticed that she had the grace to blush. 'Well, don't bother. The fire's out.'

'I'm sorry, Hamish,' she muttered miserably, swinging round to slot the phone back in its rest. 'I'm making a terrible mess of things.' She had buttoned her rather oversized cream blouse and stood desolately by the kitchen table looking like an old-fashioned shirt advertisement of the *It looks even better on a man*' variety, her long legs disappearing up into its voluminous folds. To Hamish she was a she-devil, at the same time infinitely desirable and thoroughly murderable.

'Yes,' he remarked sourly. 'I think that is one matter on which we totally agree. What I don't understand is exactly *what* you are trying to do.'

Catriona did not see the Jekyll and Hyde fighting behind Hamish's eyes. She pulled out a kitchen chair and sat down with a bump, as if her legs wouldn't hold her up any more. 'I'm trying to please all of the people all of the time and my father always told me that was impossible.' She sank her head in her hands, hiding under her mane of bright hair.

Hamish gave a humourless laugh. 'Hah! Pleasing *some* of the people some of the time would be nice. Especially if the some happened to include me.'

She looked up at that, tossing back her hair and gazing at him with troubled eyes. 'That's just it actually, Hamish. It's you I've been trying to please most and now I realise that I can't.'

He stared at her incredulously. 'Excuse me? You've been trying to please me? Well, I hate to disillusion you but your good intentions have not been very obvious. Frankly I can't remember when I have felt less pleased.'

She stood up again suddenly and walked into the hall. 'I need some clothes on if I'm to have a serious conversation,' she said, passing him in the doorway.

Somehow he controlled his urge to grab her and merely watched as she slipped on her skirt and jacket, assuming a businesslike air in a matter of seconds. Her legs were still bare and, without comment, she removed her tights from the umbrella stand where he had thrown them earlier. The aftermath of their unfulfilled passion seemed to her a sad and arid thing. Silently she picked his silk shirt off the floor and handed it to him. Equally silently he put it on, his movements jerky and stiff, like a marionette.

He followed her into the sitting room where they sat awkwardly on the two upright chairs which flanked a Victorian Pembroke table in the bay window. Outside the sun was sinking behind a blanket of grey cloud, turning the sky a weird luminous lilac. Both inside and out a storm threatened.

'I feel awful,' confessed Catriona with the briefest of apologetic smiles, twining her fingers together in agitation. 'I tried to tell you how things were on Friday but somehow I couldn't make the words work properly. You didn't seem to hear them.'

Hamish folded his arms and crossed his legs, putting up his defences—but whether against his own temper or her words he did not know. 'Try again,' he said gruffly. 'What do you want to tell me?'

'That I can't be your lover any more, or your mistress or the other half of an "item" as you put it. I can't because I don't feel that way about you any more and it isn't any use pretending I do.' She avoided his eyes, stared past him instead at the little Uig landscape on the wall, wishing she could dissolve into its surface and become part of that small, secure corner of the world again.

'You mean I upset you, repulse you in some way?' he asked in an ugly tone. He had no reference for this situation, had never been faced with outright rejection before.

'No! You are attractive and charming—gorgeous in every way! I was incredibly flattered when you took me out, bowled over when you fancied me and intoxicated when we first made love.' She blushed as she said this, her voice dropping to a whisper. 'But when I came to my senses I realised that there was no more to it. It was infatuation, not love. It had no firm foundation, Hamish. It was just a fabulous fling and it's over.'

'I see. Just water under the bridge, you mean? Ships that pass in the night? Take it or leave it?' He uncrossed his legs, unfolded his arms and leaned forward belligerently. For the first time she felt a frisson of fear, an inkling that he was not far from striking out. 'And I'm supposed to do just that? Take it on the chin and leave it alone?' He stood up and began to pace across the hearth, to and fro like a caged tiger. 'But supposing I can't? Or won't? Supposing I don't accept that it was just a fling? May I remind you that there is the small matter of a million-pound investment at stake here—to say nothing of a substantial bank balance which might find its way elsewhere!'

'Is that a threat?' asked Catriona nervously. She knew he was capable of it, suspected he might be capable of backing up his threats with violence. 'I hope not. I was hoping that we could remain friends, Hamish, friends and colleagues.'

'No!' he yelled, turning on his heel to loom over her. 'No, we can't do that because I shall never be able to look at you without wanting you. You've got right under my skin and the sight of you will always make me itch!' He paused suddenly, aware that something odd was happening. 'Why are you laughing? What the hell is there to laugh about?'

It was really a means of self-defence. Catriona had her hands over her mouth and her flaring silver eyes were full of helpless hysteria. She shook her head and gasped, 'I'm sorry! I didn't mean to laugh. But being "under your skin" as you put it just struck me as so ludicrous!' She took a deep, steadying breath. 'I'm not something glamorous out of a Frank Sinatra song, Hamish, I'm just a girl—a woman if you like—a simple Highland soul—flesh and blood with arms and legs and a skinny body and no boobs. I'm not some *femme fatale* who eats men for breakfast and spits them out. I made a mistake, OK? And I'm really sorry. I should never have let you show me the Picasso. I should never have gone with you to London. I should never have pretended to you that everything was all right when it wasn't. But I did it because I'm stupid and naive, not because I'm devious or manipulative, not because I wanted to con you out of a million pounds for my own benefit, and not because I want to hang on to my job at the bank. I don't even like my job any more. I don't like the situations it gets me into, I don't like most of the people it puts me in contact with and I don't like the way money rules everything. I shouldn't be a banker obviously and I shouldn't be a mistress and I shouldn't be giving you or anyone else an itch just because my legs and eyes and hair and mouth are put together in a certain way. Brains, money, even beauty—if that's what you call what I've got—these all seem to me to be dubious assets, which I have come to the conclusion I can well do without.'

All trace of mirth had dissipated in the course of this speech and she sat slumped on her chair, as if all her energy had ebbed away. Hamish stared at her for several seconds. 'Where did all that come from?' he asked bemusedly. 'Who the hell were you talking to on the phone?'

Catriona wrinkled her brow. 'On the phone?' she echoed, puzzled. 'No one in particular. All this has nothing to do with him.'

'No? Well, whoever it was certainly triggered some change of attitude. I arrive here to find a melting moment and after three minutes on the phone she becomes a lemon sherbet. I think I'd rather be the man on the line. He seems to stir you up in a way that I don't any more, apparently.' Hamish hovered by the hearth, casting thunderous glances at her from under a knotted forehead.

Taking a calculated risk, Catriona stood up and moved to his side, reaching out to place her hands on his shoulders and a kiss on his cheek, not a kiss of passion but of compassion. 'This has nothing to do with anyone else,' she told him firmly. 'The phone call triggered a train of thought, that's all. It made me see that I've been

419

stupid and selfish and that I must start getting my priorities right. And one of them is you. Not Hamish Melville, millionaire, but Hamish Melville gentle man—nice, kind, generous man whom I want very much to keep as a friend and whose son I want to see happy and secure and whose wife probably loves him for all the right kind of married motives—much more and much better than I do.'

Hamish took her hands off his shoulders and held them tightly in both of his. 'Catriona, Catriona,' he said sorrowfully, manfully acting mournful when he felt mutinous. 'What am I to make of you? Reluctant bank manager, amateur Agony Aunt and complete enigma.'

'A friend, that's what you're to make of me.' Her eyes fixed on his pleadingly. 'Please?'

'Bloody hell,' he swore loudly, maintained a long, tense silence and then shrugged with reluctant resignation. 'Damned witch! I can refuse you nothing.'

Alison stared at Catriona in disbelief. 'I can't believe you got away with it,' she said. 'You did a "Dear John" on Hamish Melville and he's still speaking to you and still banking with Steuart's. I consider that deserves the Nobel Peace Prize. You should be in the Diplomatic Corps.'

Catriona laughed. 'MI5 more like—Head of Dirty Tricks. But you must tell John he's not to reveal any of this to Bruce or Donald. I don't want Lord Nevis to know how near he came to losing his best customer.'

It was Monday and once more she and Alison

were lunching in the wine-bar opposite the bank, but this time the atmosphere between them was considerably warmer than it had been the last time they'd eaten there.

'Perish the thought. Anyway, your revered Lord Chairman must be feeling flush at present because he just bought a painting through my good offices—a fantastic McTaggart landscape which a beleaguered Lloyds Name was selling in order to settle his astronomical account. It was a private deal and I consider it my best transaction this year.' Alison preened visibly as she spread pâté on toast.

'How long are you going to go on working, Ally?' asked Catriona suddenly. 'Have you thought about how you're going to juggle dirty nappies and fine art?'

'Not really.' Alison grimaced. 'John wants me to stop working altogether but I want to keep my hand in. I can't let all this knowledge of brushwork and patina disappear under a flood of breast-milk and gripe-water, can I?' She tapped her dark head exponentially.

'I suppose it depends how you feel at the time,' remarked Catriona. 'It's hard to imagine you pursuing pram-pushing as a full-time career but you never know.'

Alison gave her friend a quizzical look. 'Are you sure you want to continue this conversation?' she asked.

'Why shouldn't I?' came the surprised response.

'Because I've had the distinct impression that babies are a subject you find hard to discuss,'

421

commented Alison. 'Or perhaps it's just my baby you avoid mentioning.'

A slow flush crept up from Catriona's neck to inundate her whole face. 'Oh God,' she said with mortification. 'I hoped you hadn't noticed. The last thing I've wanted to do is upset you, especially now.'

'Why especially now?' enquired Alison with spirit. 'Do you think being pregnant makes one emotionally fragile all of a sudden? Or totally self-centred? What upsets me is you becoming clam-like about such things. You're the one who's fragile, Catriona Stewart—like Edinburgh crystal, and just as transparent.'

'Not too good at dissembling, eh?' asked Catriona sheepishly. 'A wee bit obvious?'

'Just a wee bit. What is it? Don't you like my baby?' Alison looked affronted but there was a twinkle in her eye.

'Yes, of course I do—or I'm sure I will when it's born,' declared Catriona. 'I'm just horribly, unforgivably and reprehensibly jealous, if you want to know the truth.'

'I don't think that's horrible, unforgivable or reprehensible,' said Alison gently. 'I've been jealous of anyone who's pregnant for years now, until I fell myself.'

'Have you?' Catriona giggled with relief, adding with amusement, 'Why do we say "fell pregnant"? As if pregnant women were fallen women! It conjures up images of Adam and Eve and original sin and apples.'

Alison frowned. 'Well, apples fall, don't they? Don't forget Isaac Newton. Anyway, your being jealous is a good thing. It might stir you into looking for the right kind of "lurve".'

Catriona took a sip of her white wine and made a face. 'I'm not sure I can be as calculating as that.'

'Who said anything about being calculating? Hormones can't count as far as I know,' Alison chuckled. 'But at least you might stay away from married men in future.'

Catriona shivered. 'I don't need any extra discouragement on that score. It's funny, you know—when I first heard you were pregnant it was as if you became a different person. Not the old familiar Ally but someone grown-up and important and way above my level. And you weren't one person any more but two, one of whom I didn't know at all.'

'Am I still this daunting two-faced creature?' Alison asked with concern.

'No. I don't know why but you seem to have reverted to type. Perhaps I've just got used to the idea of you growing a bump.'

'Thank goodness for that.'

'And since that is the case you can give me the benefit of your sage advice. What do you think I should do about Rob Galbraith?' Catriona continued earnestly.

'Rob Galbraith? Oh yes—Mr Completion Bond. How did we get on to him all of a sudden?'

'He's asked me up to his country seat at Easter. You know, the Lochaber place in Glen Doran.' Catriona explained this rather diffidently, being still rather nonplussed by the invitation, about which she had yet to call Rob back. She wondered why a man who knew only too well what had transpired between herself and his brother should nevertheless want to pursue a friendship with her. She felt a certain wariness, exacerbated by her suspicion that all members of the Galbraith family were heartless hedonists, without conscience or scruple.

'Really?' responded Alison with surprise. 'But he's Andro's brother, isn't he? I thought you wanted to sever the Andro connection.'

'I can't altogether,' Catriona reminded her, 'Hamish still expects me to keep an eye on the film investment and I can't refuse him that after what's happened, can I?'

'I don't know,' Alison pondered. 'You seem to reach parts of Hamish Melville that no one has ever reached before! However, since I have not had the dubious pleasure of meeting the Galbraith brothers I don't feel very qualified to advise you on what you should do about Easter. Do you want to go?'

'It is on my back from Skye and I could visit the Carruthers too, who've also asked me...' Catriona's voice tailed off indecisively.

'You *are* in demand,' put in Alison, smiling. 'Perhaps you'd better spread yourself around and see how the cookie crumbles.'

'You think I should go?'

'Why not? It's only a day in your life and you never know what may come of it.'

'You've changed your tune. When it was Hamish doing the asking you couldn't discourage me enough.'

'This is different,' insisted Alison, undeterred. 'Whatever you say about him, in my opinion Hamish is still a snake, but this invitation comes from the boss's son.'

'*Noblesse oblige* and all that?' enquired Catriona, one eyebrow arched.

'Absolutely, darling!' agreed Alison with a wink.

Andro returned from London with the contenders for the parts of David Balfour and Catriona Drummond whittled down to two for each. The American director who had been appointed by Minerva, a quiet self-contained man called Sam Fox, had expressed his preferences but these did not coincide with Andro's and he flew back to Edinburgh armed with videotapes of the screen tests for Isabel to throw in an opinion.

'I'm happy with Andrina Gordon as Catriona,' he said, winding the two-inch tape on to the VT viewer in the editing channel below the mews flat. 'She's hardly a model of Highland innocence in real life but she's sparky enough to play Catriona and she can *act* the innocent admirably, as you'll see. Also her accent is almost perfect without coaching. But Sam's choice for Davy Balfour is a classic case of American misjudgment, if you ask me. Take a look.'

Isabel touched the VT controls and the image of a good-looking dark-haired young man sprang to life on the television monitor in front of them. Mark Sole was a young English actor who had made a big impression in a television drama series playing the sensitive son of a business tycoon, full of insecurities and infatuations and possessed of an endearing naivety about the opposite sex. He brought all the qualities that had earned him acclaim in that part to the test for David Balfour and achieved a convincing performance in every aspect, save for his voice which was indisputably and indelibly English, much too English!

'He'll never latch on to the right accent, however much he's coached,' complained Andro who, to Isabel's annoyance, had winced and tutted all the way through the playback. 'I've met him and he's thick. His mother brought him to the audition, can you imagine? The lad is nineteen! Sam Fox thinks he looks the part and says the accent will come with practice, but I *hae me doots*. Severe doots!'

'If you hadn't made so much fuss during the screening I'd have got a better idea,' grumbled Isabel, winding the tape back at high speed. 'Why don't you go and make a cup of tea and leave me on my own to view it again. I might be able to express an opinion then.'

So Andro climbed the stairs, albeit grudgingly, and was incensed on his return to hear Isabel on the telephone to Sam Fox. 'I agree with you, Sam,' she was saying in her most decisive tones. 'Mark Sole looks great. Just the right mixture of bashfulness and intelligence. What does the voice coach think?'

'Jeezus!' expostulated Andro in fury, slopping tea over the VT console in his disgust. 'You can't cast him. He's a girlish, churlish, *English*, numbskull!'

'Just a minute, Sam,' Isabel called down the phone, turning to add to Andro, 'Careful, darling—your xenophobia is showing.'

'This isn't xenophobia,' retorted Andro. 'This is artistic assessment—my brief, remember? The boy's a liability—take my word for it.'

'Yes, Sam, good idea, do that,' Isabel said in agreement to a suggestion from the other end of the phone. 'I'll wait to hear from you.' She replaced the receiver and turned to Andro again. 'Sam's going to ask the voice coach to give him a session and then get him to record the scene again but I think he's the one. He's got charisma, for all that he's still only a boy.'

Andro was furious. 'Charisma! When did that ever butter bannocks? The boy's a buffoon. He'll trash the film single-handed!'

Isabel eyed him speculatively. 'We'll see him again,' she confirmed stubbornly, 'and then we'll decide. You've got your choice with Andrina Gordon, Andro. You can't win them all.' Privately she suspected that Andro found Mark Sole, with his dark, smooth good looks, too much competition. He saw himself, in the part of Alan Breck, as *the* romantic heart-throb of the film and he didn't want any comparatively unknown juvenile stealing his thunder.

'The name Andrina is the female equivalent of Andro, isn't it?' he mused vindictively. 'Perhaps fate is throwing us together. What do you think, Izzy darling?'

'I think you had better look to your acting

laurels, lover-boy,' returned Isabel sharply. 'Those high cheekbones of yours won't make up for low standards!'

'I'm so glad you could come tonight, before Easter,' said Felicity, taking Catriona's coat and hanging it on a hook in the cloakroom to one side of the entrance hall of the Finlay house. 'I have an apology to make to you and I wanted to do it sooner rather than later.'

'An apology?' echoed Catriona, pretending ignorance. 'For what?'

Felicity led the way up the stairs, turning sideways to address her guest at the same time. 'I'll tell you over a drink. Bruce isn't home yet and the children are doing their homework so we have half an hour or so before supper. It's just us, I'm afraid. I hope you didn't mind being asked to a simple family supper.'

'I love it,' Catriona assured her. 'Family meals are the thing I miss most about leaving home.'

'In here.' Felicity opened the drawing-room door. A coal-effect gas fire glowed cosily in the Adam-style hearth and the smell of spring flowers drew the eye to a huge bowl of bursting daffodils on the central sofa-table. The room was bright and fresh with pastel-coloured chintzes and modern floral paintings. Catriona had seen it before when she came for dinner but then it had been full of people and noisy chatter. Now it was serene and welcoming.

'This is such a lovely room,' she remarked with enthusiasm. 'You have a very deft touch.'

'Heavens, do you think so?' exclaimed Felicity, visibly gratified. 'I just like colours to be bright, that's all. Nothing subdued about me, I'm afraid.' Her blue and green checked trousers and yellow cashmere sweater bore witness to this characteristic. Beside her Catriona, for once in grey and pink, felt rather insipid. 'What shall we drink? Do you like whisky or gin or would you prefer wine? I have some Chablis on ice.'

'That sounds perfect,' agreed Catriona, taking one end of the sofa in obedience to Felicity's directional gesture. 'I still can't think what you have to apologise to me about, though.'

'For being a suspicious old cow, that's what about,' proclaimed Felicity flatly, pouring wine into two stemmed glasses. 'For crying foul where it was not due.'

'If you mean for suspecting that it was me Bruce was having an affair with, then that's OK. Apology accepted,' grinned Catriona, taking a glass from her hostess. 'And if it means being given family supper in recompense then I might almost be glad you suspected me.'

'You haven't met my family in full force yet. I must say, you seem amazingly unruffled about being labelled a scarlet woman,' observed Felicity, sitting at the opposite end of the sofa. 'How did you know I'd suspected you anyway? Was it so obvious?'

'No,' Catriona laughed. 'Elizabeth told me.'

'The gossipy old goose,' complained Felicity indignantly. 'How could she!'

'Don't blame her,' responded Catriona hastily. 'She thinks you're a bit of a honey, by the way.'

'Does she?' Felicity looked slightly mollified by this information. 'Now who's telling tales out of school?'

'At least we all know what we think of each other now,' Catriona said. 'That is, as long as you've stopped seeing me as a scarlet woman.'

'Well yes, but you're still a bit of a mystery to me.' Felicity frowned.

'Alison reckons I'm transparent as glass.'

'Well, she knows you better than I do, of course. Personally I find it hard to understand what a gorgeous girl like you is doing unmarried and buried in a bank, that's all. I suppose I'm old-fashioned.'

'A little narrowminded, maybe. I dispute the gorgeous bit but if I am, why shouldn't I be as acceptable in a bank as anyone else?' Catriona displayed a touch of indignation.

'Oh, you are acceptable, of course you are. I can't help thinking it's a rather uninspiring occupation for someone with your intrinsic glamour.'

'I'm not the least bit glamorous. I'm a crofter's daughter, brought up among sheep and fish and tatties and tractors. Sometimes I wonder what on earth I'm doing among all you sophisticated city sinners.'

'Do you? You look so much the part, though. Career-girl born and bred.' A shadow crossed Felicity's face. 'Not like me—I'm no city sinner. Super-mum and mega-drudge, that's me. Sometimes I can understand why Bruce might be tempted elsewhere.'

'Well, I can't,' retorted Catriona, incensed.

'He's dead lucky to have you and I'm not the only one to think so. Anyway, he only took a detour off the straight and narrow because it happened to beckon like a beacon. Linda Melville was looking for a way to get back at her husband for his infidelities and Bruce was her hapless choice.'

'Huh!' was Felicity's dry reaction to this notion. 'I don't think he was as hapless as all that. Gutless, perhaps.' She shrugged eloquently. 'Anyway, we're not discussing me or Bruce, we're discussing you. Are you happy here in Edinburgh?'

Catriona was in two minds about how to answer this question. Should she confess her full-blown IDS to her managing director's wife? 'I have to admit that sometimes I pine for Skye,' she compromised by saying. 'But I don't think I'll ever lose that entirely, no matter how long I stay away.'

'Won't you go back there one day?' Felicity asked sympathetically. 'Surely you must if it's so much a part of you.'

Catriona nodded. 'Lately I've been devising wild schemes to become a Highland banker but none of them seem to work out in detail. Still, my father's got to leave the croft to someone and I daresay it'll be me. So perhaps when I'm a grizzled old maid I'll be able to swap the bonny bank for the bonny brae.'

'Do you have to be a banker? Couldn't you set yourself up as a financial consultant or something? Your knowledge of cheques and balances would be of great value on the receiving end of a bank statement, surely,' observed Felicity. 'Not that I'm encouraging you to leave Steuart's. I know that Bruce wouldn't want to see you go.'

'I expect my bout of restlessness will disappear in due course,' mused Catriona without conviction.

'I'm sure it would if some gorgeous hunk of a man diverted your nostalgia into romance,' commented Felicity slyly.

'Now you *are* being old-fashioned!' cried Catriona with amusement. 'I don't think it's politically correct any more to assume that all a girl really needs in life is a good man.'

'It may not be politically correct but I bet I could still find a good few girls who agree with me,' returned Felicity unrepentantly. And a good few executives' wives who would like to see all their husbands' beautiful female colleagues well and truly attached and out of harm's way, she added cynically to herself. Catriona was charming and sweet but in Felicity's eyes she still represented a sexual challenge to many a red-blooded professional male, whether married or unmarried.

'Who agree with you about what?' asked Bruce, striding into the room and moving straight to the drinks cupboard. 'Catriona, your glass is looking a bit sad. Shall I give you a refill?'

Both women held their glasses up for attention and the subject of man's necessity to woman was tactfully dropped.

'You can load the car now, Minto,' Hamish shouted through the kitchen door to the manservant who was watching television in his private quarters waiting for the summons to take his employer to the airport. Several suitcases and a long body-shaped ski-bag were stacked waiting in the hall. 'I'll be out in a few minutes.'

Walking through to his study Hamish keyed-in his self-made safe-combination and opened the recessed stainless-steel door. He sorted through the contents, searching for a particular item, and when he found it opened the thin, grey-velvet hinged jeweller's box to inspect the contents. The fabulous snake-link diamond bracelet winked at him in the light of a lamp. There was nothing about it to suggest that it had ever been stuffed unceremoniously into Catriona's duffel-coat pocket and then dropped disdainfully back through the letterbox of the Melvilles' Moray Place flat. Few women, least of all Linda, would imagine that it was second-hand goods, a gift spurned by another. It looked irresistible lying on its bed of royal-blue satin, Hamish thought, and decided that since it had failed to achieve the purpose for which it had originally been bought, it would serve another just as well. It would be a gift of reconciliation, a symbol of forgiveness. He would give it to Linda in front of Max so that they should both know that the family was still a unit and the bracelet was its link-chain.

He snapped the box shut with a sigh. He had spent two confusing days trying to come to terms with Catriona's rejection. For some hours on Sunday night he had struggled against it, telling himself that she would change her mind, that it was only a matter of being patient and waiting for the penny or, as he wryly acknowledged in this case, the million pounds to drop. But when he woke on Monday morning from an unrefreshing sleep he realised that he was fooling himself, that Catriona had extricated herself as gently as possible from a relationship which she felt unable to continue and the most that he could hope for was to remain on friendly terms with her.

He wondered if he would be able to do that or if it would be better to cut and run, transfer his funds and his accounts from Steuart's to another bank and appoint another agent to handle his investment in the film. For most of a day he had weighed the pros and cons of these two courses of action and eventually decided that his feelings for Catriona were such that he would rather keep in touch with her than cut her completely out of his life. He found it impossible to imagine never teasing her again, or sharing a restaurant table with her, or feasting his eyes on what he considered her perfect physiognomy. There was too much he liked about Catriona apart from the glorious sex they had enjoyed together. He decided that though they might not sleep together they might still be friends. Curiously, in a way he had never felt towards Linda or his first wife or any of his various mistresses, he felt protective towards Catriona—the only woman who had ever tired of him before he tired of her.

He tucked the jewel-box into his inside jacket pocket, folded the receipt into his wallet in case of customs enquiries, and switched out the lights. The Range Rover was waiting in the drive, loaded with his baggage. 'See to the burglar alarm for me, please, Minto,' he instructed, climbing into the passenger seat. 'Damnit man, d'you know I'm rather tired? I'm really looking forward to this holiday.'

Seventeen

The Cuillin rose like far pavilions, snow-capped against a livid sky. 'By Tummel and Loch Rannoch and Lochaber I will go...' ran the famous 'Road to the Isles' song but in modern terms there was no road leading west from Loch Rannoch. The old route to Skye over the wild moors and mountains of Lochaber was only possible on foot but, when driving home, Catriona loved to take the roads which most closely followed it because, on a clear day, the spectacular Cuillin range was in view for the last half of the journey, and she concurred with the song's lyrical cry, 'O the far Cuillin's a-puttin' love on me...'

Driving up the Skye coast from Ardvasar where the Mallaig ferry docked, she stopped the car and watched a rain squall race like a sea monster across the Sound of Sleat, corrugating the water into a sinister swirling serpentine. On the opposite shore, through the approaching sheet of rain, she could just make out of the dark humps of the Sandaig Islands which sheltered Gavin Maxwell's 'Ring of Bright Water'. It was a place of myth and magic, of poetry and legend, of sudden calm and violent change, where men and creatures fought together to stake their claim to a patch of inhospitable earth and where nature battled always for supremacy. A place where money meant nothing and human beauty was dwarfed and eclipsed by the splendid grandeur of mountain, sea and sky.

That's the trouble with city-folk, thought Catriona, taking shelter in the car as the squall hit land with ferocious force. 'They lose the natural yardsticks against which all life must be measured. And I stand in danger of losing mine.'

'I have a confession to make,' Catriona told her parents hesitantly when the three of them were gathered around the fireside after supper.

A surprised look widened Jamie Stewart's good eye. 'Very well, *a nighinn*,' he responded, rising to his feet. 'In that case we need a dram.'

Apart from attending a lengthy church service the island folk traditionally kept to their hearth and home on a Good Friday. It was a day for taking stock, for reviewing the winter past and planning the summer to come and for considering man's position in the universal scheme of things. Those choosing to mortify the flesh spent the day on bread and water, others philosophised over oatmealed-herring and whisky. The Stewarts had feasted on herring and now they saw no reason why they should not consume a little of the 'water of life'.

Catriona was grateful to be alone with her parents. Marie and Donnie were by their own hearth with their children, much heartened by her delivery earlier in the evening of the financial documentation that would enable them to renovate the coveted croft in the Fairy Glen. What she had to say now was not for their ears since it might cause them to fear for the loan's security.

'I want to come home,' she began, swirling the tangy liquid in her glass so that the aroma of whisky rose from it like a blessing. 'Not here to the croft, but home to the island, to the people I understand and the place I belong.'

Nothing was said for a few fertile moments but the atmosphere filled with unvoiced thoughts and opinions which hovered almost tangibly about the room.

Jamie was the first to speak. 'You want to give up your career?' he asked, trying not to express the level of disappointment he felt.

'Not entirely,' replied Catriona. 'Obviously I should have to work, to earn a living. But my career in the sense of maintaining a high managerial position in banking, yes. I want to give it up. Not tomorrow, or even probably this year, but in the near future.' She glanced at her mother but Sheena sat mute, her usually quick, blue eyes pensively hooded.

'But why?' Jamie was compelled to ask. She has spent half her life preparing for a career, he thought incredulously, which she now proposes to give up just when she's starting to reap the benefits! It seemed to him both illogical and ill-advised.

'Because I'm not suited to it,' replied Catriona calmly. 'I thought I was but I've discovered I'm not.'

'But you're brilliant at it!' expostulated her father. 'Look how you've bounded up the ladder. No one, no woman anyway, has achieved such quick promotion in so short a time. Even I know that, living out here in the sticks.'

'Two things—' Catriona broke in swiftly, 'two things you've just said which I can pick up on. First—I have done what few women do. Well, I'm proud of that but I've also paid a price. Second—you live "in the sticks". You used the expression sarcastically, Dad, but not without a secret sense of superiority. And you're right. Island life, island values, are superior, certainly to anything I've witnessed in Edinburgh. I don't want to be an outcast any more. I want to come back.'

'But to what?' persisted Jamie. 'What is there for you here?'

Catriona smiled at her father's bewilderment. 'Everything. There's everything here. Tell him, Mum.' She turned her gaze upon Sheena who was silently keeping her counsel in her armchair on the other side of the hearth.

'You came back yourself, Jamie,' Sheena

438

pointed out. And you never regretted it, as far as I know.'

'I'd been injured,' protested Jamie. 'I was retreating. The island was my saviour.'

'And how do you know that the same does not go for Catriona?' suggested Sheena gently. 'What do we know of what has been happening to her since she left?'

'She's not hurt—are you, Cat?' enquired Jamie doubtfully.

'No, Dad, not physically. I have been damaged perhaps by things that have happened, but if I came back I wouldn't be retreating, I'd be advancing, looking for some way of using my skills here in the island. Highland enterprises need financial expertise as much as any other, don't you think?'

'How do you mean, damaged?' Sheena asked with instant concern. 'You said you'd paid a price. Has something occurred since you were last here? What happened to Andro?'

Catriona gave a hollow laugh. 'Good question. Andro turned out to be not quite what he seemed. It's a bit of a story.'

'We'll hear it. We have plenty of time,' said Sheena determinedly. 'I get the impression though that he is a symptom rather than the disease.'

'That's right,' Catriona nodded eagerly. 'You're spot on, Mum, as usual. And the disease in question is the whole money-grubbing, image-conscious, two-timing world of glittering prizes into which I have strayed. I don't like it. I don't like what people do to get there or what

439

they do to stay there, and I don't like the fact that I have been drawn into behaving just the same way for just the same worthless reasons.'

Jamie downed his dram in a gulp and flung himself back in his armchair with an exasperated exclamation. 'Well, it all sounds cock-eyed to me, but if you do genuinely want to come back you know that, in time, this croft will be yours and of course we hope you'll use it and work it rather than let it fall into neglect as so many have. Continuity is important, that's one thing we know on the island.'

'One thing among many,' nodded Catriona. 'So you'd like to see me back, Dad?'

'Yes, right enough, of course,' agreed her father solemnly. 'But I still don't know what you're going to do for a job. You can stay here with us as long as you need to, but I have to tell you here and now that we have no intention of leaving our home before we're ready to go.'

'I should think not! Don't worry, I'll buy a flat or a wee cottage or even a caravan. And I'm not talking about tomorrow or even next month, I'm talking about maybe a year's time. I have to see this loan through for Marie and Donnie first anyway. I just wanted you to know what's in my mind.'

Sheena gave her daughter a motherly look. 'I doubt if you've given us one per cent of that,' she remarked. 'Don't get me wrong, Cat, it will be lovely to have you near us when you come back, but the workings of your mind, my dear, remain a closed book.'

'You suspect my motives?'

Sheena shrugged and sipped her whisky. 'Only because I think there is much more behind your decision than a mere value judgment between island ways and city ways. You're talking like someone who has seen the future in crystal and rejects its portents.'

'What future could be more secure than a bank manager's?' asked Jamie, puzzled.

'Security is not what's at stake here, Jamie,' Sheena said a little crossly. 'Cast your mind back to when you were thirty-something, like Catriona is now. What were the most important things in your life?'

Jamie frowned and opened his mouth to speak but then thought better of it. He glanced at the mantelpiece where a framed photograph showed himself and his family gathered, smiling, in front of the crofthouse. It had been taken when the two girls were about eight and nine and he and Sheena were in their mid-thirties. They looked wind-blown and sun-kissed, arms about each other, happy and contented together.

'Yes,' he said slowly, rubbing his dented skull. 'Yes, I see.'

Easter Saturday was cold and wet. Marie and Donnie brought the children for lunch but they were fretful and fractious and even playing horsey with Catriona did not keep them quiet for long. 'There's a new indoor playpark at Portree, let's take them there,' suggested Donnie.

So Catriona spent an energetic afternoon rescuing Niall from the ball-pool and taking Katie Mac down the bumpy slide, giggling

441

deliciously as her tummy flipped over each unexpected dip. Marie was looking larger than ever and confessed to her sister that she had got her dates muddled up and the baby was due in July, not August. 'So Donnie's got to get on with rebuilding the Sheader croft pretty quickly,' she said earnestly. 'As it is I doubt if we'll be in it before the autumn. Thank God for your loan, Cat. I don't know what we'd do without it.'

'You deserve it,' Catriona told her warmly. 'You'll have no trouble getting a mortgage once the house is built, and the Fairy Glen has been crying out for people for years now. Just be sure you make friends with the ghosts.'

'Niall and Katie will do that for us,' Donnie chuckled. 'I defy any restless spirit to dislike that little elf.' He nodded at his tiny daughter, poised on the top of a foam-rubber castle, her copper curls tangled and wild. As he spoke she threw herself off into the soft, bouncy moat and lay shrieking with delight at her own audacity.

'I defy them to take against any of you,' Catriona declared. 'They're lucky to get such special neighbours.'

'You will come and stay with us, won't you Cat? It will be almost as much your croft as ours.' Marie put a pleading hand on Catriona's arm.

'Try and keep me away,' her sister assured her. 'I intend to see much more of all of you in future.'

She caught the Sunday afternoon ferry from

Ardvasar, leaving the rain behind on the island. The road from Mallaig to Glendoran was dry and relatively traffic-free, only a scattering of early caravans impeding her swift progress along the winding and splendidly scenic route. She was looking forward to seeing the Carruthers and inspecting the improvements at the steading but Monday loomed beyond this pleasant interlude as an impending ordeal. After the reassuring visit with her own family she couldn't help regretting having accepted Rob's invitation to Glen Doran House. He and his family seemed to epitomise the world on which she wished to turn her back.

Although it was still far from finished the steading had been transformed from the blackened shell she had seen on her previous visit. Was it only five weeks ago, she pondered in silent disbelief, that I came here after the fire? Only a little more than a month since I first met Andro? So much had happened since then that she felt she must have changed radically herself.

'You look thinner, Catriona,' said Sue disapprovingly, greeting her with a kiss and eyeing her tight jeans and body-shirt which were no longer quite tight enough. 'And you don't need to. What have you been doing?'

Catriona laughed diffidently. 'Nothing. I don't think I've lost weight.' She tucked her hand unconsciously into her loose waistband and flushed a little. 'Well, perhaps a pound or two.' She pulled her duffel coat out of the car and put it on, snuggling into it not so

443

much for warmth as disguise.

'Or five or six, excuse me,' contradicted Sue. 'You'll lose your beauty if you get any thinner.'

'Perhaps that's why I'm doing it,' mused Catriona thoughtfully. 'I'm dubious about the value of beauty.'

Sue exclaimed in disbelief. 'Huh? Only someone who had it in abundance could say such a thing.' She ran her hands through her no-longer-highlights, pushing the straggly layers of hair off her face. 'I reckon I'm in overdraft at the beauty-bank.'

Catriona assessed Sue's comfortably bucolic appearance—rosy cheeks, faded jeans and wax-less Barbour—and grinned. 'You look like a woman who means business. There'll be plenty of time for playing the glamorous restaurateur.'

'As to that,' exclaimed Sue wryly, 'you haven't yet seen me in my chef's whites. Glamorous or what!'

'Well, the buildings look pretty good,' remarked Catriona, 'and so do you, actually. Happy and healthy.'

'And hardy, thank God.' Sue waved eagerly to two teenage boys who strolled into view from behind the re-roofed steading, a large brindle Alsatian bounding in their wake. 'Peter, John, come and meet Catriona!' she called to them. 'These are my new Highland laddies,' she said proudly. 'Don't they look great? They've been working like men since they arrived. I don't know what we'll do when they have to go back to school. And this is the fire-guard-dog I told you about—Bran.'

444

Catriona shook hands with the boys and fondled the dog's ears. Their very presence seemed to give the steading project a new depth of meaning, an investment in the future as much as the present. Peter, at fourteen, was as tall as his father but with the just-grown look of sheepish surprise that stringy adolescents often acquire along with their spots and sudden inches. His younger brother, John, still had some of his boyish roundness, his so-far-unblemished face slightly blurred by puppy fat and his eyes not yet shadowed by teenage insecurity. They were both brown-haired and fresh-complexioned, unmistakably Anglo-Saxon. They exchanged pleasantries with Catriona with well-drilled solemnity, aware that 'manners maketh man'.

'So these are your potential Hell's Angels?' Catriona teased Sue, glancing around the littered forecourt. 'I don't see the motorbikes anywhere.'

'Too young yet, thank God,' declared Nick, coming up behind them. 'Peter's a demon with the dumper truck though, aren't you, Pete?'

The older boy blushed and mumbled a reply and his less-shy brother commented cheekily, 'Don't ask why there's a chunk out of the steading wall though, will you?' and received an elbow in the ribs as a reward. 'Ouch!' he cried, retaliating with a fist in his brother's bicep. 'I can't help it if you can't steer straight.'

'But you can help being a little creep,' retorted Peter angrily. 'At least I don't mention your attempt to cement yourself into a corner.'

445

'You just have,' grinned John, unabashed at the memory of his classic DIY error.

'Now then boys, no arguing,' ordered Sue. 'Go and get washed and tidied up for dinner, and stoke up the fire and lay the table while you're at it, please. We're going to have a quick inspection tour. Come on Catriona, the stairs are in now. You can come and see the view from what will be the bar and restaurant.'

The picture windows on the new upper floor of the steading were still unglazed but framed a spectacular vista of folding hills and ruffled water, tunnelling away into the distance behind a budding furbelow of birch trees. Even in the fading light the panorama snatched the breath away with its epic grandeur and ever-changing mood.

'There'll be no idle chatter in this restaurant,' remarked Catriona. 'Your customers will be too busy gazing out of the window.'

'So we won't give them food for thought so much as food for sitting and staring,' chuckled Sue.

'Have you thought of a name for the place yet?'

'We've got a few ideas,' replied Nick. 'Mostly based on the fact that Bonnie Prince Charlie mustered his army down the road at Glenfinnan. What do you think about "The Prince's Standard"?'

'So that people will flock to it,' added Sue helpfully.

'Or just "Charlie's Caff"?' suggested Nick.

Catriona laughed. 'Well, that might do for the

snack bar downstairs but it certainly won't do for this.' She gestured around the unplastered walls and the gaping windows, imagining all their luxurious potential. 'This needs something wild and romantic.'

'And digestible,' Sue reminded her. 'Knives and forks and Michelin stars and all that.'

'The Dirk and Claymore,' suggested Catriona triumphantly, 'speaking of knives and forks.'

'Well, if you want that sort of thing, what about The Well-filled Sporran?' proclaimed Nick, getting in the mood. 'Or The Swirling Plaid!'

'The Forty-Fiver,' giggled Catriona. 'The Young Suspender!'

'The Don't-Mention-Culloden!' gasped Nick, clutching at her arm in helpless mirth.

'I can see we're going to have to give this some serious thought,' observed Sue caustically, eyeing the two jokers. 'Otherwise we'll end up a laughing stock.'

'Speaking of serious thought,' remarked Catriona, her mirth subsiding, 'when you're up and running, do you think you might use the services of a financial consultant, if there was one available locally?'

'How do you mean?' asked Nick with interest. 'Book-keeping, VAT, that sort of thing?'

'Yes, but also tax advice, insurance, employment regulations, pension services—the whole complicated mine-field of business practices.'

'Well, I would if I could get it all under one roof,' said Nick. 'As it is my accountant is in Kent, my insurance broker's in London and my bank is in Edinburgh. Not terribly practical really.'

'So you're going to have to rationalise in the near future?'

'I suppose so, although I've been too busy getting the walls up to worry about such things at present. Why?'

'You'll have to keep this under your hat for the time being but I'm thinking of setting up such a consultancy in the Highlands.' Catriona shrugged off their exclamations of surprise and concern. 'Oh not immediately, don't worry about your overdraft or anything. I'll tell you all about it over supper.'

Sue shivered. 'I don't know about supper just yet but I could do with a dram. It's getting cold. We'll go up to the cottage, shall we? The boys will have stoked up the fire by now. It should be warm and cosy.' She gave Catriona a slightly worried look. 'You did bring your sleeping bag like I suggested, didn't you? I'm afraid the accommodation is rather basic.'

'I think tonight is the least of my worries,' Catriona assured her. 'It's what's going to happen tomorrow that bothers me.'

'Tomorrow? Oh, yes. You're braving the laird's lair, aren't you?'

'It's not visiting the laird that I mind,' Catriona confided. 'He's quite an endearing character. It's the rest of his family I'm wary of. Lord Nevis is my boss, you know, and rather daunting, to say nothing of his wife.'

'So you'll be minding your Ps and Qs,' laughed Sue. 'Well, you don't have to worry about that here. What with the two boys and Nick hurling their clothes into any old corner and a distinct lack of drying facilities, our cottage looks like a bear pit, I'm afraid.'

'Sounds wonderful. I may go into hibernation.'

The kitchen of Glen Doran House hadn't been modernised for fifty years. Its cooking facilities were cast iron and enamel and its sinks were deep and white with scrubbed wooden draining boards. Above shoulder-high cream tiles the ceiling and upper walls were still painted the vibrant shade of blue which Victorian cooks believed kept flies at bay. An ancient refrigerator made companionable gurgling sounds and vibrated violently every time the door was opened and it was flanked by two magnificent pine dressers which housed a gold-edged and crested white porcelain banqueting service—thirty of every size and shape of plate, copious lidded vegetable dishes, piles of enormous ashets, tureens that were works of ceramic art, sauce-boats and soup cups, salad bowls and coffee cups. Some of these elegant articles had been removed from the shelves to places at the central refectory table, which had been spread with a damask cloth for the occasion and laid with crystal glassware and ancestral silver. Lady Nevis might be producing kitchen-supper but she was doing it in style.

Lochaber was seated at one end of the table, his son at the other, and the candleflames flickering between them successfully prevented too much eye-contact. Toleration was the

449

watchword between this father and son. Rob and his mother, seated opposite each other on the long sides of the table, found conversation easier and even relayed messages between the Earl and his heir from time to time. A plump middle-aged woman in a floral overall padded patiently about, placing vegetable dishes on the table and distributing the plates as Lord Nevis carved the haunch of venison.

'Thank you, Kirsty,' Lady Nevis said, when the last portion was served. 'You go on back to Angus now and we'll manage the rest. You can wash up in the morning.'

'Very well, my lady.' Kirsty and Angus Mackinnon were the only staff resident at Glen Doran House, enough to cater for the old laird's meagre needs except when a visit from his family stretched their resources. The main salons of the house were under dust-sheets, so it was only the few rooms which the Earl used that needed regular cleaning, and when Lord and Lady Nevis visited they usually brought meals up from Edinburgh, ready-prepared by an outside caterer.

'Rob's invited someone to lunch tomorrow, Gamps,' said Queenie Nevis in her clearest talking-to-old-people voice.

'There's no need to shout, Reine,' grumbled Lochaber, who alone used his daughter-in-law's given name. 'Must I keep reminding you that I am not deaf?'

'But did you hear what I said?' asked Lady Nevis patiently, trying to regulate her tone. 'We have a guest for lunch tomorrow.'

'Male or female?' enquired the Earl, ignoring her and addressing Rob.

'Female,' Rob replied, grinning slyly at his grandfather. 'You know her actually, Gamps. You lent her a clock.'

'I lent my rowan clock to an island girl who turned up at my workshop out of the blue one day,' said Lochaber, cutting into his venison with the same kind of vigour that he applied to his woodcraft. 'Come to think of it, she said she worked with George's crew. I advised her against it.'

'Thanks very much,' muttered Lord Nevis in a tone that *was* inaudible to the Earl.

'She said you told her she should be back on Skye making babies,' remarked Rob, to his mother's amusement.

'Did he?' asked Lady Nevis. 'You saucy old thing, Gamps!'

The laird said nothing, chewing his meat methodically.

'I don't think she minded,' Rob added to his mother. 'She seemed to take to the old boy.'

'Don't call me an old boy, you cheeky young weasel!' exclaimed his grandfather, swallowing suddenly. 'She was a rather lovely young lady as I recall. What's she doin' acceptin' an invitation from you?'

'Succumbing to my irresistible charm,' retorted Rob, who held his grandfather in great regard but scant respect.

'Kow-towin' to the boss's son more likely,' sniffed the Earl. 'Though it would be good to think you could attract a nice girl like that.'

'Are we sure she *is* a nice girl?' asked Lady Nevis tartly, then added hastily on fielding Rob's angry glance, 'Nice in the old-fashioned sense of the word, I mean.'

'Whatever is the difference between old-fashioned nice and modern nice, Mother?' Rob asked acidly.

'I don't care what kind of nice you mean,' rumbled the Earl. 'I remember her well. She was pretty, polite and pleasant and she had Celtic gold hair and gleamin' silver eyes. A man could live with that on any scale of niceness.'

'It would be *nice* if we could use the house properly to entertain our guests,' grumbled Lord Nevis, who disliked taking his meals in what he called 'the servants' quarters'. 'I can't remember when I last ate in the dining room here.'

Lochaber's hearing was acute enough to pick up this remark. 'When you bring anyone here that's worth entertainin' I'll order the dust-sheets removed,' he said huffily. 'But I'm not spendin' money openin' up the house just for your infrequent visits.'

'We might come more often if we were made more comfortable when we got here,' his son declared loudly down the table.

'Tell your father I don't want to make him comfortable,' retorted the Earl with spirit, via Rob. 'He'll only bring a bunch of bloodthirsty bankers up here to shoot the birds and stalk the deer. This is a protected estate—protected from serpents and vipers!' He favoured his grandson with a wicked grin. '*You* might merit some dust-sheet removal one day, my boy, if you

452

play your cards right.'

'The rooms used to be beautiful when I first came here,' recalled Lady Nevis nostalgically. She was used to what she considered the pointless sparring between her husband and his father and chose to ignore it rather than endorse it by taking part. 'Full of sunshine and they smelled of beeswax and flowers. We used to have some wonderful house parties.'

'Well, Rob knows how to get them opened up again, don't you, laddie?' A wrinkled wink accompanied this sally.

'I wanted to talk to you about something like that actually, Gamps,' replied Rob after a hesitant glance at his parents. 'With your permission I'd like to move into Glen Doran House permanently in the not too distant future.'

'Would you, Rob? Now that *is* music to an old man's ears,' crowed the Earl with surprised gratification, smiling and nodding over his venison.

'Move in? Actually live here?' asked Lord Nevis incredulously. 'What would you do, for goodness sake?'

'What do you mean, what would I do?' Rob ejaculated indignantly. 'This whole estate could do with an overhaul, for a start.' He held up his hand at his father's exclamation of anger. 'Oh, I know strictly speaking that's none of my business—yet. But I just thought I'd make the point. Grandfather can't go on handling things almost on his own. He needs some help and I'd like to give it to him. But I'd also like

453

to set up my own business here, something that would use the land profitably and provide some employment for local people. I've been away long enough.'

'That's perfectly true, laddie,' agreed Lord Lochaber vehemently. 'And if your father doesn't think so then that's too bad.'

'I didn't say that,' returned Lord Nevis sharply. 'I'm just a little surprised, that's all. Rob has always seemed firmly hooked into his job in London. It's a very good job, with the added bonus of a bit of glamour. After all, you refused to come into the bank because you preferred it.' He glared at Rob accusingly.

'Eight years ago, when you started the bank, yes, that is how I felt. And I still don't want to work in banking. I haven't the aptitude or the qualifications. But nor do I want to go on living in London. I belong here and I want to be here.'

'When can you come?' asked Lochaber, plainly delighted by this notion. 'The sooner the better!'

'This needs more discussion,' insisted Lord Nevis ponderously, laying his knife and fork neatly together in the centre of his plate.

'Stuff and nonsense. He wants to come—he can come—end of story,' announced Lord Lochaber gleefully. 'You can discuss it as much as you like, George, but at the end of the day he is the ultimate heir and he belongs right here. You should be glad! From now on you can leave Rob and me to handle the estate and you can get on with featherin' your nest of vipers.' He leaned forward to place his gnarled fingers on Rob's sinewy hand. 'You just get yourself organised and get up here, Robaidh my boy. The sooner the better.'

'But what about Andro? enquired Lady Nevis doubtfully. 'Won't that cut him out completely?'

'Don't worry about Andro, Mother,' Rob remarked with heavy irony. 'He won't miss out; he never does. In fact, as always, he'll probably get a great deal more than he deserves.'

'What do you mean?' she demanded hotly, defending her younger son. 'He's done terribly well lately. Your father says he's rescued a film project from ignominious failure almost single-handed.'

'Quite right,' nodded Lord Nevis. 'At the eleventh hour he managed to persuade Hamish Melville of all people to invest a million pounds.'

'I'm aware of that, Father. I drew up the contracts and supplied the Completion Bond.'

'Did you, dear boy?' enquired Lord Nevis in surprise. 'Well, it was quite a coup. I believe Andro's beginning to pull himself together at long last.'

'Really?' intoned Rob with sarcasm. 'I advise you not to ask how many knives he plunged carelessly between how many shoulder-blades in the process. I just hope it's the start of a long and brilliant screen career because that will keep him well out of my hair.'

'I wish you two boys wouldn't differ so much,' sighed Lady Nevis. 'It's bad enough having these two bickering all the time.' She gestured to each end of the table and addressed the two noble lords in strident tones. 'I hope you're going to behave yourselves tomorrow both of you, in front of poor Angus Mackinnon. Sometimes I wonder what he must think of us after one of these estate tours of yours. I sit there red with embarrassment while you two squabble and he grits his teeth and drives.' She turned to her son pleadingly. 'Why don't you come with us, Rob? You always seem able to keep the peace.'

But Rob shook his head and grinned. 'No way! I wouldn't want to spoil their fun. Besides, Catriona is due around midday and I want to be here when she arrives.'

Driving up to Glen Doran House, Catriona was struck once more by its welcoming aspect. From early morning the sun had gilded the surrounding hills and now, at midday, it shone warm on the mellow stone of the house's façade, glinting off the long, square-paned sash windows.

The polished-oak storm-doors stood wide at the main entrance and Rob had obviously been looking out for her car because as soon as it drew to a halt he opened the inner glass door and strode down the front steps. 'Hello again,' he said, clasping her hand in both of his. 'Welcome to Glen Doran.'

'Thank you,' she smiled. She had forgotten how kind his eyes were, soft, speckled blue-grey irises with clear unveined whites, fringed by thick, dark lashes. And they looked at her straight and frank, surely hiding nothing...?

'But it's not your first visit, is it?' he remarked, shutting the door of her car. 'You've been here before.' They began to climb the steps.

'Yes, but it's nice to come in the front door,' she said appreciatively. 'So far I've only seen the back premises and the loch path.'

'Ah yes. Andro was hardly playing the charming host, was he? Well, no Andro today—only the Olds and they're all out and about at this moment so we have the place to ourselves. What would you like to do before lunch? See over the house?'

'Yes please, I'd love to. It looks so friendly and hospitable from the outside, not at all daunting like some stately homes.' She stood and gazed upwards into the lofty moulded-plaster ceiling of the hallway. 'But it is obviously very grand.'

'Quite grand,' he murmured diffidently. 'You may find that hard to appreciate at present since everything is covered with dust-sheets but there's some rather special oak panelling and the plasterwork is elegant. Keep your coat on though, it's freezing cold.'

Despite the shrouded furniture, the fine proportions of the rooms were apparent and the Adam-style restraint of the embellishment was noticeable. White pilasters and cornices were picked out in pastel blues, grey and greens and the oak panelling was unstained, a little dusty but with a depth of polish which shone through the dull film. As they wandered from room to room they chatted about styles and decorations

457

and speculated about the use to which each may have been put and Catriona gradually lost her nervousness. Rob seemed relaxed and easy, unpretentious about his illustrious heritage but at the same time quietly proud of the beautiful house that was his ancestral home.

There was a suite of five rooms on the top floor of the west wing in which he lingered longer than the others. 'These are the nursery quarters,' he confided, standing in the middle of a corner room which boasted windows overlooking on one side the rugged brown hills enclosing the glen and on the other the slate-grey loch, gleaming in the dip of the landscape, drawing the eye from the wide sweep of forest and peak that lay to the south. 'This was my bedroom when I was a little boy. Andro had the one next door and our nanny had two rooms off the central sitting room. We had lessons in there with a governess for several years. Until we went to prep school.'

'This is a lovely room,' commented Catriona, entranced by the double view and the sunlight pouring in through the smeared panes. 'Why don't you sleep here when you come home?'

Rob shrugged. 'It's cheaper to heat the other wing of the house. I have a room on the first floor now but it's rather soulless, I must say. I may change it if I come back permanently.'

'Are you going to?' she asked with surprise.

He nodded. 'I've been talking to Grandfather about it. He's getting on a bit now and although he doesn't say so I know he'd like some help with the estate. He's let things slip a bit. It's not his fault but I'd like to sort it out. Anyway, I can't stand much more of London. No one is ever gruntled there.'

'Gruntled?' echoed Catriona curiously, then smiled. 'Oh, I see. And that makes you *dis*gruntled?'

'Very,' he concurred. 'So I'm jacking in my job and picking up my crummock.'

'That's funny. I've been talking with my parents this weekend about doing much the same thing.' She was struck with a sudden thought. 'But for God's sake, don't tell your father. I'm not leaving the bank immediately or anything. Just thinking about it.'

'Really? Leaving Edinburgh? No, I won't tell Father, don't worry. He'll take a lot of telling anyway.'

'Why?'

'He can't imagine that everyone isn't deliriously happy working for Steuart's. It's just a big family, he always says.'

'Well, to be honest it's not so much Steuart's that gets me down as banking in general. I'm sick of the "money rules, OK" scenario.'

'What do you plan to do, then?' Rob asked. 'I mean, when I leave London I've got a job to do here but if you're dropping out of banking...?'

'I may end up in Queer Street—is that what you think?' She laughed. 'Oh ye of little faith!' She shoved her cold hands into her coat pockets. 'You're right about these rooms. Even in the sunshine they're freezing.'

'We'll go down now, shall we? That's one advantage of eating in the kitchen—it's warm, and Gamps will probably have the sherry bottle out by now.'

Rob stood back to let her precede him through the door. He noticed that she kept her distance, wary of even accidental bodily contact. The observation perturbed him. 'So what *are* you going to do?' he persisted gently as they walked down the gloomy second-floor corridor. With all the doors firmly shut, the only light filtered through the cupolas over the stairways which were grimy with neglect.

'I thought I might start some kind of financial consultancy. Give a service to small businesses in the West Highlands.' She frowned uncertainly. 'Does that sound like a pipe-dream to you? I want to get back to where I come from, you see. Like you.'

'No, it doesn't sound like a pipe-dream. It sounds a really good idea. It might need a bit of financial backing at first though, had you thought of that?'

She shrugged expressively. 'Not really. I haven't given any of it much thought yet. I only know I don't want to stay in banking and live in Edinburgh for ever. Everything else is in the air.'

'Like a castle! Good for you. I hope it works out.' They had reached the first-floor landing where the carpets were deeper and the dados more elaborate. 'This is where the grown-ups sleep,' he said, and added on a note of regret, 'I'm down with the grown-ups nowadays.'

'Shame!' she exclaimed softly. 'I bet you had an idyllic boyhood up there in your eyrie.'

'Well, at least Nanny loved me.'

Catriona skipped down the graceful central staircase. 'Did Nanny love Andro too?' she asked.

'She was infatuated,' Rob declared. 'He learned how to seduce females at an early age.'

'At his brother's knee?' she teased.

'Certainly not. I am the soul of probity. Come with me below stairs.' He pushed open the door beneath the staircase which led to the back quarters. 'All manner of excitements await you there.'

But as they made their way down the rather dingy brown-tiled passage they heard sounds of consternation coming from the kitchen. Before they reached it Kirsty burst through the door, her face pale and shocked. 'Oh Master Robaidh!' she exclaimed with anguish. 'There's been an accident!'

Eighteen

A bedraggled and distraught-looking man in a torn green all-weather jacket stood in the kitchen, blood trickling down the side of his face from a flesh-wound in his scalp.

'Angus! What's happened?' demanded Rob. Pulling a chair out from the table, he placed it behind the gasping, swaying man and gently pushed him into it. 'Here, sit down.'

461

'Call the ambulance!' insisted Angus Mac-kinnon urgently, panic in his pale blue eyes. 'They're injured, the laird and your mother and father. I don't know how bad!'

'Catriona, dial 999,' ordered Rob briskly. 'Kirsty, show her the phone.' He turned back to Angus. 'What exactly happened? Where are they?'

'Up on the brae—near the reservoir. The embankment gave way at the wee bridge there—the stone one, you know? The Land Rover just rolled down the slope—there was nothing I could do!' The man's breath came in rasping jerks, as if his lungs hurt.

'Take it easy, Angus. You've run a long way and you're bleeding. You stay here and tell the ambulance where to come. They should be able to get up the track as far as that. How badly are they hurt?' Rob had filled a glass with water as he spoke and held it to Angus's trembling lips.

The breathless man took a sip and choked slightly but managed to say, 'Your mother's no' bad. She's lookin' after the others.'

'Right.' Rob began to open and shut one drawer after another in the kitchen dressers. 'Kirsty! Where's the first-aid kit?'

The flustered woman dashed to the required drawer and pulled out a small red and white plastic case. 'Here. The ambulance is on its way.'

Catriona replaced the receiver. She saw Rob pull a plastic container from a cupboard and start to fill it from the tap. 'I'll come with you,' she said.

'Good,' he nodded, thrusting the container at her. 'Finish filling this. I'll get some rugs. We'll take your car. It'll cover the terrain better than Father's Merc but I want to get his mobile phone. I'll meet you round the back.'

The little silver Golf bounced and slid on the stony track, climbing the brae as fast as Catriona dared to drive it. It seemed to her a desperately long way along the winding, unmade road, up through a pine plantation and down between thick banks of dead bracken until the track began to follow the path of a burn which debauched into a small, manmade reservoir. Beyond a low grey-stone bridge which spanned the burn they could see the overturned Land Rover lying at a crazy angle just above the water level.

'Christ! It was lucky it didn't roll into the reservoir,' exclaimed Rob. His face was white with anxiety, his hands clutching the dashboard as Catriona wrestled with the wheel of the Golf.

'There's your mother!' she cried as a hunched figure became visible, bent over something lying on the steep, stony slope between the Land Rover and the track. A scar of newly exposed earth and rubble showed where the side of the roadway had caved in, hurling the vehicle down the embankment.

'Put the car off the track—up there,' Rob suggested, pointing to a flat grassy area on the nearside of the bridge. 'Leave a passage for the ambulance.'

As soon as they came to a halt he was out of

the door with an armful of rugs, bounding over the heather and rocks to where his mother was. Catriona followed more slowly, slipping in her not-quite-so-suitable leather boots. Lady Nevis was kneeling at her husband's side, her face scratched and muddy, her eyes anguished but dry. She seemed oblivious to the darkening bruise on her temple. When she spoke her voice was remarkably steady, as if she was staying calm for the sake of the wounded man.

'He's in terrible pain,' she said softly. 'It's his leg. I haven't moved him.'

Lord Nevis had been thrown out of the Land Rover as it rolled and his right leg was twisted at an impossible angle to his body. His face was contorted in agony, his breathing short and juddering. He was conscious but incapable of speech. Blood was seeping through his torn trouser leg where it looked horribly as if shards of bone had pierced both flesh and fabric.

Rob dropped to his knees and opened the first-aid kit. 'Don't worry Father, the ambulance is on its way,' he said, feeling for a point on his father's thigh where he might put pressure on the blood vessels to slow the bleeding.

'Where's the Earl?' asked Catriona, looking anxiously around. She could not see another body anywhere.

'He's still in the Land Rover,' Queenie Nevis told her. 'I couldn't get him out.' From the sound of her voice, she didn't believe there was much point in doing so. 'They weren't wearing seat-belts in the back.'

Catriona stifled a gasp of dismay and stumbled

over to where the heavy vehicle lay on its side, the wind-rippled water of the reservoir lapping at its battered roof. There was no engine noise but a strong smell of spilled diesel mingled with the scent of fresh-turned earth. Angus and Lady Nevis had clearly struggled out of the front of the vehicle by pushing open the now-horizontal passenger door, for it was unlatched. Catriona picked her way round the exposed chassis to peer in through the rear window which was caked with mud but unbroken. She could just discern the pathetically crumpled figure of the old Earl lying against the lower rear door, his head wedged between the front seat and the roof-brace. She could not see his eyes, nor could she tell whether or not he was breathing.

Gingerly she hauled herself on to the back wing of the Land Rover. It shifted slightly but did not seem unstable. She heaved the front door open and managed to wriggle under it, easing the lower half of her body into the cab so that her feet were resting on the steering column. 'I'm going in,' she called to Rob, who had raised his head to observe her actions.

He glanced apprehensively at his mother, placed her hand gently on the pressure bandage he had applied to his father's thigh and said, 'Press hard here, dear—I'll be back in a moment.' Then he grabbed a gnarled, silver-grey section of dead branch which had fallen years ago from a nearby pine tree and hurried across a stretch of churned-up ground to the Land Rover. Using the branch as a lever he wedged the door of the vehicle open, allowing

465

Catriona to slide completely inside.

'He's breathing,' she called, having contorted her body to push her hand down near the Earl's face. 'I can feel it on my fingers.'

'We're going to need some heavy equipment,' said Rob gruffly, shoving a rug into the cab. 'Try and put this over him. Can you hang on in there in case he comes round? I'm going to ring for more help.' He saw Catriona's ashen-faced nod and smiled grimly at her. 'Great girl! I think Mother and Father will be all right till the ambulance comes. She's shocked and concussed but she's hanging on and he's in pain but not losing any more blood.'

'Get on the phone quick,' urged Catriona, stretching over the front seat to ease the rug around the frail body. 'He's too old to survive this for long.'

But it was an hour before the firemen who came could cut the Earl out of his metal cage, an hour during which Catriona dangled, cramped and uncomfortable, over the vertical front seat and kept him steady, talking to him continuously even though she couldn't be sure that he heard her. The noise of the hydraulic cutting equipment was deafening as the sturdy steel of the Land Rover's coachwork put up a stiff resistance. Its impressive strength had protected the passengers from being crushed to death when the vehicle rolled but now, that very strength hampered the work of the rescuers.

Meanwhile the RAF had sent a helicopter with a team of paramedics who prepared Lord and Lady Nevis for transportation to the Belford

Hospital in Fort William by ambulance and laid out a special cradle upon which Lochaber might be winched to safety in the aircraft when they eventually managed to release him from the Land Rover. Sadly he never made it.

Soon after they arrived, with Catriona's help, the paramedics managed to get a drip into the old man's arm and just as the firemen were finally hauling the roof back, working up to their waists in water, Lochaber's eyes flickered open.

He gazed straight at Catriona with instant recognition. 'You came back then,' he murmured. 'Did you bring the clock?'

She had to strain to catch his words, but was able to bend nearer as the roof moved back. 'You'll be out soon,' she told him clearly. 'Not long now. You're all right.'

His head moved a fraction, even jammed as it was. 'No. Can't stay. Just glad you're here.' His voice trailed away and his breath rattled loudly in his chest.

She saw his eyes roll upwards under the wrinkled lids and cried out despairingly, 'No! Don't go! You're free now!'

And perhaps he was, but not on this earth.

'God, you were brilliant,' Rob said later that afternoon as he and Catriona slumped over the kitchen table drinking hot sweet tea. 'I don't know how you stayed with him in that position all that time. You must have been in agony.'

After she had crawled out of what remained of the Land Rover, Catriona realised that she could hardly walk. Her legs, which had been folded under and around the steering wheel, were rigid with cramp and her head was buzzing with the noise of the hydraulic cutting tool. She was also devastated that it had all been for nothing, terribly distressed to have seen the Earl slip away just as relief became imminent.

She did not cry for long, however, being more concerned to help Rob deal with his grief at the death of his grandfather. 'I'm just glad someone was with him who knew him,' she said gently. 'It's a shame it couldn't have been you but you wouldn't have squeezed into the space. I'm so sorry he couldn't hang on. He was amazingly tough to last as long as he did.'

'They said they thought his spleen was ruptured,' murmured Rob. 'He may not have made it anyway. I just hope he wasn't in terrible pain at the end.'

'No, he wasn't,' she told him. 'He was quite lucid and calm and he knew who I was. That was so extraordinary! He opened his eyes and he knew immediately who I was.' She told Rob what the old man had said to her.

'You made more of an impression than you think,' was Rob's comment and he smiled briefly at her. 'I think he was probably happy with his last sight on earth.'

Catriona bit her lip and hung her head. Into it came regretful memories of the bitter thoughts she'd had recently about the Earl and his family.

'I must phone Andro,' said Rob wearily, heaving himself to his feet. 'He worshipped

Gamps more than anyone.'

'Did he?' murmured Catriona, wondering why some of the old man's wisdom had not rubbed off on his younger grandson.

Rob spent ten minutes talking to his brother and another five getting a hospital report on his parents. When he returned to Catriona she and Kirsty were making sandwiches with cold beef which they should have had hot for lunch. 'You need some food, Master Robaidh,' the housekeeper said in motherly tones. 'And the young lady looks half-starved.'

'Catriona. My name is Catriona,' said she, butter-knife in hand.

'Very well, Miss Catriona,' agreed Kirsty, taking the knife from her. 'Why don't you and Master Robaidh go to the sitting room and I'll bring you a tray.'

Her rather subservient mode of address sounded strange to Catriona, more used to an egalitarian approach, but Rob didn't appear to notice.

'Andro is coming up this evening, Kirsty,' he said. 'Come on, Catriona, we'll go and light the fire in the snug.'

'It's all lit and ready. You just relax,' Kirsty said kindly. 'I'll see to this.'

'What about your husband though?' asked Catriona with concern. 'Wasn't he hurt?'

'Angus is fine. A bit shocked and wi' a big bump on his head but the doctor came and looked at him and said he'd just to sleep it off. I thank God for his safety, Master Robaidh, and pray for the soul of His Lordship. I hope you do not hold Angus responsible.'

'Not in any way, Kirsty. I've already told him that,' Rob assured her. 'Let him rest easy on that score.'

When he wasn't in his workshop, the late Earl had used a small morning room near the kitchen quarters as his regular retreat. In there he had listened to the radio, read copiously and written letters and, very occasionally, watched television. It had a tiled fireplace and cosy furnishings which had all seen better days but it was comfortable and its atmosphere reeked of its missing proprietor. Examples of his woodwork were scattered about—wooden goblets, a bowl made of beautiful burred walnut and a large, pale polished beech platter heaped with fruit shapes in woods of many shades and grains.

'I just can't believe he won't sit here any more and listen to *The World At One,*' mused Rob sorrowfully, avoiding the chair nearest the fire which had been his grandfather's. 'He's always been here, in this house, all of my life.'

'What did Andro say?' asked Catriona dully, curling up in the corner of a sofa.

'He wanted to know how it had happened of course, and where the parents are. He's going to call in at the hospital on the way up.' As he said this the telephone rang from a writing desk in a corner of the room. He rose to answer it and spoke rather formally for several minutes to the caller.

'*The Inverness Courier,*' he said laconically, when he replaced the receiver. 'Some stringer has been monitoring the emergency frequencies.

470

They wanted Grandfather's death confirmed.'

'There'll be more calls,' observed Catriona. 'The stringer will sell the story to the agencies. It'll be on the wires already.'

Kirsty entered at this juncture with a trayload of sandwiches and steaming mugs of soup. Despite the sombre atmosphere Catriona realised she was ravenous. Shock had sharpened her appetite. Rob, too, seemed hungry and they consumed the meal in companionable silence, both wrapped in their thoughts, exchanging only occasional reassuring glances.

When they had finished, Catriona wiped her mouth on her napkin and said awkwardly, 'I should be going.'

Rob looked stricken. 'Don't go,' he said instantly. 'I don't want you to.'

'But I shouldn't be here,' she murmured, shifting to the edge of her chair. 'I'm not part of the family.'

'What does that matter?' he asked in bewilderment. 'I wish you would stay. I really don't want to be on my own.'

'Andro will be here later. I'll stay until he comes, if you like.'

'Stay whether he comes or not,' Rob urged. 'Grandfather liked you. He'd want you to be here.' The phone rang again. 'Oh God, I suppose it'll ring all evening,' he said wearily before answering it.

Catriona watched him as he dealt with another reporter. Despite the businesslike style of his conversation his pale, drawn face held a touching vulnerability. He looked younger than his years, like a youth facing his first experience of bereavement rather than a mature adult, familiar with life and death. She wondered sympathetically if this was perhaps his first close encounter with the Grim Reaper. It had certainly been the first time she had ever watched someone die and she had found it a cathartic experience, even though it had not been her own relative. How much worse it must be when it was your long-lived, much-loved grandfather who was snatched away before your eyes.

'That was the *Scotsman*,' he muttered when he put the phone down. 'There are bound to be more.'

'You look exhausted,' she said. 'Let me take the next one.'

'Yes,' he responded, 'I'd be grateful. It seems so dreadful talking about him as if he's no longer here. They're all asking questions about him in the past-tense.' He sank down beside her on the sofa and buried his face in his hands.

She moved up beside him and put an arm around him. 'Cry,' she said softly. 'No one is looking.' She felt his shoulders shake under her embrace and the sobs followed, long, racking sobs which tore at her own emotions so that slow, waxy tears slid down her cheeks also. The telephone rang again but she let it ring. She remembered the time, not so long ago, when she had been unable to do so and it had been he, Rob, on the line. Hamish had begged her not to answer it that time but she had. How different was this occasion!

The ringing stopped and Rob's sobs subsided.

She withdrew her arm and felt in her pocket for the tissues she usually kept there. 'Here.' She handed him one and waited while he mopped his eyes and blew his nose.

He stood up and threw the used tissue on the fire where it blazed up and disappeared into ash. He turned and gave her a rueful smile. 'Thanks,' he said. 'I needed that.'

She returned the smile. 'There are better-padded shoulders to cry on,' she observed.

'Yours was fine,' he said quietly. 'Much appreciated.'

Andro arrived at about ten o'clock looking white and shaken. 'They've operated on Father's leg,' he told Rob, 'so I waited until he was out of theatre. They've put a pin in it and they say it will knit in time but he'll have a limp. Mother's had a head X-ray and has a hairline fracture of the skull. She'll be in hospital for several days until they're sure they've controlled any swelling. She wanted to come home but the doctor said there's a risk of brain damage if she does.'

'Poor old things,' said Rob with concern. 'Still, they're in the best place. It's been mayhem here. Press calls, television and radio. Did you hear it on the radio news?'

'No, I didn't.' Andro looked ill-at-ease, as if he was containing his emotions only with great difficulty. He strode to the cupboard where he knew his grandfather kept the drinks. 'I need a dram,' he declared defiantly, as if they might declare it out of bounds. 'Anyone else?'

'Yes, I'll have one,' responded his brother. 'Catriona?'

She shook her head without speaking, fearing that if she did Andro might explode. The look he had given her on his arrival had demonstrated all too clearly his antipathy to her presence. Perhaps it put him under some restraint, she thought. Perhaps he, too, wanted to cry and couldn't allow himself to do so in front of her. She felt uncomfortable, undecided about what she should do.

Andro brought Rob's dram over to him, standing very close and muttering, 'What the hell's she doing here?'

'Catriona is my guest,' responded Rob in his normal voice. 'She was with Grandfather when he died and she's been wonderful since. Do you have a problem with that, Andro?'

'Yes I do! Why should she have been with Gamps when he died? She's nothing to do with us!'

'Well, you weren't here old man, were you? And by chance Catriona was. I don't know why you should object to her being here. She's done a lot for this family—not least for you.'

'Look, I'll go,' said Catriona cautiously. 'It might be best.'

'You're not going down the road at this time of night,' Rob said indignantly. 'It's fine for you to stay.'

'In that case perhaps you'd tell me where I can sleep because I must admit I'm tired out.' It was true, she was, but she also thought it would be better if she left the two brothers alone together.

'You can have Mother's room. I'll show you,' said Rob, glaring angrily at Andro. 'I'll be back down in a few minutes. Don't go away.'

On the way up the stairs he said to Catriona, 'Don't worry about Andro. He's just feeling bad about our grandfather and guilty about you. The combination is too much for his manners. They crack under the strain.'

'I don't want to be his enemy,' she said wearily. 'Try and make him understand, will you? He doesn't have to feel guilty. I treated Hamish just as badly as he treated me.'

Rob frowned. 'I dispute that,' he said roughly. 'You never set out to deceive Hamish Melville deliberately. But if it might help I'll explain that you don't bear any grudges.'

'Yes,' she agreed with relief. 'That's right. I don't.'

'This is Mother's room. My parents' marriage has survived on the premise that those who sleep apart stay together.' He shrugged. 'I wouldn't bet on it myself but it seems to have worked for them. My room is just down the corridor and Andro's is over there.'

'I might lock my door, just in case you don't calm him down,' she exclaimed half-jokingly.

'I'll sort him out, don't worry. See you in the morning,' he said. 'I hope you sleep all right.' He kissed her gently on each cheek and once softly on the lips for good measure. The kisses were a benison and left her feeling less bewildered. They didn't tell her precisely why he had invited her to Glen Doran but they gave her a hint.

'Why are you such a shit to women?' Rob demanded when he returned to Andro who had downed at least two measures of whisky in his absence.

'Why are you such a bloody doormat?' retorted Andro indistinctly. 'You let them walk all over you every time. Catriona's doing it now. She's got you right where she wants you.'

'Rubbish. She's not like that, as you know. At least I treat women like human beings.' Rob picked up the tumbler he'd abandoned earlier and took a swig, holding his temper in check. 'I don't rut and run like a stag on the hill.'

'I hardly think Isabel would agree that I rut and run,' sneered Andro. 'I reckon she's been around a good few months longer than any of your women seem to stay.'

With an effort Rob ignored this jibe. 'Isabel is no ordinary woman,' he said. 'She has more interesting things to worry about than whether you're flitting from hind to hind. But even the Isabels of this world have their length of tether. It wouldn't surprise me if she reached hers quite soon.'

'And then you'll move in on her, isn't that how it goes? You seem to like my cast-offs, if Catriona's anything to go by.' Andro was not letting up.

'Why are you deliberately trying to rile me?' enquired Rob gruffly. 'Is this your way of mourning Gamps? Because it's a bloody peculiar way.'

'Gamps understood me,' muttered Andro darkly. 'He's the only one who did.'

'Oh, I understand you, Andro, I just don't like you very much. Perhaps Gamps felt sorry for you, that's why he put up with all your bloody nonsense. He thought you were searching for something and, being the man he was, he also thought he could help you to find it. He didn't realise that everything you find you suddenly don't want any more.'

'He knew that I love Glen Doran. He knew that I was prepared to fight to keep it safe.'

'Safe? What do you mean safe?' Rob frowned as Andro slopped more whisky into his glass. He noticed that his brother's hands were beginning to shake and picked up a plate of sandwiches which Kirsty had left wrapped in cling-film against the actor's arrival. 'Here, you need food if you're going to drink at this rate.'

Andro curled his lip at the sandwiches. 'Trust you to think of food. Is it comfort-eating that gave you that cuddly figure?'

Standing side by side the two brothers were much the same height but there was no denying that Rob was broader and fleshier than his lean, ectomorph brother. 'Cuddly' however, was exaggerating. Once again Rob did not rise to the bait. 'Comfort-eating is preferable to solace-drinking on the whole. Are you going to tell me what you mean by "safe"?' he asked.

'Free of incomers. Safe for the real people of the glen,' Andro responded sulkily. 'Gamps agreed with me there.'

'No, he didn't!' Rob cried incredulously. 'He thought people should give something back to the land that spawned them, certainly, but he didn't deny others the opportunity to make their contribution as well. He wasn't an exclusionist.'

'Oh, what the hell does it matter what he was now?' muttered Andro angrily. 'He's dead and I suppose you and Father will start to haul Glen Doran kicking and screaming into the tourist millennium. We'll have a theme park and log cabins and an all-weather Bonnie Prince Charlie leisure centre. Gamps will be turning in his grave before the first sod has hit the coffin.'

'You must be joking!' exclaimed Rob. 'Whatever gave you that idea?'

'Well, those English loons have already started to build their fast-food drive-through down at the old steading. Unfortunately a good dose of cleansing fire didn't manage to scare them off. Your friend Catriona has been wet-nursing them along, hoodwinked by their plausible English bonhomie. And I thought she was a good Highland girl.'

Rob screwed the top firmly back on the whisky bottle and shut it away in the cupboard. 'You talk drivel when you're drunk,' he declared. 'Today has been a shock for all of us but don't use Gamps's death as an excuse to start flinging accusations around. You have no idea what Father will want to do with the estate and no more do I, but I can assure you that if I have any say in it, it won't include a theme park or a fast-food joint.'

'At least you'll *have* a say in it,' Andro persisted. 'I suppose you'll be Viscount Nevis now, won't you? Just don't expect me to tug my forelock.'

'Christ! Now we've got jealousy to add to the paranoia,' observed Rob with a sigh. 'The only thing I wish you'd tug is the insides out of one of these sandwiches, you bloody idiot. Then you might be fit to make arrangements for Grandfather's funeral tomorrow. As it is you'll be no bloody use to anyone.'

'Won't there have to be an enquiry or something?' asked Andro, suddenly flopping into a chair and ripping the film off the plate. He began to eat two sandwiches at once, greedily, as if it was his first food of the day. 'People can't be killed suddenly without someone asking questions, surely?'

'The Procurator Fiscal's been informed and I suppose there could be a Sheriff's enquiry. But it was just a tragic accident. We're lucky it was no worse.'

'What could have been worse?' demanded Andro with his mouth full. 'Oh, I suppose Angus could have wiped out the whole family while he was at it and still walked away without a scratch.'

'It wasn't Angus's fault,' Rob said patiently. 'He couldn't know that the rain had weakened the road. It could have happened at any time and to anyone. Don't go looking for scapegoats.'

'I want to!' yelled Andro with his mouth full and his eyes brimming with tears. He swallowed hard. 'He was such a great old boy! He could have gone on for years yet and died in his bed the way he wanted. It's bloody unfair!'

'Well, for once we agree,' his brother nodded wearily.

'You're not going to go on seeing Catriona, are you?' asked Andro suddenly, taking Rob by surprise.

'I don't know,' he replied. 'I might. Why?'

' 'S bloody awkward,' Andro said in a muffled tone, still chewing.

'You shouldn't play around with people's lives,' said Rob implacably. 'At least I won't be using her and discarding her like a paper handkerchief. And if there is anything between Catriona and me in the future you can just keep your big mouth shut about your part in her past—otherwise things could get very unpleasant around here. You wouldn't want to be cut off from Glen Doran for ever, would you?'

'Christ,' muttered Andro mutinously, grabbing several more sandwiches and standing up to leave. 'You haven't even inherited Paradise yet and you're already playing God.'

Catriona fell asleep instantly, hardly taking in Queenie Nevis's elegant bedroom with its solid mahogany furniture and aquamarine silk wall-coverings. She had feared that when she closed her eyes she would see the old Earl's face, jammed beside the seat of the Land Rover, bruised and vulnerable, his white hair dishevelled and wild. But instead she lapsed immediately into oblivion and woke after what seemed only a few minutes' sleep to find dawn creeping through the carelessly drawn curtains. Only ten weeks from midsummer the Highland nights were already quite short. Peering at the small carriage clock on the bedside table she saw that it was five-thirty.

She sat up, wondering briefly where she was, and then all the events of the past twenty-four hours came crowding back. For several minutes she lay back against the pillows and analysed her situation. Everything that had happened the day before had been dictated by chance, chiefly of course, the death of the Earl and the removal of Lord and Lady Nevis to hospital, but Glen Doran House was no longer a place for a stranger who had only been passing by on her way back from her Easter break. Rob had been grateful for her company the previous afternoon but Andro's arrival had changed her status utterly. She now felt like an unwanted guest, a spare part, surplus to requirements, however hard Rob might kindly try to reassure her.

Decisively she swung her legs over the side of the bed and stood up. The trousers, shirt and sweater that she had been wearing the previous day were hanging over the back of a chair. Swiftly she pulled them on and, carrying her boots, she tiptoed to the door, opened it and slipped through into the corridor. She wanted to get away, back to her own territory. She was not needed here any more and it would be better not to confront either of the two brothers again but just to melt out of their lives. Andro hated the sight of her and Rob had just moved one step nearer to becoming the Earl of Lochaber.

He had responsibilities and duties which could only be hampered by a girl he just happened to have asked home for lunch.

After driving back from the scene of the accident she had left the Golf parked in the stableyard so she was able to creep down the stairs and out of the house through the kitchen quarters where the bolted doors were easy to open. But before she left she had one final thing to do. In the back of her car was the rowan clock. She had meant to return it to the Earl during her visit, had wanted to tell him that she no longer needed it because she had discovered what he had meant her to discover—the preciousness of time and the stupidity of wasting it. Gratefully she realised that before he died the old man had known this, had appreciated that her very presence there at the scene was evidence of her discovery and had been glad. It may not have been his greatest achievement in life, but it had been his last.

Hastily she carried the clock through the kitchen and into the little sitting room where she and Rob had sat together the previous evening. Using a pen from the Earl's desk and a sheet of his headed writing paper she wrote a note.

'Dear Rob, Here is your grandfather's clock,' it ran. *'He knew that I would return it and that it had achieved its purpose. I am so sorry he is dead. He was a wonderful man—kind and perceptive. I wish I could have known him better. Please pass on my condolences to your parents and to Andro and tell your father that I will make sure everyone is*

informed at the bank. I hope they both make a swift recovery. I will be thinking of you. Catriona.'

She propped the note against the clock and turned away, thinking it would successfully close a chapter in her life.

Nineteen

'All right, settle down now, please—camera rehearsal! Quiet, everyone, and let the crew concentrate.' Although he was equipped with a megaphone, the First Assistant Director, a small, wiry Glaswegian called Kenny, preferred to use the full volume of his substantial voice-box to call the film location to order. It was the middle of May and Precipitous City Productions' filming of Robert Louis Stevenson's *Catriona* was nearing the end of its first week.

The camera was mounted on a mobile dolly set on a metal track laid through a narrow alley leading off Edinburgh's Royal Mile. Normally Brodie's Close gave access to the studded wooden entrance doors of several restored tenements and to a café housed in a quaint, vaulted chamber where tourists mingled with lawyers from the nearby courts. For the film, however, the Close had been shut off and cosmetically returned to its original fetid mid-eighteenth-century state—an example of the many cramped and filthy thoroughfares which had criss-crossed the old walled city of

483

Edinburgh. From these had led hundreds of overcrowded and foul closes in which everybody, from lords and ladies to prostitutes and water caddies, had lived stacked one above the other in tall stone 'lands' clinging to Castle Rock. In it, on this sunny twentieth-century May morning, would be filmed the crucial first meeting between Catriona Drummond, Jacobite, and David Balfour, Whig, a scene of Montague and Capulet significance and love at first sight.

'Jeezus Alex, fur a wee squirt you dinna half weigh a ton!' puffed Tony the Grip, as he struggled to push the camera along the track with its operator clinging precariously to the dolly.

Alex Duncan grinned wickedly. When he was working he exchanged his dapper pinstripe for an equally immaculate black tracksuit. 'It's all the money in my pockets, Tone,' he quipped. 'You'll have to eat more porridge.'

'Drink mair ale y'mean!' scoffed the barrel-shaped Tony. 'Hey, Shona. Flash the WD40 will ye?'

A perky girl with plaits who was busy writing shot details on a clapperboard dropped her black marker-pen and whipped an aerosol can out of a capacious black camera-bag. Shona was the Runner, the lowliest member of the camera-crew. She began to spray mist-fine lubricant carefully on the stainless-steel rails.

'We could do wi' some more wedges i' this track,' grumbled Tony as, yet again, he heaved the dolly back to its starting-place. 'She's shifting about like a ship at sea.'

Ian, the Best Boy, right-hand man to the Grip and a younger and smaller version of Tony himself, complete with incipient paunch and thinning hair, produced a mallet and several wooden wedges which he proceeded to hammer under the sleepers of the track.

Sam Fox, the director, was leaning against a wall, watching the rehearsal on a small TV monitor which received instant pictures from a video camera mounted under the wide lens of the ciné camera. It showed him the framing and gave him an idea of continuity and composition before the shot was actually taken. What it couldn't do was supply the unique luminosity and depth of perspective that distinguished film from video—only the processed product of the big 35 millimetre camera could do that.

He was interrupted by a fresh-faced, good-looking young actor in costume who wandered disconsolately on to the set. Mark Sole was dressed in fawn britches and a brown high-collared jacket, ready to play Davy Balfour, the diffident hero of *Catriona*. Many had remarked on his likeness to the famous Alexander Naysmith portrait of Robert Burns which adorned the lids of shortbread tins, but at this present moment he looked more like a schoolboy victim of playground bullying.

'Someone's been in my dressing-room, Sam,' he complained, a bewildered expression clouding his clear brown eyes. 'It's been turned upside down and there's graffiti everywhere.'

'What?' responded Sam, who always wore a baseball cap to disguise his balding pate. 'I don't believe it. Show me. Carry on, Alex. Back in a moment.' Sam was a kind, intellectual New Yorker, slow of speech but quick of brain, who liked his actors to be happy. He clasped a fatherly arm around Mark's shoulders and led him out of the close.

The actors' facilities were located in a temporary off-street enclosure further up the Royal Mile. The superstar Gil Munro merited a whole mobile home to himself and there was always a small crowd of assorted fans hanging around the control barriers hoping for a sight of the famous expatriate Scot whom Hollywood had transformed from an Edinburgh dustman into a world 'personality'. But the location dressing-rooms of the other stars were situated in a vehicle known as a road-train because its compartments closely resembled the partitioning of an old-fashioned railway carriage. Sam Fox strode past the security guard, who acknowledged him with a nod, and opened the door to the first compartment, stopping short with an expression of shock.

Mark Sole had covered one section of his dressing-room wall with photographs of his family and these were now almost obliterated by a stark and ugly message sprayed in violent red paint: *English Pig Go Home.* On the mirror, SFS was scrawled several times and the same three letters in the same blood-red paint were repeated at irregular intervals, over any available surface—table, wall, cupboard and wash-basin. The soft furnishings were slashed and ripped and the contents of drawers and hanging space had been flung indiscriminately about the room, whilst bottles and jars of make-up and toiletries had been emptied over them. The whole shambles was the work of a vindictive and malicious hand.

'Shit!' muttered Sam Fox, taking it all in at a glance and then firmly shutting the door on it. 'Have you got the key?' he asked Mark, who wordlessly handed it over and watched the director turn it in the lock. 'We'll let the cops have a look at this before we get it cleaned up,' he said sympathetically to the actor. 'God, I'm sorry Mark. I never dreamt anything like this could happen.'

Dazedly Mark shook his head. 'Me neither,' he said faintly. 'I know some people object to me playing Davy but I didn't know they were *that* fanatical.'

'What's happened?' A face as sweet and delicate as a porcelain doll appeared around the door of the next dressing-room. 'What are you all looking so cross about?' Andrina Gordon's baby-blue eyes were wide with curiosity.

'Have you been here for the past half-hour or so, Andrina?' asked Sam, ignoring her question. 'Did you hear any noise coming from here?'

Andrina pursed her soft pink lips and shook her head. 'Nope. Not a thing. Has there been a break-in?'

'Yeah. Sort of,' admitted Sam. He plucked the two-way radio transmitter from its hook on his belt and called to his assistant director. 'Kenny, could you take five and call the cops,

487

please? Tell them to come to the road-train a.s.a.p.'

'The police!' squeaked Andrina, excitedly. 'Wow! Does that mean we won't be doing the scene this morning?'

'No, it doesn't,' returned Sam instantly. 'It means we'll be half an hour behind schedule at most. Stay in costume and don't go away.' He could see his day's filming disappearing if Andrina decided she had time for extra-curricular activities. He didn't know who she was dallying with but he was aware of Andrina's reputation and, as far as he could tell from recent evidence, she was living up to it.

A shadow fell over them from the doorway. Andro loomed there, not in costume but lounging in his habitual jeans and leather jacket. He was not due to appear before the camera that day. 'What's all this about calling the police?' he enquired laconically, and raised an eyebrow at Mark. 'Do I detect a Sole in distress?' His tone of voice indicated that if this were the case it did not cause *him* much distress.

'Mark's dressing-room has been vandalised,' Sam told him curtly. 'Some bastard with an IQ of zero has been spraying paint around—and worse—I've called the cops.'

'I heard you over the radio. Is that really necessary—just for a bit of harmless graffiti?' Andro sounded incredulous.

'Racist slogans are hardly harmless in my view,' Sam said tightly. 'Mark is pretty shaken up by it and I don't blame him.' He turned

488

to the perturbed young actor and added, 'Why don't you go to the canteen, man, and get yourself a cup of coffee or something? I'll send the cops down to see you there and they can take a statement. We'll go for a take in about forty minutes, OK?'

Mark nodded and ducked past Andro as if he couldn't get away from him fast enough.

'I want this incident cleared up and sorted out as soon as possible,' said Sam urgently. 'I don't want it affecting Mark's concentration.'

Andro gave a cynical laugh. 'What concentration? A few slogans scrawled over his pictures of Mummy and Daddy won't destroy what was never there in the first place.'

'How d'you know they were scrawled over his family snaps?' asked Sam sharply. 'I didn't say so.'

'Where else would they be?' enquired Andro languidly. 'He's got his fat-faced relations stuck all over his bloody room. He's a Mummy's boy—a mewling, puking, knicker-wetting infant.'

From her doorway Andrina sniggered. 'Poor Baby Mark,' she cooed softly, winking at Andro.

'He should crawl back where he came from,' sneered Andro. 'Re-attach himself to his mother's Surbiton apron strings.'

'For Chrissake, Andro!' snarled Sam, edging past him into the sunshine. 'You made your feelings about Mark perfectly clear at the original casting conference. It would be best for the successful completion of this movie if you now kept them strictly to yourself.' The director flung this opinion over his shoulder as he strode off down the pavement.

'Best for this movie would be if Marky-baby dropped out and let us hire a real actor who can speak the lines without sounding like Prince William buying sweets in Kensington High Street,' remarked Andro slyly to Andrina, insinuating himself forward. 'Are you accepting visitors, Ms Gordon?' he asked, sliding his hand around her waist and bending to kiss the pale half-moon of breast exposed by the décolleté of her tightbodiced costume.

'Depends on who they are,' she demurred, making no effort to deter him. 'Thanks to the demon spray-painter I happen to have an extra half-hour before shooting begins...'

'Excellent,' he said, pushing her gently back into her dressing-room and closing the door.

Her male co-stars had often been heard to remark that it was surprising Andrina Gordon ever appeared before a camera, so busy was she entertaining in her dressing-room. One had coined for her the meritorious clapper-board nickname 'Scene-One, Bonk-One', but she remained unabashed. 'If you need it, get it,' was her motto, and she did.

Precipitous City had taken over a church hall near the Castle as a production base. Twice a month St Columba's reverberated to the sound of unaccompanied psalm-singing as the 'Wee Frees'—or the Presbyterian Free Church of Scotland to give it its Sunday name—held a service in Gaelic but in this busy period of

490

location shooting it was thronged every day with film technicians in jeans and sweatshirts, actors and extras in wigs and petticoats, and production personnel carrying clipboards and two-way radios. Lunch was the busiest time, when specialist caterers laid on a buffet of tempting dishes ranging from low-calorie salads to rich ragouts in cream sauces. Seating was at a series of long refectory tables on a sit-as-you-come basis. Thus it was that Hamish and Catriona, making their first visit to the set of the film, sat by coincidence next to Isabel.

'I don't think you two have actually met before, have you?' asked Catriona rather awkwardly. 'Hamish Melville—Isabel Carlisle. You have a million pounds in common.'

When Isabel blushed she did so very prettily. Her long, rather sallow face took on a peachy bloom and her copious dark lashes fluttered becomingly as she cast down her eyes. Unusually for her she was wearing a bright colour, a tailored trouser suit in warm, sunny apricot with a scarf in a darker shade of the same hue, and her trade-mark round-lensed spectacles were framed in tortoiseshell instead of metal. It was an outfit which Catriona thought took almost a decade off her age.

Hamish, too, was clearly impressed. 'I had no idea that I'd invested in such charming talent,' he crooned, taking her hand with the eagerness of a sales manager. 'How very gratifying.'

Catriona hid an amused smile. Since Hamish's return from his Easter skiing holiday there had been a complete change in their relationship. She now rather enjoyed her regular meetings with him, meetings which were entirely dictated by his financial affairs and made no reference whatever to any love affair. Hamish treated her more like a favoured sister than a coveted mistress, so it seemed that the past was truly over and done with. It had been his suggestion that they visit the set of *Catriona* together and she had been happy to do so. However, although his seductive charm was no longer beamed at her, it seemed he had lost none of it. Now it was focused on Isabel instead, with super-megawatt power.

'I'm sorry that I have not made a point of meeting with you, Mr Melville,' murmured Isabel, her becoming blush showing no sign of subsiding. 'Particularly since you have been in my thoughts. We're all very aware that we wouldn't be here today if it weren't for you.'

'No, you wouldn't,' agreed Hamish frankly. 'And I'm beginning to realise just how much of a crying shame that would have been. I hope you have a little time today to explain things to me personally?'

'Of course,' said Isabel, almost too readily, taking no interest in the prawn salad she had selected for her lunch. 'What would you like to know?'

This is a turn-up for the books, thought Catriona with irony. Obviously I should have introduced Hamish to Isabel before.

At this point she noticed Andro stroll into the dining hall in close proximity to a diminutive actress in a sprigged muslin period gown which made her look the image of a Royal Doulton figurine. Isabel and Hamish were too deep in conversation to notice them but most of the other people in the room looked up at their entrance, some merely intrigued by the affecting sight of the handsome young actor and the beautiful 'Jacobite' lady, others, who were more in the know, whispering between themselves about this latest development in the film's first and fastest-growing off-screen affair. Many also knew of Isabel's partnership with Andro and cast surreptitious glances at her, expecting fireworks, but she remained oblivious, enthralled by Hamish.

'Catriona might like to join us there too, wouldn't you?' Hamish asked suddenly.

Catriona realised that she had no idea what he was talking about. Her mind had slipped back to Glen Doran and the awful day of the accident. She had seen Rob only once since then, at Lochaber's funeral which, as befitted a clan chief, had been a huge and ceremonial affair, not conducive to intimate conversations. Nevertheless she found he was much in her mind, never more so than now for, after working his notice in London, he would be moving back to Glen Doran permanently this weekend.

'Sorry,' she said contritely to Hamish. 'I wasn't listening. What would I like to do?'

'Come and watch them filming out on the beach tomorrow. Isabel says they're shooting an escape by sea,' Hamish told her. 'Max comes home for half-term this evening and I'm sure he'd like to go.'

'Oh? No, I can't, I'm afraid,' murmured

493

Catriona. 'I'm going up north.'

Rob had invited her to Glen Doran and this would be the first time she had been there since the accident. Their relationship, if it could even be called that, had not changed or progressed and she, for one, had been grateful for the breathing space. Both of them had plenty to come to terms with and had taken time to do so, as if treading water in a rough sea. This weekend would tell if the period of caution was over, perhaps establish a pattern for the future.

'I'm sure you'll get VIP treatment though, won't he, Isabel? Is Andro working that day?' So much the better if he is, she thought. It means he won't be at Glen Doran.

'Yes,' Isabel said evenly. 'It's one of his main action scenes so he'll be flashing his sword about.' She caught sight of Sam Fox approaching across the hall and stood up. 'Excuse me, I think the director wants a word with me.'

Sam was frowning deeply. 'Have you heard about Mark Sole's dressing-room?' he asked, shifting his baseball hat to a more comfortable position on his head. 'Some bastard trashed it this morning.'

'No! What happened?' Isabel's voice rose in agitation.

'Some crackpot crowd calling themselves SFS sprayed their calling card everywhere and scrawled racist remarks over poor Mark's family photos. I called the cops but he doesn't want to press charges. Says he'd rather forget

494

all about it. We've given him another dressing-room and the other one is being cleaned and redecorated.'

Catriona pricked up her ears at the mention of the SFS. She kept an eye out for newspaper reports but the protesters had been quiet lately, apart from spraying slogans at tourist centres, particularly those popular with the English.

'How did they get past the security guards?' asked Isabel furiously. 'We pay two men to patrol those road-trains full-time!'

'They claim they were *in situ*—said no one went in who shouldn't have,' said Sam. 'It looks like an inside job. That's why Mark's not taking it any further. He says he reckons he knows who did it.'

'Who?' asked Isabel urgently. 'We must do something about it.'

Sam shook his head. 'Nope. The boy won't give a name. He's being very British about it—y'know, all that stiff upper lip crap.'

'Is he very upset?'

'Yeah, he was at first. But afterwards he gave a real good performance to camera and his accent was perfect. Even the voice coach was impressed,' Sam drawled. 'I have to say I was surprised.'

Isabel laughed dryly. 'Well, our crackpot may have done us a favour then,' she remarked. 'Good for Mark. I always suspected there were hidden strengths behind that baby-face.'

'Did you?' asked Sam with surprise. 'I admit that I just thought the camera loved him enough to make it worthwhile disguising the voice problems with post-syncing. But right now his Rs are rolling like ball-bearings.'

'And Andro reckoned Mark Sole couldn't tell his Rs from his elbow,' crowed Isabel. 'Bully for Andro!'

'Does Andro have it in for Mark?' Catriona asked Isabel when Sam had wandered off again.

'He doesn't hold with an Englishman playing a Scottish literary hero,' Isabel revealed. 'And there are plenty who agree with him. There's no doubt that Mark looks the part however.' She sighed. 'Casting is never perfect.'

'Ask Andro if he's got a can of spray paint,' suggested Catriona, wondering grimly if, back in March, he might also have manufactured a few petrol bombs. She knew that Andro was a complex and disturbed character, very good at appearing to be what he was not. Was he also a fire-raiser? Could the man who had cheerfully drunk with the Carruthers on the night after their steading fire be the very man who had actually done the burning?

'If he has, you'd better sort him out pronto,' advised Hamish angrily. 'Another incident like that could scupper the film.'

'Oh, I'll sort him out OK, have no fear,' Isabel promised. 'He might be surprised to find that his actor's contract isn't as water-tight as he imagines.'

Hamish studied Isabel with interest. He had been struck by her unusual looks but now he was equally struck by her obvious spirit. Hamish was attracted to strong women. He liked to test their determination against his. So far Catriona had been the only one to defy him. He was resigned now to a platonic relationship with her—a relationship which he was enjoying more than he'd expected—but Isabel would be a new and interesting challenge. On a mountain-top in Switzerland he had given Linda the diamond bracelet as a pledge of reconciliation, but he could not stay faithful for long...

Rob sat listening to his parents giving him the latest bulletin on their recovery and was grateful for his reviving gin and tonic. They were wrapped up in their medical trials and tribulations and totally oblivious to the enormous change that was occurring in his life, leaving London for the challenges of Glen Doran. He felt as if he stood at the start of some daunting obstacle course, fraught with all kinds of unexpected hazards and without the guiding hand of his grandfather. He would have liked to discuss it with his father but the new Earl was still in a wheelchair and could talk only of the frustration of not yet being declared fit enough to pick up the reins at the bank.

'Bruce Finlay assures me that everything's under control but I won't feel satisfied until I can get my knees back under the boardroom table,' the invalid grumbled. 'A ship never sails a true course with a strange hand on the tiller.'

'You just want to believe that you're indispensable, Father,' Rob said in a tone of mild rebuke. 'You have to let others handle things for a while.'

'I have done,' his father snapped. 'But it's

gone on long enough. The doctors are too cautious. Next week I'll go to the bank come hell or high water.'

'How will you get there, George?' asked his wife reasonably. 'You can't get into a car with your leg stuck straight out like that and you can hardly call even a private ambulance just to take you into work.'

'I'll get one of those Handicabs you see driving around the town. You can get a wheelchair in them,' Lochaber told her irritably. 'Plenty of people do full-time jobs from one of these things.' He tapped the arm of his chair and grimaced. 'I'll regard them with considerable admiration in future.'

'But you still get very tired very quickly,' Lady Lochaber reminded him. She herself was still suffering blinding headaches as a result of her fractured skull and couldn't lift her head off the pillow some mornings. 'You'd probably get to the bank and fall straight to sleep.'

Rob ran a hand over his brow. He had heard all this on the telephone numerous times from each of his parents and found it hard to contain his patience. In his state of relative youth and health he did not comprehend the daily misery of not being certain of full recovery. 'So I take it you won't be coming up to Glen Doran for a while,' he said, sipping his drink.

'Not while I'm like this, dear boy,' said his father impatiently, gesturing at his leg which protruded horizontally in front of him in its plaster cast. 'I couldn't even get up the front steps.'

'Angus and I could lift you.'

'No, I don't want to go. You sort the place out and we'll come up when we're more mobile. Just don't do anything too radical without consulting me first.'

'Get the dust-sheets off if you can, Rob,' said his mother earnestly. 'It would be so nice to see the place in all its full glory again.'

'I'll do my best. I'm taking Catriona up with me tomorrow.' Rob caught his mother's sharp glance as he said this and grinned. 'Now, now, Mother! Don't start hearing wedding bells. I just fancy a bit of company. It's going to be rather depressing not finding Grandfather there as usual.'

'I'm not hearing wedding bells, dear,' 'Queenie' demurred. 'But I do detect a stirring of romantic interest in my normally indifferent son, do I not?'

'I'm not "normally indifferent" as you put it,' exclaimed Rob indignantly. 'I'm just a bit choosy, that's all.'

'That's what I mean, dear,' she responded evenly. 'And you seem to have made some kind of a choice. That's all I'm saying.'

Rob thought about this. 'Well, maybe I have,' he nodded, 'but it's very early days and I don't know whether the feeling's mutual.'

His mother sniffed a little censoriously. 'Well, she's made some pretty questionable choices in her time, if our London sighting is anything to go on. Perhaps you'd both be sensible to look before you leap.'

Rob stared at his mother and shook his head

in bewilderment. 'You were full of concern for her at the time, Mother, as I remember. You said she was an innocent abroad.'

'That was before you showed any interest in her,' she retaliated. 'Now her track record doesn't look so marvellous.'

'But you like her, don't you? Admit it! And you don't want me producing some naive little virgin like Diana Spencer, do you? Look what happened in that set-up.'

Frowning hard, Lady Lochaber pondered this statement for several seconds, then her brow cleared suddenly. 'You're right, I do like her. And she was wonderful with your grandfather on the day he died.'

'She's a good banker, too,' offered the Earl, putting in his pennyworth. 'Intuitive and reliable.'

'Oh well, there you are then,' commented his wife with heavy irony. 'Just what we need for our son and heir.'

'God! We're only going to Glen Doran for the weekend,' Rob pointed out. 'Not walking up the aisle of St Giles's Cathedral!'

'Your father proposed to me beside the loch in Glen Doran,' Lady Lochaber reminisced nostalgically.

'So I did,' muttered her husband glumly. 'The mud-stain never came out of the knee of my trousers.'

'Well, at least we stuck as tenaciously as the mud,' returned Queenie.

'Not to Glen Doran though,' mumbled Rob under his breath.

'It was you, wasn't it?' Isabel confronted Andro with her suspicions about the dressing-room incident that evening when he returned home to the mews. In response to Catriona's suggestion she had searched his wardrobe and found a bag full of aerosol paints on a top shelf. 'You trashed Mark's room.'

'What?' He looked astonished, as if such a concept were ridiculous. 'Why should I?'

'To try and frighten him off. You thought he'd blub and run, but instead he performed better than ever. You boobed there, Handy-Andro, didn't you,' she gloated.

'What do you mean he performed better than ever?' Andro sounded rather peeved.

'Sam told me. You didn't watch his scenes afterwards. They were excellent. We cast the right actor after all.'

'You mean the thicko turned into a boy wonder overnight? Impossible!'

'No—not overnight. It was all down to SFS, or whatever you call yourselves. It was you—I know it was.' She pulled one of the cans out of the carrier bag on the chair beside her and waved it in his face. 'And so does Sam—and Mark! You knew his photographs had been ruined because you ruined them. No one else had seen them. It's only thanks to Mark that you haven't been charged with malicious damage and inciting racial hatred. He refused to press charges.'

Andro's face darkened dangerously. 'How bloody magnanimous of him—Marky the martyr!

501

Sod him and sod the bloody English who take all our best jobs. I'd like to trash the lot of them!'

'And I'd like to trash you!' yelled Isabel furiously. 'But I'll settle for seeing the back of you. I think you'd better leave and take your filthy spray-cans with you.' She stuffed the one she was holding back into the bag and threw the whole lot at him. Only by displaying the instinctive catching skill of a slip-fielder did he avoid a clout on the head.

'You bitch!' he yelled back. 'You nearly gave me a black eye and I'm filming tomorrow.'

'Only just,' retorted Isabel. 'Precipitous is quite prepared to resile on your contract if you don't get out of here right now.'

'What do you mean get out? I live here, remember. This is my home.' Andro's lip curled. 'And resiling on my contract will take more money than the budget can stand.'

'That's just where you're wrong,' she crowed gleefully. 'Your agent cocked it up because he knew you were a partner and therefore thought he didn't need a fine-tooth comb. Your contract has got more holes in it than Emmenthal cheese, so if you want to appear in this picture, and I know you do, you'd better toe the line. And that means finding somewhere else to live.'

'You're power-mad, aren't you?' Andro observed acidly. 'You belong in the Mafia, making people offers they can't refuse. But the real truth is that you're jealous—just because I poked Andrina a few times. Christ, she's the cast bicycle—anyone can ride her. You know she means nothing.'

'That's the whole point,' groaned Isabel, despairing of his ability to comprehend. 'No one means anything to you, Andro. I realise that now. I thought you loved me even though you couldn't keep your hands off other women, but I was wrong. You're a heartless, self-centred prick. I know you've been bonking Andrina at every possible opportunity but that's not why I'm kicking you out. You nearly scuppered the film and I won't share my bed with a racist and a saboteur, that's why.'

'Who wants to share your stinking bed anyway,' he snorted with derision. 'Lately I've had to close my eyes and hold my nose just in order to get into it. And you may have noticed that they're not exactly queuing up to take my place.'

Isabel wanted to shriek that Hamish had made it clear only that afternoon that he was extremely interested in doing just that, but she held her tongue. If she did let Hamish into her bed it would be on her terms and they would not include giving him a key to the door. She'd made that mistake with Andro and now she wanted her life back.

'Don't be crude and don't be rude, Andro,' she said calmly. 'Just pack up and go.' She stood up, slinging her bag over her shoulder. 'I'm off out for dinner—don't be here when I get back. And be on set tomorrow or face the Emmenthal factor.'

'Don't threaten me, you fucking cow!' Andro

screamed at her departing back. 'And don't expect me to go on working in the fucking production office either. As far as I'm concerned I'll act and go.'

Isabel popped her head back through the door. 'Well, that'll make a change,' she exclaimed caustically. 'Normally you fuck and go. And not very well, either!'

Climatically May was often a magic month in Scotland. The Home-Muirs had decided to celebrate the long, sunlit Friday evening by wheeling out the barbecue and inviting a few friends for supper in their walled back garden. By now Alison had 'popped' and was wearing a loose sweatshirt, wildly decorated with multi-coloured balloons which drew attention to, rather than disguised, her bump.

'If you've got it, flaunt it,' she chuckled when Donald Cameron made some witticism about 'carrying it all before her'. 'At least I've found a premature use for nappy pins,' she added gaily, hoisting the front of her jumper to reveal one of the said pins joining the gaping placket of her jeans.

'When is the baby actually due?' enquired Gillian, as usual to be found not far from Donald's shoulder.

'In September, so I've still got three and a half months to go—by which time I won't dare to wear anything with balloons on it for fear of encouraging comparisons,' joked Alison, whose dark good looks had blossomed with her pregnancy.

Gillian failed to find anything funny about the idea of inflating to balloon size. 'Ugh!' she shuddered. 'I think I'd rather adopt.'

Alison laughed. 'Don't be daft. Adopting's much more difficult. You have to be an upright citizen for that.'

'Which is something few people are when they get a baby by the normal method,' remarked Donald mischievously and winced as Gillian indignantly dug him in the ribs. 'Sorry, darling. Am I offending your Morningside sensibilities?'

'You'll have to get used to that, Gillian,' warned Alison with a smile. 'You'll never clean up Donald's dirty mind.' A couple of weeks previously the Banking Hall Manager and the Commercial Manager had surprised no one by announcing their engagement. It was Steuart's first bank-born romance and so was cause for much in-house celebration, of which this barbecue formed merely a part.

'It'll be your turn next, Catriona,' declared John, happily sizzling sausages to a charred turn. 'We can't have an unmarried member among such managerial connubial bliss.'

'There's just one vital ingredient missing,' laughed Catriona who was pouring sparkling wine around the assembled company. 'No conman to go with the nubial.'

'But she's working on it, aren't you Cat?' declared Alison roundly, grabbing her friend's arm and steering her out of the chattering circle around the barbecue. 'What's the story on tomorrow?' she persisted. 'Or is it "Lochaber no more"?'

Catriona made a face. 'I'm terrified, to be honest. Rob is such a lovely man but I just can't imagine there ever being anything between us. There is already too much, if you see what I mean?'

Alison made a rude noise. 'Bah! No, I don't. Just because you flung yourself at his crazy mixed-up brother and lived to rue the day doesn't mean you have to shy away from him. If he doesn't mind, why should you?'

'Because I think he must mind.' Their conversation was being held in muttered whispers in the semi-darkness, away from the rest of the group but Catriona felt uncomfortable. It was too sensitive a subject to be made part of a party atmosphere. She had lain awake for several nights since Rob's invitation pondering her feelings for him. She knew the weekend had to be some kind of watershed and felt she must be quite sure which way she wanted events to flow. 'Put yourself in his position. Wouldn't you think twice about dating your brother's cast-off?'

'I don't think one can climb inside another person's head like that,' Alison remonstrated. 'After all, he's had time to think about it more than twice and he's obviously decided he doesn't mind. It's how you feel about him that matters, not how you imagine he feels about you.'

'That's just it—I don't know!' wailed Catriona. 'I think he's dishy and kind and generous and lots of other things that go to make up Mr Right but I haven't felt the mountains tumble.'

'Oh, really Cat!' Impatience sharpened Alison's tone. 'As far as I can tell, the earth was heaving about like a bouncy castle when you fell for Hamish and there was lightning and thunder in Andro's fingertips, but much good all that did you. Have you ever stopped to think that perhaps a little old-fashioned courting first might make the going steadier?'

Catriona bit her lip. There was no denying that Alison was right. In her relationships with both Hamish and Andro she had been much too impetuous and metaphorically her fingers were still blistered. It would be the worst kind of foolishness to rush into another without due care and attention. Yet the rowan clock seemed to tick loudly in her brain. Someone, somewhere had to be out there for her. She was not meant to be forever a lonely, efficient banker, counting other people's assets, and she wasn't meant to stultify in the streets of the city. Rob seemed to be drawn back to a rural existence as irresistibly as she was herself—an attitude she found as attractive as his curly blond hair and his kind, twinkling eyes. On the other hand he came packaged with some pretty formidable extras which would be difficult for a crofter's daughter like herself to handle. The prospect of meddling with the heir to an earldom was a daunting one. However much she fancied him, this was one man whom she couldn't approach with light-hearted abandon.

'Don't worry. If I do anything at all, I'm certainly not going to throw myself at him,' she told Alison a little primly. 'Quite the opposite, in fact.'

'But you're already friends, and he obviously needs company now he's moving back to Scotland. Isn't that enough for now? Just be his friend, Cat, and let him be yours and take it from there.' Alison took the bottle she had been carrying from Catriona's hand and refilled her glass for her. 'There. I may not be able to have a drink on it, but you can.' She raised her orange juice. 'To absent friends and future Countesses,' she quipped, grinning.

'You rat,' cried Catriona, laughing despite herself. 'You put your finger on the problem straight away—as usual!'

Twenty

Rob had ordered a new Land Rover to replace the one in which his grandfather had died. He collected it from the Edinburgh dealer on Saturday morning and drove straight to collect Catriona from her flat. Heading north, the big, all-purpose tyres gobbled up the miles effortlessly but the mood between the two people riding above them was less tractable.

'I feel quite peculiar,' Rob confessed as they crossed the Ballachulish Bridge on the later stages of their journey. 'The nearer I get to Glen Doran, the more nervous I become. Even though I was brought up there and have driven this road a hundred times, it's as if I'm going there for the first time.'

'I wonder why?' asked Catriona, who was experiencing an equal fluttering of butterflies in the stomach, though for totally different reasons. 'Maybe it's because you're more or less the boss now and you're afraid it will change you. You know—"Power corrupts and absolute power corrupts absolutely".'

He took his eyes off the road to glance at her curiously. 'Do you think I'll end up absolutely corrupt?' he asked.

'No, of course not,' she laughed. 'It's just a quotation. I don't even know who said it.'

'It was someone called Lord Acton. An eminent Victorian.'

'Oh, another Lord. There seem to be a lot of you about.'

'Do you mind?'

'What? Lots of Lords a-leaping?' There was still mirth in her tone. 'No, not at all. Why should I?'

'Not lots—one in particular.'

She frowned. 'Well, my Lord Nevis, I only have one problem with your title...'

'Which is?'

'That you're called after a mountain. Being with you might easily be seen as social climbing.'

'Cheeky!' He lifted his hand off the steering wheel and pushed her playfully on the arm. 'You'll be all right now though,' he chuckled. 'I've just pushed you off.'

'That's what happens to social climbers. People cut them dead.'

They fell silent. The road rushed on under the Land Rover's wheels like a roller belt. And after a minute Catriona asked, 'How did you know?'

'Know what?'

'That it was Lord Whatsisname—Acton?'

'Anyone who did history at Cambridge knows that.'

'Did you? Gosh!'

He grinned. 'No. I read law—but Lord Acton was a famous past professor of history. He was a bit of a Liberal—a friend of Gladstone's. He worried about the State smothering the small man and the freedom of minorities.'

'Good for him. In that case, perhaps he would have been on my side,' Catriona remarked.

'Your side?' he echoed curiously.

'Yes. On the side of the small crofter against the oppressive landlord.'

'Are you implying that I am now an oppressive landlord?' he asked indignantly.

'Absolutely,' she cried teasingly. 'And absolutely corrupt.'

'A great help you're going to be this weekend, inciting all the tenants to revolt.'

'Isn't it peasants who are always revolting?'

'And you want to be considered one of them?' he enquired dryly.

'No, no. Crofters are not peasants. We are independent, self-employed taxpayers with full security of tenure.'

'Help!' he exclaimed. 'Thanks goodness I did read law at Cambridge.'

They drove round the big house into the

stableyard. 'Only visitors park at the front,' Rob commented.

Kirsty Mackinnon met them at the back door. 'Welcome home, my lord,' she said solemnly. 'And welcome, Miss Catriona. I've some cold chicken waiting if you've not had lunch.'

'We stopped at Fort William, thanks Kirsty, at that nice fish restaurant on the lochside,' said Rob, who had wanted to delay the moment of arrival. Strangely, now that he was here, inside the house, he felt quite different—elated and excited, full of energy.

'I prepared your usual room and put Miss Catriona in the yellow room,' Kirsty went on. 'I hope that was all right.'

'It's fine, Kirsty,' Rob assured her. 'The first thing I'm going to do is go through all the principal rooms and remove all the dust-sheets. I can't even remember what's under most of them, they've been there for so long. So let's hope the weather stays fine over the next day or two and we can open all the windows and let the place have a breath of fresh air.'

Kirsty smiled delightedly. 'It's a breath a fresh air just to hear you say that, my lord,' she said. 'I've stocked up on dusters and polish and I've got some of the local girls standing by to man the vacuum cleaners. You only have to say the word.'

'Excellent. How is Angus? Has he got over the accident?'

'Well, he still has nightmares about it but the track's been repaired and you can hardly see where it happened now. We miss your

511

grandfather terribly though.'

'Yes, you must. We all do,' said Rob soberly.

He carried Catriona's overnight bag to a pretty room at the front of the house. It was large and bright and decorated in various shades of yellow, cream and deep gold, the soft furnishings faded but neat and clean, and it had a view of the loch, lying sapphire blue in its crowding circle of hills, their slopes patchworked with bright green as the birches and rowans began to sport their summer livery. Spring had come late in the Highlands but now there was something magical about the contrast of stark grey granite with the verdure of burgeoning bracken and the splendour of gold-flowering gorse engulfing the ochres and browns of winter's dead grasses. Catriona stood for some minutes drinking it in, realising that she never tired of the Highland beauty parade.

'Are you feeling strong?' Rob asked her when she came downstairs after unpacking her few belongings. 'I'd like to remove the dust-sheets in the main drawing room and I could do with some help.'

'Aha, now I know why you asked me here,' she cried. 'Peasant labour!'

'Right,' he nodded, adding as an afterthought, 'I'll just fetch my whip in case you revolt.'

After half an hour of hauling and shoving and shaking in the main ground-floor room, all the splendours hidden for so long beneath the dust-sheets were at last revealed—a set of gilt armchairs upholstered in dark blue damask, two beautiful rose-wood commodes, a pair of marble-topped side-tables, several hand-embroidered fire-screens and a stunning blue silk carpet with a design of peacocks and lions.

'This is so gracious and elegant,' Catriona pointed out as they stood back to admire the results of their efforts, 'but not very clannish. Where's all the Galbraith tartan? Where are the stags' heads and spittoons?'

'Clan tartans were banned after Culloden, don't forget. And my great-great-great-great-grandmama was a very refined lady, by all accounts,' Rob informed her gravely. 'Only tea was taken in her drawing room and no one was allowed to spit in the fire. However, the chiefs tended to be coarser characters and the other reception rooms are more oak and leather.'

'I wonder which side you take after?' speculated Catriona. 'The refined elegance or the rough and ready?'

'Oh, the riffraff element without a doubt,' he replied. 'But I can be relied on not to frighten the horses.'

'Speaking of which, will you fill up the stables, now you're going to live here?'

'Why, do you ride?' he asked with interest.

'A crofter who rides is a rarity,' she declared. 'But I always wanted to learn.'

'Why do you make such a point of being a crofter's daughter?' he enquired somewhat tersely.

'Because I am proud of my background, as you are,' she retorted.

'Or because you constantly want to remind

me of it for some reason?'

There was an edgy moment while she considered this accusation. Then she shrugged uncomfortably. 'I find you easier to talk to as a mister than as a lord,' she confessed.

All at once he grinned, relieving the tension. 'Doesn't everyone?' he said. 'Being a lord is a liability! A dubious asset, just as you once told me beauty and brains are.'

Catriona nodded, much relieved. 'Yes, I can believe that,' she said and added teasingly, 'but thousands wouldn't!' A glance at her watch told her it was five-thirty. 'I don't know whether you want to come with me but I'd very much like to visit the Carruthers down at the steading, and now might be a suitable time.'

'Yes, good idea,' Rob said. 'Of course I'd like to come. I've never met the Carruthers. Kirsty wants to cook dinner for us though. Shall I tell her we'll eat about eight?'

'Yes, fine.'

Catriona was unaccountably nervous about introducing Rob to the Carruthers. It seemed so important that they should get on together, mainly because they would be living in such close proximity but also because they were all her friends and she wanted them to like each other. If the Carruthers agreed that Rob was special it would bolster her own growing regard for him, and if he took to them it would prove that he shared her taste for what was honest and of good report.

At first she thought it was going to be a disaster. When they turned into the car park behind the steading there was a man on a ladder painting the window-frames bright orange. 'Bloody hell,' swore Rob, who couldn't help feeling a certain proprietory interest in the place, despite the fact that it was no longer part of the estate. 'They can't paint them that colour!'

The Carruthers abandoned their various tasks when they realised who their visitors were and Catriona could see by the way Rob kept glancing at the windows while she was introducing him that he was dying to broach the subject of the colour so she decided to do it for him.

'What's with the windows?' she asked when the niceties had been observed, names exchanged and hands shaken. 'Is this to be a new branch of the Orange Lodge?'

Nick laughed uproariously. 'No!' he exclaimed, catching his breath. 'That's an undercoat. Why? Did you think we'd decided to go anti-Jacobite?'

'I thought I might be in for another Battle of the Boyne,' said Rob, whose relief was obvious. 'Crimson or white are the accepted colours in the Highlands.'

'Yes, so we've noticed,' grinned Nick. 'But this undercoat is supposed to protect against wet-rot and other nasties. Apart from that, how do you like the improvements? I think we might say that the SFS did us a favour. We'd never have done such a radical re-design if it hadn't been for the fire.'

Rob stared around him, taking in the sturdy stone walls, the steep slate roofs and the extensive dry-stone terracing which retained the gardens and service areas. Despite its newness the development still retained the impression of being part of a traditional pattern, nestling unobtrusively in the enclosing landscape. 'Very good,' he approved, 'as long as the windows are white.'

'They'll have to be,' agreed Sue with dancing eyes. 'Because of the name we've chosen. Look at the new sign.' She pulled back a canvas cover which had been spread as protection over a large, flat wooden board leaning against the wall. On a green background was painted a famous Jacobite emblem in white and gold and underneath were the explanatory words 'The White Cockade'. A wrought-iron bracket could be seen already in place, bolted to the side of the building, from which the sign would be hung. 'Couldn't have orange windows with that, could we?'

'Hardly,' agreed Rob, smiling. 'When do you open?'

'In two weeks,' confided Sue with a grimace. 'I can't really believe we'll be ready but Nick says we've got to be.'

'Absolutely right,' averred Nick. 'We can't afford to miss the peak three months of the year.'

'I trust you've got the Bonnie Prince coming to do the honours?' enquired Rob. 'They say his ghost rides Glenfinnan, so he hasn't far to come.'

'We'll send a fax—see if he's free,' chuckled Nick, then grew more serious. 'Actually we had been going to ask your grandfather. We were so sorry to hear about the accident.'

'Yes, we all miss him,' responded Rob soberly. 'He'd have been pleased to cut the ribbon but he'd have made you swear to employ local labour in exchange.'

'Oh, we'll be doing that anyway,' Nick assured him. 'We've already hired two lads to do the dry-stone walling and they'll be staying on to work in the garden. We want to grow fresh vegetables—over there behind the kitchen. And we've several youngsters lined up to train as waiters and waitresses, plus two trainee chefs already working under Sue, so we're doing our bit for community productivity.'

'Perhaps you might do the honours for us in your grandfather's stead, Lord Nevis?' suggested Sue shyly. As opening day approached she had begun to discard the scruffy appearance of the bad months. Her hair was smartly cut and coloured a soft, wheaten blond, and although she'd been working hard in the new kitchen she looked fresh and pleasing in a white cotton shirt and dark pink trousers.

Rob was taken aback by the invitation. He had still to become accustomed to being the heir to Lochaber and as such, he supposed not without some qualms, a pillar of the community. 'Well, that's very kind of you,' he said with slight hesitation, glancing at Catriona as if waiting for her to give him the yea or nay. 'Do call me Rob by the way,' he added. 'I'm not used to being called Lord Nevis yet and I don't know if I ever shall be.'

'I think that's a great idea, Sue,' said Catriona, smiling gratefully at her friend. All her worries about whether the three would get on had been needless, she thought. 'If Rob opens the place he'll have to dine here at least once a month.'

'In that case I hope he likes the food,' Sue said. 'I'm planning a fairly simple menu to start with, using local fish and game of course. Is it you I should talk to about getting supplies of game and venison off the estate, Rob?'

'From now on, yes,' he replied happily. 'And rabbit and hare if you want them—I'm even thinking of rearing quail in some of the outbuildings. It would be good to have a reputable outlet for them locally so that people can taste the finished product.'

'In that case I think we can do a deal,' Sue declared, 'as long as the price is right. I'll start working on some recipes.'

'I think we should try one of my wines out now,' remarked Nick hospitably, leading the way into the restaurant. 'The décor isn't finished yet but you can get some idea of what it will be like.'

The style was eighteenth-century, a period when, appropriately for a Jacobite theme, paintwork was predominantly green and fixtures refined and delicate. The reproduction ladder-back chairs were sturdy but elegant, ambient lighting was to be from shaded wall-sconces, augmented, Nick told them, by candle-lamps on the tables. There would be white linen napery with, whenever possible, Jacobite white roses as floral decoration.

'I considered putting the traditional goblet of water on the tables so that people could drink to the "King Across the Water",' Nick confessed, wrestling with a corkscrew and a bottle of wine selected from an extensive rack set into the end wall of the restaurant. 'And then we decided that might be going OTT.'

'We thought Americans would drink the water and the French would use it as a finger-bowl,' laughed Sue.

'This is a fairly light red wine from the Rhône,' Nick informed them, pouring a little into four glasses. 'I can get it at a good price so I think it may become our house wine.'

They all drank and passed favourable comment and then Catriona said, 'Where are the boys? It's too early for a disco, surely?'

'They're both away for the day. Peter has taken to hill-walking and John joined the school shinty team, believe it or not. They've become little Highlanders in no time,' Sue told them with obvious gratification. 'We only ever see them on Sundays when I insist they're at home for roast lunch.'

'So it's been a good move as far as they're concerned?'

'Yes, I'm relieved to say. And when we're up and running we hope to be able to say the same for ourselves. As long as we don't get any more visits from the SFS brigade.'

Catriona exchanged glances with Rob who said with grim determination: 'I don't think you'll have any more trouble from that organisation.

In this area at least, I happen to know they're a spent force.'

Sue asked Catriona if she'd like to see the new 'Ladies' and led her into a pretty pink and green room fitted with chintz-skirted dressing tables as well as the usual basins and toilet cabinets. 'I wanted to make it a bit more like home,' she explained. 'Not too much whiff of disinfectant and Harpic.' Then she moved closer to confide, 'I like the new laird, by the way. And he seems to like you all right.'

Catriona blushed. 'Well, he's not really the laird yet but I think Rob will be the one with the hands-on approach as far as the estate is concerned. His father doesn't seem very interested.'

'Well, that's his loss and our gain,' Sue observed. 'And do I take it we might see rather more of you, now that Rob's here as well?'

'I don't know,' Catriona shrugged. 'We're just good friends, as they say in the best scripts.'

'Just before they ride off together into the sunset?'

'That's only in the movies,' Catriona demurred. 'At the moment I still have a job to do and he has thirty thousand acres to run. I should think the only place we'll ride off together is to the railway station so that he can put me on a train.'

'But that's not until tomorrow, is it?' insisted Sue mischievously. 'Before that, anything could happen!'

In the moonlight the loch lay mysterious and

dark with only a hint of silver reflecting off its smooth surface. There was the merest breath of a breeze, and as Rob and Catriona strolled along the rutted track they were serenaded by the musical slap and trickle of wavelets on the shoreline pebbles and a chorus of frogs provided percussion accompaniment from some invisible backwater. All was peace and tranquillity, and the concealing blanket of night lay between them.

'Are you still thinking of setting up in business on Skye?' asked Rob. The mood of teasing jocularity which had existed during the afternoon had changed subtly to one of measured reflection. They'd dined cosily in the kitchen on Kirsty's cullen skink and roast lamb and then strolled out to witness the dying of the long day.

'Yes, I am. I was talking to Hamish Melville about it only yesterday. Ironically he offered me financial help.'

'Why ironically?'

'Well, it seemed so strange after I'd more or less conned him out of a million pounds. I told him I didn't think I was a very safe investment and he said he liked to take a risk now and then. He really is a fraud, that man—makes out he's a ruthless operator when really he has a heart of gold.'

'Perhaps he just has a soft spot for you,' suggested Rob. 'Are you sure there isn't still a flame flickering somewhere?' He tried to make the question sound casual but they both knew it was far from that.

'Certain sure,' she answered swiftly and almost vehemently. 'As sure as I'll ever be about anything.'

'Will you let him help you?'

'No. I'd like his advice but I won't take his money. I'll borrow through the usual channels.' She felt her Wellingtoned feet squelch through a patch of soft dark mud, and wondered if she had extracted herself completely from the metaphorical mire. 'What about you?' she asked. 'Have you decided what kind of business you're going to start here?'

'No, not really. I mentioned quail-raising to the Carruthers but I'm open to other ideas if you have any.'

'I'll give it some thought. What did you think of them?'

'Who—the Carruthers?' She heard him take a deep breath while he chose his words. 'Interesting, industrious, determined, fun—I can understand what you see in them.'

She sighed, pleased. 'I'm glad,' she said.

'I hope they'll fit in in Glendoran. The villagers can be a bit awkward if people try to steamroller them. They take their own pace and the Carruthers may find that a little frustrating at first. They'll need patience, but it'll pay off in the end. Loyalty doesn't come any stronger than that which is earned in the Highlands.'

'Meanwhile they needn't expect another fire ceremony, I hope?'

He gave a hollow laugh. 'No, I think that was a one-off.'

'Why? Do you know who did it?' She was

testing, wondering if he would admit his brother's involvement.

'I might do,' he replied cautiously.

'Do you think, for instance, that Andro might be a member?' Catriona suddenly found herself plunging off firm ground into hazardous territory.

'Of Scotland for the Scots? Why do you ask?'

She couldn't tell from his voice if he was angry or wary but she told him about her suspicions after the Mark Sole incident at the film location. 'And he was up at Glen Doran when the buildings in the district were torched—on both occasions,' she added grimly. 'If you put two and two together they do tend to make four.'

'He is a little unstable at times,' Rob admitted. 'But I can't believe he's that stupid. There's no proof, is there?'

'No. And we don't want anyone to find any, do we?'

'Preferably not. I can just see the newspaper headlines: EARL'S SON FIRE-BUG!'

'THE HONOURABLE ARSONIST!' was Catriona's offering, made with a tight smile. She added cautiously, 'It may be a small point but for a start I don't think the Carruthers would like to know that they're living down the road from the family of the man who fired their steading. As long as he doesn't do it again.'

'I'll talk to him,' Rob promised. 'Try and put the fear of God into him.' He ran his hand distractedly through his hair. 'But I don't know...Grandfather was the one who could always make Andro toe the line.'

'Well, you're the boss now, so you'll have to do it,' said Catriona firmly.

'Is this the dreaded absolute power?' he asked gloomily.

The tight smile came again. 'No. This is being your brother's keeper.'

For a few minutes they listened to their feet swishing through the grass and heather.

'I'd like us to see much more of each other, Catriona,' Rob said at length, boldly addressing her bleached white profile, fringed by the moon-dark mane of her hair. 'Does the idea appeal or appal?'

Catriona's heart fast-forwarded. This was the moment of truth. She felt her throat constrict so that the words would hardly come. 'Appeal, I think,' she said faintly, then threw back her head and peered at the wistful set of his shadowed mouth. 'Yes, definitely,' she declared. 'It appeals to me, if it appeals to you.'

Even in the darkness his face lit up. He stopped in his tracks. 'Really? Despite the mountainous drawback?'

She understood him to mean his title. 'I suppose I could get used to being a social climber,' she nodded sheepishly. 'It's not your fault, after all.'

'It isn't so far from here to Skye,' he reminded her.

'Only a hundred miles!' she exclaimed, laughing. 'Thomas Carlyle used to walk that far to visit Jane Welsh.'

'Did he?' asked Rob in amazement. 'He must have been keen.'

'He was. He courted her for five years before she agreed to marry him.' Catriona began to walk on again but Rob caught her hand, guided more by instinct than eyesight for it was hard to see.

'Hey,' he called gently, pulling her back. 'Must I make a five-year plan? If so, can we start now, please? I don't want to waste any time.'

She felt unaccountably shy as he put his arms around her and pulled her close to him. There was something tantalising and breathtaking about his embrace, something important and significant that she could not name. They were so close now that they could see into each other's eyes, colourless in the moonlight but far from expressionless.

'I have a strange and fundamental feeling,' he said softly, 'that something is happening here which may not take as much as five years.'

She said nothing but moved slightly to reach his lips with hers. Their kiss was full of contradictions, sweet and sharp, joyful and solemn, satisfying and disturbing all at the same time. It spoke of hope and fear and laughter and tears and it left them both breathless and filled with awe.

'I don't want to jump the gun or anything,' he murmured hesitantly, studying her face, 'but what is your view on separate bedrooms?'

Solemnly Catriona put a hand up to her ear and shook her head. 'I heard no shot,' she said, then added with a wicked smile, her lips against his ear, 'I'm against them.'

With a great sigh of contentment Rob buried his face in her hair. 'Thank God for that,' he said. 'So am I.'

This Large Print Book for the Partially sighted, who cannot read normal print, is published under the auspices of

THE ULVERSCROFT FOUNDATION